MW01713345

The Holy Road

Book Two of The Rifter

GINN HALE

Blind Eye Books

blindeyebooks.com

The Holy Road
Book Two of the Rifter
By Ginn Hale

Published by:
Blind Eye Books
1141 Grant Street
Bellingham, WA 98225
blindeyebooks.com

All rights reserved. No part of this publication may used or reproduced in any manner without the written permission of the publisher, except for the purpose of reviews.

Edited by Nicole Kimberling
Cover art, maps and all illustrations by Dawn Kimberling

This book is a work of fiction. All characters and situations depicted are fictional. Any resemblances to actual people or events are coincidental.

First print edition March 2013
Copyright © 2013 Ginn Hale

ISBN 978-1-93556 0-25-8

Amura'taye

Stair to Rathal Pesha
Common Mill
Bousim House
Payshmura Hostle
Candle Alley
Blood Market
Gates
Prison
Fairgrounds
Gates
Pyre
Holy Road

Basawar Year 153
Rathal'pesha
Wastes
Bousim Lands
Vundomu
Samsira River
Nurjima
Naye'ro
Du'yura
Silaun
Tushoya
Lisam Lands
Anyyd
Umbhra'ibaye

Fai'daum North Year 185
Greenhills
Westcliff
Silverlake Islands
Iron Heights
Vundomu fortress
Ssahn'illev

The Story So Far:

After using a key intended for his roommate, John Toffler and his two closest friends—Laurie and Bill—are thrown into the harsh world of Basawar. John and his friends survive the winter wilderness with the aid of a rebellious young priest, Ravishan, and eventually join Basawar society in the city of Amura'taye.

While Laurie and Bill find shelter in the household of the exiled Lady Bousim, John ascends the Thousand Steps to the monastery of Rathal'pesha where he reunites with Ravishan. He hopes that among the mysterious teachings of the Pashmura priesthood he can find a way to return home. After a year of service in the monastery, he has made many discoveries and a few friends, chief among them the aged priest, Samsango, and the healer, Hann'yu. But the way home still eludes John.

Soon John begins to fear that Laurie's newly developed powers could be those of the destroyer god, the Rifter. If she were to be discovered, it would mean the end for all of them. Complicating matters further is the fact that Laurie continues to practice the forbidden arts of witchcraft under the tutelage of Lady Bousim.

In the midst of John's turmoil, Ravishan confesses his attraction to John. But Basawar is a world where such desire is punished with death. And after a frustratingly brief kiss in Candle Alley, John orders Ravishan away from him—for both their sakes.

Chapter Thirty-Four

Bright beams of morning light streamed through the windows and warmed the infirmary as if spring had at last reached the mountains. But outside, snow still lay across the monastery grounds and deep drifts blanketed the surrounding peaks.

In the midst of so much snow and ice the pungent scents of fresh herbs seemed strange, out of place, and too much of a reminder of things John did not want to think about.

He glowered at the bright emerald herbs filling his mortar and then pounded the pestle into them with unnecessary force. Thick stems and glossy leaves rapidly dissolved into a frothy green pulp under his ministrations. He took what satisfaction he could in that.

"Good spirit, Jahn, but I think you may have gone past paste to liquid." Hann'yu offered the criticism without much concern as he leaned across the long wooden table and peered into the mortar. He appeared somewhat amused by John's overly enthusiastic preparation of the herbs. "Something isn't bothering you, is it?"

"No," John replied, though he couldn't bring himself to meet Hann'yu's speculative gaze. Despite his unconcerned manner, Hann'yu could be a very insightful man.

In truth, John had spent most of last night attempting to purge his mind of the memory of Ravishan's warm body pressed against him—the taste of his mouth and the longing in his handsome smile. John had tried to concentrate on anything else, and yet the tempting sensations of Ravishan's bare skin, his willing lips, and his strong hands had suffused John's dreams with both desire and terrifying visions of persecution. He'd woken sweating, frustrated, and lonely for Ravishan's company.

But the monastery of Rathal'pesha was the last place to indulge himself. Or Ravishan, for that matter. So John had chosen instead to put his energy to use in the infirmary.

"I suppose I'm just a little nervous about preparing all these medicines correctly," John told Hann'yu.

John looked meaningfully at the heaps of fresh and dried herbs that engulfed most of the table and lay bundled in parchment on the windowsill. He'd bought them in Amura'taye less than an hour before he'd met with Ravishan in Candle Alley. Yellow pollen from several of the blossoms still clung to his gray cassock. He wondered how much of it had brushed onto Ravishan's black coat during their one brief kiss.

"You'll do fine." Hann'yu offered him a charming smile; the expression betrayed more of his cosmopolitan, southern background than did his dark skin and delicate features. "Just go a little more gently with the fresh herbs. Treat them more like you would ladies."

John glanced between the phallic-looking pestle in his hand and Hann'yu's lascivious grin.

"You mean pounding them?" John lowered his voice, despite the fact that all of the infirmary beds were currently empty. Someone might be listening from the common sickroom on the floor below them.

Hann'yu simply laughed at John's expression. Then he schooled his features into something close to contrition.

"I'm sorry, Jahn," Hann'yu said. "I shouldn't tease you."

"You shouldn't," John agreed, though he suspected that wouldn't stop Hann'yu.

And despite Hann'yu's occasional lewd joke, John found the work and conversation relaxing. He passed most of the morning grinding, pounding, and mixing the plants into various pungent concoctions, while Hann'yu observed from across the wooden table.

The sunlight grew stronger and the infirmary warmed. Now and then Hann'yu offered John instructions or made a face at the smell of a particularly rank herb. After hours of work, the entire infirmary smelled of strange medicines. The sharp, astringent scent of the herbs clung to John's hands and only one last bundle remained on Hann'yu's table.

It was nearly noon, and he still hadn't seen Ravishan. After weeks of regular visits, John found himself routinely glancing up, expecting to see him at the door or standing silently among the rows of beds. The long hall of the infirmary seemed oddly abandoned without him.

John unwound the kidskin vellum that held the last bundle. The tannic scent of leather evaporated as he spread the vellum and exposed the dark knots of dried gray leaves and thick roots. An earthy, almost living, aroma rose from the clumps of gnarled root, reminding John of both the musky weasel nests and the acrid tang of sweat.

"Don't touch that one with your hands." Hann'yu nudged a black-glazed clay jar toward him. "Use the vellum to funnel it into this."

"What is it?" John carefully slid the leaves and roots into the jar. A fine dust wafted up and John held his breath until it had settled.

"Not much in itself. Eastern physicians used to call it goatweed. Eat some and it will be right back up with you in a few minutes. If you get some of the sap into your blood, though…" Hann'yu shook his head. "It could well be the end of you."

"It's poison?"

Hann'yu nodded. "You should close the lid and wash your hands well."

John frowned. The tips of his fingers where he had touched the vellum felt hot and tender. There was quite a bit of fine residue left on his skin.

Then Hann'yu burst into laughter. "You'll be fine. It has to be specially prepared to be deadly. Whole and dried it won't affect anyone but a witch."

The definite tingling in John's fingertips and knuckles continued. He suppressed the guilty urge to hide his reddening hands behind his back.

Hann'yu went on, "You should wash up before you touch any of the ushiri'im, though. They're sensitive to it as well."

"Witches and ushiri'im?" John went immediately to the washbasin. He poured water from the pitcher and then soaped up his hands and rinsed them. The water felt bitingly cold, yet soothing. He emptied the basin out the window, poured more water and plunged his hands into it.

"Witches and ushiri'im." Hann'yu gazed at him evenly. "Odd, isn't it?"

"Is it?" John eyed Hann'yu back, wondering if Hann'yu was making an oblique reference to something he should have known about or if this was more of the intellectual sedition that had gotten Hann'yu exiled to Rathal'pesha in the first place. From Hann'yu's expression, John guessed it was the latter.

"A man who didn't know better might make some connection between the two that could get him exiled or worse." Hann'yu drifted to John's side, in the way that he always did when he seemed to feel the subversive urge to educate John.

"But you wouldn't be that man?"

"Oh no." Hann'yu lowered his voice. "That man was a colleague of mine who now has a price on his head. He joined the Fai'daum."

John raised his brows at such a frank admission of familiarity with a member of the revolutionary group.

Hann'yu simply peered down at John's hands. Beneath the water, they looked deathly white, except the tips and knuckles, which were bright red. John glanced to Hann'yu, trying to read his expression. He didn't appear alarmed, only curious.

"Often in backwaters like Amura'taye, town chiefs pay exorbitant sums for powders made from the scrapings of goatweed roots. They call it whores-torch. Usually it's used to ferret out a suspected witch. They could as easily be finding ushiri candidates. But they don't know that, of course. Church secret." Hann'yu kept his circumspect gaze on John's hands as he casually said, "I won't have you handle goatweed again. It affects you worse than it does me."

"Thank you for that."

Gradually the burning sensation receded. John watched the redness fade from his knuckles, wondering if it had been some kind of allergic reaction or possibly a sensitivity to the fungus that formed the mycorrhizae sheathing the plant's roots.

"Where you grew up—" Hann'yu began.

"Shun'sira," John supplied quickly. Years ago he and Ravishan had decided on Shun'sira as the safest district for John to claim for a homeland. It was a remote district at the ragged edge of the Bousim tithing lands and was populated mostly by subsistence hunters who lived distant, scattered lives in the rugged hills and bogs. John had memorized the names of the few settlements that dotted the otherwise barren map of the area in a single afternoon.

"Did they have many witch burnings there?" Hann'yu inquired, still passively inspecting the progress of John's inflamed knuckles.

"They didn't have much of anything there." John kept his answer deliberately vague.

"The town chiefs preferred to skin the witches for their bones, then?"

"I don't know... probably. My family lived in the hills. We didn't see too many other people, unless it was on market days." John didn't want to talk about burning or flaying anyone. Just the thought of witches' bones and how they were acquired revolted him utterly.

Months ago, John had read about the sacred bones in the holy texts. Bled and skinned, the still-living remains of certain women were bound together with copper wires and used in divination rituals. Apparently, in the southern convent at Umbhra'ibaye, the remains of thousands of women had been assembled into something called the Issusha'im Oracles. The text had contained a small drawing, and since then, the image had worked itself into the worst of his nightmares.

Now it was too easy for John to picture their white teeth and hollow eye sockets; readily he conjured the stale, rotted scent of them and heard the clatter of their thin arm bones against their ribs as they twisted amidst the red wires restraining them.

A cool breeze drifted through the open window and John shuddered. Hann'yu cast him an oddly mournful look.

"Did you know that, once, it was only the holiest of women who were allowed to sacrifice themselves and become Issusha'im Oracles?"

"No," John replied flatly.

Hann'yu plainly wanted him to understand something about the connection between the issusha'im and goatweed, but John didn't know exactly what. Though he now spoke Basawar fluently, there were many aspects of the language and the culture that John suspected only a native understood innately. All he could do was drift along in the conversation and hope that, eventually, he would perceive the implications.

"Before the war with the Eastern Kingdom, there were no witches. Women with witches' powers were considered Parfir's holy brides, equal to the Kahlil in the depth of the god's blessings upon them. Look back through the books for yourself. You won't find a mention of a witch until after the first siege at Ganaa." Hann'yu glanced up at him. "Am I scandalizing you?"

"No." John lifted his hands from the water experimentally. His fingers felt slightly stiff but the burning was gone. "Were you hoping to?"

"A little," Hann'yu replied. He tossed John a cloth to dry his hands.

John smiled tiredly, sad to see Hann'yu disappointed, but there was nothing he could do. He couldn't be surprised by heretical disclosures when he lacked the instinctive knowledge of what was normal and what was profane here in Basawar.

"You just don't believe me, do you?" Hann'yu asked.

"I believe you," John assured him, and he did. "Even holy doctrine is bound to be altered by wars. A church can't remove itself from the society in which it exists." John dried his hands. His skin felt tender against the rough cloth.

Hann'yu studied him. "You're a strange man, Jahn."

"How so?"

"You seem so unconcerned sometimes, as if even the most startling revelation means nothing to you. It makes a man want to surprise you."

"You could just jump out from a dark room," John suggested. It was something of a shame that the provocative, social impact of Hann'yu's conversation was so wasted on him.

"Jumping out of closets might be just a little beneath my station," Hann'yu replied. "I may just have to stop trying to shock you. Parfir only knows what I might end up saying."

John shrugged. "So long as you don't confess to a burning passion for me, we'll be fine."

Hann'yu's dark eyes went wide with shock. His face drained of all color. John instantly recognized the expression of horror, but the words were already out of his mouth. He had unintentionally struck upon a subject far more profane to Basawar society than either immolating women or skinning them alive. Backtracking would only get him in worse trouble, so he pushed on. "You're not in love with me, are you?"

"No." Hann'yu coughed. "My god, what a thing to say."

"I haven't scandalized you, have I?" John asked in a deadpan voice. He gazed levelly at Hann'yu with a slight, sardonic smile.

Hann'yu stared at him for a moment, and then laughed. It was loud, relieved laughter.

"I see your point, Jahn. It is a little cruel of me to just say things to you in hopes of getting a startled reaction." Hann'yu shook his head and then lowered his voice. "But you truly must take care, as far as such desires are concerned. Before you came here there was an…incident…" Hann'yu looked a little sick and John felt afraid to ask what the outcome had been.

"A young man was put to death," Hann'yu said at last. "Now Dayyid will not tolerate the mention of such abominations, not even in jest."

"Not to fear. Dayyid and I don't share many jokes." John forced a smile.

Hann'yu nodded but his expression was bleak. He stepped back to the table and picked up the sealed jar of goatweed roots. He studied it for a moment, and then placed it back among the smoked glass jars and dark bottles on one of the tall shelves behind him.

John watched him and wondered what would be done with the poisonous, knotted roots. As if sensing his curiosity, Hann'yu said, "The goatweed will be distilled into a poison, potent enough to lay even a god low. Though for now it is nothing but an ugly irritant."

He sighed heavily and turned back to John. "You know, I don't just say things to you to see if I can disgust you—"

"You didn't disgust me," John assured him. "It's just that sometimes I don't know why you tell me these things. I know it isn't just to shock me. There are obviously simpler ways."

"Yes, obviously," Hann'yu agreed. He offered John a half-smile. "It's not easy to be alone, not even when it's just in knowledge. A man wants someone else he can talk to. In Nurjima, there were dozens of us who would gather at teahouses and discuss these things. The conversations could go on for hours, and sometimes people got angry. We'd argue and rant, but I always came away from the discussions feeling alive with thoughts. But here, no one wants to know more than they have to. No one wants to ask questions. You'd think knowledge was a poison." Hann'yu glanced briefly to the dark jar of goatweed, then returned his attention to John. "You don't seem like the other men here. You're not afraid to learn new things. You pursue knowledge. I suppose it makes me nostalgic, talking to you like this."

John nodded. "I know what you mean."

"Do you?" Hann'yu smiled at the idea. "There was a large intellectual circle in Shun'sira?"

"No, but I understand isolation—" The rest of John's words were cut off by a loud pounding on the infirmary door. John strode across the room quickly and pulled the door open. Fikiri and another ushiri stumbled in. Their arms, chests, and faces were crisscrossed with long, narrow gashes.

John led them both to beds and had them sit down. He had now seen enough of the ushiri'im's injuries to be unsurprised by the profusion of blood. These kinds of long, narrow slices weren't usually lethal. They bled a great deal and were obviously very painful. But it was the deep, organ-piercing punctures and bone-shattering impacts that killed most ushiri'im.

Those internal injuries could be easy to miss at first glance. Often, the shocked ushiri'im weren't even aware of the extent of the damage to their bodies.

Hann'yu walked quickly to them. "All right, let's get a look at the two of you."

While Hann'yu undressed the other ushiri, John swiftly and efficiently removed Fikiri's clothes. The heavy wool of Fikiri's coat was still cold from the Gray Space. Jagged rents marred the coat's front and back. The leather vest Fikiri wore beneath his coat had fared better. Only one cut punched all the way through it. A single, tiny scratch marked Fikiri's thin chest and that had already stopped bleeding. His legs, too, were unharmed. His worst injuries seemed to be a deep cut along his right arm and a gash across his chin.

From the next bed, John heard a quiet hiss escape from Hann'yu. John glanced up to see Hann'yu tossing aside the other ushiri's blood-soaked underpants. The ushiri's face was white and he shook violently. His hands were folded over his groin.

"It looks worse than it is," Hann'yu assured the ushiri. "A few stitches will patch everything up good as new." Hann'yu glanced to John. "How's Fikiri?"

"Two superficial cuts. He'll need stitches in his arm and maybe his chin. Otherwise just bandages." John studied Fikiri for a moment. There was a dark bump on the side of his temple. "Did you hit your head?"

"In combat practice two days ago," Fikiri said. "Ravishan did it."

John nodded. Nothing life threatening, then.

Hann'yu moved swiftly, gathering his needles and stitching thread. "Get Fikiri's cuts cleaned up and bandaged. I'll start sewing up Thuum."

"Will you need my help with him?" If the wound was very bad Hann'yu would want John to bear it for Thuum. John didn't relish the thought, but if absorbing some of the ushiri's injuries would save Thuum's life, then John would do it.

"No." Hann'yu gave him a quick smile. "This will just require stitches. It would be most helpful if you could prepare Fikiri."

John nodded, relieved. As Hann'yu pulled the canvas panels shut around the bed where Thuum lay, John turned back to Fikiri.

"Is he going to live?" Fikiri asked.

"He'll be fine." John didn't know if that was completely true, but it was what Fikiri and Thuum both needed to hear right now.

John filled the washbasin with water and brought bandages and towels over to Fikiri's bedside. He sat down on the stool next to the bed and kicked Fikiri's discarded clothes out of his way. Bright red splotches of blood spattered the sheets all around Fikiri. The boy looked scared. He held his right arm close to his body and pressed his left hand over his slashed chin.

John tore a strip off one of the towels, folded it into a pad, and held it out to Fikiri. "Hold this against your chin."

Fikiri obediently did as John told him.

Gently, John cleaned and bandaged Fikiri's injured arm and then the deep gash in his chin. Then, John turned his attention to the smaller scratches that slashed across the skin of his arms, neck, and face. Fikiri looked like he'd gone a few rounds with a gang of angry cats. After John was done with him, he resembled a poorly wrapped mummy. Tufts of his blond hair had come loose from his tight braids and now hung like wisps of smoke around his pale face. John found the blood-stained sheets beneath his skinny body and the heap of torn, bloody clothes at the foot of the bed too depressing to look at. A fifteen-year-old boy shouldn't have to endure this kind of life.

"Come on, let's get you into a clean bed." John easily lifted Fikiri's thin body and carried him to the next bed. Fikiri lay back into the pillows and pulled the blankets over himself. John thought the boy might just go to sleep, but instead Fikiri looked up at him with a strange, yearning expression.

"Do you want me to get you something for the pain?" John asked.

Fikiri nodded and John brought a cup of yellowpetal water. Fikiri took the small clay cup with his left hand and sipped the liquid. After taking several more drinks, he set the cup aside on a small medical tray that stood beside the bed.

"When we were on the Thousand Steps…" Fikiri's voice was just a whisper. John stepped closer to the bedside and knelt down to hear him.

"What about it?" John asked.

"We could have turned around," Fikiri murmured. "You could have let me turn around, and we could have gone back to Nurjima."

John didn't say anything in response. He didn't even move.

Fikiri continued to fix him with that intense look. "Why didn't you let me turn around?" His voice wasn't angry, but soft and confused.

John stood and retrieved the empty cup. He didn't want to look at Fikiri. Seeing the boy's pain and knowing that he was complicit in it made him sick with himself.

"I'll get you another drink," John said.

"My mother promised to take you and your family with us," Fikiri persisted in a whisper. "Didn't you believe her?"

"I had to bring you, Fikiri—" John cut himself short, knowing he couldn't explain himself to Fikiri. He turned, found more yellowpetal water, and refilled the cup. Without looking at Fikiri, he set it down on the bedside tray.

"I have duties in the common sickroom." John forced the words out with a mechanical flatness. "You should rest. Hann'yu will be with you soon."

"Why can't you tell me?" Fikiri persisted in a whisper. "Even Behr and Loshai don't know why you did it."

"I'm sorry," John said. Then he turned and walked away.

☾☾☾

The common sickroom was located outside the infirmary down a flight of wide stairs. It was a larger, open chamber with more beds arranged in close rows. The shelves that lined the back wall were not packed with medicines but with bedding, canvas panels, and bedpans. Hann'yu rarely sent John down to the common sickroom to work. He seemed to think that it was in some way beneath John.

John surveyed the few men who occupied the beds. Most were older and sleeping. Two gray-haired ushvun'im stood near the large windows that opened to the gardens. They held buckets and scrub brushes, but seemed lost in conversation. Neither of them took note of John, which suited him.

There were several baskets of clean sheets and beds that needed to be remade. John needed to do something. So he started with that.

He didn't want to think about what he had done to Fikiri. At the time, he hadn't really known what would be expected of the boy. But even if he had, John knew he would have forced Fikiri up those steps anyway. He would have done it because Rathal'pesha was the key to his return home.

He could offer himself the excuse that Laurie and Bill were both depending on him. He could tell himself that it was only a matter of numbers—the needs of three to that of one. He could say that Fikiri wouldn't have been alive at all if it hadn't been for him. John had simply made the best of the options he had been given. He had done what needed to be done. He wanted to take some consolation in the truth of all that, and yet none of it made him feel good or just. It made him feel sick with himself and with the world that surrounded him.

Sometimes his life seemed like nothing but a series of ugly choices. Putting his dog down or having it live on in crippling pain, lying to his family about his life or losing them for the sake of honesty. There never seemed to be a painless option, only degrees of what he could live with and what he could not bear.

John made the beds quickly, with focused intensity. Crisp, tight corners came to him easily, as did high polish on boots and miles of silent marching. His father would have been proud of that, at least. These were beds the old man could have flipped a quarter on.

John stopped, staring at the basket of sheets. He didn't know why he was suddenly thinking of his father. That was pointless. Even if John did ever get back home, his father wouldn't spare him a word.

It was regret, John supposed. Another right choice that he had made that hadn't been much better than the wrong choice. And what for? So that he could end up here, in this stronghold of repression, lying awake at night fantasizing about Ravishan and praying that he didn't get them both killed. What consolation was he supposed to take in knowing that his father, an entire world away, knew he was gay?

Pointless, John thought. Sometimes life was simply pointless. He supposed that this entire silent rant of his was much the same. No matter how bad he felt, there was nothing to be done about it. He had made hard and even cruel choices, but in the end they were the ones he knew were right. There was no use in regretting them.

John made another bed, more slowly this time. He wondered, not for the first time today, where Ravishan was and what he was doing. He was probably training, taking his frustration out on some undeserving opponent—or possibly taking it out on Dayyid.

The thought of that, at least, brought a slight smile to John's lips.

He supposed he should go back upstairs and see if Hann'yu needed him. He picked up two sets of new, clean sheets and folded them to take with him. He'd need to change the beds Fikiri and Thuum had used.

When he reached the infirmary, he found Thuum tucked into a clean bed and lying in a sedated sleep. The canvas panels were drawn closed around the bed that John had left Fikiri in. John poked his head in. Hann'yu glanced up from where he sat on the stool next to the bed. His delicate needles, his spool of fine black thread, and a bottle of astringent sat on the tray beside him. Fikiri stretched across the bed in an unconscious sprawl. A fine track of black stitches arced over his chin. Hann'yu continued his work over Fikiri's arm, stitching Fikiri's flesh as if he were sewing nothing more than a shirtsleeve.

"He'll be fine," Hann'yu assured John. "It was good you gave him the yellowpetal water. He was beginning to babble."

"I didn't mean to knock him out."

"Oh, you didn't. I did that myself." Hann'yu bent back over Fikiri's arm. "He was going to end up saying something that would embarrass him later, so I gave him a little prick of something. It ensures better stitches anyway. No tossing and twitching."

"What was he saying?" John asked. He hoped it wasn't more about Lady Bousim's offers to him.

"He hates it here. He hates all of us. He wants to go home. He wants his mother. The kind of thing that boys say when they're hurt and scared." Hann'yu tied off one stitch and started another. "I suppose you heard a lot of the same when you brought him up the Thousand Steps."

"Not much," John replied. Though he vividly remembered Fikiri curled up and sobbing on the frigid steps, it wasn't something he needed to share with Hann'yu.

"Two years ago this behavior might have been acceptable, but now he's getting a little too old for it."

"He's only fifteen," John argued, though he didn't know why except that it seemed that someone should defend the boy.

"He's an ushiri. A couple of cuts like these are the least of his problems, and calling for his mother isn't going to do him any good."

John guessed that Hann'yu was right. Still, what harm did it do anyone when Fikiri cried or complained? It didn't hurt Fikiri.

But John was beginning to realize that Fikiri's obvious misery pained the men around him. It pricked at their guilt, knowing that they put these demands upon a child. It would be so much easier if he were strong and silent, if he shrugged off his injuries the way Ravishan did. It would have allowed them all to think that the ushiri'im were made of tougher stuff than other men, that they didn't feel the hurt as deeply and weren't terrified in the face of their own agonizing deaths.

John frowned down at Fikiri's pale face. He really was just a boy. John found that he had to look away. Like the rest of them, he couldn't stand to think about it.

After a moment, John asked, "Do you need me for anything?"

"You could clean up the beds."

"I thought the same thing." John lifted the clean sheets slightly and Hann'yu offered him an absent nod.

John turned aside and let the canvas panel fall back into place. He stripped the stained bedding off one of the beds and quickly spread and tucked in the new sheet. John had just started towards the next bed when he felt that slight shudder of air and that whisper of a chill behind him. Though he disliked the sensation of the Gray Space opening, John also associated it strongly with Ravishan's arrival.

He turned, expecting to greet Ravishan, only to find himself smiling inanely into Dayyid's glowering face.

"Is he with you?" Dayyid demanded.

"What?" John was too startled by Dayyid's unexpected presence to reply properly. "Who?"

"Ravishan?" Dayyid almost growled the name.

"No." Then a worrying thought came to him. "Is he missing?"

"He's been gone since last night." Dayyid's scowl deepened the lines of his weathered face. "Even when he is disobedient, he doesn't stay away for a whole day."

"Maybe he's lost," John suggested. Though he thought that Ravishan was just avoiding him. This was probably wise for both their sakes…though it seemed somehow very unlike Ravishan.

"He doesn't get lost," Dayyid stated flatly.

"I'm sure he gets lost sometimes." John remembered Ravishan telling him that he had claimed to be lost when he had wanted to slip away and visit him. He would probably make the same claim now.

"No." Dayyid gave him a look of sheer contempt. "He claims to have been lost, but he never is. His bones are the god's own. There is no place on this world unknown to them."

Because the world itself was the god's body, John quickly filled in the unspoken reasoning that Dayyid had to be following.

"Perhaps he's tired."

"Or injured," Dayyid countered.

The thought sent a sharp stab of worry through John. He'd left Ravishan in an ugly part of Amura'taye. Ravishan obviously hadn't returned to Rathal'pesha.

"He's never stayed away for an entire night before?" John asked.

"Never."

"Is there any way of tracing where he might have gone?" John asked.

"Certain men can feel the Gray Space." For the first time, Dayyid looked directly into his face. "I have the ushiri'im looking for him, but it never hurts to have another man."

"What do you need me to do?" John asked.

"I didn't mean you." Dayyid smirked. "Tell Hann'yu that I want to see him as soon as he is done here."

John scowled at Dayyid. But Dayyid had already turned away. He didn't spare John a glance as he strode out of the room. The door simply fell shut behind him. John hurled the clean sheet onto the mattress with unnecessary force.

"Ravishan really hasn't been up to see you today?" Hann'yu called from behind the panel.

"No." John frowned down at the sheet.

There was no further response from Hann'yu. John picked up the sheet but didn't move on. Finally, he said, "Do you think that I should go look for him?"

"Do you think you could find him?" Hann'yu asked back.

"I might."

"Then go," Hann'yu replied. "The beds will still be here when you get back."

John hardly heard the rest of Hann'yu's response. He was already heading for the door.

Chapter Thirty-Five

John closed his eyes, allowing himself to simply feel the scored lines that the ushiri'im often left when they tore into the Gray Space.

The walkways, walls, and the very air of Rathal'pesha were rough from the countless invisible abrasions. If he concentrated, John could feel them all. Lifting one hand into the air, he traced the finest imperfection, a sensation not unlike running his fingers across a pane of glass and having his skin catch on the razor thin scratches marring the surface.

In the wastes he had occasionally been able to feel Ravishan's passage by following the abrasion in space. But here in Rathal'pesha, the constant practices of all the ushiri'im made it impossible to distinguish one from another, much less track a single trail.

He supposed it wouldn't have mattered in any case. Ravishan hadn't returned to the monastery.

If he wanted to find Ravishan, he guessed that he would have to hike back down to Amura'taye. It would take the better part of the afternoon. He would arrive well after sunset. An ushiri could traverse the distance in an instant, so Dayyid probably already had several of them searching the town.

If Ravishan was there, they would eventually find him.

But then, there was no guarantee that Ravishan would be in Amura'taye. He was the strongest of the ushiri'im, able to cross mountain ranges in a moment. He could be anywhere in Basawar.

John leaned his head against the stone railing of the walkway. He shouldn't have left Ravishan the way he had. If anything happened to him, John knew he wouldn't forgive himself. He wished that he could just know if Ravishan was safe. Even if he couldn't find him, just knowing would make all the difference.

The entire walkway seemed to sway beneath him. John bolted upright, staring around him, but nothing moved. The stone walkway remained solidly where it had always been. There were no signs of a tremor in any of the surrounding towers or trees.

It hadn't seemed like an earthquake in any case. The movement had been silent and smooth. The land had seemed to simply slide beneath him as it so often did in his dreams. John remembered the same sensation coming to him the night before he had arrived in Amura'taye. Miles of land had whipped beneath him, leading him up from the flood plains, through the thickening forests, over the terraced farms of the mountain, and straight up to Rathal'pesha. It had taken him directly to Ravishan.

John lowered his head, again resting it on the railing. He closed his eyes, concentrating. Slowly the walkway slid out from under him. He drifted over the monastery grounds, seeing gardens and stone paths pass beneath him. He recognized Samsango, lounging beneath a twisted pine with two other elderly ushvun'im. A moment later, John swept up over the walls and the watchtowers and then began to rise up the face of the mountain itself. The air was colder and thinner. The few trees that grew there were scrub, and as he ascended higher, even those disappeared. Soon, there was nothing but jutting stone and deep drifts of snow.

Ravishan was there, crouched beneath an outcropping of gray rock, staring down at the monastery below. His black hair blew across his face and he pushed it back. Absently, almost carelessly, he turned his black-bladed knife through his hands.

John opened his eyes.

He felt a slight shock as the surrounding stone walls and walkways of Rathal'pesha instantly rushed over him. Reflexively, he gripped the walkway railing, as if the world had truly shifted beneath him. For a few minutes, John simply stood where he was, wondering how he had just seen Ravishan.

His first instinct was to disregard the experience. For all he knew, it had just been an effect of a sleepless night, deep guilt, and wishful thinking.

It wasn't as if he'd opened the Gray Space or caused spontaneous combustion. He'd just imagined Ravishan, whose image came to him all too often and too readily.

Still, John decided that it was worth following. Seeing Ravishan turn the sharp knife through his hands so carelessly had disturbed him. Even if his vision had been completely wrong, John knew he had to go up the mountain.

He went quickly, only stopping to get a heavy coat and gloves.

☾☾☾

John followed the narrow animal tracks leading up between the outcroppings of rock and scrub pines. A few wild goats paused atop jagged stones to watch him pass beneath them. He climbed higher and the air began to burn in his lungs. Despite the snow and wind, sweat beaded his body.

It was tiring work, and yet not as difficult as he had expected. He had anticipated more trouble keeping his footing, but that, at least, seemed to come easily. Even scaling the face of a steep incline, with his body pressed against the frigid rock, hand and footholds seemed to simply open where he needed them. It gave him an odd feeling of security, as if the mountain itself were cradling him, and it would not let him fall.

Just the kind of thought that would come to a man suffering from oxygen deprivation, John told himself. He shook his head and continued climbing. He was almost there. He could already see the outcropping where Ravishan knelt. John picked his way closer. Ravishan's black coat and hair stood out sharply against the white snow.

Ravishan's gaze was distant, almost unseeing. He raised his empty hands to his mouth and breathed over his fingers, presumably to warm them. A rush of relief washed over John as he saw that Ravishan had sheathed his black curse blade. Slowly, Ravishan shifted his gaze from the distant sky to the field of gray stone and white snow surrounding him. When he suddenly saw John, he looked as startled as if John had leapt out from nowhere.

John smiled and gave a tired wave.

Ravishan seemed expressionless. He straightened and stood. For a moment, John thought Ravishan might just slip away through the Gray Space. Instead, he remained where he was, watching as John closed the distance between them.

It was only when John stepped in close to Ravishan, sharing his shelter beneath the stone outcropping, that a red blush spread across Ravishan's cheeks. Then it seemed incredibly natural for John to wrap his arms around the other man and draw him close. Ravishan surged into the embrace, hugging John so hard that it was almost painful. When he pressed his face against John's neck, his skin felt icy. The fragrances of incense and pollen still clung to Ravishan from the night before. His body felt so good in John's arms.

"Are you all right?" John asked.

Ravishan nodded, not lifting his face from where it was pressed against John's neck.

"I shouldn't have left you the way I did," John spoke softly, his lips brushing Ravishan's cold hair. There was no one to overhear them, but secrecy had become a reflex to him. "I'm sorry."

"It's not your fault." Ravishan finally looked up at him. "I've been thinking about the things you said—"

"You shouldn't." John wished he could have taken the whole thing back somehow and been less of an arrogant bastard. "I don't know half of what I'm talking about."

"But you were right," Ravishan told him. "I hadn't thought about what could happen to us. When I did... when I thought of what Dayyid could do to you if he discovered us…" Ravishan bowed his head against John's chest.

"It's all right," John whispered. "We aren't going to do anything. So nothing will happen to us."

Ravishan lifted his face again. The afternoon light lit golden flecks in his dark eyes. Traces of a blush still colored his cheeks, but his mouth remained pale from the cold.

John bowed his head and gently kissed Ravishan's lips. He only meant it to be brief and sweet. But then Ravishan closed his eyes and opened his mouth to him. Desire surged through John's body. He pulled Ravishan against him hard, kissing him with a savage hunger.

Then John caught himself and drew back.

"Nothing's going to happen?" Ravishan asked. Slowly, he opened his eyes and offered John one of his dazzling, rare smiles.

John loved that smile—the joy in it, the honesty of it, and most of all the fact that it was meant just for him. Suddenly, John desperately wanted Ravishan. The wind, snow and stone surrounding them didn't matter. All he wanted was to kneel with Ravishan beneath the shelter of this outcropping and make love to him. It took all of his will to stop himself from pulling Ravishan back into his arms.

"I told you, I didn't know what I was talking about," John answered.

John forced himself to let go of Ravishan and step back. Ravishan released him hesitantly.

John's entire body ached with an almost overpowering longing. It had been years since he'd touched another man and felt his arousal returned so fervently. And Ravishan wasn't just any other man. He was strong, smart, beautiful, and so very eager—everything John could have wanted.

But neither of them could afford to embark on this affair. Only this morning Hann'yu had warned him that at least one man had lost his life for such a thing. Homosexuality wouldn't be tolerated even in jest here.

John had to look away out over the frigid mountains for several moments before he could regain his composure.

"It's so cold," he said just to fill the silence. "You wouldn't even know it was spring."

"It always feels like winter up here," Ravishan replied.

John didn't trust himself to look at Ravishan, so he occupied himself by digging through his coat pockets for the pair of heavy gloves that he had brought.

"Here." John handed over the gloves. "Your hands looked cold."

"You could see them, behind your back?" Ravishan asked.

"Not just now. Earlier." John glanced to him and watched as Ravishan pulled the gloves on and flexed his fingers against the stiff leather.

"Thank you."

"It's the least I could do." John fell silent, unable to find anything safe to say. His mouth still burned from Ravishan's kiss. His body ached.

"So…" Ravishan said, but then didn't add anything else.

At last, John said, "I suppose we should get back to Rathal'pesha. Dayyid has the ushiri'im looking for you."

Ravishan sighed. As he gazed down at the monastery, that distant, hopeless expression returned to his face. From so far above, the stone walls and dark green trees seemed so small. John could blot the entire monastery out with one raised hand.

"I don't want to go back," Ravishan murmured. The words were so soft that John wasn't sure that he had been meant to hear them. "I hate it there."

John opened his mouth to tell Ravishan that he was sorry, that it was unavoidable, but then stopped himself.

When he had climbed up here he had only been thinking of Ravishan's safety. Obliquely he'd imagined shepherding Ravishan back down to Rathal'pesha, as if he would be bringing Ravishan home. But now it struck him that the monastery offered Ravishan none of the security or protection of a home.

John knew that Ravishan's right arm, hidden beneath his coat sleeve, was swathed in bandages. John realized that at some point he had stopped thinking of the perpetual injuries those bandages masked. He had begun to accept the countless small scars and fresh cuts tracing Ravishan's body as if they were natural. Scars on the skin of an ushiri seemed as harmless as freckles. But they weren't natural, and they weren't harmless. They were years of pain carved into flesh.

Those injuries were all that Rathal'pesha offered Ravishan. Of course he hated the place. Of course he wanted to run away. Who wouldn't? He didn't cry like Fikiri, but John knew that Ravishan had endured far worse for much longer.

John frowned down at the monastery. In his own way, he needed Ravishan to be an ushiri and become Kahlil as much as the Payshmura priests did. The Kahlil offered him a chance to get back home. But if that meant that Ravishan had to endure injury and agony so routinely that pain became commonplace, then it wasn't worth it. Ravishan deserved better, and if there was nothing else John could do for him, he could at least give Ravishan his freedom.

"There must be somewhere you can go where Dayyid and the other ushman'im can't find you," John said softly. "Somewhere far from here. Nurjima, maybe."

From Hann'yu's descriptions, John knew it to be a vast city with a diverse and liberal population. It seemed like just the kind of place where a smart young man like Ravishan could remake himself and his life.

"You want us to run away to Nurjima?" Ravishan asked as if John had suggested something unimaginable and wondrous.

You want us to run away…

Yes, right now he wanted to go anywhere, so long as he could be with Ravishan. But John stopped himself from saying as much. He couldn't travel through the Gray Space and it would be idiotic for Ravishan not to. If he was going to escape from Dayyid, then he needed to go very far as fast as possible.

Besides that, John knew he couldn't just abandon Laurie and Bill here.

"You should go," John told him. "You could probably be there in a few minutes. Dayyid would never be able to track you down."

Ravishan studied his face for several moments and John could see the realization dawning in his expression. Ravishan shook his head.

"I'm not going to leave you." He scowled down at the distant grounds of Rathal'pesha but then looked back to John. "I promised you that I would take you home and I will."

"You made that promise years ago—"

"I want to keep it. For you," Ravishan said firmly. He shoved his gloved hands into his pockets. "And in any case, you aren't the only one I made a promise to. There's Rousma as well."

"Rousma?" John thought he might have heard the name before but he couldn't remember when. Then he recalled the girl who Ravishan secretly spoke to through the Gray Space. John recalled her strange cadences and awkward sentences whispering through the air. The same tones often hunted him through his dreams of the holy bones.

"When we were children, they took her to Umbhra'ibaye," Ravishan said. "Now she's one of the Issusha'im Oracles."

"They're going to skin her?" A shudder of revulsion coiled through John's stomach.

"They did that years ago. At least she's still alive. By holy law, we both should've been executed along with our parents. But there was too much power in our blood and bones for them to let us go." Ravishan kicked at the snow beneath his feet. "If I run away they'll take it out on Rousma."

It was so wrong, John thought. He wanted to curse the sheer injustice of Ravishan's entire life. But Ravishan's determined silence held him back.

"I swore to her that once I was Kahlil I would find a way to free her. So, you see, there's no running away for me," Ravishan said at last. He leaned into John's shoulder and John instinctively wrapped an arm around him, offering his silent comfort.

"Don't look so grim, Jahn," Ravishan told him. "Before I met you, becoming Kahlil was something I had to do to keep myself and my sister alive. I endured my training. But after I met you I began to truly want to become Kahlil. I want to cross into Nayeshi with you and…I want the life I can have there with you."

John met Ravishan's gaze and Ravishan flushed and looked down at his boots.

"Things are very different for men like us in Nayeshi," John assured Ravishan. He didn't want to brood over the liberties he'd lost in Basawar, because it would only depress him, but in comparison Nayeshi was a welcoming haven.

"When we reach Nayeshi..." Ravishan began, but then faltered.

"Yes?" John asked.

"Will you live with me? Will you be my lover?" Ravishan asked in a rush.

Despite the surrounding snow, John felt a flush of warmth. He didn't know quite what to say. There were so many reasons that they shouldn't even be discussing such a thing.

"You don't have to say yes." Ravishan shied immediately, taking a step away, eyes downcast. "I'll take you back no matter what you say."

"Of course I'll be your lover," John said quickly. "I can hardly keep my hands off you now. Do you think anything would stop me once we're in Nayeshi?"

Ravishan looked up at him, as if he were startled, then slowly his expression melted into a radiant smile.

John realized that part of what made Ravishan's smiles so charming was the sense of surprised delight that they conveyed. He never seemed to expect happiness and that made giving it to him so much more of a pleasure.

John leaned forward and stole one last quick kiss, then turned and started back down the steep trail.

Despite the fact that he could have stepped through the Gray Space and reached Rathal'pesha in an instant, Ravishan followed John on foot. When the path grew wide enough, they walked side by side, their arms brushing in an easy communion.

Chapter Thirty-Six

As the short months of northern spring passed quickly into summer, John managed little more than a furtive embrace and one desperate kiss with Ravishan. The rest of his time seemed dominated by Hann'yu's need for assistance in the infirmary.

It seemed that Dayyid pushed the ushiri'im harder every day and steadily more and more of them suffered greater injuries. In early spring, John feared that bearing the brunt of the ushiri'im's wounds would kill him, but his body adjusted and by the time the taye flowers were blooming on the mountainsides he found himself shrugging off even the deep punctures that seemed to plague Fikiri.

John took some consolation in the fact that he saw less of Ravishan because he was by far the least likely ushiri to be badly injured.

When Hann'yu didn't need John to bear the wounds of the ushiri'im, he kept busy with ushvun battle practice and studying holy texts for his formal initiation. Steadily his knowledge of the Payshmura history increased and his skill in dispatching an opponent became a reflex.

The only interruption of John's routine came one summer afternoon when Hann'yu attempted to teach him the spells that healed lesser injuries and eased pain. The result was disastrous.

Hann'yu had brought up two injured lambs for John to practice on. But the moment John had laid his hands on them, their skins had ripped open as their bones tore through their flesh. Shrieks of pain had choked as vertebrae had exploded into their throats. In an instant, they'd become nothing but blood, gristle, and fragments of bone.

John had staggered back in horror and vomited into an empty water basin.

"I don't think you were meant to be a physician," Hann'yu had remarked, his face pale.

John had nodded but hadn't been able to bring himself to look at what he'd done. After that, Hann'yu hadn't attempted to instruct John in any healing spells, much to John's relief. He continued to bear wounds, clean beds, bandage injuries, and prepare medicines, but did nothing beyond that.

Once he passed the trials of his initiation, winning the right to wear a single honor braid, he gained a little more free time.

Now as the summer neared an end, John took to visiting Samsango down in the kitchens. After long days in the heights of Rathal'pesha, bearing deep wounds, feeling the air tear asunder, and overhearing whispers of oracles and rumors of the destroyer god, he found Samsango's company relieving. They did simple work and often discussed the mundane news that the other ushvun'im brought up from Amura'taye.

"Another witch," Samsango said sadly. He settled his frail, aged body on a bench before one of the weathered cooking tables. "When I was a boy, there was only one witch that had to be burned. Now, it's nearly one a year."

John frowned at the pale flames flickering in the bread oven. Waves of heat rolled out over him. He shoved the tray of uncooked loaves inside and closed the oven door. Outside, predawn light had yet to soften the night sky. It would be hours before the majority of the ushvun'im woke.

John sat down at the table across from Samsango.

"It's the Fai'daum, you know," Samsango told him. He slowly measured out two more handfuls of ground taye into the mixing bowl. John cracked three weasel eggs into the bowl and began mixing as Samsango looked on. Slowly the red yolks of the weasel eggs colored the dough dull pink. John turned out the dough. Samsango scooped up the soft mass and began to expertly knead it.

"Their leader is in the thrall of the demoness, Ji Shir'korud," Samsango informed John.

John nodded. He recognized the name and remembered the large yellow dog he'd seen addressing the Fai'daum on the night he had been taken in by the Bousim. It felt like ages ago.

"The demoness teaches all the girls witchcraft and heresy. Then the poor, pretty things end up being burned. Such a waste."

John gazed at Samsango. A cold unease gnawed at him. The old ushvun went on working the bread dough as if the brutal murder of these girls was of no more consequence than wasted food. Samsango glanced up and gave John a gentle, warm smile.

"Up all day in the infirmary and now working all night with me in the kitchen," Samsango remarked. "You must be exhausted, Jahn."

"I'm fine," John said. He knew Samsango to be a caring man, who had gone out of his way to help John settle in the monastery when he'd first arrived. Samsango took pains to see to the health of even the most ill-tempered goats and weasels. Yet, he could also easily conclude that a girl accused of witchcraft must be burned. He didn't seem able to even imagine any other course of action.

Intellectually, John knew that it was just a matter of culture. Samsango had no way of perceiving any morality apart from Payshmura holy law. Within the Basawar culture, Samsango was perfectly consistent. He was kind and just. It was only from John's point of view that a contradiction emerged.

John wondered briefly if this was how vegetarians felt watching their companions eat meat. Or how pacifists felt watching popular war films.

He didn't want this sensation of revulsion. He liked Samsango. That was why he had come down to the kitchens in the first place. But he couldn't think of anything to say, any way to stop feeling alienated by the other man. He suddenly thought of Kyle, recalling the way his old roommate had, at times, just stood there staring at him. He, too, must have been shocked by the society around him. John wondered which of his own actions had sent waves of secret revulsion through Kyle.

"You look like you're about to fall asleep where you're sitting," Samsango said. The dull red glow of the kitchen fires softened the deep wrinkles of the old man's face. Samsango's expression was gentle, fatherly. John couldn't help but smile at him.

"I suppose I am. I'm probably slowing you down tonight," John said.

"No." Samsango patted a ball of dough down onto the cooking sheet. "This is the last. After it's baked, I'll be done. Though I have a little more room on the sheet…perhaps I should make a treat for our brothers who will be marching down the mountain."

He collected scraps of dough and worked them quickly into fat little buns. Once he was done, he laid a thin cloth over them and pushed the cooking sheet aside to allow the rolls to rise. Taye flour still caked his hands. He wiped them on a spare dishcloth, then looked up at John again.

John wanted to say something more, but he couldn't stop thinking of the girl who would be burned. Did she have friends or family? Was there anyone who would want to help her? Could they help her? What would he do if Laurie were ever discovered and condemned? The heat of the bread oven seemed suddenly more intense.

He didn't think he could imagine anything more painful, or terrible, than burning.

"I can see that you're troubled, Jahn," Samsango commented. "Would it help to tell me why?"

John didn't respond immediately; keeping his inner thoughts secret had become too much of a habit for him. But this was something he did want to share with Samsango, he realized.

"Did you know that before the first siege at Ganaa there were no witches?"

Samsango's bushy gray eyebrows shot up. "You have been listening to Ushman Hann'yu too much. He's from the south. They don't know anything there except what they read in books."

"But it's true. I looked it up."

Samsango cocked his head, seeming to contemplate something just past John.

"Long ago they might not have been called witches," Samsango said at last, "but there have always been people who are tempted to misuse Parfir's blessings. They are not always bad people, but when they do wrong, they must be punished."

"But to burn a girl to death—"

Samsango held up a silencing hand. "I understand your turmoil, Jahn. If I'm honest, I will tell you that I share your sorrow for the poor child." He sighed heavily. "But remember, if the prior hears you repeating the things that Ushman Hann'yu tells you, you won't just be whipped. You might endanger Ushman Hann'yu as well. And you could lose that braid you fought so hard to earn or be barred from the presence of the ushiri'im!"

Samsango looked truly distressed by the thought of this. He placed a callused, flour-caked hand over John's fingers. His touch felt surprisingly warm.

"For the sake of the ushiri'im, if not yourself, you should keep your peace. They need your strength."

"The ushiri'im just need a body to bear their wounds. It doesn't matter if it's mine or not," John responded.

"You do them a great service," Samsango pronounced. He glanced at the raw scar that wound around John's wrist as he did so. The injury was recent and had been Fikiri's.

When the boy had been brought into the infirmary, his fingers had been gashed down to the bone. He had fixed John with a look that was half-shock and half-accusation, but he had said nothing. John had taken as much of Fikiri's wound as he could without losing his own fingers. Now both their palms and wrists were crossed with the same tender, red scars like some blood-brother pact gone terribly wrong.

"Modesty is good." Samsango's voice cut through John's wandering thoughts. "But you should take pride in your station, you know. Not many of the ushvun'im can serve the ushiri'im so well as you do. It's a great contribution."

John gave a lackluster nod. If it wasn't him, then it would have been someone else. But Samsango wouldn't see it that way.

"And to live up in the holy chambers." Samsango closed his eyes as if he were savoring a delicious sweet. "To be so near the holiest of the holy. I envy you a little."

"Only a little?" John teased.

Samsango opened his eyes. "Not so much that I'd want to be wrapped in bandages every day of my life."

"It's not the bandages that are so bad," John replied. "It's what's under them."

"Indeed."

The warm air hung thick with the smell of taye flour and faint dry spices. The moist scent of the loaves baking in the ovens began to spread through the kitchen. John took in a deep breath, knowing that the scent should have conjured images of his mother or grandmother, but neither of them had ever baked bread. His only association with the aroma was here in Rathal'pesha. When he returned to Nayeshi, he thought, the smell would remind him of sitting here in the flickering light of the cooking fires, watching Samsango.

"I imagine you're excited about the Harvest Fair," Samsango said.

Most of the men in the monastery were anticipating the annual fair with obvious excitement. Even Dayyid had mentioned it with a tone that struck John as almost enthusiastic.

"Now that you've earned your braid, you'll be allowed to attend. You won't believe everything you'll see there. I still remember the first time my father took me. The air was like perfume, with so many scents. Southern apples and honey sweets. Wine. And there were dancers and singers all the way from Vundomu. And the things there, glass lamps in every color you could imagine, embroidered bolts of silks, fat roasting dogs." He grinned wide, exposing the few teeth he had left. "I feel like a boy again just thinking about it."

John found himself smiling at the innocence of Samsango's nostalgia.

"You'd better watch for the game tables, though, and the wine sellers." Samsango's expression grew stern and John couldn't tell if he was joking or not. "They'll take advantage of even a poor old ushvun and then coldly turn him away when his few stones are gone."

"I'll be careful," John assured him.

"It's easily said, but harder to do. You get swept up in the music and colors and all the strange new people. And the dancing women. A young man like you has to watch out for them particularly. They're so lovely that it's easy to forget yourself. Then the prior will be shouting at you for months."

"Do you want me to keep an eye out for you?" John asked.

"At my age?" Samsango laughed. "The prior would proclaim it one of Parfir's miracles if I were to get up to trouble with a dancing girl. No, I'm just warning you. Some of these girls come all the way from Nurjima. They're clever and beautiful and some are a little wicked. A young man like you has to be careful."

"I will be."

"Should you keep an eye out for me?" Samsango shook his head as he repeated John's offer. "You can be so naive, Jahn. As if a lovely city girl is going to chase down an old prune like me."

"Some people like prunes," John replied.

"Not poor prunes," Samsango said. "Nobody likes a poor prune."

"I like you."

"I like you as well, Jahn. But you're not much of a substitute for a dancing girl." Samsango patted John's hand, as if he was indulging a child. "Now that bread needs to be turned, doesn't it?"

Taking the old man's implicit suggestion, John opened the oven door. Heat washed over him like a sudden afternoon sun. He wasn't very experienced at turning trays of bread, having spent far more time on the practice grounds than in the kitchens. He slid the large, oven peel under the tray of bread and rotated it, careful not to upset the tray and send the rolls bouncing into the fire. The heat swallowed his arms and rushed over his face. Beads of sweat immediately rose across his brow and just as quickly evaporated.

Heat rolled over him in waves, growing steadily more encompassing. Flickers of discomfort built into an intensity. John could smell the fine hairs on his arms scorching. His fingers trembled as the sensation grew to searing pain.

When he finally finished and jerked the peel out of the oven, the warm air of the kitchen felt frigid against his hands.

"Oven too hot for you?" Samsango asked.

John only nodded.

"I used to be the same way," Samsango assured him. "But, you know, it's like anything. You get used to it."

"I don't know if I want to get used to it." John scowled at his red fingers.

"It can't be helped." Samsango shrugged. "You do something enough and it becomes part of your nature."

John frowned at the inherent truth of Samsango's words. It was intrinsically human to adapt to his current surroundings. He had been living in Basawar for two years. Soon, it would be three. His body had grown used to hard labor. His skin was tanned and callused, his hair drawn back into an ushvun's braid. On the rare occasions that he caught his own reflection in a polished mirror, it looked strange to him. He could stare at himself and find nothing that marked him as foreign from the other men of Rathal'pesha.

Basawar vocabulary came to him easily. Even in his dreams, the words and images all arose from this world. When he thought of his home, he thought of Nayeshi, not Earth.

John suddenly realized why he had been so focused on his alienation from Samsango this evening. He hated it, but he also needed it. He needed that feeling to remind him of who he was. He needed its discomfort to keep him from becoming the man he played at being, because it would be easy and natural to adjust and settle into this life.

But he couldn't allow himself to overlook witch burnings just because they took place out of his sight. And he couldn't be proud of helping children like Fikiri learn to endure the pain of wounds that could kill or cripple them. No matter how much he wanted to feel at ease with Samsango or Hann'yu, no matter how desperately he wanted to lose himself in adoration of Ravishan, it couldn't come at the cost of his identity.

Once Samsango had settled back down at the kitchen table, he said, "You still look troubled."

"I'm just tired."

"Then you should sleep." Samsango smiled. "If man's hungry, then he should eat. If a man's tired, he should sleep. There are very simple solutions to most problems. It's only that men resist their natures."

John took in the pragmatic wisdom of this and nodded. "You're right. I'll go."

He started for the door and Samsango called out to him, "Thank you for coming down to see me. It's nice not to be lonely, even if you're not a dancing girl."

Chapter Thirty-Seven

A day later, John was immersed in the exuberant atmosphere of the Harvest Fair. Grim, muddy Amura'taye had been transformed into something beautiful. Just as Samsango had predicted, the displays of color and noise did amaze him.

After living so long within the monastery, where the sacred quiet was broken only by solemn chanting, John had almost forgotten about the existence of music and dance. Now, the air seemed alive with it. As he walked through the rows of tents, makeshift wooden stalls, and painted carts, the sweet tones of flutes and stringed instruments whirled around him. Different melodies rose from different directions. They tangled with the scents of strange foods, strong perfumes, and living bodies pressed close in the afternoon heat.

In front of John, under the shade of a dull yellow tent, three women sang as they patted flatbread between their hands. Two of the women were older, their white hair partially hidden under red widows' veils. Doubtless, they had both lost the same husband. The third woman was younger, the daughter-in-law of the older two, John guessed. She, like most of the married women at the Harvest Festival, was obviously too poor to afford silver wedding rings. Instead, her fingers were banded with black tattoos.

Her voice rose in a pure clarity, striking notes as if she were ringing bells. Beneath her song came the constant, rhythmic slap of the flatbread cakes striking against palms. The three women worked in harmony, singing and pounding out the cakes, tossing them easily onto a thin sheet of heated metal and then flipping them up to the narrow counter where the vendor stood.

They sang of the Samsira River and the spring floods that fertilized the fields of Amura'milaun. John found the song beautiful despite its simplicity.

"Yellow honey cakes!" a man called out. "Fresh and sweet!"

His voice hardly carried over all the other vendors' cries. Countless tents, wagons, and stalls wound around each other, creating their own billowing bright streets. The Harvest Fair grew up like a second brighter, louder city outside the gates of Amura'taye. Crowds of people had come from all across the north to sell, buy, and gawk at the exotic goods of the farthest lands.

Hundreds of strangers moved around John like a living liquid, surging forward, rocking back, spilling into narrow spaces between wagons, then flowing back into the constant push and brush of bodies. Every human and animal odor washed over him and seeped through the scents of flowers, perfumes, fruits, and foods. The voices of hawkers cut through one another, only to be lost under the constant roar of the crowd. Children's squeals and screams split the air, as did the shrieks of caged birds and the bleats of agitated goats.

And yet, the music somehow carried through it all. It became a delicate stream of order flowing through the rolling chaos. As John walked further into the din of shouts and murmurs, he could still pick out the voices of the three women.

Only when John left the avenue of food and flower vendors did he lose the thread of their song.

He stood in a new maze of merchants that appeared to be dedicated to textiles and jewelry. Bolts of embroidered cloth and long swathes of delicate lace hung from racks. Strings of glass beads and beaten metal charms lay in heaps on tables. He wondered if he was getting any closer to where he should have been: Binders' Row.

None of the ushvun'im were supposed to travel outside the monastery alone, particularly not when they would be exposed to the delights and temptations of gambling tables and dancing girls. Before any of them had been excused to attend the Harvest Fair, they had been assigned partners. John had known better than to hope that Ravishan would be his. Ravishan's earlier transgression and his recent disappearance had inspired Dayyid to designate himself as Ravishan's partner for all three days that the priests were allowed to attend the Harvest Fair.

Hann'yu had requested John's company and Dayyid had agreed offhandedly. However, the moment they had reached Amura'taye, Hann'yu had simply wandered off, saying he would meet John in the Binders' Row after fifth bell. John hadn't minded at first. He could keep himself entertained easily enough. But soon he realized that without Hann'yu, he couldn't let Dayyid see him, and that meant that he couldn't see Ravishan either.

Twice already he'd been forced to duck into a tent to avoid Dayyid. And there were other ushiri'im, ushman'im, and ushvun'im at the fair as well. John didn't know any of them well enough to assume that they wouldn't report him to Dayyid. So John had spent the whole morning and most of the afternoon cagily scanning the gaudy crowds for dull gray Payshmura cassocks. Every time he glimpsed an approaching pair of his fellow priests, he was forced to plunge deeper into the crowds or hide in random tents. The situation had infused John's entire morning with a paranoid and furtive feeling of criminality.

Now, with fifth bell finally approaching, he could not find the rendezvous point. Sighing, he pushed his way forward through the throng of packed bodies. He watched enviously as two barefooted children darted between a bearded man and his wives. They dashed ahead and ducked through the flaps of a tent. His own progress had to be slower and more gentle. He was too big to easily slip between people unobtrusively. Though, he had noted that people tended to move aside the moment they noticed his gray cassock and holy braid.

Among the poorer population, the deference was most notable. The women bowed their heads and drew back beside their husbands or brothers. The men often averted their eyes or held up their hands in the Payshmura symbol of peace. John returned the gesture and passed on.

As a family of raggedly dressed herders pulled quickly aside for him, John caught a glimpse of a party of silk-clad women moving through the crowd. Their skirts were all made from the same shimmering swathes of green silk—the vivid color worn only by the Bousim family. John quickened his pace. He guessed that he looked particularly intimidating moving fast and with obvious intent. Young mothers jerked their children out of his way and men stepped aside. Only a few seconds later, he had caught up to Lady Bousim's entourage.

Pivan and his commander, Tashtu, both strode at the head of the large group. Their deep green uniforms looked crisp and the silver emblems of their rank and honors gleamed from the straight collars of their jackets. Polished pistols hung from dark leather holsters at their hips. Their black riding boots shone with the luster of oil and snakeskin.

Behind them, Lady Bousim walked slowly, seeming hardly aware of the crowds of awed farmers and herders. Her black hair was strewn with silver, emeralds, and pieces of polished jade. Her long flowing dress shimmered like nothing worn by any of the surrounding throng. The silver rings on her fingers and the silver chains linking them swung and chimed like precious bells.

Even as tall and blond as he was, John realized that he was not as out of place as Lady Bousim. Among the poor herders and farmers of Amura'taye, Lady Bousim's wealth and noble rank placed her absolutely beyond their grasp. One glance at her smooth skin, her deeply curved breasts and hips, her luxurious clothing and lustrous hair informed any onlooker that she had never toiled in a field nor gone hungry through a hard winter.

She was lovely and unobtainable. Even standing among common men and women, walking the same tight confines, she was distant. Her armed guards kept people away with just a glance. Her maids encircled her, smiling and talking, moving constantly, so that the lady herself could only be seen in brief glimpses.

Beside Lady Bousim, both Inholima and Ohbi wore their glossy black hair in long twisting masses of braids and tiny silver beads. Pale, translucent green veils floated over the long straight lines of their dresses. Laurie stood nearest to Lady Bousim, dressed just as Ohbi and Inholima were, but her platinum hair and pale skin lent her a radiance. The silver beads adorning her hair were nearly as long as Lady Bousim's. Strings of polished jade cascaded from her necklace down over her thin chest and shoulders.

Behind the women, John recognized Bati'kohl's round face and Rashan Mou'pin's startlingly vicious smile. Then there came another young rashan in a dark green uniform and beside him, Bill.

Bill looked out of place with the other men. His pale skin appeared almost blue beside the tanned arms and faces of the rashan'im. His blue eyes looked like cut stones and his black hair spiked out from his face like strokes of ink. His slim body appeared delicate, almost girlish, in comparison to the thickly corded muscle of the rashan walking beside him.

At first, John thought that the rashan had slowed his pace to accommodate Bill, but then he noticed the limp in the man's step. The rashan laughed quietly at something Bill said and nodded.

Bill glanced up and immediately picked John out of the surrounding throng of onlookers and waved him over.

"Jahn," Bill said, "this is Alidas. Do you remember him?"

John regarded the rashan. He was younger than Bill but stood taller. His brown hair fell around his face, softening the sharpness of his jaw. He returned John's gaze with a knowing intensity.

"I don't think..." John said softly and then cut himself off as the man's features and his limp made a sudden connection. This was the rashan he had ridden behind that night on the Holy Road—the young man whose leg had been crushed beneath his fallen mount. He had looked so pale that night, like a corpse.

"You were to be Fikiri's attendant?" John asked, though he was sure of the answer.

The rashan smiled and nodded. "I didn't know if you would remember me. It was so dark when we met and so long ago."

"I saw you a few times after that, but you weren't well. I think you were sleeping most of the time," John said.

"I told you he'd remember," Bill said to Alidas. "Jahn doesn't forget much."

John didn't say anything to that. In truth, he had tried to forget as much about that night as he could. Before then, he had never seen men struggle, beat, and kill each other. He had never been responsible for a single life or death before that night. Involuntarily, he recalled the dirty face of the Fai'daum youth he had hidden. He had scrupulously avoided thinking of the entire matter, and yet he could still remember the boy's name. Saimura.

"I never had the chance to thank you," Alidas said. "Pivan says you saved my life."

"I don't know that I did that much—" John cut himself short, realizing that his words could seem insulting. It was Alidas' life after all. "I'm glad that you were all right and that you've recovered," he added quickly.

"Recovered is a kind word for it," Alidas replied. "But near enough."

"We're going with the ladies to pick up some bolts of cloth for winter," Bill said. "Then we'll head back to the Bousim tents for a meal. I'm sure it would be fine if you joined us."

"I know Rashan Pivan would like to see you," Alidas added.

"And Fikiri should be meeting us there as well." Bill peered over his shoulder at the retreating backs of the rest of the Bousim entourage.

"I have to go to Binders' Row," John said. He didn't particularly want to see Fikiri. And he doubted that Fikiri wanted to see him. Still, it would be nice to talk with Bill and Laurie. "But after I'm done there, I should be free to come by. Seven bells?"

"That would be great." Bill took a half step back and bumped into a woman. She wheeled around about to hiss something at him and then went silent as her eyes fell on John. Immediately, she bowed her head and scurried deeper into the moving crowd.

Bill frowned after the woman and then eyed John. "Were you just declared scariest man at the fair, or did I miss something there?"

"It was probably just the Payshmura robes," Alidas remarked before John could explain. "You know what they say: the woman who crosses a priest steps straight into a fire."

"Sounds like something Rasho Tashtu would say." Bill gave a disgusted scowl and Alidas, too, displayed clear antipathy at the mention of his own commander. Then he glanced back through the clusters of people pushing past them. The Bousim entourage was nearly out of sight.

Alidas said, "We had better get going, or we'll never catch up."

Bill nodded. "But we'll see you later, Jahn?"

"Seven bells. I'll be there." John started to step away from them, but then paused. "You don't happen to know where Binders' Row is, do you?"

"Keep following this street south." Alidas pointed along the rows of cloth vendors. "You'll pass the leather tanners, then the binders."

"Thanks," John said.

"Tell me if you find any good books," Alidas commented. "I haven't had a chance to look yet."

"I will." John watched them go. It was strange to see Alidas, as tanned and muscular as he was, gripping Bill's slim shoulder for balance as they walked. An instant later, strangers closed in around them and John continued on his way.

He reached Binders' Row in a little under half an hour. Distantly, he could hear the city bells of Amura'taye ringing out the fifth hour. The sun was slipping from its blazing summer zenith. This far north it would still be a while before darkness, but at least the heat was beginning to relent.

The smell of leather hung over the two short corridors of wagons and wooden stalls that made up Binders' Row. Booksellers sat or leaned under the shade of their stalls, most of them quietly reading passages from their own merchandise. It wasn't a busy area. Only a few men and boys passed by John. None of them made eye contact with him or each other. John didn't see any women. It reminded him a little of his walk through Candle Alley.

"And a thousand bulls were tithed by the Lisam gaunsho to the Black Tower," an old man read slowly and solemnly as John walked past. "And the lands of the south were blessed a thousand times over by Parfir. In blossoms and fruit, in boundless fields of white taye and red, Parfir gave his holy blessings."

John leaned into the stall, peeking over the narrow shelves of books to search for Hann'yu. There was no one inside, so he walked on.

As he wandered farther along Binders' Row, the readings began to stray from purely religious works. He overheard passages that sounded more historical in nature, then those of technical works. John caught the partial descriptions of a miraculous steam engine, new printing presses, and the brilliant street lamps of Nurjima. Then he began to pick out hushed murmurs of 'bare fingers, full breasts' and 'red lips, sweet as nectar.' Just once John caught a whisper of the word, 'Fai'daum.'

John paused, trying to locate the man who had said the name of the Fai'daum; even after a few minutes of listening, he didn't hear the name of the group again. Instead the air hummed with low murmurs of hushed longing and erotic desire. John continued his search.

At last, John caught sight of Hann'yu's gray cassock and black coat. The streaks of silver that twisted throughout Hann'yu's eight braids were hidden by the deep shadows of a covered stall. He stood, eyes half closed between shelves of books, listening intently. His expression was gentle and appreciative, like a man hearing exquisite music.

The bookseller looked about thirty. He sat on a tall stool with the small leather book across one of his legs. He glanced up as John stepped into the stall but didn't stop reading.

"As she lifted the hem of her skirt to step across the stream, I caught sight of her dainty white ankle." The bookseller flipped the page. "I knew at once that she was no mere milkmaid as she claimed."

John supposed he should have predicted that he'd find Hann'yu in this section of Binders' Row.

"I've been looking all over for you," John whispered.

"What?" Hann'yu turned and swayed, then squinted at John. "Oh, Jahn. You should listen to this. Receive the wisdom of the more worldly...world." The thick, honey-like scent of mead poured off his breath.

John didn't find it unpleasant, but it struck him as too strong for so early in the day. He asked, "Are you drunk?"

Hann'yu frowned, as if he were concentrating on a difficult algorithm, and then slowly nodded. "It's really the only way that I get through the Purification Ceremony with Dayyid."

"Ceremony?" John couldn't recall any mention of a ceremony. "When?"

"Tonight." Hann'yu made a sour face and then turned his attention to the man reading. He made a quick gesture and in response the man lifted his book to display the title embossed into the leather spine. *The Journey from Innocence.*

"You'd think, with such fine literature as this, that more boys would be interested in reading even in a cold, ugly wasteland like Amura'taye." Hann'yu paused, then added, "Especially in a cold ugly wasteland like Amura'taye."

John waited for something more, but Hann'yu had fallen silent. He rocked back slightly and John realized that he was again listening to the reading.

"Her pink-tipped fingers worked apart the buttons of her wet blouse," the reader softly intoned.

"You say Dayyid is holding a ceremony tonight?" John prompted.

Hann'yu nodded, but offered no further explanation.

"What kind of ceremony?" John asked. "Is there something special we'll be expected to—"

"No," Hann'yu cut him off. "All we'll be expected to do is remain silent. Say nothing, do nothing. Just watch like corpses."

It wasn't a reassuring turn of phrase. John whispered, "But what exactly—"

"Hush." Hann'yu held his hand up in front of John's mouth. "This is a sweet story. We shouldn't ruin it. Just listen."

Hann'yu closed his eyes and John relented. He waited while the man on the stool read on to the end of the story.

The milkmaid turned out to be a noble girl fleeing an abductor. The hero was revealed to be her intended husband in disguise. Everything tied up at the end and finished with the passionate couple still in perfect moral standing. It wasn't much to John's taste, but Hann'yu seemed to enjoy it.

"Eloci Nass'ilem." Hann'yu smiled fondly. "She wasn't allowed to write nearly enough in her time."

"Yes, it sounded interesting," John said automatically. "But what is the Purification Ceremony for?"

Hann'yu gave John a weary look. "Don't look so concerned, Jahn. The ceremony won't begin until the last hour of the day at twelfth bell. There's nothing you'll be expected to do but chant and look holy. Nothing you need trouble yourself over."

"If it's nothing to worry about, then why are you getting so drunk?" John asked quietly.

"So drunk?" Hann'yu smirked. "You have no idea. You'll wish you had a whole vat of wine in you later tonight. It's the only good excuse a priest can claim for a weak stomach."

The man who had been reading watched them for a few moments, but then looked away as John caught his gaze. He flipped through the pages of the book on his lap but didn't begin reading again. John wondered how common it was for a pair of priests to be seen arguing in one of these bookstalls.

Hann'yu pulled a book out from the shelf and gave it to John. He chose another for himself. John looked down at the slim volume Hann'yu had given him. A circle enclosing a tree was embossed on the cover, but there was no title. John turned it over in his hands. The spine was bare.

"*Poems from Milaun*," Hann'yu supplied the title. "Even Dayyid couldn't complain. Well, I suppose he could, but not much."

Hann'yu took his book and approached the bookseller. John followed him to the front of the stall. Hann'yu passed the man two black-lacquered coins. One side was etched with the image of a tower, the other with gold sun.

"Thank you for coming so far from civilization and reading so well," Hann'yu said. "We will take these two."

The man smiled at Hann'yu and handed the coins back. "The compliment of Parfir's blessing would be a greater payment than any other."

"Of course." Hann'yu drew a small polished stone from the pocket of his cassock and placed it in the man's palm. "May Parfir protect you in the darkness of his sleep and lavish you with joy upon his waking."

The man lowered his head and remained bowed until after the two of them had left his stall.

As they worked their way through the rest of the Harvest Fair, John discovered that this was a routine interaction. Earlier in the day, he had been so focused on avoiding other priests that he hadn't watched them make any purchases. Now, with Hann'yu, he realized that they never really paid for anything. Hann'yu either gave out blessings and polished pebbles or lacquered wooden coins. Many of the vendors' wagons displayed large dishes of the polished stones. Others hung strings of the black coins above their entryways.

Hann'yu paused against the side of a seed-seller's wagon.

"We should find a wealthy merchant or one of the city judges to invite us into one of their tents," Hann'yu said.

"Not necessary. I've already been invited to the Bousim tent."

"That's right. You were Fikiri's attendant." Hann'yu grinned. "That's better than I could have hoped for. We'll drink ourselves sick and pass out."

"I really don't think that would be a good idea—"

"Don't be so serious, Jahn." Hann'yu rolled his eyes.

"I wouldn't be, but I'm not entirely sure you're joking."

Hann'yu sighed. "I would never embarrass myself or you in front of such esteemed company as Lady Amha'in'Bousim."

Knowing the kind of man Hann'yu was, John believed him. Hann'yu's warmth and reverence for noblewomen seemed innately ingrained in his nature. The presence of Lady Bousim would probably do more to encourage sobriety in him than anything John could do or say.

"All right. Let's go then," John decided.

It didn't require much effort to locate the Bousim tents. They rose up in swooping emerald arcs behind the rows of flower sellers. Wealthy families of Amura'taye had erected tents for themselves as well, but none were as vast or as pleasantly placed. The natural perfume of cut blossoms and live flowers drifted over the heavier scent of tahldi hide and human sweat.

Rather than merely providing temporary relief from the sun, the main Bousim tent impressed John as a work of architecture. Massive, carved timbers had been driven into the earth and secured with thick viridian-dyed ropes. The huge lengths of green cloth that stretched across the timbers were reinforced with worked leather displaying a pattern of the Bousim crossed arrows. Polished jade baubles hung from the timbers and lengths of silky green cloth, and silver bells were strung across the entry.

The four rashan'im who guarded the front of the great tent watched Hann'yu and John as they approached but didn't challenge them. As they entered, the faint sound of bells announced their presence. Inside, the air was cool. The tent's interior was suffused with an emerald glow from light passing through the cloth walls. Hann'yu's dark skin took on a pine tone. John imagined that his own pale hair had turned the color of a lime.

Aside from an open circle at the center of the tent, the rest of the floor was littered with low tables and embroidered cushions. Men, wearing the badges of city judges, guild fathers, and scholars, sat at the tables surrounded by their wives, unwed daughters, and favorite sons. Some glanced up as John and Hann'yu entered, but most seemed too engrossed in their conversations to take any note.

Every table was laden with dishes piled high with fragrant cut fruit or sliced meat. As he eyed these, John became suddenly aware of the absence of the flies and bees that had filled the open fairgrounds. He surmised that the veils of cloth and strings of bells over the entry weren't purely ornamental.

At the far end of the tent, Lady Bousim lounged with her maids and attendants. Two younger men were seated across from her. Their clothes, like those of the guild fathers, city judges, and scholars were well made and new. They wore clean, polished shoes, instead of sewn goatskins or scuffed work boots. That alone marked them as better off than most of the people at the Harvest Fair. But compared to Lady Bousim and her entourage, they might as well have been peasants.

Lady Bousim looked up as John and Hann'yu approached. She gave John a gentle smile, but when she took in Hann'yu's face, her expression suddenly became radiantly happy. She stood.

"Please forgive me if I'm wrong, but you are the very image of Hann'yu Shim'arun of the Lisam House," Lady Bousim said.

"I never did the name service enough while it was mine." Hann'yu bowed smoothly and then straightened. "Now I am only Ushman Hann'yu."

Both Hann'yu and Lady Bousim turned expectantly to John. His grasp of Basawar etiquette was poor when it came to women, but he knew that it was rarely desirable for them to introduce themselves to unrelated men, particularly if the men were of a rank close to or higher than their own. Hann'yu cleared his throat quietly. Suddenly, John realized that they were waiting for him to introduce Hann'yu to Lady Bousim.

"Ushman Hann'yu, please allow me to present the benevolent Lady Amha'in'Bousim to you."

Hann'yu bowed a second time and Lady Bousim invited them both to sit and dine.

Once the formality of the introduction had been dispensed with, Hann'yu installed himself at the table across from Lady Bousim and the two of them immediately began discussing their native city of Nurjima. The two handsome young men who had been attempting to entertain Lady Bousim were all but forgotten. Hann'yu opened the book he had purchased and read a brief passage. Lady Bousim recited the passage that followed from memory. A classic of Basawar literature, John supposed.

He worked his way back to where Bill sat, just behind Laurie. He wasn't surprised to see that Alidas was seated there too. His right leg jutted straight out over a pillow in an awkward fashion. The maids and rashan'im all around Lady Bousim were talking to each other but with their voices lowered. The sound created a soft, almost insectile hum.

"You just missed Fikiri," Bill remarked.

"He brought me flowers." Laurie held up a small bouquet of red blossoms. "It was so cute. He ran off like a little kid right after handing them to me."

"I'm seething with jealousy," Bill said.

"I'm quite attracted to the bouquet myself," Alidas told Bill. "I would try to steal it, but I'm sure your wife would break my good leg."

Laurie snickered and lifted one tiny, white fist. "Yeah, watch out, Alidas. I'll take you out."

"If you keep bullying me like that, Behr is going to take pity on me and you know where that could lead," Alidas murmured.

"Brutal fists of fury for you both." Laurie held up her balled fists and made a tiny jabbing motion.

"Is there anything you'd like to eat or drink?" Bill asked.

"Anything really," John said. "But no wine. I'll just pass out."

Bill waved one of the Bousim serving girls to him. He ordered white taye cakes and roast lamb and blossom water.

"And spring cheese," Laurie added. "Be sure to bring a big block of spring cheese."

The servant girl nodded and slipped away.

"Did you find something in Binders' Row?" Alidas leaned forward slightly, as if to read the title of John's book.

"*Poems from Milaun*." John offered the slim volume to Alidas.

Alidas took the book and held it with reverence. He didn't flip through the pages as John had; rather, he treated them with care and read with interest.

"These are the old plains songs. You hear field women singing them in rounds when you ride through the southern countryside. They sing them in the kitchens as well." Alidas turned the page that he had been reading. "You can tell that some of them come from the apple orchards near Umbhra'ibaye because of the mentions of the bones. The Issusha'im Oracles are there, you know."

"Yes, of course," John replied. He was only half listening to Alidas.

He hadn't realized how tired he was until he sat down and relaxed. He'd been up since dawn and the walk down from Rathal'pesha was always tiring. He noticed that a number of people had stretched out on the ground with their cushions propped under their elbows or beneath their heads. He lay back.

The green tent above him glowed like the underside of an immense leaf. John closed his eyes.

"Would you like me to read some aloud for you?" Alidas offered.

"Certainly," John replied. Laurie laughed.

"I think Alidas was asking the ladies, Jahn," Laurie whispered. John shrugged in reply.

Alidas' voice was soft as he read, and the cadence of the poem reminded John of a lullaby:

"Fine men may court you with silver and stone.
Spring blossoms will promise an autumn delight.
But bless us, our sisters of holy white bone,
Lest day breaks too swiftly and turns into night..."

Alidas continued reading, but John's thoughts lingered on the words of the first poem: *sisters of holy white bone*.

The existence of the Issusha'im Oracles seemed too strange to be believed. Living bones. They frightened him and fascinated him at the same time. Eyeless skulls somehow watching, searching, looking into the unknowable future. Yet Ravishan's sister was one of them.

John didn't know exactly when he drifted into sleep. But his thoughts began wandering from the oracles to the great stone gateways that they commanded. With the Nayeshi'hala, they could tear apart the fabric of existence. John's dreaming mind created images of black holes ripping through the skies, tearing away color and light from the land the way a rupture in the hull of an airplane could whip away all life within. He shuddered in revulsion—as if those two lambs were once again dying in his hands and he couldn't stop it from happening.

John bolted upright.

The tent was darker, lit now by hanging oil lamps. More people had gathered inside. Many of them were in the open space at the center of the tent, dancing. John straightened his cassock. He could only catch glimpses of the people around him as they moved between the luminous oil lamps and the deep shadows of the night. Their bodies melted into one another, forming one swirling silhouette.

Music rose up from the far left side of the tent where a dozen musicians were gathered on a raised dais. John was a little surprised to see Bill among them, strumming an instrument that looked like an overgrown mandolin. Alidas leaned at the edge of the musicians' dais, watching Bill play. He held a small bone flute in his hands. John guessed that he, too, would be playing along with the musicians.

For a few minutes, John simply watched Bill play. In Nayeshi he had never shown any aptitude for music. Or perhaps, he just hadn't shown any interest in it. He hadn't shown any interest in anything, really. He was the friend who everyone thought was smart enough to be outstanding in any field he chose, but who never made a choice. He had seemed content to do nothing but rent odd videos, memorize obscure, useless trivia, and wander through dance parties dispensing misinformation.

Now it was strange to see him so deeply focused and eager. John noted the way Bill's fingers slid and jumped along the strings. He could pick out the distinct tones of Bill's music as it floated through the surrounding pipes and drums. The purity and skill of it was obvious.

John searched the wide space of the tent for Laurie. He caught sight of her at the entry, nearly opposite him. She stood beside Ohbi, watching Bill. A moment later, she glanced to the pile of cushions where John had been sleeping. Seeing him awake, she waved and held up a small hunk of what looked like bread and began working her way around the edge of the crowded tent toward him.

John caught glimpses of her between the raised arms and turning bodies of the dancers. For a second, she dropped into a deep shadow and then emerged again, her pale hair gleaming in the lamplight. She wasn't far from him when, suddenly, a dark form seemed to melt out of the silhouettes of the dancers and jerk her back into the darkness. At first, John mistook it for a play of the flickering light.

But Laurie didn't reappear.

A sudden fear seized John. He rushed forward, brushing dancers and onlookers aside, hardly taking note of them as he raced along the edge of the tent.

He could feel some strange power, radiating from within the curtain-like folds of the tent wall. It shimmered through the darkness like heat waves dancing across a desert horizon. It drew him.

John tore back one of the deep folds of the tent to discover Rasho Tashtu holding Laurie from behind in a tight grip. One of his thick arms crushed across her throat, while his other hand groped at her breast.

"If you don't let me go," Laurie hissed, "I swear I'll make you wish you were dead."

John knew she could and would. He could feel the fury and power emanating from her in waves.

"You need a little training." Tashtu's words were slurred. "A real man—"

John didn't let him get any further. He caught hold of Tashtu's hands and ripped them off of Laurie. She immediately bolted free.

"Who the hell do you think you are?" Tashtu roared. The alcoholic flush in his face looked almost black in the shadows of the tent.

"Release me, peasant!" Tashtu snarled. "I'll have your head for this."

He attempted to jerk free but John held him, grinding his thumbs into the soft flesh of Tashtu's wrists. He wanted to snap the man's hands off. He wanted to feel the bones crack and the tendons tear. But Tashtu was too high-ranking in the Bousim house. Harming him would only end up endangering Laurie and Bill. John knew that, and yet it was incredibly hard not to keep twisting the man's arms, grinding into his bones.

John released him and Tashtu stumbled sideways.

John glanced back to Laurie. Her jaw was clenched, her lips pressed tightly closed as if she were fighting to remain silent. Her pale eyes looked unnaturally bright. Her entire body trembled, but John didn't know if it was with fear or rage.

"Are you all right?" John asked.

Laurie managed a tight nod.

John caught a movement from the corner of his eye and turned in time to see Tashtu straighten. His hands were clenched into fists.

"Fucking priest!" Tashtu swung for him.

John blocked Tashtu's punch and then caught the man's throat in one hand. John's fingers felt hot as they closed around the supple muscles and delicate column of cartilage that encased Tashtu's trachea. John flexed his hand and Tashtu choked.

"I could kill you." John's words came out evenly, as if he was not seething with anger, as if it was a simple statement of ability and not a driving desire. He was so enraged that he could hardly think of anything else. His attention locked on the kick of Tashtu's desperate pulse against his palm.

Only slowly did he become aware of how quiet the tent had become. Distantly, he registered the circle of startled and fascinated men and women surrounding him.

Tashtu swayed in John's grip, his mouth wide open, his face dark purple. John instantly released him. Tashtu collapsed to the ground. This time, he didn't struggle back up. He lay, sprawled out and gasping.

John turned back to find Laurie, but she had disappeared into the crowd. John thought he saw her far back with the other members of the Bousim household, her face buried against Bill's chest.

"Interesting choice of entertainment, Ushvun."

John turned to meet Dayyid's unamused face. John opened his mouth to offer his explanation but then realized that Dayyid appeared to be in no mood to hear anything he had to say.

Chapter Thirty-Eight

John hung back between Ravishan and Hann'yu as they trailed Dayyid back across the fairgrounds. In the depths of the night, John expected the stalls to have been locked up and the vendors to have bedded down. Instead, torches had been ignited, and oil lamps lit and hung. Fairgoers still packed the narrow avenues between the stalls, tents, and wagons. There were fewer children but far more men.

The smell of burning oils and strong wine wafted through every other scent on the air. The music that John picked out through the roar of fast bargaining and loud drunken voices was oddly slow. Smoky, sensual melodies curled out from the closed flaps of the tents they passed.

Dayyid glanced back over his shoulder at Hann'yu.

"I would have thought that you'd have remained sober enough to keep Ushvun Jahn from embarrassing himself in a common brawl."

Hann'yu grinned. A red, alcoholic flush spilled across his nose and cheeks. The strong smell of wine and mead clung to his breath. There was no denying that he had been drinking. But compared to Tashtu, Hann'yu only seemed slightly tipsy.

"It was hardly a *common* brawl." Hann'yu gave John a slightly lopsided grin. "That was a rasho that our Jahn took down. And the man had been mistreating ladies all evening. Jahn may very well have been acting as Parfir's wrath for the offenses. It was magnificent."

John glanced to his right to see Ravishan's reaction. So far he had been silent, keeping his eyes focused on Dayyid's back. Ravishan looked over to him at the same moment and gave him a brief, approving smile.

John imagined that an entire day spent with Dayyid had to be miserable and exhausting. He wished he could offer Ravishan some consolation.

"You would have been proud to see him move, Dayyid," Hann'yu continued. "It was like lightning. Something to put the fear of god back into the masses."

"Ushvun Jahn's prowess does nothing to excuse you," Dayyid responded coldly. "I shouldn't have to come and fetch you for the Purification Ceremony every year. If you had minded the hour and kept your eyes on Jahn, none of this would have happened."

"But as it was, Jahn saved a very pretty girl," Hann'yu countered.

"For all you know she was one of the whores who follow the fair," Dayyid said.

"She was Jahn's sister." The playful tone dropped from Hann'yu's voice.

Dayyid glanced back, this time to John. John met his gaze. Dayyid's scowl seemed to soften. He turned his attention back to their path.

"Was she...is she unharmed?" Dayyid asked after several minutes of silence.

"I think so," John said.

Dayyid nodded and said nothing more.

They continued threading their way south through the fairgrounds until they reached the last wall that enclosed the terraced steps of Amura'taye. City guards, armed with archaic-looking bows and spears, stood on duty at the heavy gates. They bowed as Dayyid approached and remained bent down until John, Ravishan, and Hann'yu had all passed through the open gates.

Outside, John expected to only see the flat expanse of the Holy Road, the small shrine to Parfir, and the surrounding forest. Instead, he found that they had stepped out into a second fairground. But a single whiff of the air told John why this one was kept so far from the city.

The air was choked with the smells of blood, meat, excrement, urine, and fires. Makeshift pens held fattened goats, young sheep, and old gaunt tahldi. Dogs crouched together in cages. Coops of weasels hung from the eaves of wagons. Smoked and salted carcasses dangled from walls and over entryways.

Tahldi bellowed and dogs whimpered as they were dragged from their pens. Teams of sweating, muscular men wrestled the animals down. Butchers slashed open the animals' throats with fast, practiced strokes of their gleaming knives. Blood splashed and sprayed. Almost immediately, women and girls took over the work of skinning, gutting, and butchering the slaughtered creatures.

In the flickering red torchlight, the bodies of butchered animals seemed to melt into the blood-stained sweating forms of the men and women moving between them. Crowds of buyers shoved their way to the pens. They pointed and shouted out which animals they wanted, many demanding the same dog, goat, or sheep. Arguments seemed to break out constantly.

"You haven't been here before, have you?" asked Hann'yu.

John shook his head. He had tried to hide his revulsion at the vast, open-air abattoir, but Hann'yu must have noticed it.

"I was astounded the first time I came as well. I couldn't believe how many people were up and about this late. They don't even have proper lights." Hann'yu shook his head. "But the blood market is always busiest at night, when the air is cooler and there aren't so many flies."

John simply nodded. The fact that it was so busy at night hadn't really made an impression on him. His deep familiarity with the twenty-four-hour conveniences of Nayeshi made the idea of nighttime shopping unremarkable.

It was the way the blood and butchery seemed so routine, the straightforward brutal slaughter that shocked him.

"The night brings out its own kind of vermin." Dayyid threw a pointed look to the shadowy alcove between two wagons where a group of men seemed to be lounging. John wasn't sure what Dayyid was referring to. The men looked bored, but hardly like vermin. In fact, some of them seemed very well dressed. Then John saw a woman farther back in the shadows. The thick body of the man thrusting between her sprawled legs hid most of her nudity. Her thin arms absently clung to his back as she stared up at the dark sky.

Noticing John's stare, one of men waiting his turn lowered his gaze. Others shifted so that that John wouldn't see their faces.

"It wouldn't be half so bad if the girls were allowed to ply their trade indoors," Hann'yu said. "In Nurjima, the laws have been changed and the diseases—"

"This isn't Nurjima," Dayyid cut him off.

Hann'yu sighed and didn't make a reply. His amused energy seemed to be evaporating. His steps had grown steadily slower and clumsier as he continued walking.

John looked to see how Ravishan was responding to all of this. His expression was distant, his eyes still fixed on Dayyid's back. He didn't even seem to be listening to the conversation.

As they pressed through a crowd gathered around a bull calf. John very briefly allowed his hand to brush against Ravishan's. Ravishan's expression didn't change at all, but he grasped John's hand in a tight, almost desperate grip. John held his hand for an instant and then broke away before anyone could notice the exchange.

They continued working their way through the crowds until they reached the middle of the blood market.

There, two small braziers stood about four yards in front of the aged building housing Parfir's shrine. Other ushvun'im and ushiri'im had gathered outside the weathered wooden walls. John recognized Samsango and Fikiri among them. Samsango gave him a brief wave.

Dayyid stopped just short before the open doorway of the building and turned, scowling at Hann'yu. "You're sober enough to inspect her, I hope?"

Hann'yu nodded.

"Go on then." Dayyid waved a hand at the shrine. "We don't have much time, so try to be quick."

Again, Hann'yu only nodded. His lips were pressed closed in a hard line. His face looked pale even in the warm red firelight. John wondered if he was going to be sick. Hann'yu took a deep breath and then walked into the shrine.

"My brothers." Dayyid raised his voice, addressing the rest of the ushvun'im and ushiri'im. "It is time to begin our prayers."

Immediately, the gathered men knelt in rows along either side of the doorway. They filled the entire space between the shrine and the two lit braziers, only leaving a narrow path between the two. John wasn't sure where he was supposed to sit. The ushiri'im seemed to have taken the spaces closest to the braziers. John guessed that he should be back farther with Samsango and the other ushvun'im. He began to go but Dayyid caught him by the arm.

"Harvest wines affect Hann'yu more than they ought to," Dayyid whispered. "When he's done in the shrine, make sure he doesn't come back out and embarrass himself in front of the ushvun'im. Wait for him by the door."

John strode quickly to the doorway and crouched down, leaning his back against the wooden frame. He had a terrible feeling about all of this.

The small flames in the braziers snapped and flashed behind Dayyid.

Dayyid remained standing, making sure that all of the men were properly spaced and solemn. Behind him, Ravishan also stood, waiting. When Dayyid turned and strode to the closest fires, Ravishan followed him.

Dayyid raised his hand, signaling the prayer with a quick motion of his fingers. Instinctively, the words came to John, as they did to the priests surrounding him. The low, deep invocations rolled from them like a sudden flood. Their voices washed through the air, engulfing the cries of animals and drowning the noise of commerce.

Behind him in the darkness of the shrine, John thought he could hear a faint sound, a whimper. He turned his head just slightly to look back into the dark chamber. Inside, five city guards stood circled around Hann'yu and the naked girl he knelt over. One of the guards absently toyed with the head of a sledgehammer. Another held a small lamp out over Hann'yu. Its light cast Hann'yu's face in shadow but burned into the girl's features.

She was young, probably still in her teens. Her head had been carelessly shaved. Dirt and scabs mottled her bare skin. She tossed her head and cried out, but a tight leather gag muffled her voice.

Her scraped, bruised arms were bound back behind her. The guards held her legs apart as she struggled to pull them closed.

"Well?" The guard's voice hardly carried over the waves of chanting that enveloped John. "Has she got a whelp in her, or not?"

Hann'yu glanced up at the man. His skin looked deathly pale as it caught the light. He lowered his face again before he spoke. "No, she isn't carrying a child."

"Then it's the fire for this bitch." The guard holding the lamp grinned. "Ring the bell."

Hann'yu didn't look at any of the guards, but simply walked away from them as if he were half-asleep. He reached the doorway of the shrine but didn't come out. Instead, he slumped down to the floor and pressed his forehead against the wall. His eyes were clenched shut, but tears still dribbled down his cheeks. He clamped his hands over his mouth to cover the sound.

John looked away as a brassy bell clanged overhead.

Ahead of him, men and women from both fairgrounds were gathering. More city guards arrived, leading tahldi hitched to wagons bearing wood, kindling rags, and oil.

He could hear the girl whimpering and moaning behind him as he watched the unlit pyre steadily growing in front of him. He tried to imagine what he could do to free the girl. But there were too many guards. Even if he could overpower all five of them, then what would he do? There was nothing.

Women from the city threw bundles of dried herbs and flowers into the heap of kindling. Many of them knelt and added their voices to the prayers of the priests. The men seemed less solemn. Several youths passed drinks among themselves and exchanged jokes with the guards building the pyre.

John closed his eyes and chanted along with the priests around him. He all but shouted the words out, drowning out the pathetic noises of the girl behind him and the laughter of the gathering crowds of men.

"Let the flames shine," he called out, "and this darkness will be consumed. It will not share your breath, holy Parfir. It will not touch your flesh. It will not taste your sacred blood. It will burn away from you and never have shape again."

The prayers went on. John had recited them before. He had practiced them with Pivan and Bati'kohl here in the shrine. He had recited them almost daily in the monastery. He had known them for years, but he had not understood them.

A sacred fire, parting shadows from forms, it had seemed so abstract. But it wasn't. A genuine pyre was being built in front of him and it was a real girl who they would strip of her living form.

John glanced back to Hann'yu. He lay on his side now, his face buried in his arms. John guessed that he had passed out and envied him.

Dayyid stood, overseeing the construction of the pyre. There was a focused intensity to his expression. The light from the two braziers gleamed over his long black braids and glowed in his eyes. He chanted, his low strong voice carrying over all the rest. He held an unlit torch in one hand.

Ravishan knelt beside Dayyid with his head bowed, his loose black hair hiding his face. Fikiri sat a little further back among the rest of the ushiri'im. He stared out past the pyre into the gathered crowd of townspeople, tradesmen, and city guards. His mouth barely moved with the words of the prayers.

John heard the squeal of a hinge from behind him and then the five city guards marched out of the doorway, dragging the girl between them. She sobbed and made pleading noises around her gag. The fingers of her bound hands were swollen, black, and horribly bent back. Her legs scraped the ground like broken branches as the guards dragged her past the line of priests.

Dayyid held up his hand to end the prayers. All of the gathered ushvun'im and ushiri'im went quiet. The city guards stopped in front of Dayyid, lowering the girl to the dirt at his feet.

"Unholy creature." Dayyid glanced down at her for only an instant. "You have been found barren of even Parfir's smallest blessing. Once, he fed you with his own flesh, quenched your thirst with his very blood. He brought you the abundance of summer and gave you shelter in winter. You knew only his kindness and yet made yourself like a poison to him. You gave yourself to his enemies as a whore gives herself to greed.

"You have so defiled the blessings that he placed upon your flesh that even your woman's womb is a place of desolation."

The girl's mouth worked around the gag, making the motions of denials and pleas, but only choked animal sounds came out. Dayyid scowled down at her, then glanced to Ravishan. At first, Ravishan simply remained where he was, head bowed, arms hanging limply. Then he stood. He didn't look at the girl. Instead, he stared at the small clay pot in his hand. There were markings on it, little gold suns and silver moons.

"Unholy creature," Dayyid began again, "you have fouled yourself beyond repentance or redemption. You have refused his love and now you can only know his wrath."

Dayyid stepped to the side as Ravishan spilled the glistening contents of the jar over the girl. It was lamp oil, John realized. The city guards heaved her back up off the ground and dragged her to the pyre. With a swing, they hurled her onto the low mass of oil-soaked wood, sticks, and flowers. In a panic, she tried to get to her feet. Her broken legs collapsed under her. She flailed and jerked, trying to push herself off of the kindling. Her motions only seemed to tangle her further in the broken wood and slick oil.

"Do not pity her!" Dayyid shouted over the girl's howls. "Evil feeds on honest men with teeth carved from pity!"

Dayyid turned and handed his unlit torch to Ravishan. "Look upon her and do not flinch. Her despair is Parfir's triumph. Make yourself worthy of him."

Ravishan took the torch. His face was nearly expressionless. John could see the muscles of his throat working, swallowing back sickness. He lowered the torch into the brazier on his right and then into the one to his left. Flames immediately rushed up the torch. Ravishan stepped up to the pyre. The girl screamed at the sight of him, the sound coming out like the raw shriek of a crow. Ravishan lifted the torch. His arm trembled but then he steadied it.

John clenched his mouth shut. His hands curled into tight fists. He didn't want to see this and yet he couldn't make himself look away.

Ravishan leaned forward slightly and touched the flame of his torch to the pyre. It was a graceful motion, almost a bow. Flames gushed up over the oil-soaked wood. The girl screamed again. This time it was a purely animal sound of agony. Ravishan stepped around the pyre and lit it again and again, until it was engulfed in flames. Black billows of smoke churned up against the much paler night sky. Then the air began to fill with the smell of burning hair and flesh.

Cheers rose up through the gathered crowd. Somewhere farther back, someone was playing a happy melody on a flute. People were laughing.

Ravishan stood in front of the pyre as the flames gushed and hissed outward. His face was like a corpse's. His dark eyes were wide, staring into the writhing fire. John could see droplets of oil spattering down from the torch in Ravishan's hand. He didn't flinch from them.

Revulsion and sorrow welled through John. He wanted to be sick, to cry or rage. Anything to exorcise the horror in him. Anything to get it out. But none of those courses were open to him. He closed his eyes and simply dug his fingers into the hard-packed earth beneath him.

Above them, the sky split with a massive crack of thunder. Then a heavy, hard rain began to pour down on them all.

Chapter Thirty-Nine

Most of the ushiri'im and ushvun'im took shelter from the pounding rain in the shrine. Others fled with the crowds of men and women. All around, people scattered, rushing back to the cover of their wagons and stalls or running farther to their homes in the city. Lamps and small fires died out. But the burning pyre only snapped and hissed in the face of the rain. Flames floated on thin slicks of oil and dribbled down the heaps of wood. The heat of the pyre seared the rain to white steam.

John felt the earth slowly softening beneath him. His fingers curled through the mud. Slivers of lightning splintered through the smoke-blackened sky. Thunder crashed. The music and laughter of a few minutes ago had changed to shouts and curses as lamps guttered and people tripped. Farther back in the blood market, John thought he could hear an old woman shouting. Someone had crashed into a pen and knocked the gate loose. John glimpsed escaping goats bounding between clusters of human bodies.

In the midst of it all, Ravishan stood, still staring into the flames of the pyre. Rain beat down on him, plastering his black hair to his face and drenching his clothes. The flame of his torch crackled, spit sparks, and then went out with a hiss. He remained, the firelight of the pyre illuminating his dark form.

John got up. He expected to slip in the mud, but the ground felt oddly firm beneath his feet. He walked, hunching against the pounding rain, to where Ravishan stood shuddering from the cold. His eyes were like black chasms against the bloodless white of his face. His jaw was clenched so tightly that John could see the muscles bulge and tremble.

"You need to get out of the rain." John gently took the dead torch from Ravishan's stiff hands and let it fall to the ground.

"We can't just stand here all night," John said firmly. He grabbed Ravishan's hand and started for the city gate. Ravishan didn't resist him, but he didn't throw himself into action either. He followed John in clumsy, stumbling steps. The normal grace of his motions seemed utterly lost.

John led Ravishan past floundering drunks, through the city gates and up along the now nearly deserted avenues of the Harvest Fair. John tried to think of a place to shelter. He certainly wasn't going to turn back and join Dayyid and the other priests in the shrine. The church hostel in the middle of Amura'taye, where they would have slept, was too far. And in any case, John didn't know if he could stomach any more sanctimonious exchanges with the other men who would be staying there.

Briefly, John considered taking Ravishan to the Bousim tents, but he hadn't left there under the best circumstances. The last thing he wanted was to get into another fight with Tashtu or the rashan'im who served under him.

The surrounding tents and stalls were crowded with people taking shelter from the rain. Men bumped and pushed each other, trying to get further under the cover of eaves. Women huddled close, keeping the few children still awake protected between them.

John headed for the city proper, but once they arrived he found that he had no more idea where to go than he'd had when they'd left the shrine. Dozens of streets shot out between countless hunched buildings. He looked to Ravishan for guidance.

"You know this city better than I do. Where should we go?"

Ravishan stared at him blankly, not seeming to understand his words.

"I'm getting soaked here, Ravishan," John prompted.

"The hostel in the Carvers' District." Ravishan pointed to the road to their left.

John nodded and started down the muddy street. He doubted that he needed to lead Ravishan by the hand any longer, but he didn't want to let go of him, either.

The hostel was a small wooden building with a reed-thatched roof and an outdoor toilet. Because it was the Harvest Fair, few rooms were available. The man at the door seemed relieved when

John told him that he and Ravishan could share a room. John gave the man three wooden coins and a polished blessing stone. While the man didn't look too pleased with the payment, he didn't argue about it either. He accepted John's quick blessing and handed him a cut-tin key.

The room was hardly more than a closet with several blankets and a straw-stuffed mattress on the floor. It was dark with a pungent scent reminiscent of a stable. There were no lamps or even candles. After John closed the door, he had to wait for his eyesight to adjust.

Once inside, Ravishan just leaned against the door, wet and miserable and seemingly unaware of how violently his own body shivered.

"You should get out of those clothes," John said. He winced at the words as he said them. It sounded like some kind of cheap come-on. John supposed that if Ravishan hadn't looked so pathetic and if the evening hadn't been so utterly ugly, it might have been.

As it was, John simply turned his back and quickly stripped off his own soaking clothes. He took one of the blankets and wrapped it around himself.

When he turned back to hand the other blanket to Ravishan, he found that Ravishan still wore his wet cassock. Some color had come back into his face and a blush was spreading across his cheeks. His expression was a weird mix of arousal and misery.

John sighed.

"I don't think your clothes are going to drip dry anytime soon, do you?"

Ravishan flushed and then began pulling at his heavy cassock. His hands were still numb and clumsy from the cold. The sodden fabric slipped out of his grip. John stepped closer and took hold of the dripping wool, saying, "Here, raise your arms."

Ravishan quickly lifted his arms over his head. John pulled the cassock up and off him. He tossed it into the pile with his own clothes. He'd worry about getting them dry later. For now, he concentrated on Ravishan.

The thin white material of the undershirt and pants was plastered to Ravishan's body. The wet fabric did nothing to hide the deeply tanned expanses of Ravishan's lean chest and muscular legs. Even in the dimness of the room, John could see the dark hair of Ravishan's chest and the way it tapered into a fine line leading down to his groin.

An instinctive flush of desire surged through John. His skin felt suddenly much hotter. John forced his thoughts past it. The night had already been too desperate and repugnant. Ravishan was a stunned, shivering mess. The last thing he needed was a seduction. John doubted he was up to it himself.

He quickly untied the knotted laces of Ravishan's pants. Then he straightened and stepped back. Ravishan could handle the rest for himself. Once Ravishan had undressed, John handed him a blanket, which he wrapped around himself. His black hair was beginning to dry and curl just slightly.

He looked like he could have been some young, biblical prophet draped in shadows and flowing cloth.

"Are you tired?" John asked.

"I don't know. I think I am but I don't feel—" Ravishan cut himself off. "I don't want to go to sleep."

"I don't either," John said. His own mind was in too much turmoil to sleep. Still, his body ached with exhaustion and hunger. There was nothing to eat, but at least he could get off his feet. John sat down on the mattress. Ravishan joined him. Despite the dousing of rain, the smell of smoke and roasting meat still clung to both of them.

John didn't want to think about it. And yet each time he tried to think of something to say, his mind was overwhelmed with the image of that girl, struggling, shrieking as she burned. He didn't know if merely witnessing an atrocity could harm a man, but it seemed that way.

Somewhere in him there had been a self-image of a man who was brave enough to suffer for his convictions. A man who would not stand by as a girl was murdered in front of him. Now revulsion and recrimination were eating that ideal away.

He glanced to Ravishan. He knew it was a double standard of the deepest affection that kept him from applying the same expectation to Ravishan. He wouldn't have wanted Ravishan to fight to save the girl. He wouldn't have wanted Ravishan to die for her.

"I can't think of anything to say," Ravishan whispered. "I can't stop seeing the fire."

"You did what you had to."

"I know," Ravishan replied far more easily than John expected. "She murdered her husband's first wife. She misused the power that Parfir had entrusted to her. But..."

John frowned. The revelation that the girl was a murderer herself shouldn't have mattered. It didn't justify her brutal treatment. But it seemed to make it easier for Ravishan to accept.

"I don't know why, but this entire day I've felt like I was eight again. I felt like I did when my mother burned, like a stupid little child who couldn't do anything." Ravishan's voice choked. He lowered his head so that his loose hair hid his face. "I haven't thought about her or my father in years. I don't know why now..." Ravishan wiped the back of his hand across his face. He kept his head lowered. "I think I always knew they were criminals, but they weren't bad. They never hurt anyone. There was even a big, golden dog. Nobody tried to kill her or cook her. They were people who never hurt anyone...god, I'm babbling like a baby."

Again Ravishan wiped his face. He drew in a deep breath. "How am I going to be Kahlil when I can't even burn a witch?"

"You did burn her." The words came out with a flatness that John wasn't used to hearing in his own voice. Ravishan didn't seem to notice it.

"But I didn't want to," Ravishan said quietly as if it were the worst confession. "It made me feel sick, like they were making me burn my mother again."

"They made you burn your own mother?" It seemed too horrible to be true. Even as he asked, John knew it had to be. It would have been the only act that could have proven Ravishan's loyalty to the Payshmura. It would have been the only way he could have saved himself and his sister.

"She was a traitor, a holy sister who turned to witchcraft. She aided the Fai'daum. The punishment had to be burning."

"And your father?"

"They shot him. I didn't see it, but Rousma did. She still has nightmares about it."

"I'm sorry," John said. He wished he could say something else, something that would make it all less terrible.

"It could have been worse." Ravishan shrugged and leaned back against the wall. It was an act of boyish bravado, an attempt to regain his composure. John could see that Ravishan's face was streaked with tears but he didn't say anything. Anyone else sitting in the darkness with him wouldn't have known.

"They were going to shoot me as well." Ravishan gazed up at the ceiling. "They had me on the ground with a gun right up to my head. But I moved."

"Through the Gray Space?" John asked.

Ravishan nodded. "Then Dayyid wanted to keep me alive to train me."

John leaned back beside Ravishan. "You've had a crappy life."

Ravishan looked startled for a moment and then laughed.

"Yeah, I have." He leaned his head against John's shoulder. John slid his arm around Ravishan and held him. "But it doesn't seem so bad right now." Ravishan closed his eyes.

John held him until he fell asleep.

Chapter Forty

John awoke early. Thin predawn light seeped in through cracks between the planks of the walls. Ravishan's warm skin pressed against his own. Their legs and arms had curled around each other as they slept. John pressed his lips lightly against Ravishan's.

Slowly, Ravishan responded. He opened his eyes and smiled, still half-asleep. Lazily, he brushed a hand across John's chest. John leaned in to kiss Ravishan a second time, but then John's stomach let out a growl of hunger. John felt a small flush of embarrassment spread over his cheeks. "I haven't eaten since yesterday afternoon."

"And I smelled too delicious?"

"You are delicious," John replied.

"Am I?"

"Yes." He kissed Ravishan again, much more deeply this time. Ravishan leaned into him. John slid his hand over the edge of blanket that lay across Ravishan's waist. His fingers curled around it and he forced himself to uncurl them. Anyone could be outside that door. Listening. Maybe it was just paranoia, but he had a strange sense of being watched.

John drew back from Ravishan and forced himself to sit up. "We have to get to the church hostel before Dayyid notices that we're missing."

Ravishan groaned but sat up as well. "What will we tell him if he's already noticed?"

"The truth, I suppose," John said. "We picked the closest hostel we could find and got out of the rain."

John picked up his pants. They were cold and still damp from the night before. His undershirt and cassock lay crumpled together on top of his sodden wool socks and filthy boots. Ravishan's wet clothes flopped beside his own in a second, unappealing mound. Not for the first time, John wished he had access to a washing machine and dryer.

He sighed and pulled the pants on. A clammy chill slid up his legs.

"Dayyid probably spent all last night sharpening his razors for what little hair I've managed to grow out," Ravishan muttered.

"Maybe not? He wasn't paying much attention to you when we left."

"He always notices when I'm gone and he's going to be in a foul mood. He hates to get wet." Ravishan scowled at his soaking clothes. "Right now I'm not relishing the idea myself."

"I'd tell you that it's not so bad, but I'd be lying," John replied.

Ravishan took his own clothes and dressed quickly. John did the same. It did no good to draw out the unpleasant sensation of the damp cloth folding over dry, warm skin. And after a few minutes, John found that the heat of his body had at least warmed the wet clothes.

They left the hostel without even a nod from the man who had rented them the room. Now the man lounged in a chair beside the door, sleeping. John imagined he'd been up most of the night allowing drenched strangers in. John left the room key in his lap.

Outside, the sky was still dull and the streets were muddy. Little white seabirds clustered together under eaves of many of the buildings. No one else seemed to be up yet.

"If we cut through the Smiths' Rows—" Ravishan began then stopped and scowled at the countless rows of stone buildings before them.

"We cut through and…" John prompted.

"We'll run straight into one of the inner city walls." Ravishan shook his head. "I'm not used to traveling with someone who can't cross the Gray Space."

"Would it be better if you arrived alone?"

"No. If I was out with an ushvun, Dayyid might suspect I was up to some mischief, but if he thought I was alone, then he'd be sure," Ravishan said. "We'll just have to take the main road."

"He doesn't trust you much, does he?" John asked as they walked.

"Dayyid? Not even as far as he can throw me. But I'm his best chance for a Kahlil so he can't afford to be rid of me." Ravishan glanced up at John and smiled. "Your braid is a mess."

"You're on the scruffy side yourself."

They walked up the slow incline of the main road. As they traveled, the gold edge of the sun began to rise. People awoke and began the first activities of the morning. The scents of cook fires drifted through the air. Wisps of smoke curled up from chimneys. The strong aromas of cooking meat floated out from the buildings.

It was normally a smell that John would have welcomed—the promise of a warm meal wafting on the cold air. But this morning the fresh memory of the girl burning on the pyre choked his appetite.

"Rousma says that the Issusha'im Oracles have almost found the Rifter," Ravishan said casually.

"Here?" John's thoughts jumped immediately to Laurie.

"Of course not. In Nayeshi. You think I'd be this calm if the Rifter were here?" Ravishan shot him a disbelieving look. "They could find him in a year or so. Then they'll have to send out the Kahlil."

"That's not too long," John said absently. A sweet, fruity scent rolled over him. Someone was baking apples.

Ravishan dropped his voice to a whisper. "It means we could be leaving for Nayeshi in a year."

"We might miss the next Harvest Fair."

"I wouldn't mind that a bit," Ravishan replied and he looked suddenly hurt and haunted. Ravishan needed the escape Nayeshi offered. Perhaps he needed it as much as John did.

As they walked on, the buildings they passed appeared better kept. John picked out shop signs hanging over freshly painted doors. A few blocks away, a street vendor called out that daru'sira and taye cakes were for sale. If they hadn't needed to reach the church hostel as soon as possible, John thought he might have hunted the vendor down. A taye cake would have settled his stomach. As was, they kept walking. John caught the voices of other street vendors offering more dishes and passed them by.

John could see the gilded silver dome and golden filigree of the church hostel a few blocks ahead of them. It was the only building in Amura'taye adorned with such extravagance. While the last few decades of crops and grazing lands had been stunted and sickly, the tithes the Payshmura church demanded remained high. With their massive holdings and wealth the gaun'im could afford it, but most common men and women barely managed subsistence. With such blatant inequity, it was no wonder that the Fai'daum had come into being.

He wondered what Ravishan made of the Fai'daum. Before John could ask, Ravishan suddenly waved to someone ahead of them. Hann'yu rushed down the block toward them. As he came closer John saw that he was carrying a bundle of blue leaf cakes. The smell reminded John of sage.

"I've been looking for you," Hann'yu said. He smiled with obvious relief.

"Dayyid isn't already sending people out to find me, is he?" Ravishan glanced up and down the street with a hunted expression.

"I don't think so," Hann'yu said. "Are either of you hungry?"

"Starving," John admitted.

"Have some. They're best when they're still hot. A very kind woman made them for me, though I think she over-estimated my appetite." Hann'yu offered them the bundle of blue leaf cakes.

Both John and Ravishan helped themselves to the steaming, fragrant loaves. John ate his with a famished intensity. Once he had something in his stomach, he seemed to realize how hungry he really was. Ravishan smiled at him as he eyed the last cake in Hann'yu's bundle. Hann'yu, too, noticed John's attention.

"Have it," Hann'yu told him. "I've already stuffed myself on them."

"Thank you." John picked up the warm cake but years of Nayeshi etiquette stopped him from just devouring it. "Would you like half?" he asked Ravishan.

"Yes, thank you," Ravishan replied.

John handed him half the cake and they both ate quickly.

"I've found myself in something of a bind," Hann'yu said while John and Ravishan chewed. "I was thinking that the two of you might be able to help me out."

John simply nodded and took a last bite. Ravishan made an affirmative noise around his food.

"Last night the rain woke me up and I saw the two of you leaving so I followed. I had thought we three could share accommodations but I lost my bearings before I even got out of the fairgrounds. I wasn't in the best state." Hann'yu gave John a slightly embarrassed smile. "In any case, a widow took pity on me and allowed me the shelter of her home since it was close."

"That was nice of her," Ravishan said. He took the last bite of his cake.

"She's a kind woman," Hann'yu replied. "But you can see my predicament. It looks bad if I return saying I spent the night alone with a woman. Dayyid might make a fuss over it. It would be a terrible way to repay the woman for her goodness."

Knowing so little of women, Ravishan seemed to accept Hann'yu's story with no apparent suspicion. But John suspected that Hann'yu might actually have something to hide. It wasn't just any woman who invited a strange man into her house and then who got up and baked him breakfast. Especially not in Basawar, where most women wouldn't have gone near a Payshmura priest for fear of offending him in some manner. Hann'yu plainly needed a cover story even more badly than Ravishan and he did. Their mutual corroboration could shield all three of them.

"Why don't we tell Dayyid that all three of us spent the night at the same hostel," John suggested.

"That would be an excellent idea," Hann'yu replied.

"It's nothing." Ravishan shrugged. "If the weather hadn't been so bad, you probably would have been with us."

"Yes, absolutely," Hann'yu agreed. "The rain certainly came on suddenly."

John didn't know why, but a slightly guilty feeling crept through him at the comment, as if he were somehow responsible. Perhaps it was just that he had been so relieved that the storm had broken. If only it had come earlier.

They reached the hostel and found Dayyid. He seemed angry until he heard that Ravishan had not been alone. After that, he sent the three of them down to breakfast with a warning not to wander away before prayers. It went much more easily than John had expected.

He supposed that was because he wasn't used to having alliances. He was accustomed to thinking of himself as a lone foreign man set against the world around him. But he had friends now and soon he discovered that he'd also gained a kind of respect.

He noticed it throughout the next two days at the fair when his fellow ushvun'im as well as several of the ushiri'im paid him passing compliments on his battle prowess. Samsango pronounced him Parfir's protector of all men's sisters. Ravishan grilled him about which holds he'd used to defeat a rasho so quickly. John noticed two other ushiri'im listening intently to his response, though Hann'yu looked immensely bored by the entire exchange.

After they returned to Rathal'pesha, the ushiri'im's interest in him only seemed to grow. Most of them already recognized him from the times that he treated them in the infirmary. But after the Harvest Fair, they seemed overtly friendly toward him. In the halls of Rathal'pesha, they greeted him casually and struck up conversations with him as they would never have conversed with the other ushvun'im.

Soon it became obvious that they wanted to test their own battle prowess with him. John agreed to it, so long as they fought without blades. It was a good excuse to see more of Ravishan. Dayyid couldn't criticize them for practicing battle forms together.

Familiarity with the ushiri'im gave John another advantage. They often allowed him into forbidden chambers, if he was walking with them. Slowly, over the course of several months, he gained access to room after room of Rathal'pesha's greatest heights.

Soon he was familiar with the barrack-like chambers where the ushiri'im slept as well as the small treasuries where relics from Nayeshi were housed. Locked cabinets held tattered white T-shirts, work pants, a baseball and a wide variety of postage stamps. One glass case contained bills and coins from a scattering of years. The earliest John could find seemed to be 1935, but he didn't look too long or too intently. He wasn't supposed to be capable of reading any of it.

An ushiri named Ashan'ahma even pointed out that John's ignorance rendered his presence in the sacred rooms harmless. "It isn't as though he could carry our secrets to the Fai'daum. He can't read a word of the holy script."

Ravishan had added his agreement to Ashan'amha's and the matter had been settled among the ushiri'im. None of them mentioned it to Dayyid. They simply allowed John to go where he pleased.

The highest chamber both drew and repulsed him. It was like a scabbed injury that he wanted to forget about but always found himself scratching. When he stepped onto the stairs leading up he felt a change, as if the stones themselves had become infused with something terrible.

As he ascended, John heard voices. They were not the clear human sounds of the ushiri'im speaking through the Gray Space. These were quiet and strangely distorted, almost indiscernible. They piled over each other. They bumped and muttered through each other, building hundreds of tones, thousands of words. As John came closer, the voices grew louder but not more distinct. He only became more aware of the chaos of them. Their disjointed sentences crashed and jarred, hissed and murmured, like the ramblings of a hundred paranoid schizophrenics.

At the top of the stairs, the gray stones of the floor and walls seemed to have been infected with the same disorder. They were pitted and yellowed, like diseased teeth. The grain of the stones jutted in one direction and then abruptly broke into a different formation. Wisps of bluish smoke curled out from the edges of the single iron door in front of him. The smell of seared ozone mixed with an odor of taxidermy.

John stepped closer and placed his hand against the cold iron. A feeling of utter revulsion swept over him. He pulled his hand back. The same feeling had come to him from the yasi'halaun and from the broken stones of the Great Gate.

"The men in red ride south. We holds them back. Then men in red ride north. We cannot sees them. We cannot sees..."

John picked out one murmuring voice only to lose it in the hisses of another. "We sees the tower. Falling. The tower is falling. The tower falls. The tower burns..."

"It is near water. The water knows it, loves its flesh..."

"Blue eyes. We sees it. Yellow hair. Running. Dirty feet..."

"The convent burns. We smells our bones blackening. We smells us..."

"Traitors in the palaces. Gold and guns to the men in red. Traitors..."

Then a shriek suddenly broke through all of the soft whispers. "NO! IT HURTS! I HATES YOU! It hurts! It hurts, it hurts, it hurts..." Slowly the cry died to a whimper and then was lost in the depths of countless other murmuring voices.

"Quiet her, can't you?" This time the voice was distinct and familiar. It was Ushman Nuritam.

"Forgive us, Ushman." The response came from a strong, female voice. "Rousma is young and still not broken into the collective of the issusha'im. But her potential is great. She has given us our first glimpses of the Rifter."

Rousma. Ravishan's sister. She had sounded like a little child. It was wrenching to hear her in such obvious pain and yet John knew there was nothing he could do. She was one of the issusha'im now, pared down to a skeleton, strung together with copper wires and carved with Payshmura incantations.

The issusha'im were kept in the southern convent of Umbhra'ibaye and yet it had seemed like they were just behind that door. There had to be some kind of gateway between the two places, here in the highest chamber of Rathal'pesha. He remembered Ushman Dayyid and Hann'yu both mentioning conversations with the ushman'im in the Black Tower of Nurjima. Perhaps there was more than one gate.

"I dislike her outbursts." Ushman Nuritam's harsh voice cut through John's thoughts.

"She will be reprimanded," the woman assured him.

"Very well. What of the Rifter?"

"Rousma has caught glimpses. We hope to bind him to the Kahlil within two years. That is, if a Kahlil has been ordained by then."

"He will be." Ushman Nuritam sounded slightly annoyed at the question. "The issusha'im have seen as much, have they not?"

"What they have seen changes, Ushman," the woman replied. "You have heard them yourself. Since Fikiri'ro'Bousim survived his passage over the Holy Road, their visions have broken and altered. They have become divided even among themselves."

"And there is nothing to be done about it?" Ushman Nuritam asked, but his tone was more accusatory than questioning.

"The problem does not originate from the Issusha'im Oracles, Ushman." The woman's voice remained supremely calm. "They can only look into the future. They cannot alter it. That is the work of the Kahlil. Perhaps your question should be put to him."

"Yes, I'm sure it will be," Ushman Nuritam responded coldly. "But, for now, you can tell me nothing?"

"We can tell you many things, but none are certain and many are lies."

"Spoken like a true sister of the bones, Ushvrun Polima," Ushman Nuritam said.

"I could hope for no greater compliment."

John heard Ushman Nuritam's derisive snort, but if the woman did, she made no response. The voices of the issusha'im continued to mutter and mumble. John caught whispers of ruin and fires, the lost key, the demoness, the Rifter, and Jath'ibaye.

"If there is nothing more for you to tell me, then I will be going," Ushman Nuritam said after a moment. "I have no wish to further exhaust the bones."

"Of course," the woman responded. "Peace to you, Ushman."

"And to you, Ushvrun."

Outside the door John felt a sudden shudder of cold pass through him. He knew the feeling from witnessing the ushiri'im move through the Gray Space. The gateway inside the room had closed. The place went instantly silent. Then John heard Ushman Nuritam's footsteps slowly approaching.

"The greatest compliment, indeed," Ushman Nuritam muttered to himself.

John rushed back down the staircase. The ushiri'im might allow him into forbidden chambers but Ushman Nuritam wouldn't so easily overlook his trespass.

He reached the hall a floor below and hurried back to the scroll room. He was supposed to meet Ravishan there after the next bell. It was a relief to escape the staircase and those voices.

Hundreds of small deep nooks had been carved into the walls of the scroll room. Delicate silver grates hung from hinges over each one. Inside were dozens of cloth and leather scrolls enclosed in wooden cases. The writings here were older than the books in the library. The Basawar words were archaic and difficult for John to read.

But oddly, no matter how old a scroll was, the Nayeshi words it contained were always modern English. Ages passed between writings, but the Nayeshi that they described was always within the same few decades. It made John suspect that the Great Gates could only allow travel between a very limited area and age of Nayeshi. That was good, in that it meant he, Bill, and Laurie would be sent back to the same region. But it also brought up a far more troubling thought. One that John had never considered before. It was time as well as space that they would be crossing.

At first, John had hoped that each of the Kahlils' crossings into Nayeshi had progressed chronologically in Nayeshi history as they had in Basawar history—the first crossing into the forties, the second into the fifties, and so on. That would have ensured that he, Laurie, and Bill would return a few years after they'd left. But reading the scrolls, he had discovered that this was not the case.

The issusha'im hunted the limited window of access that they had to Nayeshi. They searched back and forth, past and future. They accepted the first Rifter they could find. Then they cast a spell that bound the Rifter and the Kahlil together. That bond drew the Kahlil to the correct time and place.

That meant that whatever decade this new Rifter was living in, it would be the decade that Ravishan would be taking them into.

John drew out one of the scrolls. A perfume that almost smelled like cinnamon drifted off of it. The supple leather was familiar in his hands. He had looked over this scroll several times already, slowly deciphering the ancient script. Faded sepia images of flowers ran along the top of the scroll while skeletons knelt in prayer on the bottom. He read the first lines easily.

The holy bones, the Issusha'im Oracles, saw far and spoke the words of ruin. They spoke of the end of kingdoms, of the fall of those who had crafted them.

And so we called the blood of the seas and the breath of the air, the rage of fire and the strength of stone. We called Parfir to us and would have given him form, but it would not hold. For he was all life, land, water, fire and sky. No body of this world could contain all his vastness. Only cut away, only wounded and severed, could he be captured in flesh.

And that flesh was of Nayeshi, near as the night, distant as the day.

And the world of Nayeshi held him, for it did not know him as god. And he did not know himself.

John felt the chill and heard the hiss of the Gray Space. He turned, expecting to see Ravishan. Instead, Dayyid stood frowning at him. John rolled the scroll closed.

"Already reading the divine history." Dayyid glanced at the scroll in John's hands. "Hann'yu said that you learned your letters quickly. I see that he was right."

"He's an excellent teacher," John replied offhandedly. He had no idea how Dayyid could find fault in any of this but he suspected that the ushman would try.

"Indeed." Dayyid gave John a piercing look. "I've heard the same said of you."

"What do you mean?" John asked.

"My ushiri'im seem to have taken to practicing battle forms with you." Dayyid watched John like a cat preparing to pounce on an unsuspecting robin.

"I think they just enjoy beating me." John returned the scroll to its case, then slid it back into its nook and closed the silver grate over it.

"I've been told that they rarely have that pleasure." Dayyid stepped up next to John. "In fact, none of them have bested you. Isn't that so?"

"I'm sure some of them have. They're probably just being modest." John wondered who had passed all this information on to Dayyid. It wasn't like one of the ushiri'im to brag about being beaten.

"Who's bested you?" Dayyid asked.

"I don't know," John replied as casually as he could with Dayyid staring so intently at him. "We've been practicing so much that I don't recall all the matches."

"When I asked, each of them told me that you had won every bout." Dayyid remained standing just a little too close. "Why do you think they would wish to lie to me?"

"I'm sure that none of them would have lied to you," John said quickly. Lying to Dayyid could get an ushiri whipped mercilessly. "We just practiced holds and defenses, so it's hard to say who's won."

"You seem to be the only one who is uncertain of the outcomes," Dayyid replied.

John sighed. A year ago he would have just bowed his head and apologized until Dayyid sent him away in disgust. But John didn't think he could stomach any more of that. It wasn't that his fear of Dayyid had lessened, but rather that his anger toward the man had grown.

There had been the beatings during his first days in Rathal'pesha. There had been the slights and only half-veiled insults; he'd constantly reminded John of his lowly rank. But none of that infuriated John as much as the memory of how easily Dayyid had condemned that girl to burn while knowing that Ravishan would be the one to take her life.

"I beat them." John straightened so that Dayyid had to look up to meet his gaze. "So what?"

Dayyid stepped back just slightly. His dark eyes narrowed, as if taking John in for the first time. Distantly, John heard the bells ringing out the new hour.

"Hann'yu is expecting me in the infirmary," John said. It was a lie that meant that he would miss Ravishan, but he couldn't stay in this room with Dayyid. He was too likely to lose control of his temper and lash out at the man. That wasn't something he could afford to do.

John walked out before Dayyid could make a response. It was one of the only times he had gotten in the last word. Not much of a victory, but John supposed it would be enough to enrage Dayyid.

At the moment he didn't care.

Chapter Forty-One

Autumn passed quickly in Rathal'pesha and deep winter soon settled over the monastery. John searched out work that would keep him clear of Dayyid. He had spent most of this day chopping wood for the fires and hauling casks of oil up from the storerooms. It had been dirty, tiring work but at the end of the day he felt good, knowing he'd accomplished so much.

Now John gazed down from one of the raised walkways. Snow swirled past him. The empty grounds below appeared deceptively still and peaceful. Thick white drifts smoothed the stone paths and raised garden beds into a single flowing plane. The perfect white was broken occasionally by stone walls or the exposed branches of a dark pine. Just below him, smoke billowed from the kitchen chimneys like clouds.

"You're going to freeze out there," Hann'yu commented loudly from the shelter of the kitchen doorway two stories below. The two ushiri'im standing next to Hann'yu studied John. The shorter of them waved John over. He crossed the walkway and then took a staircase down to meet them.

All three men wore heavy wool coats and scarves. Their thick wool caps were pulled so low that their eyes were barely visible. It took John a moment to recognize Ashan'ahma. He could have been any of the ushiri'im in those clothes. Only the loose strands of his light brown hair and the sharp crescent scar that bit into his right cheek identified him.

Ravishan, however, John knew instantly. He had hit his last burst of growth this winter and now stood only a hand shorter than John himself. Of the rest of the ushiri'im and ushman'im, only Dayyid came close to Ravishan's height. His summer tan had faded and the dark stubble along his jaw stood out clearly. Deep shadows showed beneath his eyes as well, a sign of the intensity of his training.

Now that the Rifter was so close to being found, Dayyid was working the ushiri'im relentlessly. At the center of Dayyid's attention was Ravishan, his best hope for a Kahlil.

Ravishan leaned against the doorframe, letting the building take his weight. His hands were loosely tucked into the pockets of his coat while his arms hung slack. No twenty-year-old should have looked so at ease with exhaustion.

Behind Ravishan John could see the oven fires flickering. He thought he smelled bread. Samsango must have started baking already. Normally he waited for John to join him.

John regarded Ashan'ahma, Hann'yu, and Ravishan curiously. The kitchens were one of the last places he expected to see any of the ushiri'im, much less two of them and an ushman. Hann'yu's mouth kept curling up at the edges as he tried to suppress one of his huge grins.

"Dayyid gave all three of you scullery duty?" John asked.

"He can be so cruel," Hann'yu said.

"If he had me cook, it would be more than cruel," Ashan'ahma said. "It could kill us all."

Ravishan simply yawned.

"So?" John asked. "What are you doing down here?"

"You'll never guess." Hann'yu was beaming.

"All right," John said. He waited a moment. "You're not going to tell me?"

"No, you have to try," Hann'yu insisted.

"You've baked Dayyid into a giant cookie which we will offer to the unsuspecting leaders of the Fai'daum?" John responded glibly. Both Ravishan and Ashan'ahma exchanged a brief smile.

"No. Where do you get these ideas?" Hann'yu shook his head. "I can't believe you can't guess. It's so obvious."

John frowned. What could be so obvious and yet elude him? Snow continued falling. The tops of John's boots were slowly being hidden under a layer of white.

"I have no idea," John admitted at last.

Hann'yu looked at him in disbelief. "You have no idea what might be special about today?"

"It's snowing?" John guessed. Hann'yu's exasperated look told him that he had given the wrong response. Then Samsango stepped out through the doorway. He wore only his undershirt and pants and his cheeks were still red from the heat of the cooking fires.

"With all respect, Ushman," Samsango lowered his head slightly to Hann'yu, "Ushvun Jahn is going to freeze to death if we keep him out here guessing all night."

Hann'yu sighed. "All right. But I can't believe you, Jahn. Such a sharp mind and then to miss something like this."

"I told you he wouldn't remember," Ravishan said. "We common people don't celebrate our births the way you gaun'im do."

A celebration of his birth, John thought, and then he suddenly remembered.

Today was the tenth day of the Snow Month, the day John had supplied to Samsango as his birthday. That had been years ago. It hadn't come up again and John had almost forgotten about it. The tenth day of the Snow Month was nowhere near his real birthday. At the time, John hadn't been sure of the names of the summer months so he had simply chosen a date that he knew how to say.

"None of us are gaun'im any longer," Ashan'ahma said.

"A tree can never forget its roots," Ravishan replied. Then he glanced to Hann'yu. "We should get inside."

They hurried into the warmth of the kitchen. John pulled the door shut. When he turned back, he saw that the worktable had been covered with a cloth. Two bundled gifts were placed on it, as well as a pot of daru'sira and a platter of stuffed rolls.

"Goat cheese," Samsango said to John. "I'm afraid this late in the winter there wasn't much else to make them with."

"You shouldn't apologize," John said. "They smell delicious."

They all seated themselves. Ravishan dropped down next to John on the long bench. Ashan'ahma and Hann'yu sat across from them. Samsango remained on his feet, obviously unsure of where he belonged at the table. Normally, he would never have been allowed to seat himself next to an ushiri or ushman. He eyed the edge of the bench next to John, but it was too short for him to fit. John started to move, but then Hann'yu invited Samsango to sit with him.

"Jahn has spoken so highly of you," Hann'yu said.

"Has he?" Samsango looked almost bashful.

"He certainly has." For his part, Hann'yu seemed amused by Samsango's obvious awe. John could see why. Of the two of them, Samsango was certainly the more pious. "Jahn said you were originally from the Hishii Monastery."

"Yes."

"You must have come here before the fire."

"No," Samsango replied, "I was there when the Fai'daum burned it down. After that, the few of us who escaped fled to Rathal'pesha."

"The winter march," Hann'yu said. "I've read about it. I can't imagine how you lived through it."

Samsango looked a little embarrassed. But the attention had to be expected. Even John had heard of the winter march from Hishii. Over three hundred ushvun'im and ushman'im had started out and fewer than twenty had survived. The mountain winter had been harsh and the Fai'daum relentless.

"Parfir was watching over me." He glanced to the steaming stuffed rolls as Hann'yu started to reach for one of them.

"Perhaps we should have a blessing so we can eat." Samsango bowed his head.

"Yes, of course." Hann'yu drew his hand back from the rolls. John caught Ashan'ahma's grin at the exchange. John had only seen Hann'yu say a blessing on the most formal of occasions, when Dayyid or Nuritam was present. Otherwise, he was known for being lax.

"Jahn," Hann'yu said, "why don't you speak for us?"

"You should wake Ravishan up first," Ashan'ahma said.

"I am awake," Ravishan answered. His eyes remained closed and his head was bowed to his chest. Under the table one of his hands rested against John's thigh. Even through his cassock John could feel the heat of Ravishan's skin.

"I'll make it fast in case you nod off," John said quietly.

Ravishan frowned slightly but didn't open his eyes.

John bowed his head. "Holy Parfir, we thank you for your blessings and your bounty. From your sacred body you have fed us and given us shelter. You are with us always and we are forever thankful—"

"Well spoken," Hann'yu cut in. "Let's eat." He snatched up one of the rolls.

Samsango seemed surprised by this new abbreviated blessing, but he said nothing. Ashan'ahma helped himself to a roll, and then John took one for himself and handed a second to Ravishan. Samsango took one of the rolls as well but just held it, obviously watching for the others' reactions.

Hann'yu let out a groan of delight as he took his first bite. "This is delicious. These aren't the rolls we normally have, are they?"

"No, they're something I like to make for special occasions."

"I haven't tasted anything like this since I lived in Nurjima." Hann'yu sighed. "You could have been a private cook to a gaunsho."

"Delicious. Truly delicious," Ashan'ahma added. He took another.

Bald, weathered and nearly toothless, Samsango still managed to take on the air of a star-struck girl as he beamed and blushed at Hann'yu's and Ashan'ahma's compliments.

John smiled and ate his roll. The bread was soft and simple while the hot cheese inside burst with a subtle sweetness of toasted spices.

Ashan'ahma helped himself to a third with a look of slight guilt. Hann'yu had his second. Ravishan gazed at the roll in front of him, his eyes only half open. John imagined that he was assessing whether the sustenance was worth the effort of eating it. After a moment Ravishan picked up the roll and ate.

"It's good," Ravishan said.

"I think that you've outdone us all in our gifts, Samsango." Despite their difference in rank, Hann'yu's manner was effortlessly gracious. He addressed Samsango not as a lowly ushvun but with the warmth and familiarity of a respected elder. Both Ashan'ahma and Ravishan followed his example.

Briefly, John wondered what Rathal'pesha would have been like if men like Hann'yu were in charge of it instead of Ushman

Nuritam and Ushman Dayyid. He didn't get far with the thought before Hann'yu pushed a bundle of cloth in front of him.

"Here, open it up and see what you think," Hann'yu instructed him.

"Thank you." John took the bundle. It was light and soft. He unwrapped the scrap of cloth and lifted out a pair of supple leather gloves. Fur lined the insides. John carefully pulled them on and flexed his hands. The leather stretched and gave without binding.

"You're a hard man to fit," Hann'yu remarked.

"I know." John gazed at the tiny stitching that decorated the backs of the gloves. It was a simple pattern of two leaves curling out from a single vine.

"Thank you," John said again. Hann'yu smiled.

Ashan'ahma handed a second bundle to John. "Just remember that we aren't all able to appropriate funds from the treasury as easily as Ushman Hann'yu."

Like Hann'yu's gift, Ashan'ahma's was wrapped in rough scrap cloth that would later be used as rag for making paper. John unwrapped it and found an ivory and silver pen inside. It had obviously been used. Most likely it was one of the few things that Ashan'ahma had been allowed to bring with him when he had been tithed to the Payshmura. The arching Basawar letters of John's name had been freshly carved into its body.

"It's not so bad, is it?" Ashan'ahma asked.

"No, not at all. It's beautiful." John held the pen. It looked incredibly white against the dark leather of his new gloves. "It was yours?"

"Yes." Ashan'ahma nodded. "Before my ushiri talents were discovered, I fancied the life of a writer for myself. Everyone gave me pens, of course. So, now I'm passing one on to you."

"Thank you," John said.

Ashan'ahma smiled and then looked oddly embarrassed. He squinted at Ravishan's still form. "He's asleep, isn't he?"

"No." Ravishan's voice sounded rough but the response came quickly.

"So what have you got for Jahn?" Ashan'ahma asked.

"I've got some laundry." Ravishan yawned.

"You're not fooling anyone," Ashan'ahma said.

Ravishan frowned at him but then straightened. "All right, but it's not much to look at." He dug into the deep pockets of his coat and then brought out three small red apples. The flesh of each of them bore a number of sharp gashes, the kind of injuries that came from the Gray Space.

"Fresh apples," Samsango gasped. Hann'yu and Ashan'ahma looked amazed as well. It was the dead of winter. The last fresh fruit or vegetables any of them had eaten had been bitter greens a month ago. It would be another three months before they had anything better than leathery pieces of dried berries.

John could smell the sweet tang of the apples rising from their sliced skins.

"How did you get them?" Samsango asked.

"I picked them this afternoon from an orchard in Umbhra'ibaye." Ravishan smiled slightly.

"No wonder you were so torn up in the infirmary," Ashan'ahma said. "Umbhra'ibaye is too far to go."

"I'll go farther when I'm Kahlil." Ravishan shrugged. "Anyway, it was only a few scratches."

John glanced questioningly to Hann'yu. Hann'yu only gave a small shake of his head. John glanced down at the apples again. Their red skins and pale white flesh were split and torn. One of them was sliced all the way to the core. It was no wonder Ravishan was so exhausted.

"Well?" Ravishan asked. "Are they too ugly to eat?"

"Not at all," John replied. It embarrassed him to feel so touched while staring at three small apples.

"We should cut them up and share them," John decided.

All five of them carried knives. But only Samsango's short paring knife wasn't infused with curses or carved from sacred bone. John stood and found clay cups for all of them. He poured out servings of the strong daru'sira.

The sweetness of the apples balanced the bitter edge of the daru'sira. John closed his eyes, savoring the taste. In Nayeshi this would have been nothing to him. He could have gotten all the varieties of apples he liked at a grocery store. The gloves and the pen, even the stuffed rolls were things that he would have taken for granted.

But here, he knew the kind of rarity and effort that they represented. Because life was harder here, because resources were more scarce and convenience virtually unknown, each offering meant much more. Hann'yu couldn't just pick up a pair of gloves at a department store. Ashan'ahma wouldn't ever be able to replace his pen with another. Samsango couldn't just order a meal in. And Ravishan had bled to bring him these three sweet apples in the dead of winter.

If he had never lived here, he never would have been able to understand how precious each of these gifts was. For a brief moment John was so moved that he felt tears begin to wet the corners of his closed eyes. He quickly drew in a breath and stopped himself from going any further with these thoughts.

"So," John said, "do you think that the sisters in Umbhra'ibaye would like to trade residences with us?"

Hann'yu laughed.

"Wouldn't that be a treat?" Ashan'ahma asked.

Samsango nodded. "I suppose it's warm there, even now in the Snow Month."

"It's like a nice day at harvest," Ravishan said. "You can smell the ripe fruit and the leaves are just beginning to turn gold. I don't think it ever snows there."

"It doesn't," Hann'yu said. "I lived in Amura Milso when I was young. I never saw snow until I went north to Nurjima for my schooling."

"In cold months like these I imagine you miss it." Samsango refilled his cup of daru'sira.

"I miss Nurjima more," Hann'yu said. "But there's no point in brooding over it. And Rathal'pesha has its good qualities."

"Does it?" Ravishan asked.

"Certainly it does." Samsango smiled. "It is the most sacred honor to be so near the holy ushiri'im."

John could see how that wouldn't be much of a consolation to Ravishan or to Ashan'ahma, for that matter. But for Samsango it truly was a kind of blessing. The ushiri'im were living testaments to Parfir's power. They were men who carried the god's own bones.

"There is something very sacred about the presence of the ushiri'im," Hann'yu agreed. "At times the very air feels different in the rooms where they have been housed for so many generations."

"And there are all those fine lines left behind from where they've passed through the Gray Space," John added. He poured more daru'sira into his cup.

Hann'yu regarded him questioningly. "Fine lines?"

"Well, not obvious lines but, you know, scratches. You can follow them..." John trailed off as he became aware that none of the other men at the table were showing any sign of recognition of what he was describing.

"You can follow where we've gone?" Ashan'ahma asked.

"Yes, but..." John tried to think of a way to retract what he had said. "It's just what Hann'yu was describing, the texture of the air is different. It's scratched. You can feel it like a scrape in the grain of wood."

"You can, perhaps," Hann'yu said. "But I certainly can't."

"I've never noticed it either," Ashan'ahma said, "and I am an ushiri. You, Ravishan?"

Ravishan shook his head.

"I'm probably not describing it correctly," John said.

"No, I think you're describing it perfectly," Hann'yu said. "I've never seen it but I've read about it. The Kahlil Vash'illoun wrote about a current running through all of Parfir's creations. When an ushiri opens the Gray Space, he cuts into that current and either moves with it or against it. Most ushiri'im can't sense it and so their movements are at odds with Parfir's currents. The paths they leave were described as the marks a sharp blade leaves on ice."

"Exactly," John said.

"And you've seen this?" Samsango stared at John.

"Just once or twice," John lied.

"That's how you can always find Ravishan for me. You can see the path he's left." Hann'yu shook his head. "Dayyid really should have accepted you as an ushiri."

"It wouldn't have made a difference if he had," John said. "Ravishan is going to be the Kahlil."

"But having you with the others might have allowed you to share your sense of the currents sooner," Hann'yu said. "From what I've read it's moving against those currents that causes injuries to the ushiri'im when they are within the Gray Space."

"What do they look like?" Ashan'ahma asked.

Ravishan also looked intently at John, waiting for his answer.

"The currents or the paths?"

"The currents," Ashan'ahma said.

"They don't look like anything. They just feel right. I don't know how to describe it except...You know when you're swimming and you can feel the water flowing around you? It's like that."

"Just like that," Ashan'ahma said ruefully.

"If you can feel these currents," Ravishan said quietly, "you ought to be able to open the Gray Space."

"I can't," John said. The idea of touching, much less creating, an opening to the Gray Space repulsed him utterly. He had no idea how Ravishan or any of the ushiri'im managed to overcome the feeling of revulsion that the Gray Space generated.

"But you can feel Parfir's living current?" Ravishan asked. "Right now in this room, can you feel it?"

"Yes," John admitted after a moment.

"So," Ravishan held up his hand over the table, "if I were to open a space, you could tell me which way the current was running?"

John gazed at Ravishan's hand. His long fingers were nicked and scraped. Faint red lines streaked across his palm where earlier cuts had only half healed.

"I think so," John said.

"All right then." Ravishan's tone was almost challenging. This was an area that Ravishan was used to dominating. Perhaps a hint of combativeness couldn't be helped. John didn't bother to linger on it. Ravishan had a right to his pride.

John concentrated on the empty air surrounding all of them. He felt the weightless atmosphere that washed over him, caressed his skin, and rolled into his lungs. Each breath he released sent tiny breezes rolling through the room. Invisible currents slipped out cracks in the walls to rejoin the cold night sky. Outside, it was snowing and the winds chased each other like children intent on a game of tag.

John reached out and gently turned Ravishan's hand through the sweeping play of the elements.

"There," John said. He drew his own hands back.

Ravishan snapped his fingers apart, cracking open a thin slice of the Gray Space. The hiss was hardly audible but John still felt the chill. Ravishan closed the space immediately. He dropped his hand back to the tabletop.

Only the faintest trace of the opening remained hanging in the air. It was almost invisible compared to the others John had seen. No one else seemed to notice it.

"It opened so smoothly," Ravishan said. "I hardly felt any resistance." He lifted his right hand again. "Show me again."

"But—" John began.

"Not tonight, Ravishan," Hann'yu said. "You've already exhausted yourself and Jahn should be allowed to relax on this one day."

Ravishan gave Hann'yu a harsh frown that was distinctly reminiscent of one of Dayyid's scowls. "This is important."

"So is Jahn's day of birth," Hann'yu replied.

Ravishan glanced to John and then sighed. "All right. But you have to show me tomorrow."

John just nodded his agreement. He would have shown Ravishan now, but he thought the others would have been bored. And Ravishan had to rest sometime.

"You're never going to be free of him now," Ashan'ahma told John.

"But this is wonderful, isn't it?" Samsango smiled. "What a perfect thing to discover. A great talent hidden in a lowly ushvun."

Hann'yu smiled warmly at that and nodded. "I suppose it's to be expected that Parfir's gift to Jahn would be so much greater than all of our material offerings." He poured himself another cup of daru'sira and filled Samsango's cup as well, then glanced to John. "So how does it feel?"

"What?" John asked.

"To be twenty-five," Hann'yu said. "It's been so long I can hardly remember what it was like."

John shrugged. The last birthday he had celebrated had been his twenty-second. It seemed as if it had been decades ago, ages ago. He couldn't even remember what he had been given or done then.

"It feels older than I expected," John said.

"Just wait for forty-six," Hann'yu replied.

"Forty-six?" Samsango waved his hand as if brushing the comment aside. "You wait until you've turned sixty. Sixty. That's nearly the ages of all four of you put together."

Hann'yu smiled. Ashan'ahma was well into his thirties, John was twenty-five and Ravishan was twenty. Their four combined ages put them well over a hundred. But they all let Samsango's bad math pass without comment.

"You're older than the bell tower, aren't you?" Ashan'ahma asked Samsango.

Samsango nodded. "I was here when they pulled the old one down. That's when you know you're old. When you've outlived the architecture."

"So, you'd remember Gaunsho Par'taum?" Ashan'ahma asked.

"Of course." Samsango smiled broadly at the mention of the man's name. "He had such a voice! Women came from miles to hear him sing at the Harvest Fair. He was born the first son of the Du'yura Gaunsho, the heir to the entire family. But he must have felt a great calling because he disguised himself as a common pilgrim and came to the monastery. Of course they admitted him, but only as a lowly ushvun. He was the worst worker I had ever seen." Samsango shook his head. "He didn't know how to light a fire, couldn't sew a stitch, and he was scared of the goats. He complained and wouldn't eat the food. Ah, and he refused to clean out the privies. No matter what, he wouldn't do it. But when you heard him in prayer...such a beautiful, sacred voice would rise out of him. It was as if warm sunshine filled the chamber. Eventually the ushman'im noticed and sent him to the Black Tower to sing for the Usho. Then, of course, his brothers recognized him and he was returned to the Du'yura family."

"He was my grandfather," Ashan'ahma said.

"Really?" Samsango looked Ashan'ahma up and down, searching for traces of the man he remembered. "How is your singing?"

"Not as good as his, I'm afraid. But not bad."

"It's quite good," Ravishan said.

"It is," Hann'yu agreed.

John hadn't noticed it, but then he was rarely among the ushiri'im when they sang their prayers. More often he was working with his fellow ushvun'im or running errands for Hann'yu.

"You must let me hear you," Samsango said.

"You'll be disappointed," Ashan'ahma warned.

"I know that I won't," Samsango replied. "You must sing something."

"Come on," Hann'yu said. "You always want to sing."

Ashan'ahma relented easily. His voice was deep and rich. John leaned onto his elbows and simply listened. Ravishan leaned beside him, half-asleep but smiling. Both Hann'yu and Samsango seemed lost in remembrances. Doubtless Hann'yu's recollections were of the operas of Nurjima, the costumes, lights, and late night conversations. Samsango seemed to simply be recalling his youth and the sacred voice he had known.

John closed his eyes and let his own thoughts wander with the song. Despite the cold and his aching muscles, the night seemed perfect.

Chapter Forty-Two

Ravishan woke John before daybreak, demanding instruction. He bounded up the stairs to the infirmary and John followed in a groggy daze. They worked together while the sun slowly crept up over the mountain peaks.

Outside the infirmary window, the sky was a pale white expanse. The rising sun only burned a faint white circle through the walls of falling snow. John yawned and frowned at the smell of ozone and smoke that hung in the air. He turned back to Ravishan. He had expected that Ravishan would want to train with him. But he hadn't thought that Ravishan would wake him up before the break of day for it.

"Show me again." Ravishan stood, tensed as though he were preparing for an attack. His right hand was slightly extended, his left drawn back, closer to his chest. A fine sheen of sweat already covered his bare chest and arms. Wisps of his shaggy black hair hung around his face.

"Try to feel it for yourself," John said.

Ravishan closed his eyes and frowned intently. He shifted his hand slightly, but then scowled. "I can't...I thought I did, but it was just the wind."

"The wind is part of it," John assured him. The living current, as Ravishan called it, suffused the wind and rolled with it.

"Here?" Ravishan moved just a little more.

"Close," John said. "You're really close."

Ravishan shifted the angle of his right arm, turning it by slow degrees. John felt him move into and then out of the delicate current that surrounded them. Ravishan suddenly punched his hand forward, rending the Gray Space open. Flames arced through the air. The sound of tearing metal cut through the morning silence.

"Damn it!" Ravishan jerked his arm back to his chest. The Gray Space snapped closed. Ravishan squeezed his left hand over the bleeding cut in his right forearm.

"How can I be getting worse the more I practice?" Ravishan glared at his arm.

"You're trying too hard," John said. "I don't think it's something you can force. More finesse, less force. Less Dayyid, more Hann'yu."

"So I should be drunk?" Ravishan asked with a smile.

"Maybe not that much like Hann'yu." John went to the drawers and dug out a roll of bandage. "Let me see your arm."

Ravishan held it out. The cut was deep and narrow. John bandaged it. Not for the first time, he wished that he possessed a little of Hann'yu's skill at healing. He tied Ravishan's bandage. There were other, much smaller scratches across Ravishan's arm and even one thin red welt across his cheek.

"Maybe you should try this with something that's easier to feel," John said.

"What do you mean?" Ravishan asked. He was still scowling at his arm as if it had betrayed him.

"It's hard to feel the atmosphere. It's too prevalent and we're too accustomed to it. But maybe something else. Maybe water."

"You want me to go swimming in the dead of winter?"

"No, just…" John looked around the room and at last caught sight of one of Hann'yu's porcelain bowls. "Here, let's try it with this." John got up and filled the bowl with clean water.

"If you put your hand in, you can feel the pressure of the water." John slipped his own hand into the bowl. The water was icy. He closed his eyes, concentrating on the texture of the water surrounding his fingers. A moment later he felt Ravishan's hand slide into the water next to his own.

"What do you feel?" John asked.

"Wet," Ravishan replied.

"Other than that."

"I don't know."

"There are strong and weak forces," John said. "Elements like oxygen and hydrogen bond together firmly. They're the hard grain of the water. The force pulling clusters of molecules together is different...Can you feel it?" John asked.

"I don't know what you mean by oxygen," Ravishan said.

"It's a molecule. Something that you'll feel in both the air and the water."

"I don't—"

"It doesn't matter," John assured him. "It's just a name. What's important is to feel the difference between the strong and the weak forces. You want to open the Gray Space by cutting through the weak forces, not the strong ones."

John knew that what he was describing was not the whole experience of the currents he felt. But he had no words to describe the living force that seemed to saturate not just the chill water but the bowl containing it. The air, the stones, everything around them overflowed with that deep energy. When he concentrated on it, John felt as if it was surging up to meet him, churning and pressing against his skin. He could feel it twisting on the cold drafts that slipped through the window. He imagined that he could turn it through his hands or snap it apart. It was a strange sensation.

Ravishan's eyes were pressed closed in concentration. His dark brows compressed, nearly forming a single line. Ravishan turned his hand through the water, slowly. Then suddenly he stopped. His fingers straightened.

John quickly withdrew his own hand from the water. He didn't want to get hit by the Gray Space that Ravishan would open.

Ravishan flicked his fingers apart. A burst of water splashed out of the thin air a foot behind John. Ravishan looked up and grinned. "I think I got it that time."

John nodded. He'd hardly felt the chill of the space opening.

"There's a texture," Ravishan marveled. "A grain. Like you said, it's weak in one direction, strong in another." He stared at John for several moments. "How did you know?"

"That's just how it felt to me," John said. Hann'yu wasn't going to be pleased about the spill of water. John glanced to the shelf to see if there were any towels.

"John," Ravishan said his Nayeshi name in a low whisper, "you would tell me if you were...if there was something more, wouldn't you?"

John focused on the towels. There was so much he didn't say. He didn't even know why, exactly, except that he knew their lives here were fragile. He didn't want to discover something that would change the way they were, right now, together.

"I would. I—" John started to turn back towards Ravishan but something caught his attention—a distortion in the air. A faint blur hovered just a foot from him. Someone was in the room with them, spying from the Gray Space.

A shot of anger rushed through John. Without thinking, he bolted forward and grabbed the scrawny ushiri by the arm. A wave of nausea rolled through him as his hands drove into the Gray Space. John jerked the ushiri out as if he were hauling a fish out of the water. The air screamed and a frigid blast whipped across John's face. Fikiri howled in shock as John hurled him onto one of the infirmary beds.

"What do you think you're doing?" John demanded.

Fikiri scrambled upright. His face and arms were crisscrossed with scratches. His lips looked blue.

"I didn't do anything," Fikiri said quickly.

"You were spying on us?" Ravishan stepped forward.

"It was Dayyid's order," Fikiri snapped. He glared at Ravishan. "He doesn't trust you."

"He didn't trust you either. Now I can see why he's changed his mind. You've turned yourself into his little boot-licker. You're pathetic," Ravishan replied.

"And you're a pervert—" Fikiri hardly got the last word out. Ravishan lunged onto him, gripping his throat.

"I'll kill you in the Gray Space and no one will ever find your body. Not Dayyid. Not even your precious mommy," Ravishan hissed.

"Ravishan." John pulled him back from Fikiri. "No one is going to kill anyone. Just calm down."

"He—" Ravishan just clenched his mouth shut and looked away from Fikiri. "Fine. Let him go crying back to Dayyid."

John addressed Fikiri, "How long has Dayyid had you watching Ravishan?"

"Long enough," Fikiri responded.

John took one step closer. "How long?"

"Since that night he disappeared." Fikiri narrowed his eyes at John. "There are things I could tell him that I haven't...not yet."

"Such as?" John asked. A cold revulsion that had nothing to do with the Gray Space churned through John's stomach.

"I heard you two talk about going to Nayeshi together," Fikiri said.

"And?" John asked. Dread gripped him as he remembered that Fikiri had called Ravishan a pervert. They had been careful but there had still been moments when Ravishan had pressed a hand against his. There had been small gestures, brief overtures. How much had Fikiri seen and how much had he understood?

"And I want to go too," Fikiri demanded.

"What? No!" Ravishan snapped.

"If you don't take me and my mother with you, I'll tell Dayyid everything." Fikiri looked at John. "I'll tell him about the night you two spent in the hostel. I'll tell him what you did in the morning."

"You'll die before you can say a word!" Ravishan started forward again but John caught him by the shoulders.

"Calm down," John said softly.

"I'm not going to let this piece of snot blackmail me," Ravishan growled.

"You're not going to kill him," John said flatly.

"I can beat him till his tongue falls out," Ravishan countered.

"Just calm down," John told him. "Beating up Fikiri certainly won't make Dayyid less suspicious."

Ravishan stepped back again and turned away from Fikiri.

"All right," Ravishan said. John could see the muscles in his jaw working.

John turned back to Fikiri. "So you and Lady Bousim want to go to Nayeshi?"

"We're going to live there with Loshai," Fikiri said firmly.

"With my sister?" John asked. "Why do you think she'd be going?"

"Because I've watched her." Fikiri's pale face flushed slightly. "I've listened to her and Behr when they thought they were alone."

"Now who's the pervert?" Ravishan demanded.

"At least I didn't have my head shaved for whoring with a goat herder," Fikiri spat back.

Ravishan glared at Fikiri. "If Jahn wasn't here, you would have my blade through your throat, Fikiri."

"Well, he is here," Fikiri answered. "So just shut up."

John caught Fikiri's jaw in his hand and turned his face so that they were staring directly at each other. He leaned a little closer to Fikiri.

"Don't push your luck," John said slowly. "And don't insult Ravishan."

Fikiri blanched. John continued, "What are you going to do if we don't agree to take you with us?"

"Then I'll tell Dayyid everything." Fikiri lifted his chin slightly.

"Tell him," Ravishan said suddenly. "He can't afford to kill me now. I'm his Kahlil and he knows it."

"Maybe, but we all know he's dying to beat the life out of Ushvun Jahn," Fikiri replied.

A look of horror washed over Ravishan. Then his eyes narrowed and he shifted his weight into a battle stance. His right hand flexed and John could almost feel him summoning the force to create a Silence Knife. John thought he might really kill Fikiri.

"So you'll be coming with us," John said quickly. "You and your mother."

There was no point in arguing. He had to tell Fikiri what he wanted to hear, even if it might not turn out to be true.

"I want your word," Fikiri said.

"What?" John asked.

"I want your word that you'll take us," Fikiri repeated.

"All right." John agreed. "I promise that we will take you and your mother to Nayeshi when we go."

"Ravishan has to promise as well," Fikiri added.

"You have my word." Ravishan's voice sounded flat but his expression was filled with contempt.

"It's your own fault," Fikiri snapped at Ravishan. "If you weren't a disgusting pervert, there wouldn't be anything for me to tell Dayyid. But you—"

"Fikiri," John cut him off. "You've gotten what you want, so don't keep goading Ravishan into murdering you."

Fikiri bowed his head and glowered down at his scraped hands.

"You should go," John told him. "Now."

Fikiri stood and started for the door. Ravishan watched him with narrowed eyes. John could see his hands shaking with suppressed fury.

John almost swore when Fikiri stopped at the door. Why couldn't he just stop baiting Ravishan and get out? But this time he focused his attention on John.

"How did you pull me out of the Gray Space?" Fikiri demanded.

"I don't think knowing how is as important as remembering that I can," John replied. "Don't spy on us again."

A look of genuine fear crossed over Fikiri's face. He left quickly then.

John sat down on the corner of the bed. He rubbed his hand across his forehead, massaging the beginning of a headache away.

"You should have let me kill him in the Gray Space," Ravishan said.

"Would you really have done it?"

"What he said about Dayyid beating you to death is true. I think I'd kill anyone before I'd let that happen."

"Well, it's not going to happen," John assured him. "So let's just put the murder plans aside for the moment."

Ravishan nodded. He glanced down at the floor, looking almost lost. "I should probably clean this water up before Hann'yu gets here."

"I was about to do that," John said.

Ravishan had already reached the shelves. He found one of the rags and tossed it down over the small spill. John watched the water soak into the cloth. He felt tired and a little sick.

"How did you pull him out, Jahn?" Ravishan whispered.

"I don't know. I just did it."

"You have witches' blood, don't you?" Ravishan asked.

"Maybe, I don't know. No one does things like this in Nayeshi. No one walks into thin air or has witch blood or god's bones. We're just people."

"You're not a Kahlil?" Ravishan asked.

"No." John almost laughed at the thought of it. "No. We don't have Kahlil'im in Nayeshi. You know that."

"I just wanted to be sure."

"Well, be sure. I'm not a Kahlil or a witch or an ushiri. I'm just a person."

"You're something." Ravishan smiled and stepped closer. John caught the flirtatious curve of his smile. It hardly began before Ravishan stopped himself. He stepped back from John and turned to stare out the window. John understood. Who knew if Fikiri was the only spy that Dayyid would send out? They couldn't afford even the slightest overture of affection now.

"I should go," Ravishan said.

John simply nodded.

"Be careful," John told him as he opened the red door.

"You as well." Ravishan gave him a smile and then left.

By the time Hann'yu arrived, John had thrown out the water, put away the bowl, and begun the tedious work of grinding down the dried herbs that would be needed for poultices. The smell of earthy roots hung in the air, but it couldn't mask the odor of burnt ozone.

Hann'yu sniffed and pulled a sour face. "Fikiri?" he guessed.

"Ravishan," John said.

"He normally doesn't leave such a strong smell." Hann'yu contemplated the snow falling outside the window, then opened the window anyway. Icy, fresh air rushed in.

"We were practicing with the currents," John said. "I think he got a little frustrated."

"Did he make any progress?"

"He did, actually."

"Good," Hann'yu said. Then he looked John over. "But you look dead on your feet."

"I didn't sleep well." In fact his nights had been restless for months. More and more the image of the issusha'im's bones infiltrated his rest. The hollow, black chasms of their eyes stared, unblinking, into his sleep. Even in his most mundane dreams he thought he heard them whispering after him. Lately, it seemed to be growing worse.

"I suppose Ravishan woke you before the first bell?"

"He's dedicated," John replied.

Hann'yu studied the dried roots as John ground them in the mortar.

"If so much didn't depend on him, I would say that he was too dedicated." Hann'yu went to one of his shelves and opened a jar of desiccated leaves. He dropped two of the leaves into the mortar and then put the jar away.

"Yellowpetal leaves," Hann'yu explained. "They dull pain somewhat."

John ground them in with the knotted pine root. Hann'yu would use it as an antiseptic later.

"Did you get anything to eat?" Hann'yu asked. He walked back to the window and closed it.

"Cold taye and goat milk," John said.

"Sounds awful."

John didn't think it was any worse than some servings of oatmeal he'd eaten. Hann'yu wouldn't have understood that response. "It could have been worse."

"Yes, most things could be," Hann'yu said. "But it's a sad consolation to have to take, you know."

"I know." John smiled.

"Would you like a nap?" Hann'yu offered.

"I'd love one, but—"

"Go on." Hann'yu waved him toward one of the beds. "You're no use as you are now."

"No use?" John couldn't help the tone of protest in his voice. He'd been working all morning.

"Oh, you can work well enough," Hann'yu replied, "but you're a terrible conversation partner when you're tired."

"I see." John set the mortar aside. "Are you sure?"

"Positive," Hann'yu told him. "Take a nap. I need someone who can appreciate my gossip like a second wife."

"You don't have a first wife," John said.

"We can all dream," Hann'yu responded. "Especially you. Go to bed and dream me up a wife. A pretty wife."

"I make no guarantees." John wasn't sure how well he would sleep, but his body hungered for rest. He lay down and closed his eyes. Hann'yu spread a blanket over him.

"Give her red hair and big breasts. Maybe a full, pouting mouth like the women from the Anyyid lands," Hann'yu said.

"I think you're going to have to come up with her for yourself," John mumbled. He heard Hann'yu drawing the canvas curtains closed around the bed but didn't bother to open his eyes.

"I have," Hann'yu replied softly, "many times over. I've just gotten lazy. I'm hoping you'll do the work for me."

"You don't want me to. I'll get her all wrong." John yawned. "You'll end up married to a sheep. Something with a giant udder."

"A giant udder. Really?" Hann'yu asked. "Perhaps you shouldn't tell me anymore about your dreams."

"My dreams." John's words came out in a groggy murmur. "Hardly." Moments later he was asleep.

Dark insentience coiled around him and yet at the edges of his senses he felt as though he was still awake, watching as Hann'yu separated leaves and dried flowers for teas. He heard the hard snap of boot heels outside the door and knew immediately that Dayyid stood there.

Dayyid knocked and Hann'yu called him in.

"Is he here with Ushvun Jahn again?" Dayyid asked.

"Who?" Hann'yu didn't look up from his herb table.

"Ravishan." Dayyid scanned the infirmary, seeming disappointed with its emptiness. For a moment a small pile of dull green leaves and white flowers bore the brunt of his disapproving expression. Then he looked to Hann'yu.

"No, they've finished their practices. Ravishan has gone to the golden chamber, I imagine, and Jahn is sleeping." Hann'yu glanced to the curtained bed. It gave John an odd feeling of vertigo to take in the space where he knew his own body lay in a deep sleep.

"In the middle of the day?" Dayyid frowned at the canvas panels.

"He was up early training with Ravishan." Hann'yu looked up at Dayyid. "Did you know that he goes down to the kitchen after the eighth bell and helps the ushvun'im bake for the next day? He hardly sleeps at all."

"How could he, when he's so busy doing every job that isn't his to do?" Dayyid responded.

Hann'yu sighed. "You sound jealous, Dayyid. I can see why you would be. The ushiri'im practice with him and Ravishan follows him around like a milk-pup. It leaves you out. But it's unbecoming to succumb to such a petty feeling."

"I'm not jealous," Dayyid replied coolly. "If he improves the ushiri'im, then I'm glad for it."

"You don't seem glad for it," Hann'yu replied. He stood and picked out another jar. A dark golden fluid swirled in it. "But perhaps I'm misinterpreting your glares, scowls, and threats."

"I don't trust him."

"Is there anyone you do trust?" Hann'yu searched his shelves. At last he found two small clay cups. He set them down on the herb table.

John would have liked to have heard the answer to Hann'yu's question but Dayyid offered none. He stood in silence and watched as Hann'yu filled the two cups with golden liquid. It poured like honey. Hann'yu pushed one of the cups to Dayyid and took the other for himself.

"Fathi?" Dayyid raised a dark brow.

"The drink of divine truth and joy," Hann'yu confirmed. "It suits our conversation, don't you think?"

Dayyid eyed the small cup as if it were a trap of some kind.

"He hides things," Dayyid suddenly stated. "When I placed the curse blade before him he felt its power, and yet he didn't choose it."

"He has a right not to choose it," Hann'yu replied. "Anyway, you were the one who said that you didn't want him as an ushiri."

"I didn't and I don't." Dayyid picked up his cup. He held it between his hands as if it offered him some kind of warmth, but he did not drink. "He's hiding something."

"What?" Hann'yu laughed. "His dread of being cut to ribbons by the Gray Space? It's not all that desirable of a test to pass, really."

"You know that's not what I mean," Dayyid grumbled.

"I don't, actually." Hann'yu met Dayyid's intense expression with an easy smile. "So tell me what you're really bothered by."

"He holds back," Dayyid said. "When he first arrived, I took it for pure cowardice. He took his beatings like a dog. But when he came to the golden chamber, I felt something stir in him and he restrained it. He tried to hide it from me."

Hann'yu frowned. "Hide what, exactly?"

"Power. Immense power," Dayyid said after a long pause. "When he collapsed the God's Razor, I felt it for just a moment. A raw, dark power. It struck me, but then he pulled it back. During the test he suppressed it and lied. I assume you've noticed it as well?"

"There is a force to him," Hann'yu admitted. "But it's, as you say, raw and strong. That makes it no use in the infirmary. As far as I'm concerned it's best if he does hold it back."

"Then you have sensed him hiding it." Dayyid's voice rang with vindication.

"Certainly," Hann'yu agreed, but he only appeared amused by Dayyid's serious expression and tone. "But don't you think that would be natural for a man who obviously comes from Eastern blood? He has witch's child all but written across him. He's probably had to hide his power all his life just to keep clear of harvest fires."

Hann'yu frowned down at his small cup. Dayyid said nothing. John wondered if the conversation would end there. It seemed unlike Dayyid to allow anyone else to have the last word. Hann'yu drank from his cup while Dayyid simply held his.

"If he had done nothing wrong," Dayyid spoke as if the long silence in their conversation had never occurred, "then he would have no reason to hide. In itself, his power could be Parfir's blessing. Only if Jahn misused it could he have been accused of witchcraft."

Hann'yu gave a dry laugh at that.

"Well, that's the letter of the law," Hann'yu replied, "but we both know that misuse is a matter of interpretation. There are jealous, petty people willing to cry foul against anyone they can. And Jahn doesn't just have himself to think of. He has a sister as well."

"Yes, I recall that he made a spectacle of himself for her sake." Dayyid took a small sip from his cup. He closed his eyes, savoring the taste.

“Don’t pretend that you weren’t proud to see one of ours knock a rasho flat.” Hann’yu grinned. To John’s surprise a slight smile tugged the corners of Dayyid’s mouth upward.

“Perhaps,” Dayyid admitted. “But his prowess isn’t a matter of contention.”

“Of course it is,” Hann’yu replied. “You just won’t admit it.”

“No,” Dayyid replied.

John wasn’t sure if Dayyid meant that he wouldn’t admit his jealousy or if he was refuting Hann’yu completely. Hann’yu seemed not to need to pursue the matter further.

“How’s the fathi?” Hann’yu glanced to the small cup in Dayyid’s hands.

“Still too sweet,” Dayyid replied.

“Better than last year’s, though.” Hann’yu poured himself another serving.

“Much,” Dayyid agreed.

“Another five or six years and it may be quite smooth,” Hann’yu pronounced after another sip.

“If there’s any left,” Dayyid replied.

This time Hann’yu’s laugh sounded genuine and warm. “The pursuit of perfection has its costs,” he declared.

Dayyid sipped a little more of the golden drink.

“Go on,” Hann’yu said to him at last. “Sit down, before it knocks you down.”

“I have no intention of drinking it all,” Dayyid replied. He set the small cup aside on Hann’yu’s table. It was still nearly full.

“You need to relax sometime, Dayyid,” Hann’yu said. “Go ahead. Have the rest.”

“No.” Dayyid shook his head. “I should find Ravishan and make sure he’s at his practices.”

“He’s at his practices,” Hann’yu said. “He’s always at his practices. He wakes Jahn up before sunrise to practice. He stays in the golden chamber until sunset. He does nothing but practice.”

“You disapprove?” Dayyid asked.

“I just wonder what he’s going to do when he crosses to Nayeshi.”

“Find the Rifter,” Dayyid replied as if there could be no other response.

“Yes, obviously, but I mean besides that. It takes years, doesn’t it? Then he has to wait for word from the Black Tower. He hardly knows how to relax or talk about anything but becoming Kahlil. What will they make of him in Nayeshi?”

Remembering Kyle, John had a good idea of what people would make of Ravishan—a weird, knife-wielding, scarred milkman. But it would be different for Ravishan. John planned on being there with him, helping him.

“My only concern is that he becomes Kahlil,” Dayyid replied.

“He will.” Hann’yu gestured as if waving any doubt aside. “The Issusha’im Oracles have seen the Prayerscars over his eyes. They have seen him cross through the Great Gate.”

“They also saw Fikiri’s blood spilled on the Holy Road.” Dayyid reached out to the cup he’d set aside and ran a finger over the rim before drawing his hand back. “We can’t depend upon their scrying.”

“Then perhaps we should have faith in Parfir,” Hann’yu said.

“You’ll say anything not to have to drink alone, won’t you?” Dayyid picked his cup up again and took a quick drink from it. He closed his eyes.

“Even now, drinking fathi,” Dayyid said softly, “he doesn’t stop picking at my thoughts.”

“Ravishan?”

“Ushvun Jahn.” Dayyid opened his eyes and gazed back to the curtained bed.

“He’s like a splinter in my mind.” Dayyid stepped closer to the bed and caught hold of one of the canvas panels. “He learns too quickly, fights too well...What will we do if he’s one of theirs?”

“Fai’daum?” Hann’yu asked. He looked amused by the idea.

Dayyid drew one of the panels back and scowled at John. Seeing his own body stretched out in the bed utterly exposed as Dayyid leaned over him sent a shudder of fear through John. He wanted to wake up but couldn’t quite rouse himself.

Dayyid released the panel and it fell back closed.

"He isn't Fai'daum," Hann'yu stated with certainty.

"You can't know that." Dayyid turned back to Hann'yu.

"I can." Hann'yu's smile was a little crooked. His small cup of fathi sat nearly empty.

"You think you know him," Dayyid said. "You think he's trustworthy, but to me he reeks of lies."

Hann'yu rolled his eyes.

"Even if I didn't like him I would still know he isn't Fai'daum." Hann'yu leaned back in his chair. A soft pink glow had spread across his nose and cheeks. "The Fai'daum brand their men so that one can never desert the cause."

"I've heard the same thing, but it could just as easily be a rumor, like almost everything else you hear about the Fai'daum."

"No, I met members when I lived in Nurjima." Hann'yu smiled at Dayyid's horrified expression. "In the south it's not like it is here. It's not an all-out war. There are public speeches and debates... Well, there used to be. It's all changed by now, I suppose."

"Southern intellectuals making speeches and giving themselves burn scars hardly speak for the true Fai'daum. They're children compared to the real insurgents we battle here in the north."

"Yes, so I've been told many, many times," Hann'yu said. "But even if I know nothing of the northern Fai'daum, Jahn is the last person you should suspect of being one of their spies. What would he be doing? If he was going to kill the Kahlil, he's had more than ample opportunities to end both Ravishan's and Fikiri's lives. Instead, he's improving the ushiri'im by training with them. He's born wounds for all of the ushiri'im. He could have refused and let several of them die. What kind of Fai'daum member does that?"

"I don't know," Dayyid admitted.

"You do know," Hann'yu stated firmly. "He's not a member of the Fai'daum. He's a man who Parfir has blessed with strength and power and that threatens you. Jahn has the potential to become a powerful ushman, perhaps even more powerful than you. The ushiri'im sense as much and so do you. That's why you mistrust him. That's why he nags at your thoughts."

"If you weren't drunk on fathi," Dayyid glowered at Hann'yu, "I would call you out onto the fighting grounds for saying such a thing."

"But I am drunk."

Dayyid leaned across Hann'yu's table and glared down at him. "Someday you will have worn that excuse too thin," Dayyid growled.

"Today?" Hann'yu's smile faded but his tone remained teasing as he met Dayyid's glower.

"Not today." Dayyid straightened. He turned and started for the door. "When he wakes, send him to the golden chamber."

"Ushvun Jahn?" Hann'yu asked.

"Of course." Dayyid stopped at the door and glanced back to Hann'yu. "Don't make me wait too long." Then he left.

Hann'yu took Dayyid's abandoned cup of fathi and raised it toward the curtained bed. "Well, Jahn, let's pray that wasn't the wife you dreamed up for me." He tossed back the last of Dayyid's fathi. "Sheep are sounding better already."

☾☾☾

John no longer found the chill and harsh odor of burnt ozone remarkable when he entered the golden chamber. Even those faint bloodstains that marred the perfect white practice mats no longer perturbed him. He'd fought and seen blood spilled—both his own and that of the ushiri'im—in combat practice.

But the emptiness of the space bothered him. He was used to entering the chamber to find many ushiri'im practicing their battle skills. Some afternoons the number of men and the intensity of their exertions managed to warm the chamber, despite the cold that emanated from countless rifts in the Gray Space.

This afternoon only Dayyid occupied the room; John recognized him despite the fact that he wore neither his black coat, nor his cassock. Dozens of long white scars marred the dark skin of his bare arms. He knelt before the large iron statue of Parfir, dressed in simple pants and an undershirt. His long dark braids were tied back and he gripped a black curse blade in his right hand.

Powerfully built and handsome, he reminded John more than a little of Ravishan, and yet as John studied him, he felt nothing but loathing for the man.

"You sent for me, Ushman Dayyid?" John called from the doorway.

"I did." Dayyid remained where he was. John waited for him to complete his prayers. At last Dayyid stood and turned to face John directly. He didn't sheath his curse blade.

"I will not pretend to like you, Ushvun Jahn," Dayyid announced.

"I don't think you ever have," John replied before Dayyid could go on.

Dayyid narrowed his dark gaze and John knew he should have remained silent. But ever since the Harvest Festival, when he'd realized just how cruelly Dayyid used Ravishan to enforce his own brutal ideals, John had found himself overwhelmed by his outrage at the man.

"Perhaps I have not. Such deceit is not in my nature, after all. Just as honesty is not in your nature." Dayyid gave him a hard smile and made a small sweep with his curse blade, almost absently.

John ground his teeth but kept his mouth shut. He wasn't going to be baited into attacking Dayyid and being run through with that poisonous blade.

"Hann'yu seems to think differently of you," Dayyid stated. "And it seems that many of my ushiri'im have found a use for you as well."

John nodded, not trusting himself to speak just yet. He hoped this wasn't going to be a repeat of the interrogation that Dayyid had already put him through in the library.

"I won't have my ushiri'im training against an inferior opponent. After all, one cannot sharpen a blade with a soft stone." Dayyid watched John like a cat watching a fallen crow. "From this point on I will personally see to your battle training…Unless, of course, you wish to withdraw from practices with my ushiri'im."

John stared at Dayyid for a moment, almost unable to believe that the man could be so petty. At the same time he knew Dayyid was serious and would take the greatest satisfaction in beating him to a pulp while claiming that it served a higher good. The smartest, fastest way to diffuse the entire situation would be to withdraw from practicing with the ushiri'im as Dayyid wished.

But even knowing as much, John couldn't bring himself to do so. Training was the only excuse he could claim for time alone with Ravishan and it offered John a reason to be in the upper reaches of the monastery. More than that, he refused to give up his friendships with the ushiri'im and the freedoms they had won him just to mollify Dayyid's jealousy.

"When do we begin training?" John asked.

"I believe your first lesson will start right now," Dayyid replied. He sheathed his black curse blade, and then with a flick of his hands, wrenched the Gray Space open and punched it toward John's chest.

John lunged back. Dayyid pursued him with fast, sure strides and an expression of pleasure on his face. John's heel hit the wall behind him. No further retreat in that direction.

Dayyid obviously saw as much as well and pressed his assault with a quick jab for John's face.

John dropped to a crouch, feeling the sick cold of the Gray Space slash the air just above his head. He immediately pounced up, driving both fists into Dayyid's exposed torso. Dayyid stumbled back and John bounded after him. He landed another powerful body blow to Dayyid's chest and saw the look of pain and fury as he knocked the breath out of Dayyid. But in an instant Dayyid struck back with a hard kick into John's right knee. Pain shot through John's leg and he staggered.

Dayyid pressed his advantage, tearing open the Gray Space to create a Silence Knife. The air screamed and flames followed the arc of Dayyid's fist as he plunged the Silence Knife down.

Two years ago John would have been too overwhelmed, too hurt and off balance to do anything but fall beneath the killing edge of Dayyid's Silence Knife. But since then John had trained hard and constantly, not only against his fellow ushvun'im, but also against Dayyid's ushiri'im.

They fought just as Dayyid fought, because he had trained them. Their speed and relentless attacks were Dayyid's, but so too were their weaknesses. They never expected anyone to challenge their divine weapons; they could not seem to even imagine an attack across the line of their Silence Knives and Unseen Edges.

With a roar of sheer rage, John punched directly into Dayyid's Silence Knife. Agonizing pain tore across the back of his hand, but John threw himself into the blow. Blood gushed from his hand and then the frigid cold of the Gray Space snapped closed and John's bloody fist smashed into Dayyid's jaw. Dayyid's eyes went wide with shock.

John hooked Dayyid's ankle with a fast kick and pulled him off his feet.

As Dayyid hit the practice mat flat on his back, John dropped to one knee, aiming a blow straight down into Dayyid's exposed throat. A killing strike.

Then, reflexively, John pulled back. He wasn't about to kill another human being, not even someone as cruel as Dayyid.

For a stunned instant he stared at Dayyid, horrified by what he had almost done. It had come so easily that John felt almost sick with himself. Dayyid stared back up at him, his dark eyes wide and his breath coming in gasps.

"I'm sorry. I didn't mean—"

"Idiot!" Before John could react, Dayyid brought up his leg and landed a solid kick into John's stomach. John tumbled back and Dayyid rolled up to his feet. In an instant he stood over John with one foot placed on John's neck.

"The win is mine," Dayyid declared with a smirk.

"Yes," John conceded before Dayyid placed any further weight on his throat. "The win is yours."

Dayyid stepped back, allowing John to regain his feet.

The wound across the back of John's hand hurt like hell but it didn't seem too deep, despite the volume of blood spattered across the training mats.

John noted the numerous welts and scratches that stood out across both of Dayyid's hands and forearms.

"Do you understand why I defeated you, Jahn?" Dayyid asked the question over his shoulder as he strode to the dressing table where his cassock and coat lay. He dressed quickly, hiding his injuries.

Because you're a dick, John thought, but he said nothing. The last thing he wanted was to start a real fight.

"It is because I am a true servant of Parfir. My entire being is dedicated to him. I never have to question myself or fear that I am on the wrong path, because Parfir is with me in everything." Dayyid looked up to the towering statue with an expression of reverence. Then he cast John a disdainful glance. "You have not taken Parfir into your heart, and so you question your actions. You hesitate in battle because you do not know if you are just or not. I never hesitate. That is why I beat you and why I will always beat you."

John cradled his bleeding hand and glared at Dayyid's back. Very briefly he imagined himself drawing his own knife and plunging it between Dayyid's self-satisfied shoulder blades.

But John quickly stopped that line of thought.

He wasn't here to fight the injustices of the Payshmura religion or to teach Dayyid some humility. He had come to Rathal'pesha to find a way for himself, Bill, and Laurie to escape this entire world. He'd promised to show Ravishan a kinder, better life in Nayeshi. No matter what he couldn't lose sight of those things. He just needed to endure all of this. After all, Ravishan had assured him that the issusha'im were closing in on the Rifter. It could be any day now. They would escape Basawar and he would never see Dayyid again.

John drew in a deep, calming breath and slowly released it.

"You're right," John told Dayyid.

"Of course I am." Dayyid turned back to John with a smug expression. "These lessons will ensure that you never forget that."

John lowered his gaze but couldn't help noticing how gingerly Dayyid held his left hand. John suddenly realized that he must have hurt Dayyid badly when he'd punched through his Silence Knife. And then he recalled that brief expression of shock that had flickered across Dayyid's face.

John bowed his head to hide his smile. Dayyid could talk all he liked about being Parfir's holy servant, but for that instant at least, he had to have known that Parfir hadn't been with him. Though he knew it was petty, John took more than a little consolation in the thought.

That became more true, especially as the weeks passed and his training with Dayyid intensified. He always conceded the win to Dayyid, but more and more often he exalted in those brief moments when he broke through Dayyid's divine weapons and forced Dayyid to feel defeat.

Chapter Forty-Three

As the months passed, spring grew into summer and even in the heights of the mountains, beds of berries ripened and the scents of fruit and flowers carried on the warm winds.

Despite the balmy weather, John woke, shaking and clammy. He'd dreamed of the bones again. Their strange voices hissed and murmured through his groggy memory. He tried to recall the dream but it, like others, faded to fleeting impressions of black hollow eyes and thousands of skeletal hands searching for him. He'd been terrified, but now he couldn't recall exactly why. It was something he was happy to forget.

He stared at the dim white expanses of the canvas panels that surrounded his bed. The first bright rays of morning light played across the cloth. The strong scents of other men's bodies hung in the warm air of the dormitory. He thought suddenly of the one morning he'd woken with Ravishan in his arms. If only they could have lingered… Then his revere drifted to the few minutes he and Ravishan had stolen alone in the pine garden last evening.

Compared to the nights of easy, anonymous sex he'd known in Nayeshi, the simple act of holding Ravishan in his arms should have felt dull, almost chaste. And yet the warmth and strength of Ravishan's embrace had electrified John's entire body. The smell of his skin, the feel of his fingers curling along the nape of John's neck, even the soft rhythm of his breathing had suffused John with arousal.

This morning he allowed himself to remember and ease his desire.

At last he sat up and tossed his sticky blankets aside. His body ached a little as he stretched and washed at his water basin. Just looking over his chest and thighs, John could see where Dayyid liked to strike and where his own defenses were too slow. But he was improving. Most of his bruises were old and fading.

Somewhere nearby, birds called out. John listened to their tiny, shrill voices as he dressed. He recognized the songs. Brownish birds with black heads made them. Doubtless the two singing were males challenging one another for territories. By late summer they would be settled and much more quiet.

"If only Dayyid would have been satisfied with a song," John mumbled to himself.

"He's not a man like you and I," Hann'yu had told John a month ago. "Dayyid doesn't compromise. He doesn't relent for the sake of human comfort or mercy. But he's the most genuinely pious man I have ever known. It can make him hard on the people around him, but his only true concern is how best he can serve god."

John had simply nodded at the time, but he had known that Hann'yu was wrong. Piety was not the cause of Dayyid's brutality, but a tool with which he justified his abuse of those around him. John knew as much because he'd seen the best ideals of the Payshmura religion embodied by Samsango. Parfir's edicts of generosity, humility, and compassion moved Samsango to do what Dayyid never would: to celebrate the prowess of those who surpassed him while offering aid and sympathy to those beneath him. His serene piety at times made John wish he could believe in Parfir as Samsango did. Dayyid's piety only made John want to get as far from him and his church as he could.

Today, at least, his wish would be granted. Hann'yu needed him to go down to Amura'taye and fetch supplies for the infirmary. One day down the mountain and one day back up. That meant two days free of Dayyid.

John finished cleaning his face and teeth and poured the used water into the rain gutter outside the window. The morning bells began to ring and John heard his fellow ushvun'im groaning and mumbling as they too arose from slumber. He made his way out of the dormitories and back to the kitchens. The morning meals wouldn't be ready for an hour. Fortunately, Samsango always left out bread and cold cheese for the ushvun'im who would be leaving for Amura'taye. John helped himself and then went out to join the other ushvun'im at the iron gate.

The sky was pale blue and cloudless. Woody herbs displayed yellow and violet blooms from where they nestled along the path. John brushed his hand against the bare stone of the mountain wall as he strode down the Thousand Steps.

The rock beneath his fingers was cold and hard and yet it struck John as fragile at the same time. There was brittleness in its nature, like the bones of an old woman; it felt aged and depleted.

John supposed he was projecting the decay he saw in Rathal'pesha and now below him in Amura'taye. The clear sky allowed him a sweeping view of the city. It stretched out beneath him like a map. He easily picked out the white curves of the inner city walls. They arched out and enclosed each other, reflecting the city's growth and decline. He recognized a cluster of small structures that would have been the first refuge of a few dozen farmers and herders. Larger walls and buildings spilled out from there. Clearly, Amura'taye had flourished once. Its walls swept and curled out over the entire side of the mountain.

It was still a lively city but now wide stretches of the periphery stood abandoned and crumbling, like the collapsed walls in Candle Alley where he had first kissed Ravishan. Most of the buildings there had been deserted and derelict. Now, John picked out other districts that resembled abandoned ruins more than an inhabited urban area.

It was a backwater. More than one person had told him so. And seated so close to the Payshmura stronghold of Rathal'pesha, the tithes were strictly enforced. It was no wonder that the city, like Rathal'pesha itself, was being abandoned.

What young herder would choose to struggle for a living in a desolate, repressive land when there was the promise of an easier living to be made in a developing city like Nurjima? Stories of city lights, railroads, and loom factories all attested to the rise of industry there.

At the same time John couldn't help but wonder how many of those same herders might instead choose to join the Fai'daum and fight to destroy the theocracy that so relentlessly drained them of resources and drove them from their homes.

"It looks so peaceful from up here, doesn't it?" an older ushvun'im commented to John.

"Yes, it does." John turned his attention back to the men traveling with him.

"Just past the city wall there," the man pointed to a tiny cluster of huts, "you can see what remains of my uncle's farm."

"He raised taye." John guessed the obvious and the ushvun nodded.

"But the crops aren't what they used to be. He moved to Gisa and left the land to me." The ushvun gave a dry laugh. "As if I could afford to pay the tithe for a property… Still, it's pretty, isn't it, with the wild flowers all blooming across the old fields."

"It is," John agreed.

And soon other ushvun pointed out the farmlands or hill pastures that had once been their homes. John shared what he could of his own history as they descended.

His strides were naturally longer than those of the other ushvun'im, but he slowed to their pace, and when a gray-haired ushvun seemed to flag, John took the pack of oil jars that he'd been hauling to ease his burden. All of them then paused to share a flask of daru'sira.

When they reached Amura'taye, his fellow ushvun'im wished him luck in finding all of the herbs Hann'yu had requested, and one handed him a blessed stone to give to his sister. They had all heard that she had been unwell of late.

John accepted the stone and thanked them, though he knew Laurie would have no use for it. Then he marched off to find the medicinal supplies Hann'yu needed. He purchased boughs of pungent southern herbs, jars of arcane brown syrup and glistening, succulent green blossoms. Samsango's knuckles had been bothering him recently, and so John added a jar of camphor-scented analgesic. The thick musty smells of the apothecaries clung to him. It reminded him of days he had spent wandering between the cramped shelves of used bookstores.

They needed needles in the infirmary as well. John walked across town to the open streets of the Smiths' Rows. Most of the goods were crude. Rough knife blades, ax heads, bicycle chains, and scythes were common. It was only among the cases of delicate gold and silver jewelry that John at last found medical instruments. He chose twenty of the finest silver needles. Then, out of curiosity, he looked over the other devices in the medical cases.

John picked up an instrument that resembled a pair of surgical scissors. There was an odd wire loop up by the blades. He frowned at it.

"Gelding shears," a familiar voice supplied from behind John.

He turned to see Bill grinning at him. A faint tan colored his skin and his thin frame showed traces of muscle. John couldn't remember him looking so well since they had left Nayeshi. Laurie's spells were making obvious improvements in his health.

"We just heard that the ushvun'im had come down for supplies. I figured I should see if I could hunt you down." Bill eyed the shears in John's hand. "Looking for just the right gift for that special someone?"

"Something like that." John set the shears aside.

"Do you think you have time for a lunch break?" Bill asked.

"Sure. I'm done here." John shrugged. When neither the prior nor an ushman accompanied them, the ushvun'im tended to be lax. They rarely paired off or bothered to supervise each other's activities. So long as he got back to the church hostel before dark, no one would care what he did with the remaining free hours of the afternoon.

"Good. Loshai is dying to talk to you."

"How's she doing?" John stowed the needles in his pack and then swung it up onto his back. "Is her stomach still bothering her?'

"Oh yeah." Bill looked almost pleased. "Apparently, it comes with the territory."

"What?" John frowned at the reply.

"I think she wants to tell you herself," Bill said quietly.

John decided not to ask anything more, not out here on the open street where they could be overheard.

He suspected that Laurie's recent bouts of sickness were linked to the spells she poured over Bill. John didn't know much about working a healing spell, but he had been watching Hann'yu for more than a year now. Hann'yu always chose another priest—generally

John—to bear the brunt of the wounds he treated; Laurie only had her own strength to call on. It had to wear her down.

"We've heard that things are moving along in Rathal'pesha," Bill commented as they crossed the street.

"So I'm told," John said. He guessed that Fikiri had been keeping them informed.

The walk to the Bousim house went quickly. They only had to pause once, halfway up a steep hill, for Bill to catch his breath.

"Oh yeah, feeling the burn," Bill whispered between deep breaths. "I have no idea how other people walk around all day long."

"It's not nearly as easy as it looks."

"Tell me about it." Bill straightened. "Okay, let's not keep the ladies waiting."

John followed Bill to the Bousim house and up to one of the more elegant chambers of the second floor where Lady Bousim preferred to receive her guests.

Breads, fruit, and cuts of lamb had been laid out on the long wooden table. Thinner tapestries embroidered with images of summer flowers and fruit-laden trees hung in the place of the heavier tapestries that had insulated the room the last time John had visited.

Lady Bousim greeted John with a smile as he followed Bill in. Laurie beamed at him from the seat to Lady Bousim's right. A healthy blush colored her skin and she'd at last put on enough weight to make her slim figure truly feminine. Her eyes were bright.

John grinned at her, feeling overwhelmed with relief to see her looking more than well—radiant, in fact.

The other two attendants, Ohbi and Inholima, sat to Lady Bousim's left. They bowed their heads when John entered the room. Ohbi's glossy black hair had grown even longer than John remembered. Clusters of sliver beads and ribbons hardly held back all of her twisting braids.

Of the four women, only Inholima appeared ill. A sallow tone pervaded her once golden skin and dark purple bags hung beneath her eyes. She smiled faintly, showing the small gap between her front two teeth. Most disconcertingly, the tinge of oxygen-starved blue that had once colored Bill's mouth now saturated Inholima's lips.

John suddenly had a terrible idea of who had been chosen to bear the brunt of Bill's illness.

He knew Inholima was a spy, placed in Lady Bousim's entourage by Lord Bousim. If she were to ever discover the witchcraft that Lady Bousim, Laurie, and Ohbi practiced, she could get them all killed. So John could see why they wouldn't hesitate to make her weak and ill.

Still, just sitting there at the table, she seemed young and pathetic. It made John feel sorry for her in spite of himself.

"Ushvun Jahn." Lady Bousim waved him to a seat at the table. "Is it possible that you have grown even more handsome? It is such a delight to see you again."

"Thank you, Lady Bousim." John bowed to her.

"Tell me, how is Ushman Hann'yu?"

He had almost forgotten that the two of them knew each other. His memories of last year's Harvest Fair had been so dominated by the witch burning and his fight with Rasho Tashtu that he hadn't remembered introducing the two of them.

"He's well," John told her. "A little overworked, but well."

"You must inform him that I am anxiously looking forward to this Harvest Fair so that we can talk again."

"I will."

Inholima cupped her hand over her mouth and coughed. It was a sticky, gasping sound. She looked embarrassed at the ugliness of it.

"My dear," Lady Bousim said to Inholima, "are you sure you're well enough to be out of bed?"

"You look terrible," Ohbi said softly.

"Maybe you should rest," Laurie added.

"I don't think I could stand much more bed rest. Lying on my back all day, I feel like I'm withering away." Inholima smiled weakly. "I want to stay up at least long enough to hear Behr play."

Bill glanced to Inholima. "That's flattering. I had no idea you liked it so much."

"It's soothing," Inholima said.

"Well, if Lady Bousim doesn't object, I'd be happy to play for you," Bill said.

"Of course you should play, Behr," Lady Bousim said. She turned easily to John. "You must try the white rolls. The flour was brought all the way from Milaun. They're so soft, nothing like the tough bread you find around here."

"Thank you." John took a roll. It wouldn't taste like anything to him. He added a slab of pale yellow cheese to his plate as well as several slices of lamb cutlet.

Bill walked across the room to where a polished wooden case lay on top of a small table. He opened the case and gently lifted out a mandolin-like instrument. John ate while Bill tuned the instrument. A few moments later Bill began playing. The music was simple and soothing. The melody struck John as familiar. He wondered if Bill had adapted it from some popular song from Nayeshi.

Inholima closed her eyes. Laurie quietly rose from her seat and stepped back behind Inholima. She gently set her hands on either side of the girl's temples. Inholima glanced up and Laurie smiled down at her. Inholima closed her eyes again as Laurie massaged the sides of her head.

"Just relax and rest," Laurie said quietly. "Sleep."

John's head snapped up as the last word escaped Laurie's mouth. The air had seemed to shudder around her. He'd felt it. Inholima slumped forward. Laurie caught her, stopping her from falling flat onto the tabletop. Slowly, Laurie and Ohbi lowered Inholima down to the table and let her head rest there.

"Sleep, deaf, dumb, blind." Laurie's words seemed to distort the air like waves of heat. They poured from her mouth and wrapped around Inholima's head. "Sleep, free of thought and mind."

Inholima's breathing suddenly slowed. Her head lolled to the side.

"I hadn't even finished the first song." Bill placed his hand against the strings of his instrument, silencing the notes.

"Jahn doesn't have all day to wait for her to nod off on her own," Laurie replied.

"Is she going to be all right?" John asked. Inholima looked like a corpse collapsed across the table.

"She'll be fine," Laurie assured him. "A little sleep isn't going to hurt her."

"Which is a pity, if you ask me." Ohbi scowled at Inholima's unconscious face.

"There's no need to be cruel," Lady Bousim said. "If it wasn't Inholima, then it would just be another girl sent to spy on us." She turned her attention back to John. "How is the bread?"

"Very soft," John replied.

"I thought you would like it." Lady Bousim smiled.

Laurie returned to her chair. She took several cuts of lamb and a sliced apple. Bill began playing again. John was almost positive that this time it was some variation on a Led Zeppelin song. They all seemed to take Inholima's collapsed, unconscious form in stride. He wondered how often this happened.

"So, how much longer until the Great Gate will be opened?" Laurie asked.

"Soon," John said quietly.

"She's not going to wake up," Ohbi said. "You don't have to whisper."

Suddenly John wondered just how many people Fikiri had told about their plan to leave.

"Soon as in a week or soon as in this year?" Laurie asked.

"I don't think the issusha'im are good with exact dates," John responded. "Soon is all they've been pinned down as far as anyone seems to know. I would guess within the year."

"Is there any way to hurry it along?" Laurie finished off the last of her lamb and frowned. She laid one hand against her belly.

"Your stomach's still bothering you?" John asked.

Lady Bousim gave a silent shudder of laughter at this. John had no idea why. Both Ohbi and Laurie smiled at him. When he glanced to Bill, John saw that even he seemed amused.

"It's still bothering me, but it should clear up in about nine months," Laurie said.

"Nine…" Suddenly John realized why they were all looking so pleased. "You're…" John began but then couldn't go on. He hadn't thought of this, and didn't know what he should think of it. He stared at Laurie, stunned.

"Pregnant," Laurie supplied.

"You're going to be an uncle." Bill clapped him on the shoulder. John simply stared at Laurie.

"So, you can see why I would want to know when we're going to be crossing through the Great Gate," Laurie told him. "That last trip through wasn't exactly a roll in the hay."

"Maybe if the hay was mixed into a stack of needles," Bill suggested. He strummed the strings of his instrument softly.

"I don't..." John began, but then trailed off. He glanced to Ohbi and then back to Laurie. He'd been so stunned by the news that he hadn't wondered why they would be discussing Nayeshi in front of Ohbi and Lady Bousim. Both Bill and Laurie had just offhandedly mentioned their previous passage through the Great Gate.

The reason was obvious, John realized. They had informed Lady Bousim and Ohbi that they had come from Nayeshi. This meant Fikiri probably knew...

Laurie and Bill had to be planning to bring them all along. Fikiri must have told them that John had already agreed to it. John ran his hand across the back of his neck, massaging uselessly at the tense muscles there. Fikiri, Lady Bousim, Ohbi. Doubtless they would be planning to bring Ohbi's brother, Bati'kohl, as well. John had no idea how Ravishan would manage to sneak three of them through the Great Gate unnoticed. Adding in Fikiri, his mother, Ohbi and her brother was simply impossible.

He knew he couldn't say so, not in front of Lady Bousim and Ohbi. He had to find a time when he could talk to Laurie and Bill alone.

"I don't know when," John said. "It depends on the issusha'im. But from what we've heard, it sounds like the Kahlil will be leaving by the end of the year. Early in the next year at the latest."

"Earlier would be better," Laurie said. "I think I can protect our little girl as long as she's inside me, but after that I don't know."

"How far along..." John wasn't sure why he was having such difficulty even talking. It just seemed like so much to take in. He'd known Laurie since they were children themselves. He couldn't imagine her as someone's mother.

"Six weeks." Laurie grinned at John's awkwardness.

"That's really early, isn't it?" John asked. A distant memory of his developmental biology class floated up to him. The first month. At this point the fetus would be a clump of red pulsing cells clinging, fragile and microscopic. If it had been a root ball or mineral deposit, he would have been utterly at ease. Even in the animal realm contemplating gestation periods, rates of miscarriage and stillbirth, he was comfortable. But this was his friends' child. The closeness of it made him feel nervous and uncertain.

"It's early but I can feel her perfectly. She's very strong," Laurie assured him. "Still, I'd like it if we could leave in the fall."

John stole a glance back to Bill and caught him gazing at Laurie with a wide, almost goofy smile.

"Maybe after the Harvest Fair. I think that would be the best," Laurie said.

"Before would be nice." Ohbi closed her eyes for a moment. "I would be so happy not to see another of those fires ever again in my life."

"This year it isn't a witch," Lady Bousim said. "They're going to burn one of the Fai'daum, the man that killed a garrison commander at Gisa."

"I still don't want to see it," Ohbi whispered.

"I don't think any of us do," John agreed. Ravishan would be the one forced to light the fire. John closed his eyes as if it could shut out his memory of the last fire.

"You should try one of these pears," Laurie told him.

John opened his eyes to see that Laurie was already spooning several slices of poached pear onto his plate.

"Thank you," John said.

"Don't look so glum," Laurie told him. "It'll all work out. We'll make it work out."

John could have told her that he very much doubted that they had the power to do that; instead he took a bite of soft pear. It tasted like wine and honey.

"Any suggestions for names?" Laurie asked.

"It's hard to think of good names for girls," John said. It struck him as the least of their problems.

"Don't name her Ohbi," said Ohbi. "It's such a desolate name for a little girl to have to live with."

Lady Bousim nodded. "Wounin'an is sweet. It was my mother's name."

"I like Billy-Joe," Bill remarked dryly.

Laurie laughed. Both Lady Bousim and Ohbi frowned in confusion.

"Bayal'go?" Ohbi worked hard to pronounce the foreign name.

"No, Behr is joking." Laurie quickly explained. "It's a man's name in Nayeshi."

"What does it mean?" Ohbi asked.

"I don't really know," Laurie said but her tone was pondering. "Billy is a type of goat…"

"A male goat," John supplied automatically.

"Joe's another word for coffee." Bill gave John an impish grin as he spoke. "That's a drink like daru'sira."

Ohbi nodded seriously, as if committing this all to memory. Lady Bousim picked up one of the soft rolls and nibbled on it thoughtfully.

"It's a strange name," Lady Bousim pronounced at last. "A name suitable for a wily young man, but not a pretty girl."

John tried not to picture the absolute disaster of the two of them attempting to integrate with people back home. That was assuming that any of them even made it home. His head was beginning to throb. He poured himself a cup of the pale green tea.

While Laurie, Ohbi, Bill, and Lady Bousim discussed possible names for the baby, John drank his tea. At last he heard bells beginning to ring in the new hour. It would be getting dark soon.

John stood. "I should go."

"But you just got here," Laurie protested.

"I have to be back at the hostel before dark or the other ushvun'im will miss me."

"I wish you could stay here with us," Laurie said.

"Sorry." John turned to Lady Bousim. "Thank you for everything."

Lady Bousim inclined her head graciously. "It is always a pleasure to see you, Jahn. Thank you for looking after my son."

John simply nodded. He doubted that Fikiri would have shared her sentiment.

"Stay out of trouble," Bill told him.

Ohbi held her hand up in a sign of peace. John returned her gesture and departed.

When he reached the hostel, he stored away Hann'yu's supplies and then went to the room he was to share with the other ushvun'im. None of them had returned yet. Most would stay out as late as they could, drinking hard taye liquor and gambling on goat races. John sat down on a bed. The fires hadn't been stoked for the evening and the sheets felt cold. He stared at the plain wall and tried to think.

How would seven people slip unnoticed through the Great Gate? One of them heavily pregnant, or worse yet, carrying a newborn baby. It would never happen. The issusha'im were watching everything now. The full force and attention of the Payshmura Church would be focused on the Great Gate and the Kahlil.

John fell back against the bed and stared up at the ceiling as if it would offer him some new insight. For an instant he thought he glimpsed white skulls staring back at him. And for the first time they didn't seem like a dream, but a premonition.

People were going to have to be left behind or they would all be killed.

Chapter Forty-Four

Despite the heavy canvas walls of the taverner's tent, the noise and perfumes of the surrounding Harvest Fair infiltrated the air. John easily picked out the musical calls of taye sellers and salt vendors. He could smell frying dumplings and freshly cut onions. The laughter of men and children drifted past, as did the soft murmurs of women's conversations.

Inside, his surroundings felt far more subdued. The muscular, bearded proprietor and his serving women gathered around the stacked barrels of beer, wine, and liquor. They spoke quietly among themselves as they filled flagons and rough clay pitchers. One girl tended a small charcoal fire where kettles of daru'sira stood heating.

The majority of the men seated around the tables spoke in lowered voices and wore expressions that struck John as somber if not solemn. He supposed it wasn't the joyous men of the world who needed to drink themselves into oblivion before noon. Though, the dampening presence of both an ushiri and an ushman among their company could also have been responsible for the oddly sober atmosphere.

"Such a serious expression, Jahn." Ravishan swayed on the bench seat beside him. A flush colored his pale cheeks and his eyes were dark and glistening beneath the shadows of his sharp black brows. "You should have a drink." He held up his small glass and the strong floral tang of potent flower liqueur drifted from it.

"I promise you there is no point in attempting to lure Jahn," Hann'yu commented from across the table. He cupped a mead glass gently between his tanned hands but drank little from it. "Nothing tempts him."

"I'm sure something does." Ravishan's speculative stare was only interrupted by the arrival of a plump young woman with thick black bands tattooed around her tanned fingers. She placed another steaming pot of daru'sira down on the table in front of John.

He thanked her and she smiled in a long-suffering manner. Her livelihood was not made by plying men with inexpensive daru'sira. However, her expression lit up as she noted the nearly empty pitcher of flower liqueur in front of Ravishan. But Hann'yu caught her attention and requested a plate of cutlets before she could offer Ravishan a second round.

Ravishan dropped his gaze from John to the small glass in front of him. He threw back another shot, shuddered at the strong alcoholic burn, then slowly refilled his drink.

"You should probably let the first few settle before you have another," Hann'yu suggested.

Ravishan frowned.

"I'm speaking from firsthand experience," Hann'yu informed him. "You have to wait, or you'll throw up the liqueur you've been working all morning to put away."

"Just as well." Ravishan sighed. "The stuff tastes like hell." He pulled his hands back from the full glass as if he were dragging limp birds across the table.

John poured himself a fresh cup of the bitter daru'sira, aware that Ravishan was again watching him intently. A smoky breeze drifted from some nearby cooking fire. Ravishan shuddered.

John searched for something to say to Ravishan but could think of nothing of any value to offer him. He knew too well why Ravishan had fled Dayyid's company and was now drinking himself into a stupor. But whether Ravishan was drunk or sober, nightfall would come and with it his duty to bear the torch that would burn some young man alive.

John could think of no consolation for that inevitability.

And in any case, Hann'yu was certainly more experienced as far as Basawar liquor was concerned.

"A gentleman drinks as he might ravish a lovely woman," Hann'yu stated with an easy smile. "He paces himself, prolonging the pleasure and ensuring that he enjoys all that is offered."

"You imagine that I'm a gentleman?" Ravishan gave an unlovely snort of derision and stole a sidelong glance at John.

"You have the potential," Hann'yu replied, though he seemed more amused than serious.

"No, that's Jahn." Ravishan slumped against the back of the wooden bench and studied John openly. Something in the intensity of his stare warned John to look aside—at all costs avoiding that hungry, penetrating gaze. He took a quick drink of his daru'sira.

"Ah, good, decent Jahn," Ravishan murmured. "He only drinks daru'sira. Never shirks his duties. Isn't there anything bad that you'd like to do?" Ravishan's seductive smile alarmed John with both its blatancy and its effect upon him. He felt his skin flushing and then stole a guilty glance across the bench to Hann'yu.

Hann'yu took a long drink, then lowered his mead glass. He just shook his head at John.

"Pour him a little daru'sira," Hann'yu suggested. John handed his own cup to Ravishan. Briefly their hands brushed, but John quickly withdrew. Ravishan scowled at the brown clay vessel.

"I'm sick of daru'sira," he grumbled. "I'm sick of tea and taye and prayers and practice. I want to do something else. I want to get drunk and neglect my duties. Maybe I want to be seduced."

"This brew's not actually all that bad—" John was cut off as Ravishan toppled into him. He felt Ravishan's hand brush against his thigh and Ravishan's lips press against the bare skin of his neck. An instant later Hann'yu helped him pull Ravishan upright. Ravishan grinned blearily at John.

"Just don't try to move too suddenly," Hann'yu advised Ravishan. "You're not used to flower liqueur. It goes to a man's head quickly. Wait a little while."

"All I do is wait," Ravishan growled. "I want to do something. I don't even care what, just something."

"You're not doing anything in the condition you're in right now," Hann'yu said.

"Why not?" Ravishan demanded.

"Because Dayyid would be furious if he discovered you staggering around drunk in front of all the common folk at the fair," Hann'yu informed him.

John stole a glance back at the men seated nearby. Most kept their heads down and spoke softly among themselves. Only one or two openly observed Ravishan's inebriated behavior and they looked quickly away when they noticed John returning their gazes.

"And what would Dayyid do?" Ravishan lifted his head challengingly. "Take away my torch-bearing privilege? Let him."

"He'd blame Jahn and I for letting you get into trouble," Hann'yu replied.

"As if Jahn would ever let me get into trouble." Ravishan picked up the cup of daru'sira John had passed him and then set it back down on the table. "Dayyid doesn't know anything about anyone."

"He knows a great deal more than you give him credit for." Hann'yu looked like he was going to go on, but then the woman serving them approached the table again. Hann'yu offered her a silent smile as she placed a tray of bread and salt-cured goat meat in front of them. John thanked her but declined when she offered to bring them more flower liqueur.

After she drifted to the other tables, Hann'yu turned his attention back to Ravishan.

"I understand why you might want to be relieved of your duties today," Hann'yu said quietly, "but tomorrow and all the days after you would regret it if Dayyid made you step down."

"He has no one to take my place," Ravishan said.

"There's always Fikiri," Hann'yu replied.

Ravishan responded with a contemptuous sneer. "I could rip Fikiri apart with my bare hands and Dayyid knows it."

"Jealousy is unbecoming in an ushiri," Hann'yu stated. "You shouldn't hate Fikiri for his skill."

"I don't." Ravishan contemplated the platter of goat meat and bread for a moment. "I hate him for his cowardice and conniving."

In spite of himself, John smiled at the frankness of Ravishan's response. It was like him to be too honest.

"Well then," Hann'yu pressed on, "you don't want to be replaced by him, do you?"

"Maybe." Ravishan stared at the stained tabletop. He slumped forward slightly, letting his chin rest on his hands. "I think I'm ready to start drinking again."

"Have some food," John suggested.

Ravishan scowled at the tray of rough bread and salt-encrusted goat meat. He tore a piece of bread off and took a bite. He chewed unenthusiastically and didn't eat anything more. Instead he simply stared at the pitcher of flower liqueur.

Hann'yu sighed and then stood up. "I need to stretch my legs."

"You're not going to tell Dayyid where I am, are you?" Ravishan demanded.

"No, Ravishan, I'm a gentleman. And more than that, I'm your friend," Hann'yu replied offhandedly. But he shot John a meaningful glance. "If I see Dayyid, I'll tell him that I have no idea where you are, though it isn't as if Dayyid won't find this place once he decides to come looking."

John knew Hann'yu was right. Dayyid would only tolerate Ravishan's absence for so long before he'd hunt him down.

As Hann'yu departed, two young women held the tent flaps open. John watched Hann'yu disappear into the crowds of passersby.

Golden light poured in through the open mouth of the tent and John glimpsed the world outside. The common, weathered inhabitants of Amura'taye flirted and gossiped as they bustled past, all of them caught up in their surroundings. The loud calls of vendors, the songs of working women, the bright swaths of cloth, the pungent scents of food and animals, all swirled and rolled into an exotic atmosphere of constant experience. The fair sparkled and cried for all attention to be focused on the spectacle of the moment. It was not a place of recollection, reflection, or regret.

A herd of small black goats rushed past, followed by two laughing young boys.

Then the tent flaps fell closed again, enclosing him and Ravishan in this oasis of alcohol and shadows where the very air seemed to sag with loss and melancholy.

Beside him, Ravishan tossed back another shot of flower liqueur. He shuddered and glanced to John.

"I have a right to get drunk one day out of the entire year," Ravishan murmured.

John studied him and Ravishan dropped his gaze back to the tabletop. This wasn't like him and it wasn't doing him any good.

Exuberant rebellion didn't drive him to toss back drink after drink. They both knew that. Outside, in the midst of the fair, there would at least be distractions.

John stood up. "Come on. Let's get out of here before Dayyid finds us."

"I haven't finished my drink," Ravishan objected, but he rose to his feet. John started for the exit. Ravishan caught up with him just outside of the tent.

Despite the blue sky and high noon sun, a chill pervaded the air. It was particularly notable after the warm darkness of the tavern tent. John drew in a deep breath, smelling honey and the crispness of the approaching winter. At his feet, drifts of red and gold leaves colored the packed dirt. Ravishan kicked several aside, stirring up that musky autumn scent that even now evoked John's childhood memories of Halloween.

The shifting weather and changing colors of the foliage conjured memories of wild costumes and sacks full of candy. But now dread infused his sense of the season. The red-flecked and fallen leaves looked as if they'd been spattered with blood. For a moment just the smell of smoke and roasting meat brought him visions of bodies writhing in the flames of a pyre.

John searched the surrounding corridors of brightly dyed tents and painted stalls for something to distract himself from the morose direction of his own thoughts. He wasn't going to cheer Ravishan up by brooding himself.

Behind them a vendor sang out the astonishing attributes of his cast iron pots. Two older women flaunted strings of glittering beads and a shabby quartet of men strummed their instruments beside a stall displaying a variety of southern quill pens. A small black goat butted into the back of his leg and bleated loudly before being pulled away by a young man. The music all around him, the stalls of bright beads and fragrant southern fruit, only seemed to make him think of it all the more. The joy and fervent energy of the Harvest Fair struck him as a desperate deception, an attempt to overcompensate for the terrible cruelty yet to come.

Next to him, Ravishan watched a group of laughing young men with a wistful expression.

“Why don’t we try to find more of that violet ink that Ashan’ahma likes,” John suggested. “He’s nearly out.”

“I still had half a pitcher left back in the taverner’s tent,” Ravishan commented, but he didn’t look too annoyed.

“It was nearly empty,” John replied. “Come on, Ravishan, walk with me and I’ll buy you something that tastes decent.”

“All right,” Ravishan agreed. “But I should warn you that I’m a little drunk and perhaps slightly surly as well.”

“I’ll take that into consideration,” John told him. “I’m still glad for your company.”

Ravishan flushed handsomely in response.

They strolled together, their arms brushing a little more closely than other men, but in the shove and push of the crowd no one noticed. John made what light conversation he could, but often as not they fell into a companionable quiet. Somehow in the chaos of surrounding song and noise just brushing Ravishan’s hand and meeting that flash of his smile seemed to carry far more between them than any number of words.

At last they stopped at a stand selling sweet honey cakes. John remembered the dull yellow tent and the women working beneath it from the previous year. The old women’s red widows’ veils looked dull russet in the sharp noon light. They sat, as they had the year before, singing with their daughter-in-law and pounding out the cakes.

“Yellow honey cakes,” the vendor shouted over the rumble of the crowd. “Fresh and sweet! The best you’ll ever taste!”

“He should have said eat,” Ravishan commented. “It rhymes.”

“Clearly he’s not a poet.”

“Clearly not. The cakes smell good though.”

Instead of competing with the cries of the vendors and customers all around him, John simply held up four fingers. Seconds later John exchanged two prayer stones for four piping hot cakes wrapped in some large dried leaf. Reflexively, John tried to identify the leaf. It certainly hadn’t come from any of the native flora of the cold north. The big frond resembled a banana leaf.

“Here,” John raised his voice so that Ravishan would hear him clearly, “these two are for you.”

Ravishan's hands bumped John's as he took the cakes. His fingers felt hot. Both of them hung back, close to the stand while they ate. The flavor of the cakes reminded John of sweetened polenta. Beside him, Ravishan chewed carefully, obviously aware that he was still clumsy from the flower liqueur.

All around them strangers bumped and jostled through the rows of tents, wagons, and stalls. The sweet smell of the honey cakes mingled with the odors of living breath and sweat. Everywhere John looked, billowing bright tents and gaudily painted wagons hid the crumbling remnants of abandoned buildings and fissured city walls.

Ravishan leaned closer to him. "Candle Alley isn't far from here, you know."

John studied the cracked wall, trying to place it in his mental map of the city. Ravishan was right. Candle Alley would only be a few blocks away on the other side of this wall. A normal man would have to walk all the way around to the nearest city gate to reach it, but Ravishan could simply step through to it. Walls were nearly meaningless to him.

"No one would look for us there," Ravishan whispered. His hand brushed against John's hip and then quickly dropped away.

"It's broad daylight." John could hardly believe what Ravishan seemed to be suggesting. Then again, he was young, drunk, and depressed. John supposed it shouldn't have been all that surprising. And in all honesty John recognized that Ravishan's suggestion disturbed him because of his own susceptibility. The respite of even a few minutes of ecstasy appealed to him just as much as it did to Ravishan.

He yearned for it so badly that he didn't dare to think too long on the temptation. It could get them both killed.

"It's always dark in the alley," Ravishan whispered. "No one ever looks at you."

"We should try the Quillers' Row for that ink."

Ravishan gave him a hard, vexed glare. "Why don't we go to Candle Alley?"

"Because that would be incredibly stupid of us," John responded as quietly as he could. "We have to be careful. You know that."

"I'm sick to death of being careful," Ravishan snapped. "I'm tired of doing what's right and wise. And living like this, I don't feel anything." He pulled back from John.

"Ravishan." John stepped after him, keeping his voice low and reasonable. "I know this is hard for you. What you have to do tonight—"

"What I have to do tonight isn't what I want to talk about," Ravishan cut him off. "It doesn't matter right now. Now, I want to have a good time. I want to be happy. And all you want is to drag me around this crowd of goats and peasants looking for ink for Ashan'ahma. I don't care about Ashan'ahma! I don't care about his damn ink!"

People around them gawked, and then recognizing Ravishan's ushiri coat, quickly looked away. Women and girls scuttled into tents or ducked behind wagons. Men turned away, feigning interest in anything but the scene Ravishan seemed intent on making.

"This isn't the place for this conversation," John told him.

Ravishan glared around him and then turned his attention back to John. He swayed on his feet, looking furious and frustrated.

"Are you coming with me or not?" Ravishan demanded in a low whisper.

"I don't—" John began.

"Yes or no?"

"I'm not going to—"

"Fine." Ravishan cut him off again. "I'll have a good time without you. I can do that, you know. I hope Ashan'ahma really enjoys his ink."

"Ravishan…" John didn't bother going on. Ravishan was already gone. The chill of the torn Gray Space hung in his wake.

John sighed. "You idiot."

It would serve Ravishan right if he did just go off and find gifts for Hann'yu, Samsango, and Ashan'ahma. Ravishan could stagger around half-drunk, complaining to the women in Candle Alley, and then he'd see just how sorry they felt for him.

John glowered at the wall that separated him from Candle Alley as if the sheer force of his annoyance could knock it down.

Unwillingly, he wondered how well Ravishan could navigate the Gray Space at his current level of inebriation. It was a short distance and Ravishan had been moving through the Gray Space all of his life. He could probably cross through this wall in his sleep. And he would have a great time without John when he got there.

The thought of the companionship Ravishan might find nagged at John more than he wanted to admit. And despite himself he couldn't help but fear that something might have gone wrong during Ravishan's passage through the Gray Space.

For a moment, he resented Ravishan for not having the consideration to realize how all these thoughts would disturb him. But there was no point. It wasn't as if Ravishan had cunningly manipulated him. Ravishan was just angry and frustrated. He had good reason to be. But things would only get worse if John didn't go find him and escort him back to the innocuous surroundings of the fair.

Doubtless Dayyid was already searching for Ravishan, and if he didn't find him soon, he'd have every ushvun, ushiri, and ushman at the Harvest Fair hunting. If Ravishan were to be discovered staggering drunk in a gallery of whores, Dayyid wouldn't just be furious, he'd be murderous.

John strode through the rows of bread sellers and meat roasters, following the curve of the city wall. People stepped aside when they saw him coming. Vendors went quiet as he passed them. He supposed he looked menacing, bearing down through the narrow lanes in his gray coat and long priest's braid. When he reached the gate, the city guards let him pass without comment.

One breath told him instantly that he had reached the blood market. This early in the day little of the livestock had gone to slaughter. Instead the powerful odors of living animals, droppings, and urine saturated the air. Goats bleated from their pens. Dogs barked and growled. The shrieks of birds and the weird chirps of weasels drifted out of cages hanging from the supports of the herders' stalls.

Clouds of brown flies swarmed and swept from one animal pen to another. Herders and butchers swatted at them to little effect.

The last time he had been here it had been dark. He had only caught glimpses of its magnitude. The rows of tents and pens stretched all along the outer wall of Amura'taye. There had to be hundreds of closely packed animal pens. Men and women bundled in leather and fleece coats glanced up at him as he walked past but took no further note when he displayed no interest in making a purchase.

He hardly took in the families of butchers and herders as he passed their tents. Whiffs of their cooking fires drifted through the wall of animal odors. John swatted a fly away from his face, but beyond that, his concentration was not on his surroundings. His thoughts centered upon Ravishan. What would he say to him? How would he keep him from slipping away into the Gray Space?

And yet, something in the back of his mind made him glance to his left, to a small pen beside a heavily patched tent. There was nothing remarkable about it. He almost turned away. Then he saw the animal resting there. Her thick golden coat shone in the afternoon light. Her yellow eyes were half lidded, her expression thoughtful. She could have passed for any one of the hundreds of dogs in the blood market. But John knew her. Every detail of her had burned into his mind that night when she had stood in front of him, nearly black from spilled blood, barring her white teeth.

A shudder a dread snaked down John's spine as he realized that he stood gaping at the demoness, Ji Shir'korud.

Chapter Forty-Five

The sharp light of the sun seemed suddenly intense. John could feel sweat beginning to rise across his skin.

He had managed to avoid reminders of that first night he had been brought to Amura'taye. He had tried very hard not to think of the fallen men, the shrieking animals, the blood, and his own responsibility. He had pushed all those memories back so far that he had thought they were truly forgotten.

Seeing Alidas always brought him a tiny shiver of memory, but he could easily suppress that beneath the natural flow of conversation and a few jokes. Gazing at Ji Shir'korud, the Fai'daum demoness, felt entirely different. Her presence rocked through him as if that night were about to begin all over again.

John turned away quickly as Ji looked up. He didn't know if she would remember him. He didn't want to find out what would happen if she did. He strode quickly past the row of animal pens and butchers' tents.

Ji Shir'korud was a leader in the Fai'daum. She wouldn't be here alone. And she certainly wouldn't have come here just to take in the fair. It couldn't be a coincidence that this year, when a Fai'daum member was slated for execution, Ji Shir'korud hunched only a few hundred yards from the shrine where the execution would take place.

All around John the men and women standing close and talking quietly among themselves took on a sinister air. It was impossible to know which of them were Fai'daum. Their lowered voices seemed conspiratorial. Their quick glances to him and then away now took on a furtive malevolence. The meat hooks, knives, chains, and axes hanging in racks and laid out on tables alarmed him with their potential for human butchery.

He had to find Ravishan and get out of here. John quickened his pace, barely holding himself back from a run. His thoughts raced and his pulse hammered through his body. He didn't want a battle. It would be too easy for the city guards and rashan'im to mistake common folk for Fai'daum. It would be too easy for the Fai'daum to pick out the ushiri'im, ushman'im, and ushvun'im in the crowds. There would be a slaughter on both sides. Somehow, he would have to stop the ceremony and execution.

But first he needed to find Candle Alley. He caught himself as he nearly rushed past his turn. A row of weasel vendors filled the area that he remembered as a desolate plaza. He could see the tall, cracked, city wall rising behind the painted tents and stalls. A few old women stood around the stalls, haggling with the vendors over the prices of pickled eggs and reed cages of live weasels.

Despite their bowed heads, John caught the reproachful expressions on the old women's faces as he rushed past. Briefly he wondered if they could all be Fai'daum. He couldn't imagine so many small, bent women being recruited to swarm the young men of the city guard. Then he realized that he was presenting them with the spectacle of a young priest blatantly racing for Candle Alley. Of course they looked condemning.

John ducked between low-hung weasel cages, working his way to the dark, narrow entry. A wave of musky scent washed over him. It was not too different from the animal smells of the blood market, just more condensed. The odors of sex and sweat, urine and blood, seemed to emanate from the very stones of the walls and the packed dirt beneath John's feet. It hung in the shadows, as if taking shelter within the narrow alley.

John had imagined that at this time of day the alley would be deserted. He was surprised to see women already waiting in the alcoves and men wandering between them. He lowered his head. The last time he had been here it had been night and the darkness had offered him ignorance.

He didn't want to look at the women, to see if they were pretty or ugly, sick or healthy. He certainly didn't want to recognize any of the men who patronized them. He just needed to find Ravishan and get out of this place. But he couldn't search without seeing.

He walked fast, glancing into the alcoves and at the passing men before looking away. The bright afternoon light made it too easy to see too much. Bruises mottled one girl's throat and thighs. She pressed her eyes shut as if she were attempting to close out the entire world around her. A young man pushed past John into the alcove. John couldn't help but catch the strange mix of lust and disgust on the man's face as he descended upon the girl.

John moved on quickly.

He strode past alcoves, barely lifting his eyes to take in the forms within their shadows. Expanses of pale bare bodies flicked in and out of his sight as he searched. He had almost reached the massive remains of the wall where he and Ravishan had first kissed. He peered up to the saplings growing there, hoping to see Ravishan. He spied only fallen red fruit amid a litter of golden leaves. He glanced into the alcove to his right and stopped in his tracks. His body froze in place, answering an instinct of shock and pain.

Inside the alcove, Ravishan leaned against a wall. His eyes were closed and his head was tilted just a little to the right. The young man with him was slim and dark haired. He seemed to be a few years younger than Ravishan, perhaps seventeen or eighteen. He wore rough goat hide trousers and not much else. His hands looked stained and filthy against the skin of Ravishan's bare chest.

Furious hatred shot through John as he watched the young man lean forward to kiss Ravishan's mouth. For an instant, he wanted to kill the young man. His hand dropped to his knife belt. His fingers curled around the hilt of his curse blade.

Immediately, John caught himself. He wasn't going to stab some goat herder in an alley. He felt enraged—his hands shook with the intensity of his anger—but he wasn't going to let that make him into a murderer. He stepped back and tried to clear his mind.

What had he expected to find? What had he thought Ravishan would do when he reached Candle Alley? In his own life, John had been young, drunk, and desperate to escape his obligations. He understood the solace that meaningless, anonymous sex offered. He wasn't proud of it, but he understood.

In the alcove, Ravishan broke from the younger man's kiss. John recognized the troubled way Ravishan's eyes flicked from the other man's face. He looked like he was on the verge of some guilty confession.

Then John felt a frigid hiss. A rending screech tore the air and flames arced up. Instantly, Ravishan and the young man leaped apart. The young man stumbled back and then bolted from of the alcove as Dayyid stepped out of the Gray Space.

"I should have killed you with your father." Dayyid's words came out low and distorted. His mouth was drawn back in an animal snarl. John didn't think he had ever seen another human being so utterly transformed by rage.

Ravishan gazed at Dayyid, almost defiantly. He made no motion to recover his discarded shirt or cassock. He didn't move. He didn't speak.

"You are an abomination!" Dayyid grabbed a fistful of Ravishan's hair and jerked him closer. Ravishan stumbled forward, his arms hanging slack at his sides as if they were broken. Dayyid pulled his black curse blade free of its sheath and yanked Ravishan's head back, exposing his throat. To John's horror, Ravishan didn't fight. He only stared at Dayyid, his expression cold and dead.

He wouldn't defend himself, John realized. He wouldn't escape into the Gray Space.

Dayyid's knife slid down over Ravishan's face and John charged into the alcove. He caught Dayyid's arm, jerking him back. As Ravishan fell from Dayyid's grip and hit the ground, John saw blood pouring from the corners of his mouth.

Dayyid spun on John, his furious expression turning to repulsed disdain.

"And here's the dog waiting to lick up what this whore's spilled in the dirt," Dayyid spat at him. "I'll see you both burn—"

All of the rage John had suppressed for the past years welled up in him. He realized that his hand already gripped his curse blade. Dayyid moved to knock him aside. John blocked the blow, and with a fast thrust, he drove his curse blade into Dayyid's throat.

Dayyid jerked slightly. A wet, choking gasp escaped him. Then his legs buckled and he slid off John's curse blade. A hot stream of blood sprayed up over the knife and John's hand. Dayyid crumpled to the ground. Blood continued to pour from the wide gash in his throat. It pooled around Dayyid's still head and turned the dusty ground black.

Dayyid's mouth hung slack. His eyes were wide, gazing at nothing. John stared at Dayyid as the reality of what he had just done spread through him. He'd just killed Dayyid. Murdered him. It had been so fast, so easy. Dayyid had been dead before John could even consider the consequences.

Behind him, John could hear Ravishan regaining his feet.

"Is he—" Ravishan began and then went silent.

John turned back. Ravishan stood staring at Dayyid's body. Two thin rivulets of blood poured from the corners of his mouth where Dayyid had cut him.

"You should get dressed." John's voice came out hard and cold despite the panick pounding through his chest.

Ravishan swayed, looking drunk and sick. He was hardly in the best state for any of this. John feared that he would collapse, but then Ravishan drew in a deep breath and tore his gaze from Dayyid's bleeding body. He snatched up his shirt and cassock and pulled them on.

"When did you get here?" Ravishan asked the question quietly, as if he were hoping John wouldn't hear him or answer.

"Just before Dayyid," John said. He had been so angry then, seeing Ravishan with another man. Now, only minutes later, that one kiss hardly seemed to matter. "I thought Dayyid was going to kill you."

"I thought he would too." Ravishan winced as he spoke and then lifted his hand to his bleeding mouth. "I would have deserved it."

"No, he had no right to treat you like that," John told him. "He had no right to treat anyone the way he did."

Ravishan watched John with wide, dark eyes. Then John realized that he was still holding his bloody curse blade in his hand. Part of him wanted to throw the knife from himself. Instead he knelt and wiped the blade clean across Dayyid's coat. Then he sheathed it.

"What are we going to do?" Ravishan straightened his cassock and then buttoned his coat closed over it.

The instinct to run, to distance himself from the blood and the body, surged through John. He had felt the same way the night he had witnessed the battle between the Bousim rashan'im and the Fai'daum. But now he was no mere witness. He had committed murder and he couldn't afford to be stupid. The desire for flight was just a reaction, as devoid of forethought as the reflexes that had allowed him to kill Dayyid.

"Jahn." Ravishan touched his shoulder and John realized that he had been just standing there, transfixed by the sight of Dayyid's body.

"We can leave," Ravishan said. "With so many merchants and travelers coming and going we could just slip out the gates. We'll need other clothes."

John shook his head. They needed to stay if they were ever going to reach Nayeshi. They couldn't flee. They needed to hide Dayyid's murder. John frowned at the gory wound in Dayyid's throat, the wide pool of blood and Dayyid's fallen curse blade. It hardly looked like an accident. No, the entire scene looked like what it had been: a fight, a murder.

"There are people with Eastern blood in Nurjima," Ravishan said. "You wouldn't stand out so much there. We could find work of some kind, I'm sure."

"You can't run away. Your sister Rousma needs you to stay and Behr and Loshai need me here. We have to stay." Even as he spoke, John's mind raced for some solution.

"Not if it means your execution," Ravishan whispered.

"Maybe it won't have to come to that," John said. He remembered the demoness, Ji. "The Fai'daum are here."

"What?" Ravishan gaped at him in horror.

"I recognized Ji Shir'korud in the blood market. I came to warn you…" John frowned at the blood that covered his hand and the sleeve of his coat. "That didn't go quite the way I had hoped, but... they're here. I think they want to release the man who's going to be executed tonight."

"They're in the blood market now?"

"They look like they're waiting for something," John said. "My guess is that they're waiting for nightfall, when the pyre is built."

"Or for the prisoner to be brought down to the shrine this afternoon." Ravishan pressed his fingers against the corners of his mouth again to staunch the trickles of blood flowing from his wounds. He looked miserable. John caught his shoulder and gave him a reassuring squeeze. Relief flooded Ravishan's face. For just a moment he clung to John. Then he drew back.

"We can't stay here," John said. He hadn't known that the prisoner would be moved in the afternoon. If the Fai'daum were going to attempt a rescue, then it would happen soon.

"You should go find Hann'yu," John said. "Keep him away from the blood market."

"What do we do about…this?" Ravishan gestured down to Dayyid's body.

"Nothing," John decided. "Don't say anything about him. If anyone asks, you haven't seen him since you gave him the slip this morning."

"And we just hope that the Fai'daum are blamed?" Ravishan asked.

John nodded.

"What about you? What are you going to do?" Ravishan asked.

"I'll meet you at the church hostel," John said.

Ravishan nodded but remained at John's side, looking pale and scared.

"I don't want to leave you here," Ravishan said at last.

"You have to," John told him. "Go make sure Hann'yu and Ashan'ahma are safe."

Ravishan looked as if he might protest.

"I'll be fine," John said firmly. "You have to go now, before anyone sees us here."

"Be careful," Ravishan said. Then, with a whisper of cold air, he disappeared into the Gray Space.

John gazed down at Dayyid's body one last time. The blood had stopped seeping from his throat. Flies were beginning to gather around the wound. John shuddered. There was no reason for him to stay any longer. It was far too late to make any kind of peace with Dayyid. John pulled his coat closed and hurried out of the alley.

Though only a few minutes had passed, the blood market seemed busier than it had been before. Despite the flies, clusters of women roved through the lanes of stalls and pens. John noticed an unusual number of red widows' veils. Or perhaps, because of what he'd just done, the color caught his attention far more than it normally would. He pushed his bloody hand deep into the pocket of his gray coat.

Butchering had begun. A few gutted goat carcasses hung from the eves of the stalls. The smell of offal and blood mixed with the earthy scent of straw and feed. John wondered how distinctly the odor of blood clung to him. How conspicuous would the smell be when he left the blood market?

He knew he had to get out of the market quickly, before the Fai'daum made their move. Still, he stopped at a stall selling freshly butchered and skinned weasels. He bought two. Their bodies were handed to him, wrapped in waxed parchment. They felt disturbingly warm and supple. When he pushed open a corner of the parchment, a trickle of blood dribbled over his hand.

A wave of revulsion churned through John as he allowed the blood to run along his fingers and seep into the cuff of his coat. A lesser murder to hide a greater one, he thought. Then he pinched the parchment closed again and continued on his way.

He walked quickly but not with the clarity he had possessed on his way to warn Ravishan. He knew he couldn't afford to consider what he had just done. But at the same time it was hard to keep from thinking of it. All the noise and color, the widows' veils, the silver rings, the painted tents, the scent of curing brines, and the sounds of animal cries, seemed somehow muted as if they came to him from a great distance. He concentrated on the distraction they offered.

He could still feel, with intense clarity, the resistance and crack of his knife splitting through the cartilage of Dayyid's trachea. The sensation played through his hand again and again like some strange recoil. He couldn't stop hearing the muted sound of it, like a knuckle popping. The smell of blood seemed to roll off of him. He was aware of his heart beating too fast. Despite the chill breeze, sweat beaded beneath his cassock and heavy coat.

He turned onto the wider lane that led to the nearest city gate. The high stone wall loomed before him. City guards stood sentinel on the walkways. There seemed to be more of them there than usual. John counted twenty. A hundred yards or so ahead of him a huge, heavy wood wagon, hitched to a pair of dull green tahldi, rolled out from the gate. One city guard sat at the reins while four others crouched in the open wagon bed, surrounding a bound, naked man.

The guards looked bored. John couldn't see the bound man's expression. His head was bowed and his long chestnut hair hung over his face. His pale, freckled skin was mottled with bruises. Long scabbed-over lash marks covered his back and arms. Two more guards walked alongside the tahldi at the front of the wagon. They shouted people out of the way and repelled onlookers who crowded too close to the animals.

People had come out just to watch this, John realized. That was why the blood market was more crowded than it had been this morning. The lane was packed with people, making it difficult to move without bumping into someone.

John stepped back as the wagon rolled slowly closer. An older man grumbled as John jostled him but went quiet when he saw John's gray coat and cassock. The bodies of strangers pressed up against John's back, chest, and sides, resisting his every movement.

Just to his left, a skinny barefoot boy pushed his way out from between two men. He held something dull red and glistening in his hand. As the wagon came close, the boy hurled the mass of weasel intestines at the prisoner. The offal splashed against the prisoner's shoulder, but the man didn't even lift his head in response. One of the guards riding in the wagon grinned. The tall sides of the wagon were already stained with red and brown spatters where other refuse had been hurled with less accuracy.

John wanted to turn back, but there was too much of a push behind him.

Then, suddenly, the loud crack of a rifle shot burst through the air. The guard driving the wagon fell back, blood gushing from his chest. The guards on the ground rushed to grab the bridles of the startled tahldi. A second shot tore through the head of one of the guards riding in the wagon.

A wave of panic rolled through the gathered crowd. People shouted and screamed. The man beside John shoved a girl down as he tried to distance himself from the wagon. John heard another rifle shot, but he couldn't tell where it had come from or what damage it might have done. He had to fight just to stay upright as the people behind him surged forward, running for the security of the city gates. Hands and arms smacked and slammed into his back. People kicked his legs, stepped on his feet, and tripped against his body, but he didn't go down.

He heard a tahldi scream and then saw the side of the wooden wagon as it swung off the road and came crashing into the crowd. Bodies crumpled, crushed beneath the heavy wagon wheels. The tahldi charged forward, shrieking and trampling the people in their path. An arrow jutted from the neck of one of the animals.

To John's surprise, a woman from the crowd raced forward and leaped onto one of the tahldi's backs. She caught hold of the animal's bridle and seemed to be trying to rein the tahldi in. An arrow whistled past, then another, and another. The city guards were firing from up on the wall. A child crumpled, an arrow driven through her chest. All around John, people screamed, shoved, and fell beneath each other in a wild directionless flight for some kind of safety.

A second arrow sank into the shoulder of the already-injured tahldi. The animal reared, screaming, and twisted itself against its harness. The woman and the second tahldi were pulled down with it. The hitch snapped apart as the wagon continued plowing forward.

People all around John fought to get out of the way. A woman clawed at his arm, desperate to pull herself past him. John braced himself as the wagon swung toward him. It was a stupid, instinctual reaction, but there was nothing else he could do. His hands came up as if the huge wagon wheel were a baseball for him to catch. Even in the moment he thought he must have looked ridiculous.

The man in front of John screamed as the wagon plowed him under. John clenched his eyes shut. Then he heard the deafening noise of heavy timbers splitting. John opened his eyes to see planks exploding to either side of him as if an invisible saw were rending through them. A moment later, the wagon collapsed into two pieces on either side of John. The naked, bound prisoner slammed into John's legs.

Wood shavings and sawdust settled over John like a fine snow.

An arrow slashed past John and he ducked down behind the wrecked halves of the wagon. The man at his feet groaned. Many of the cuts on his arms and back had torn open. Fat droplets of red blood dribbled down his sides and spattered the dry ground. Seeing it, John vividly recalled the open wound in Dayyid's throat and the flies twitching at its edges. He suddenly felt like he might be sick.

He closed his eyes, but he couldn't block out the roar of people all around him shouting and screaming. The blast of rifles cracked through his mind like thunder. All this, John wondered, just for one man? Was this one prisoner so important that he merited so much destruction? Or perhaps his value was simply that someone loved him enough to sacrifice other lives for his.

How many men would he kill for Ravishan?

John felt the bound man bump against his leg and he opened his eyes. Lying face down, with his legs and hands trussed together behind him, the man was still trying to move, to escape. He cursed into the dirt and jerked at his bonds. John quickly unbuttoned his coat and unsheathed his curse blade.

"Hold still while I cut you loose." John wanted to whisper, but in the surrounding chaos of noise, he had to shout to make sure the man heard him. The man went still. John sliced through the ropes and helped the man sit upright. His face was filthy and unshaven. Blood from a deep gash across his forehead had left the right side of the man's face streaked with red. Though his chest was scraped and coated with dirt and wood dust, John could still see where the word 'traitor' had been painted across his skin in black Payshmura script.

"Here." John stripped off his coat and wrapped it around the man's shoulders. He didn't seem to register the action. Instead, he stared at John as if blinking might get him killed. It was understandable. The man was Fai'daum while John, from all outward appearances, was a Payshmura priest.

John studied the man. He seemed oddly familiar. Then recognition came to John. It had been years, but John remembered the man's dark brown eyes, particularly staring at him in fear and confusion.

"I'm not going to hurt you, Saimura," John said.

The man blinked. "How do you know my name?"

"We've met before. I had a beard then and you didn't."

Saimura's mouth dropped slightly open. "It's you…from the woods."

John nodded.

"Why are you here?" Saimura asked. He seemed dazed.

"It's just my lucky day. I've been showing up at all the right places at the best times." John glanced guiltily down at his hands, still coated in blood. "Put on my coat. If you're dressed, you won't be so easy for the guards to pick out in the crowd."

Saimura got the coat on in quick, jerky motions. John heard a loud knock and crack as an arrow punched into the side of the wrecked wagon. Farther away, the report of a rifle cracked the air.

"Who are you?" Saimura asked. His voice was rough and hard to hear over the noise surrounding them. Very distantly John thought he could hear the city bells ringing out an alarm.

"I'm called Jahn." John peered between the cracked planks. Waves of people crashed up against the city gate. Others huddled in clusters behind broken stalls or carts. The guards up on the wall released a volley of arrows at anyone moving in the open. In the cacophony of threats, pleas, screams, and shouting, John thought he could hear a soft gasp and weeping.

There was a movement low to the ground, close to the wagon. Someone crawled toward them for cover. It was the woman who had tried to rein the tahldi. She moved slowly, dragging herself across the ground. John was amazed to see that she was still alive. Her black hair was gray with dirt. The thick leather of her clothes was tattered and ripped. An arrow struck the ground a few feet from her.

"What is it?" Saimura asked.

"A woman." John crept to the edge of the wagon. "I think I can get her back here."

"Be careful. The Payshmura are gathering on the wall." Saimura had taken John's place, spying out through the cracked planks. "They come out of nowhere like fucking flies."

John lunged out and grasped the woman. She was small and he easily scooped her up and pulled her quickly back behind the shelter of the wagon. She seemed incredibly delicate, more like a bird than a person. He wasn't used to holding women.

A sharp pain burst through John's forearm as she bit him.

"I'm trying to help you," John said.

"Go to hell, priest," the woman growled back. She rammed a tiny sharp elbow into John's stomach. He released her and she dropped to the ground.

"Sheb'yu." Saimura hunched down beside the woman. "He's helping us."

"What?" She eyed John with open disbelief.

"This is the same man who hid me in the forest," Saimura explained.

She frowned at John. "Why are you dressed as a priest?"

"It's a long story and I don't think we have time for it." John returned to the cracked planks. Saimura had been right. The black silhouettes of the ushiri'im and the ushman'im were appearing all along the city wall. They raised their hands in an eerie unison. John could almost see the air all around them shimmering with energy.

"They're opening a God's Razor," John said. It was going to be huge. The thin edge of the Gray Space stretched nearly the full length of the city wall.

"How many priests?" Saimura asked.

"Forty or fifty," John replied. He wondered if Ravishan was up there. He thought he recognized Fikiri's blond braids.

"Ji can't handle that many," Saimura said. He looked to Sheb'yu. "She has to pull back."

"She won't leave without you," Sheb'yu said.

"She shouldn't have come for me in the first place." Aggravation and frustration played through Saimura's strained face. "None of you should have."

Whatever reply Sheb'yu would have made was lost. A rending scream tore through the air as nearly a quarter mile of the Gray

Space ripped open. Both Sheb'yu and Saimura hunched as though the sound were a physical blow. They clasped their hands over their ears and clenched their eyes closed in pain. All around, people and animals responded in the same manner, cowering in pain and fear. John found the noise grating but not unbearable. The open gash that gaped across the sky, however, seemed to wrench through his chest and sent a rush of intense repulsion through his entire being.

Flames burst up along the edge of the God's Razor, forming a narrow ribbon of fire that hung in the air just above the city wall. The grounds were suddenly so quiet that John could distinctly hear a single lamb bleating in its pen.

Then the God's Razor dropped. The flames extinguished, but John could see the deadly edge descending.

"Get down!" John shouted. Beside him, Saimura and Sheb'yu dropped to the ground. But the people gathered at the city gate continued to stare up at where the flames had been.

The God's Razor descended, slicing through everything in its path. The limbs of trees instantly shredded to splinters. Then it cut through the crowd at the city gate. Bodies tore open. Arms, hands, heads were severed as people tried to run or shield themselves. The God's Razor swept forward. It ripped through stalls, tearing apart the people and animals sheltered within as if they were paper.

John knew he should drop to the ground and hope that the God's Razor would pass over him. He wanted to crouch down and just hide from the sights and noise of the massacre surrounding him. And yet he didn't move. He fixed his eye on the edge of the God's Razor racing toward him. It had to be stopped. The people hiding in their tents and stalls couldn't do it. The children crouching beneath carts and the animals trapped in their pens wouldn't stand a chance.

John drew in a deep breath and lifted his hands. He had broken Dayyid's Silence Knives more than once. The God's Razor was just an extension of the same thing. Thousands of times stronger, but essentially the same. The wood of the wagon cracked and burned as the God's Razor ripped through it.

"Jahn, get down!" Saimura gripped the hem of his cassock and jerked desperately, but John remained where he stood.

Tremors of fear shook John's hands as he reached out to block the advance of the God's Razor. The Gray Space bit into his palms and that sick, familiar pain flickered through him, but it felt like nothing compared to the rush of fury that surged through John at the contact. He burned with rage and the single desire to destroy the God's Razor. He clenched his fingers down, crushing the thin expanse of the Gray Space closed. The length of the God's Razor trembled and then collapsed.

John slumped against the wagon. Tremors of exhaustion played through his muscles. Sweat soaked his cassock. His hands felt as if they were on fire. He didn't want to look down at them and see how deeply they had been cut. Still, he forced himself to take in the extent of his injury. The gashes in his palms were deep but not the worst he'd endured.

"How did you do that?" Saimura stared up at him from the ground. Sheb'yu slowly lifted her head.

"He broke the God's Razor," Saimura told her.

"Can he do it again?" Sheb'yu stared past both Saimura and John to the city wall. John followed her gaze. The ushiri'im and ushman'im once again raised their hands and ripped open the Gray Space. This time the sound rang out like a monstrous howl. The flames shot feet into the air. John's stomach flipped with sickness and he felt the blood draining from his face.

"You both need to run," John said. "Now!"

Neither Saimura nor Sheb'yu argued. They bolted from the cover of the wagon and raced for the woods beyond the blood market. City guards let arrows fly after them but the arrows burst into dust the moment they struck the God's Razor. All around, wounded and terrified survivors followed Saimura's and Sheb'yu's example. They ran, not for the security of the city wall, but away from it.

Behind them, the God's Razor descended with terrible speed. John didn't wait for it to reach him. He concentrated on the searing line it cut across the sky. He focused on the air around the God's Razor, willing it to withstand the advance of the cutting edge. Suddenly a wind rushed up. The air seemed to thicken in John's lungs. The God's Razor slowed—sparks and flames skipped along its length. John's skin felt hot, as if the fire were burning around him. Pain throbbed through his hands.

He felt the ushiri'im and ushman'im pushing the God's Razor against him and once again anger flared through his chest.

He would not allow them to win this.

Massive geysers of flame shot up along the gaping edges of the exposed Gray Space. Scorching sensations blazed across his outstretched arms as if he were burning along with the searing air.

He forced the God's Razor back, slowly, painfully. Narrow slashes split open across his skin. As he fought the God's Razor, the cuts ripped wider. Pain rose to blinding intensity. Sweating and swearing under his breath, John felt another pulse of rage rush over him and he welcomed it.

Lightning crashed through the sky and the wind howled. Strength surged through John. He concentrated all of his remaining will into one action. He hurled the God's Razor back from him. On the wall, the priests scrambled to collapse the God's Razor as it swung toward them. Stones split and cracked. Priests and city guards braced themselves as the wall shuddered.

Then came a perfect silence. John waited. One after another the ushiri'im disappeared from the wall. They were done.

John fell to the ground. It seemed to catch him, gently. He closed his eyes, hardly aware of the light rain that pattered down on him.

CHAPTER FORTY-SIX

Ravishan had found him among the dead and mutilated in the remains of the blood market. John remembered that but not the rest of his journey back to Rathal'pesha. Now he lay behind canvas panels, wrapped in warm blankets on an infirmary bed. He could hear Hann'yu grinding medicines. A bell rang out the hour of praise. John listened as Hann'yu set his pestle aside and went to join in the prayers.

John could have risen and followed Hann'yu. The wounds across his arms and chest were healed. The deep cuts in his palms were only scabs now. But he wasn't ready.

He wasn't prepared to meet the faces of his fellow priests. He didn't know how he would react when they told him that Ushman Dayyid had been murdered. What would he say when they described their battle against the Fai'daum demoness, Ji Shir'korud?

Already, John had overheard ushiri'im talking about it to Hann'yu. The demoness' ability to break the God's Razor confused them. She had never done it before. They came into the infirmary with minor scratches and asked in lowered voices how Ji Shir'korud had unleashed so much power. What would they do if she returned to take the city? Had the Issusha'im Oracles known this would happen? Had it been Parfir's will?

John clearly remembered Ashan'ahma's cultured southern voice inquiring how it could have possibly been Parfir's will that Ushman Dayyid deserved to die?

They asked questions that Hann'yu couldn't possibly answer. Hann'yu responded in his usual gentle manner. He admitted uncertainty and ignorance. The ushiri'im seemed to leave more disturbed than they had been when they arrived. John realized that they weren't really looking for information so much as they needed reassurance.

Dayyid's murder had left a gaping hole in their society. Whether he had been a tyrant to them or not, his presence had been the certainty of their lives. From morning to night he'd been there training, punishing, and shaping them. He had told them what to do and how to do it. If they had a question, Dayyid had the answer. He had spoken with the assurance of a prophet. His cause had been their cause; his values had been their values. For many of them, he had been the embodiment of Parfir's will. His faith had pervaded Rathal'pesha.

And now they had lost all of that.

John wanted to feel some sympathy for their confusion but he couldn't. He had been down there on the grounds of the blood market. He had seen exactly where Dayyid's regime of unquestioning faith led. Dayyid had taught the ushiri'im arrogant cruelty. He had made them unconcerned murderers, because for all the questions they asked Hann'yu, not one had wondered if using the God's Razor against common bystanders had been wrong.

John recognized his own hypocrisy. He had become a murderer himself that very day. And yet he wasn't sorry for it now.

The ushiri'im needed to have Dayyid torn from them. They needed to feel fear and vulnerability because those things were reminders of their humanity. They needed some incomprehensible force to rend their lives apart so that they might have some sympathy for the common people they so easily destroyed.

John sighed and glared into the white folds of canvas surrounding his bed. Or perhaps he just needed to feel that the greater crime of the ushiri'im justified his own actions. He wanted to reclaim that effortless sense that he was a just man—a good man.

In Nayeshi it had been so simple to think so. Decency was the default of an easy modern society. Atrocities occurred more often in the realm of fiction than in everyday life. Mass murderers were the monsters of the week on crime shows; they weren't his friends.

But John's clear distinction between a decent person and a vicious persecutor certainly hadn't existed among the crowds who had gathered in the blood market. They had been victims, but they had been no more innocent than the ushiri'im. Most had been there to taunt a condemned man. Most would have cheered and laughed while watching Saimura writhe and scream as he burned on the pyre.

At least he'd kept that from happening. That offered him consolation.

John lifted his hands, feeling the air stroke and curl around his fingers.

If only he had realized what he was capable of, perhaps he could have saved more lives. John frowned at his bandaged palms. The Fai'daum would still have attacked. Could he have stopped them as well? If he had, then Saimura would have certainly been burned.

No matter what, someone would have died.

He couldn't have saved everyone. In a way that idea was relieving. If he couldn't have succeeded regardless of how hard he might have tried, then his actions couldn't have been of that much importance. John wanted to believe that. It suited his idea of himself.

All his life he had cultivated insignificance. He had been quiet in classes, well behaved at home. Neither good nor bad, just bland. He had been that young man who could speak at length about lichens but was never asked to do so twice. He had perfected the presence of a potted plant, a form filling space where a void would have been too notable. He had taken pains to remain unremarkable. No one cared where a boring man spent his nights.

The persona he had refined from Sunday school through catechism had kept him free from invitations to games of spin-the-bottle as well as the infidelities between professors and students. It had served him in Nayeshi and saved him in Basawar. Even as alien as he was to the priests of Rathal'pesha, he had lived among them, passing for nearly ordinary.

When Dayyid had offered him the curse blade, he had suppressed his response to it. When Ravishan had asked him how he could tear Fikiri out of the Gray Space, he had passed over it as if it were a quirk—something as happenstance as finding change in the street, just a little good luck.

He had done it all so easily, so naturally that he hadn't noticed the deceptions himself. He had built an identity of being ordinary and done it so well that even he had forgotten that it was a lie.

No ordinary man, not even one from Basawar, could crush God's Razor. Nor did they tear apart wood and iron simply by lifting their hands and willing it to happen. They did not close their eyes and see into distant cities. They could not see or feel the scars left in the Gray Space. They did not sense the life within the stones, earth, air, and water surrounding them. And the issusha'im did not hunt them.

John lowered his hands back to his chest. They felt hot even through the bandages. The pale canvas curtains surrounding him swayed and then went still.

There was no point denying that the Issusha'im Oracles had been hunting him. Not after last night; not after they had found him.

At first he had thought that it was just a dream, a distant memory returning to him in his sleep.

He watched himself climbing up the sun-warmed rock faces at Emerald Lake. The stone was hot, but he hardly felt it through the calloused soles of his bare feet. His eleven-year-old body was long and lanky, and slightly absurd in his wet, baggy swim trunks. What little hair that had remained after his weekly buzz cut had been bleached nearly white from the summer sun.

Honeybees darted between clusters of goldenrod and thistle blossoms, humming. The air smelled of pollen and nectar. Dark brambles of blackberries offered glimpses of ripe fruit hanging between their thorns. He stole a few berries as he climbed. His fingers were already stained and scratched from previous plundering.

At last, he reached the outcropping. Below him, the dark waters of the lake lay perfectly still, reflecting the wide blue sky like a mirror. His father and two brothers looked like toys out on their white fishing boat. At the water's edge, his sister sat in her bright red bikini, reading a romance novel. Laurie and her mother lounged on faded beach blankets. A spread of tarot cards lay between them. Laurie's mother was telling fortunes again.

His own mother was somewhere beneath the cover of the trees, unpacking their lunch and sneaking a cigarette. At the time,

John hadn't known that. Only later, while the ambulance sirens tore through the warm air and she clung to him crying, only then would he notice the smell of Virginia Slims on her. It would make him realize that she, too, had secrets she kept from the family. It would make him wonder if anyone was ever perfectly honest.

But none of that had happened yet.

He stood on the outcropping of stone, high above the deep waters. He grinned, feeling the warmth of the sun on his skin and basking in the brief moment before his leap. He took in a breath, preparing for the rush of fear and excitement that would surge through him the moment he'd step off the rocks.

Both Laurie and Bill screamed when they jumped, but John never did. John's father had proudly pointed that fact out to Bill's father a year before. Since then John had taken pains to maintain his silence. He pushed the air out of his lungs and stepped toward the edge.

Then something above him caught his attention—a flash, like some distant mirror catching the sun. John looked up as a blinding white bolt slammed down into him.

He saw their skeletal faces then, heard them hissing and whispering through him. He felt them searing words into his bones, binding him. The boy who John had once been screamed, while the man he now was clenched his jaws shut against the burning pain. Very distantly, he heard Laurie calling out to him. Her voice sounded like a thin whistle caught within the hundreds of growls and whispers that the issusha'im poured down over him.

"Blood to bone, we binds it.
Where it goes Kahlil finds it.
Bleed the seas, burn the skies,
Tear the earth before its eyes.
Where it walks, Kahlil follows,
No respite in shades or hollows.
Fires burn, rivers flood,
Still it calls Kahlil's blood.
Break iron, shatter stone,
Still we binds it, blood to bone."

White light seared into him. The weeds and flowers near him burned to ash. The rock beneath his feet cracked like glass. John watched as his skinny body arched up as if caught in powerful electrical current. Then the light was gone and he collapsed. Later, his mother would tell him he'd been struck by lightning. She would say that he had been so lucky to come away unscathed and that a host of angels must have been watching over him.

If she had been able to see those angels, made of skulls and bones strung together on thick wires, with bright red drops of blood pouring from them like rain, she might have thought otherwise. As a child, John had been terrified by the idea of those angels watching over him.

And now he knew. They hadn't been angels or lightning. They had been the Issusha'im Oracles, binding him to the Kahlil. So now the Kahlil could cross through the Great Gates and would be drawn though the chaos of time and space straight to him.

John stared at the canvas panels beside his bed. The prayer bells had stopped ringing. Everything was so quiet that he could almost imagine that nothing existed beyond the enclosure of white canvas. The world was just him, lying in a small rectangle on a soft bed.

The dull glow of sunlight pushed through the panels, illuminating a corner of his bed. Very distantly, John heard the calls of birds. Most had already started on their migrations south. Only tiny blackbills remained. In another month they, too, would be gone. He could smell incense and the aroma of baking taye. No matter what he might want, the world intruded. Lying here behind a curtain would not keep it at bay. It would not keep him safe from the world.

Nor would it keep this world safe from him.

Before last night that thought wouldn't have even crossed his mind. But now he knew that he was the Rifter. He knew what the Rifter did. It tore down mountains, turned skies to soot. He had already felt the sky shudder and crack in response to him. Stone and soil had answered his motions. He had pulled rain from the air. It had all come so easily that he hadn't even noticed. He had no idea how easily it could slip out of his control.

He had seen the pictures of the Rifters before him. Their expressions were always wild and terrified as they stared at the earth shattering beneath their feet. The last one had cracked the entire

Eastern Kingdom down to pieces of rubble, now lost beneath the sea. The Great Chasm was all that remained of that vast empire.

That kind of destruction was something bombs did, something earthquakes and volcanoes caused. It shouldn't have been within the realm of a human being. John couldn't imagine himself doing something like that. And yet he couldn't be certain. Until a week ago, he had also believed himself incapable of murder. Then he had killed Dayyid, without hesitation or any real regret. Now a mistrust of his own nature pervaded him.

Could such destruction be a reflex, something that he would do as instantaneously as he had torn apart that wagon? Was it some inherent characteristic, a choice, or a reaction? He knew that the Payshmura had unleashed previous Rifters upon their enemies. They had to have discovered the means to trigger the Rifters' devastating capacities.

He had read the holy books. Again and again they spoke of poisoning and bleeding the Rifter. Maybe that was the means. Perhaps the destruction was a response to pain and fear. Or maybe it was controlled by the Kahlil, who was bound to the Rifter.

He couldn't know, and he couldn't afford to guess. He had to be careful. He had to keep himself from manipulating the world around him no matter how easily it came to him. He had to control himself.

John pulled the blankets closer. Laurie had taken this so much better than he had. Of course, she hadn't really believed John when he had told her that she was the Rifter. *Chalk another one up for Laurie*, John thought grimly. She'd been right. He wondered if she'd give him a smug little grin when he told her. Probably.

That revelation could certainly wait until they were all safely back in Nayeshi.

There was a soft knock at the infirmary door. Then John heard the door open.

"Jahn?" Ravishan's voice was hushed.

John wasn't sure that he was ready to talk to Ravishan. But he couldn't hide behind these curtains forever.

"Over here."

Ravishan walked to his bed quickly and opened the canvas panels. His face was pinkish from scrubbing and his black hair still wet. Thick white bandages engulfed his right arm. Ravishan crouched down beside the bed. He offered John a shy smile but then winced as the motion pulled at the tender scars on either side of his mouth.

John gazed at Ravishan's mouth. The small scars curved up from his lips, giving the illusion of a slight smile.

If John hadn't been there in Candle Alley when Dayyid had attacked Ravishan, then the wounds would have been far worse. They would have nearly severed Ravishan's lower jaw. The scars remaining after Hann'yu treatments would have formed two pale lines running almost to Ravishan's ears. John remembered stealing quick glances at those scars and wondering how a man got them. Now he knew.

John felt suddenly cold. He glanced up into Ravishan's excited eyes. Even without the Prayerscars, John recognized Kyle's face looking back at him.

All this time he had been living with Ravishan and he had never realized. He hadn't even considered the possibility that they were the same person. John had recognized the similarity between them the first day he had seen Ravishan, but he hadn't understood that the gates crossed time as well as space. Kyle had been a man in his early thirties, while Ravishan had been a boy in his late teens. John couldn't have known then that the gates had brought him back through time to Kyle's youth.

But now it was obvious.

"I have good news." Ravishan pulled a stool up to John's bedside and sat. "The Issusha'im Oracles found the Rifter."

"Oh?" John did his best to seem surprised.

"I have been chosen to be the Kahlil." Despite his lowered voice, Ravishan's tone reverberated with pride. "Last night I was bound to the Rifter."

"How did that go?" John asked. It was all he could manage.

"He's just a skinny boy." Ravishan gave a soft laugh. "I could hardly believe it until the issusha'im struck him. The ground beneath him burned to black glass, but the issusha'im's spell didn't even scratch him."

"What about you? Did it hurt you?" John eyed Ravishan's bandaged right arm.

"They needed my blood for the binding," Ravishan replied.

John gave a tired nod. Most rituals that Ravishan endured involved the spilling of his blood. So much so that, at twenty-one, he hardly took note of it.

John studied him, contemplating the future he already knew.

After fifteen years of spells, passages through the Great Gates and the Gray Space, Ravishan's right arm would be a mess of ropey tissue. He would wear bandages with the same ease that other people wore sunglasses.

"For a moment," Ravishan went on proudly, "I felt as if I were there with him. I could smell the air there and feel the heat of the sun. I even heard a girl call out his name."

"His name?" John asked. Alarm prickled through him.

"Toffee," Ravishan said firmly.

John nodded again, relieved. That was his nickname—Laurie had screamed it when she had seen him caught in that white bolt.

Ravishan grinned but then lowered his voice. "Once I receive the blessings of the Usho, it will be time to cross to Nayeshi. We'll be free of this place."

John had seen the blessings in holy texts. They were embodied by the Prayerscars, those black tattoos over the Kahlil's eyes. Tattoos that would make Ravishan's ignorant roommate wonder what kind of freak he was.

"Why are you staring at me like that?" Ravishan asked.

"Like what?"

"I don't know, you look…are you angry at me?" Ravishan lowered his gaze to his hands. "I wanted to tell you I was sorry about what happened in Candle—"

"No. It's not that." Everything that had happened in Candle Alley now seemed utterly insignificant. "I'm not angry. I'm staring because I'm amazed by you."

Ravishan flushed.

John felt almost absurdly proud of Ravishan and of the man he would become. He would endure years alone in Nayeshi. He would never abandon his duty.

"It's one thing to stumble into another world like Bill, Laurie, and I did," John said quietly. "But to choose to go—to abandon everything you know and give yourself to a foreign world—that takes true courage."

During their time together in Nayeshi, John had seen Kyle watching the world around him with fearless fascination. He had eaten apples as if they were precious rarities. He had studied coffee pots, phone bills, baseball games, and even sock puppets with a benevolent interest. John hadn't been so accepting of Basawar's alien qualities. Kyle had remained true to his purpose as a Kahlil, and yet he had seemed to cherish Nayeshi.

"I haven't done it yet," Ravishan said.

"But you will," John replied.

Ravishan nodded as if he, too, knew that it had already happened. He was so assured, and he was right to be, John supposed.

"When you arrive," John asked, "what will you be expected to do?"

"Find the Rifter." Ravishan shrugged. "Watch over him and wait until the Usho sends word to me."

"You mean once they decide to unleash the Rifter?" John frowned, thinking of the stories of destruction and the Rifters' horrifying deaths.

"Maybe they'll want me to bring him back, but who knows? They may decide against it." Ravishan sounded pleased with the prospect. "If so, I'll remain in Nayeshi and continue to watch over him my whole life."

"Just watch over him?" As he spoke, John realized that when Ravishan discussed the future he was also describing John's past. Kyle had been living with him for years, waiting for word.

"Almost nothing in Basawar can harm the Rifter," Ravishan said. "But in Nayeshi, he's vulnerable. And he's just a child. I'll have to protect him."

An odd sense of tenderness and sorrow welled through John. For at least a decade, Kyle must have been there, watching over him.

He supposed he would have found the idea sinister if he hadn't known Ravishan. It was too easy to imagine Ravishan, scarred, tattooed, utterly alien, and completely alone, looking at John's comfortable life with longing.

John leaned forward and very gently kissed Ravishan on the lips. His skin was warm. The faint fragrances of daru'sira and istana soap clung to him. John remembered that same smell on Kyle, but he hadn't known what it was then.

John said, "You've been up all night, haven't you?"

"I was too excited to sleep." Ravishan slipped his left hand under the blankets and curled his fingers around John's hand.

"We're going to Nayeshi," Ravishan whispered.

John returned his grip. Thinking of the past and future, of himself as the Rifter and Ravishan as the Kahlil, overwhelmed him. It rendered him almost unable to think at all. But simply holding Ravishan's hand calmed him. He couldn't undo the past, nor could he know how he had already altered the future. But that didn't matter. What he really cared about was captured in the warmth of their interlaced fingers. What mattered was the life the two of them made together now.

"So, you'll have to go to the Black Tower in Nurjima to receive the Usho's blessings?" John asked.

"It's a pilgrimage." Ravishan straightened reflexively at the subject of his duties. His fingers slid free of John's grip. "I have to travel overland, no passages through the Gray Space. I'll go by tahldi at first. Then I get to ride the train from Gisa to Vundomu and then all the way to Nurjima. And after the Usho has ordained me, I'll return to Vundomu to take the Rifter's bone and carve the yasi'halaun."

John frowned. "How long will you be gone?"

"It could be as long as three months depending upon the travel conditions." Ravishan leaned a little closer to him. "But I am allowed an attendant."

"An attendant?" John raised his brows at the prospect. "Who's the lucky man?"

"Any ushvun of my choosing." Ravishan gave John a coy sidelong glance and John grinned.

He sat up. "Would it be presumptuous of me to assume that I'm going with you?"

"Very." Ravishan smiled. "But you'd also be right."

"When do we leave?"

"As soon as you're well enough to travel," Ravishan replied.

John sighed and tossed his blankets back. "I suppose I'd better get out of bed, then."

It was really as simple as that, John supposed. He might feel alienated and overwhelmed, but he couldn't elude his life. He couldn't take back a single realization or action. He just had to get up and go on. Seeing the way Ravishan smiled at him, feeling the tenderness of his touch, it didn't seem so difficult.

Chapter Forty-Seven

John hadn't expected to feel so stunned by the speed and power of traveling by train. But years in Rathal'pesha had reduced his sense of distance to a matter of footsteps. Now it felt as if he were flying. There was something exciting and energizing about feeling the rumble and force of the massive engine under their feet. Swaths of white steam swept over them like walls of parting mist, revealing new lands.

Beside him, Ravishan and Alidas leaned against the guardrail of the passenger car, discussing the fortress-city of Vundomu, where they would stop before traveling on to Nurjima.

John had been surprised when he'd discovered Alidas among the multitude of herders and traders traveling south to the Gisa railway. Alidas had confessed, with an embarrassed expression, that his knee had grown worse—too undependable for Commander Tashtu to have a use for him—and he was being sent to Nurjima for treatment.

Ravishan and Alidas had hit it off surprisingly well and even before their caravan had reached the train yard in Gisa, the two of them were snickering over obscure religious jokes and amiably debating the values of the new breech-loading guns.

The smell of coal and oil rushed over John. He gazed out as autumn trees and golden taye fields whipped past. Looking back, the mountains of the north were only blue shadows against the darkening sky.

"What do you think of your first train ride, Jahn?" Alidas shouted over the roar of the engine.

"It's certainly a smoother passage than a tahldi's back," John replied and Alidas nodded in agreement.

"Just as fast, but a train doesn't tire and it can carry huge loads," Alidas informed him. "Men, tahldi, guns. These things could move entire armies in a matter of days."

"It smells terrible," Ravishan shouted. In spite of his words, he was smiling. "But I'll grant you that it is an amazing machine."

After a week of bouncing along on the backs of tahldi, John agreed wholeheartedly. His back and thighs still ached from the constant impact of the animals' bounding gaits. Alidas seemed to share John's relief. From time to time, as he leaned on the railing and gazed out at the setting sun, Alidas' hand slipped down to his right thigh, massaging the muscle just above his knee.

"I'm not sure that the rest of the passengers are taking to it so happily," Ravishan commented.

The majority of their fellow rail passengers were livestock. Goats, sheep, and tahldi filled the fifteen big boxcars behind the two passenger coaches reserved for human occupants.

The traders, herders, and farm families who boarded the train scrupulously avoided contact with either John or Ravishan. What little comfort they might have felt in the presence of Payshmura priests had been destroyed by the massacre in the blood market. The men bowed their heads and went silent at the sight of either of them. Women drew their children close as if expecting John to snatch them up for his supper.

A few traders talked to Alidas, but in a wary manner. They never looked at his face; instead they bowed their heads and stole quick glances at the rifle slung across his back.

As they had traveled down from Amura'taye, the stories of the massacre only spread and grew in the retelling. So much so that, by the time they'd found and boarded their train in Gisa, none of their fellow travelers dared to share a car with them. John, Ravishan, and Alidas had the space entirely to themselves—a full thirty seats more than they required even when they each stretched out to sleep.

Seeing the increasingly crowded conditions in the second passenger car, John felt slightly guilty, but he didn't know that there was much he could do.

So many people had been killed and word traveled quickly through grieving friends, terrified survivors, and Fai'daum members. If the Payshmura priests had seemed like tyrants to the common folk before, they'd become something just short of monsters now.

"Jahn?" Ravishan moved a little closer to him—though not so near that Alidas might think it unusual. John could see the concern in his expression and forced his brooding thoughts aside. There was no point in worrying about any of this. Soon enough he'd be back in Nayeshi and all of Basawar could be forgotten.

"I was just wondering if we'd reach Vundomu before nightfall," John said.

Ravishan clearly knew more than that troubled him, but he didn't press the matter. Instead he turned his attention to the mountain range ahead of them. He said, "At this rate we'll arrive very soon."

"Yes, Vundomu's just there." Alidas pointed to the ridge of mountains ahead of them. The golden light of sunset gleamed across the peaks as if they were polished metal.

Ravishan simply nodded. He had traveled through the Gray Space to Vundomu, so he'd seen the fortress before. John gaped at the two gray ridges and the strangely black mountain that rose between them. A dull haze seemed to hang over it, punctuated by tiny flickering fires. They spiraled up the black mountain with the perfect uniformity of skyscraper windows.

"Are those watch fires?" John asked.

"They're barrack lamps." Alidas smiled fondly at the black mountain. "Those at the top of the fortress are the kahlirash'im barracks, armories, stables, and practice fields. Below them are the servant quarters, infirmaries, and kitchens. And last are the smiths' and miners' barracks."

"That entire thing is a fortress?" John stared at its black mass and the haze of smoke that surrounded it. He could make out its seven massive, walled terraces. In a way, they resembled the terraced farmlands of Amura'taye, but black iron walls encircled every rise. Hundreds of watchtowers rose up from the walls at regular intervals. It was obviously a single structure, but one on the scale of a mountain.

"A fortress but also a temple," Ravishan clarified. "The rashan'im there are priests and the most devout of them are the kahlirash'im. They worship Parfir in his vengeful aspect, the Rifter." Ravishan stared ahead with a look like longing. “Once the Usho ordains me Kahlil, I will be counted as one of them—the holiest of them.”

Alidas, too, regarded the fortress. “The Bousim house sent me to train at Vundomu in preparation for becoming Fikiri’s attendant.” John expected Alidas’ expression to betray either relief or regret that he had not fulfilled his duty. Instead he simply continued to gaze out at the black fortress and said, “A rashan there is a different kind of man.”

“Three eyes different?” John asked. To his relief, Ravishan smiled and Alidas laughed.

“Compared to some of the rashan’im working for the gaun’im they might as well be.”

“Certainly their filed teeth are unique,” Ravishan opined.

“Yes, but the rashan’im at Vundomu are also a sacred brotherhood. They’re literate, honorable, and sworn to uphold Parfir’s laws.” Alidas sounded wistful. “A womanizing drunk like Commander Tashtu would never have been tolerated in Vundomu, much less promoted.”

“Tashtu?” Ravishan cast a glance in John’s direction. “Wasn’t he the rasho that you beat up at the Harvest Fair?”

“The very one,” John replied. It still angered John to think of how the man had accosted Laurie.

Alidas smiled slyly. “Now that we’re away from Amura’taye I can tell you how much I envied you when you did that.”

“Thanks,” John replied. But he didn’t feel proud, so much as disturbed by the fact that Tashtu was still in the Bousim house with Laurie. There was nothing he could do to change that; he simply had to pray that Pivan would keep his word and protect his friends.

“I take it, you don’t like your Commander Tashtu?” Ravishan asked Alidas.

“Hate him, really,” Alidas admitted. “He can’t do anything in moderation. He’ll have the men out on maneuvers for weeks, then he’ll change his mind and no one will be allowed off of the Bousim house grounds. He’ll want full formal dress, then get sick of it and demand to know ‘just who do you think you’re going to impress in this backwater?’ We never knew what to expect.”

"It sounds like he doesn't know how to lead his men," Ravishan said.

"He's just a drunk," Alidas pronounced firmly.

"You're as glad to be leaving Amura'taye as I am then?" Ravishan asked.

"I'm glad to be going but not so happy about the reason." Alidas' fingers only brushed his right leg. "But perhaps my leg will improve after treatment in Nurjima."

"I hope it does," Ravishan said. "Will you stay with the Bousim household there?"

"I have to. I was tithed to them, so it will be at least another ten years before I can buy my way free." Alidas suddenly sounded very tired. "But after that I'll be my own man."

Ravishan nodded. John could see him trying to imagine Alidas' life, thinking of his own obligations and his despised superior, Dayyid. "What will you do once you are free?"

"If I can't win a captain's rank, then I think I'd like to return to Vundomu, if they'd take me." As he stared at the massive fortress, Alidas' expression again turned wistful.

"Ten years is a long time to wait to become a priest," Ravishan remarked.

Alidas only shrugged in reply.

Ravishan studied Alidas for a moment, and then asked, "Did you leave a friend behind at Vundomu?"

"Several," he replied quickly, plainly startled by Ravishan's question. Despite the growing darkness, John noticed the flush that colored Alidas' cheeks.

"Perhaps you could see them again when we stop," Ravishan offered.

"It would be worse to see them for just a few minutes and then have to go again." Alidas continued to gaze at Vundomu.

"We'll be there more than a few minutes," Ravishan replied.

"Who knows if he would even remember me? It's probably best just left alone." Alidas turned away, clearly uncomfortable discussing the subject any further.

Ravishan didn't pursue it. The three of them fell silent. Only the noise and deep rhythm of the train engine surrounded them.

Ravishan stretched his arms experimentally. He was careful with his right arm. The cuts had healed, but the scars were still tender. John watched the trees whipping past.

He never would have broached such a private subject with Alidas. In part, because he wouldn't want to discover that he liked Alidas or that they could become friends. His fate was already too weighed down by the friends that Laurie and Bill had made. He didn't need or want to feel responsible for yet another person's happiness.

John found it strange that Ravishan seemed to have no such inhibition. In a month, they would be leaving. In all likelihood, Ravishan would never see Alidas or even Basawar again. Befriending Alidas would do Ravishan no good. At best, it would just give him someone to miss. But Ravishan was innately outgoing, and he obviously enjoyed his newfound freedom to commune with whomever he pleased.

John supposed that it was that same trait that had allowed Ravishan to befriend him when he had been nothing more than a ragged stranger out in the frozen wastes.

"You know," Alidas suddenly looked to John, "I still have your book."

John frowned. "My book?"

"The southern plains songs. You let me read from it the night you quarreled with Tashtu."

"Oh, yes." John remembered now. Hann'yu had purchased the book for him. So many other things had happened that night that he'd forgotten it completely. "Was it a good read?"

"Lovely," Alidas replied. "Though it made me homesick. But just a little. It made me miss the south as the poems captured it but not the way I lived in it, if that makes any sense."

John nodded. "It captured an ideal of your home."

"Yes, exactly," Alidas replied. "*Pale as stars caught in dark branches, apple blossoms shine even in the black night.*"

"That's the kind of poetry that makes you think the life of an apple picker must be wonderful." Ravishan glanced to Alidas. "They write the same sorts of things about the golden taye of the north. As a rule, they don't mention all the goat shit in the fields and streets."

"They really don't," Alidas said, laughing.

"I suppose the song loses something if you praise the golden fields and then advise visitors to bring a second pair of boots for days when they get a little too golden," Ravishan added.

"I would have appreciated the warning at least," Alidas replied. He then turned to John. "What about you? What do they sing about your home?"

"Shun'sira?" John asked. He'd seen drawings and read descriptions. As far as he could tell the place was a collision of barren rock faces, sink holes, thorn forests, and bogs. References to clouds of biting black flies and parasitic worms appeared as a common theme in all the literature.

"Most of the songs are something like, '*I'm so glad to be leaving the mudslides of Shun'sira*,'" John hummed. "Or else, '*Shun'sira, mountainous hell-hole, I hope you fall into the sea.*'"

"The honest songs of a bitter people." Alidas laughed and Ravishan smiled at John as if he'd done something truly charming. John felt a ridiculous pleasure in having amused both of them. He'd almost forgotten what it felt like to just relax in comfortable company.

Minutes later, Vundomu came clearly into view. Dark banners decorated with scarlet moons hung from the walls. As the train approached, huge gates at the base of the fortress slowly rolled open. Plumes of steam and smoke shot up from the machines that powered the movement of the gates. Beyond them John thought he could pick out the silhouettes of hundreds of people and still more banners.

"That's quite a crowd waiting for the train," John commented.

Both Alidas and Ravishan studied the faint forms gathered in the shadows of the massive black gates. Hundreds of men stood in tight lines just beyond the train platform. Their uniforms looked like Alidas' but instead of being green they were dyed black and gray—the colors of the Payshmura. They, like Ravishan and himself, wore their hair back in priest's braids.

For an irrational moment, John had thought the procession had gathered to welcome Alidas. Immediately, he realized his mistake. One or two friends might be expected to do that. But this was a gathering of hundreds, perhaps more. John couldn't see where their ranks ended deep within the fortress.

"I don't see any—" Alidas frowned as the train continued forward. "Good eyes."

"I think they're rashan'im," Ravishan said.

"They've come to greet you," Alidas said to Ravishan. "I hope you've prepared a speech."

Ravishan paled and said nothing.

Living so close to the ushiri'im, knowing them as friends, John had forgotten how sacred they were to the rest of Basawar. The Kahlil was far more rare and of even greater sanctity. It was difficult for John to recognize that when he looked at Ravishan. To him, Ravishan was a human being, a man he cared for but not an object of worship.

Now, even over the noise of the train engine, John could hear bells ringing and voices rising from Vundomu. He recognized the words of prayers as the gathered rashan'im chanted in unison. It had to be a thousand men, John thought as he caught sight of more ranks of rashan'im. Many of them were mounted on armored tahldi. Even at this distance, John could see the polished gleam of their boots and gloves. He became suddenly aware of how grungy he, Alidas, and Ravishan looked. It had been a week since their last opportunity to bathe. They'd worn the same clothes for days. All of them probably reeked of tahldi hide and coal steam.

At the last two stops the train had made, there had been drink sellers and food vendors, ragged women with babies in their arms, and beggars all gathered at the sides of the tracks. John's own comparative cleanliness had kept him from really noticing how bedraggled he'd become. Nothing like that was in evidence at Vundomu. Nothing at all. John squinted at the precise files of clean men in black uniforms.

"Aren't there any women?" John asked.

"No," Ravishan said.

"Of course there are," Alidas replied in the same moment. He gave Ravishan a slight shake of his head. "Most of the craftsmen and servants have wives and families. They keep their homes on the eastern hills. Many of the rashan'im of Vundomu have mothers and sisters there as well. The women raise crops and keep the livestock that feed Vundomu."

"I never saw any when I was there." Ravishan scowled. He wasn't used to being wrong, John thought.

"You probably only kept company with the holy kahlirash'im. Women aren't allowed inside their temple, but you can see one of the common villages up there." Alidas pointed to the eastern slope. "My friend, Wah'roa, grew up on that mountainside."

A stone wall enclosed a cluster of thatched houses. John peered up at them. The rocks of the walls and weathered wood of the buildings hardly stood out from the surrounding trees.

Glancing from the hillside to Vundomu, John was struck again by the massive presence of the fortress. It was a mountain itself. How could anyone think of attacking such a place? The black iron walls rose like huge plates of armor. A veritable sea of armed men seemed to flow from its huge, spiked gates.

John couldn't imagine an army overpowering such a stronghold. What threat could the underfed peasants of the Fai'daum possibly pose against a fortification of this scale? And if the Payshmura priests commanded such a fortress as well as the powers of the ushiri'im and ushman'im, why did they believe they would still need the Rifter?

"Who could even challenge this place?" John wondered under his breath. The metallic screech of the train's wheels braking against the track easily drowned out his undervoiced question. They had nearly reached the gates. The deep rumble of hundreds of men chanting rose over even the noise of the train.

"We should get our packs," Alidas called as the train slowed.

Ravishan and Alidas both turned back to the doors of the passenger car, though John couldn't help but note the disparity between their movements—Ravishan striding with speed and assurance, while Alidas took his steps with careful precision. John followed the two of them into the passenger car. They had packed lightly and had already devoured most of their provisions. They would need to get more water and food at Vundomu. John swung his own pack onto his back and then hefted Ravishan's onto his shoulder as well.

At this, Ravishan regarded John questioningly.

"I believe the attendant gets the baggage," John said.

"Mine as well?" Alidas asked coyly.

"As soon as you're Kahlil I'll be glad to."

"I'm not Kahlil yet," Ravishan commented.

The train had slowed and the chanting of the gathered rashan'im thundered through the passenger car.

"RAVISHAN'HIR YA KAHLIL! RAVISHAN'HIR YA KAHLIL! RAVISHAN'HIR YA KAHLIL!" Thousands of men's voices pounded through the air in unison, proudly proclaiming Ravishan their Kahlil. The words rolled out again and again. "RAVISHAN'HIR YA KAHLIL! RAVISHAN'HIR YA KAHLIL! RAVISHAN'HIR YA KAHLIL!"

"Everyone here seems pretty sure you will be," John shouted his reply.

Ravishan flushed, seeming both embarrassed and proud. The assembled rashan'im all knew his name, all called out to him as if he were their savior. John couldn't imagine what he would think if so many people were so moved by his mere presence. Most likely, he'd pretend to be someone else.

The train came to a complete stop. Outside, the thousands of rashan'im standing in organized lines fell silent.

"You should probably go first," Alidas told Ravishan. "I think Jahn or I would be something of a disappointment."

Ravishan glanced to John and, for an instant, he looked uncertain. Then, just as quickly, the expression was gone. Ravishan squared his shoulders, pushed open the doors, and stepped out onto the stairs leading down to the train platform. A deafening cheer exploded from the rashan'im.

Alidas said something, but John couldn't make out the words. Alidas just shoved him forward.

Ravishan had already descended the stairs. The rashan'im parted before him. Once again they began their chant, their voices pounding the air like thunder.

"RAVISHAN'HIR YA KAHLIL! RAVISHAN'HIR YA KAHLIL! RAVISHAN'HIR YA KAHLIL!"

John disembarked with less fanfare. He stopped on the platform to wait for Alidas and found himself, instead, gawking at the fortress like the provincial peasant he claimed to be.

The scale of Vundomu astounded him.

Huge iron torches jutted from the walls, illuminating the wide street to afternoon brilliance. Columns of rashan'im stretched back as far as John could see. Countless other men gazed down from the towering black walls above. Nothing in Rathal'pesha had prepared him for this. He had grown so used to half-abandoned halls and wilderness that he had come to think of Basawar as a world devoid of populace and technology.

Here the streets were not made from packed dirt but paved with iron tiles. The black walls gleamed like polished glass. John couldn't see a single stain of rust or any corner where a weed had gained a foothold. The air churned with steam and smelled of pungent veru oil, used to lubricate guns, pistons, axles, and engines alike.

It was like being swallowed by a huge machine. Only the distant, darkening sky reminded John that he was still outside at all.

Ahead of John, a group of mounted rashan'im rode to meet them. One of them dismounted, led his tahldi to Ravishan, and dropped to the ground before him. John saw the man's mouth move. Ravishan inclined his head slightly, then took the reins of the tahldi and mounted. As he rode forward, mounted rashan'im closed in behind him and followed him up the road. Then the ranks of rashan'im on foot also joined the procession.

John stayed put. It would have been pointless to attempt to push his way through the crowd of rashan'im. And he could tell from the smooth organization of their departure that he wouldn't have too long to wait for a clear path. Perfectly spaced columns of men poured smoothly up the road and through a second gate. There had to be ten times the number of people who had been at the Amura'taye Harvest Fair and yet the street stood half empty in just a few minutes. John supposed such efficiency was the defining difference between the chaos of a crowd and the discipline of an army.

Alidas stepped up next to him and scanned the sea of uniformed men. More than half of them had already gone. The street suddenly seemed cavernous. John could see where other train tracks formed a junction with the ones they were on. Far to his left, he made out a variety of boxcars as well as the thick cables and awkward arms of primitive cranes. There were workmen there and animals. Now that the chants of the rashan'im had grown more distant, John could hear the sounds of sheep and goats coming from the boxcars.

The few rashan'im who remained appeared to be on guard duty. One, a slim man with black hair drawn back in a multitude of warrior's braids, led two saddled tahldi toward them. There was some kind of mark on his forehead—a Prayerscar, John realized, as the man drew closer. The red, crescent moon curved upward on his brow like a set of horns. John recalled that the kahlirash'im wore a scarlet moon as a symbol of their sect.

The man waved and John almost returned the gesture before he realized that it had been meant for Alidas.

"Wah'roa," Alidas called out to the slim kahlirash. Despite the awkwardness of his right leg, Alidas bounded ahead to meet him. John hefted his and Ravishan's packs and followed.

"Alidas! Pivan wrote saying that you would be passing through, but I didn't know when. It's good to see you again." Wah'roa smiled broadly, exposing a set of unnaturally sharp teeth. Ravishan hadn't been joking about the kahlirash'im filing them.

"I've had the good fortune to travel with Ushiri Ravishan and his attendant, Ushvun Jahn." Alidas gestured toward him. Wah'roa took John in as if he were appraising an unusually large tahldi. John guessed having an animal's name never helped the first impressions he made.

"Ushvun Jahn," Alidas introduced him formally, "this is Kahlirash'im Commander Wah'roa." This close, John noticed the deep wrinkles at the corners of Wah'roa's eyes and mouth. He was older than John had first thought, probably well into his forties. His energetic motions and youthful build disguised it well.

"Good to meet you." John bowed and one of the packs slumped into the back of his head. He straightened quickly.

Both Alidas and Wah'roa smiled at John's clumsy response.

"We are well met indeed, Ushvun Jahn." Wah'roa lightly touched the Prayerscar on his brow. "I had come to fetch you so that you might join the kahlirash'im in our prayer vigil for Ushiri Ravishan."

More prayers. John tried to look enthusiastic. If nothing else, the years at Rathal'pesha had more than prepared him to meet that liturgical challenge.

"When it comes to a prayer vigil, I'm your man," John offered as gamely as he could.

Wah'roa inclined his head as if expecting as much of an attendant.

"Would you be offended if Rashan Alidas joined us for the ride up to the temple?" Wah'roa inquired.

"I'd be glad for the company," John replied. "Will we be meeting up with Ravishan there?"

"Ushiri Ravishan?" Wah'roa asked, placing a slight emphasis on Ravishan's proper title. He shook his head. "No, he will receive blessings in the golden chamber and then be honored with a feast. We will pray for the divine Rifter's swift return and righteous judgment."

"An uplifting evening, then," John murmured. To his surprise, Wah'roa laughed.

"We will be lifted up, indeed," Wah'roa replied, and for some reason, he and Alidas exchanged amused grins. Then Wah'roa strode to one of the rashan'im standing guard. They exchanged a few words and the guard hurried away. A few minutes later he reappeared, leading a third, very large tahldi.

Wah'roa and Alidas both mounted quickly and made it look easy. John only noticed Alidas' brief wince of pain because he was looking for it. John heaved himself up into the saddle. He scrambled to catch hold of the reins and get his feet into the stirrups before his buck took off. The tahldi clearly wasn't used to waiting for clumsy men to settle themselves.

They didn't take the wide road that Ravishan and the rest of the rashan'im had followed into the fortress. Instead they passed through a second, much smaller gate. The road narrowed and seemed to lead directly up into the fortress, instead of encircling it as the larger road did. The tahldi sprang easily up shallow steps that had obviously been designed to accommodate their strides.

As they continued upward, John realized that their path had cut across the wide main road at some point. John couldn't see past the walls on either side of him, but once he thought he heard the rashan'im calling out their praises to Ravishan from below him.

At last they reached the next tier of black iron walls. Rashan'im in dark uniforms stood guard at another gate. Unlike Wah'roa, none of them wore red Prayerscars on their brows or had sharpened teeth.

"Here." Wah'roa reined his tahldi to a halt. John's own mount stopped as well, seeming to realize that Wah'roa was the one to obey, not John.

Wah'roa dismounted. "We should leave the tahldi. They get nervous in the lift."

Alidas followed him. John took longer, fighting to loosen his boots from stirrups that had obviously been designed for a man with narrower feet.

"They belong to the Nassva Stable," Wah'roa told the guard. "See that they get back there."

"It will be done, sir." One of the guards bowed and took the reins of all three tahldi.

The other two guards heaved the heavy gates open, exposing a corridor leading deep into the fortress.

As John followed Alidas and Wah'roa into the gloom, he felt the weight and strength of the stone and iron closing in around him. Behind them the doors swung shut. It was dark but not pitch black, as John had expected. Instead, a pale phosphorescent light radiated from suspended glass lamps. John peered up at them in wonder.

"Moon water," Alidas told him offhandedly. "There's a well of it near the temple."

John would have liked to examine the lamp more closely, but he reluctantly had to abandon his scrutiny when he realized Wah'roa was outdistancing him. Some kind of bioluminescent protozoan probably lived in the water.

John hurried after Alidas and Wah'roa. The walls on either side were rough-hewn stone. It felt more like a cave than a man-made structure. But ahead John could smell veru oil. The air carried the humid warmth of steam engines.

The three of them passed through another set of guarded doors and stepped into a cavernous chamber. Two huge columns of girders and chains shot up from the floor through a giant black shaft in the ceiling. Behind that, a group of men in work pants and leather aprons shoveled coal into the red glowing boiler chamber of an immense engine. Thick links of chain spun out from wheels as a black iron cage descended from the shaft. It screeched and hissed as pulleys and counterweights fought its mass down to an abrupt halt.

It was an elevator, John realized, perhaps the most primitive, open, unsafe elevator he had ever seen. There was absolutely no sign of secondary brakes or fail-safe mechanisms.

Alidas grinned at the sight of it. John felt his face drain of all color. An utterly alien device might have given John pause, but he could have imagined that some detail eluded him and taken comfort in his ignorance. But seeing something that he recognized—and recognized as lacking significantly—horrified him.

"Come." Wah'roa entered the black iron cage. Alidas went quick on his heels.

"I could take the stairs," John offered.

Wah'roa laughed. "I know that this must look like the work of some foreign witchcraft, but it isn't. The lift is perfectly safe."

"It is, Jahn," Alidas assured him.

John slumped in resignation. He wasn't going to be able to take the stairs to avoid riding the substandard elevator. He didn't even know where the stairs might be. He walked to the iron cage and stepped in. Wah'roa gave him a nod of approval, then turned to shout to the workmen behind them. "All the way up!"

One of the men nodded and then cranked back a huge gear. There was a loud clanking sound and then a hissing noise. The massive chains surged forward, whipping around the wheels and rushing up past the black iron of the cage. John tensed himself for a burst of motion, but none came. The chains continued feeding past at a wild rate.

John glanced to Wah'roa. "Shouldn't we be—" The rest of John's question died in his mouth. The cage shot up, with an almost explosive force.

"What were you asking?" Wah'roa glanced to John.

"Nothing," John said. Wah'roa smiled knowingly. The eerie green light hanging from the ceiling of the cage swayed.

"I suppose they need no machines such as these in Rathal'pesha," Wah'roa commented. "The ushiri'im simply walk where they will."

"The rest of us use the stairs," John replied.

Wah'roa gave him a strangely piercing look. Alidas stiffened slightly and glanced between John and Wah'roa as if he expected some kind of a fight. John understood at once that he had provoked a subject of much greater importance than an elevator, but he wasn't sure how.

"You speak with the true humility of an ushvun." Wah'roa inclined his head slightly to John, which lent him the air of a bird of prey eyeing a rabbit. "You may do well to guard yourselves from a machine like this, after all it does not know an ushman'im from a garrison commander and so treats them equally."

"You have to make allowances for Jahn," Alidas said quickly. "Coming from Shun'sira, he's still a little awed by shaving razors."

Following Alidas' lead, John nodded. "It's true. I saw my first one a little over four years ago."

Wah'roa's expression softened slightly. "Really?"

John nodded. "When I was first offered a bath in the Bousim house I tried to eat the soap."

Wah'roa laughed, giving John a brief flash of his sharp teeth. John guessed that Wah'roa hadn't wanted to have an argument either; otherwise he wouldn't have let John's blunder go so easily. Still, he guessed that the discord between Rathal'pesha and Vundomu must be pervasive and deep to have flashed up so readily.

"We just escorted him up from the first train he has ever seen or ridden," Alidas went on.

Wah'roa cocked his head and studied John. "And what did you think of it?"

"It felt like I was flying over the land," John said. "It was exhilarating."

Wah'roa appeared quite pleased with this response. "If the ushman'im of Rathal'pesha had had their way, none of them would have been built, you know."

"I didn't," John admitted.

"It was long before your time, I suppose," Wah'roa commented. He glanced to Alidas. "Long before either of you tender youths were born. Back then, the ushman'im argued that the trains would only allow tithe debtors to evade imprisonment and make peasants take on airs, thinking that they too could travel as far and fast as ushiri'im."

"That's just asinine," Alidas replied. But then his gaze jumped to John as if expecting him to disagree.

"You'll get no argument from me," John assured him. "I was relieved to get off a tahldi."

Wah'roa gave John an approving nod.

John remembered noting before that Rathal'pesha, and most of the northlands, were nearly devoid of technological development. At the time he had thought it the result of Payshmura religious codes—part of their devotion to Parfir and nature. But if what Wah'roa said was true, then it had more to do with maintaining the hierarchy of priests, who could walk through walls and unleash divine weapons, over the common people whose lives they controlled.

Machines offered power that the priesthood couldn't strictly control. A rifle and an ushiri might both kill in an instant, but rifles could be mass-produced. They could fall into the hands of peasants, who, unlike ushiri'im, had no doctrine to keep them from joining revolutionaries.

Clearly, though, this schism wasn't just between the Payshmura and the Fai'daum. It was fueling an animosity between the priests of Rathal'pesha and the kahlirash'im of Vundomu. John felt certain that Wah'roa's earlier anger hadn't just been over an elevator or a train.

Though now Wah'roa studied him with curiosity.

"So you traveled from Shun'sira to Rathal'pesha on foot?"

"All but the last few miles," John told him. "And that was the first time I rode a tahldi."

"It was the night Jahn and I met." Alidas looked to Wah'roa. "Jahn saved my life."

"Tell me," Wah'roa said.

"Jahn had been living in the forest when I first saw him. He smelled like a weasel nest and looked like one as well." Alidas went on describing the night John had come to warn the Bousim convoy. Wah'roa relaxed, watching Alidas, smiling just slightly. Alidas described how John's solitary life had allowed him to forget speech almost completely.

"Jahn said each word as if he had just learned it," Alidas commented.

John nodded. It was a fair description. Alidas went on with the story.

As they rose, darkness closed in around them. The shadows of chains rattled and hissed as they dropped past. The air took on the warmth and humidity of exhaled breath. John wondered how far up they were. Then, unwillingly, he considered how far they would fall if one of the chains broke. Would he be killed instantly upon impact?

And that bought up another question: could he be killed by such a fall? Everything he had read about the Rifter implied that he was nearly immortal. According to Payshmura texts, he could only be destroyed through a ritual of bleeding, poisoning, and the use of a mysterious key. But John had scars from injuries. He'd been cut, beaten, and nearly frozen. He wasn't sure how much credence he should put in the depictions of the Rifter's invulnerability. He certainly had no desire to test it.

"Jahn protected me while I lay there."

Hearing his name, John glanced to Alidas. Alidas smiled at him and Wah'roa offered an approving nod.

"He took my place as the attendant to Fikiri'in'Bousim and then was chosen as the attendant to Ushiri Ravishan. Now he's here, riding a lift for the first time," Alidas finished.

"Perhaps we should recruit more men born from Shun'sira's soil," Wah'roa said. "Or perhaps just those strong enough to have escaped their births."

Alidas laughed and John smiled.

"Ah, Shun'sira, mountainous hell-hole, I hope you fall into the sea," John said softly.

Alidas laughed and then explained the joke to Wah'roa. He seemed to appreciate it.

The soft yellow glow of firelight radiated down from above them. The movement of the cage began to slow. John could hear the low murmur of men's voices. Then, at last, the cage came to a jerky stop beneath an archway of girders, chains, and pulleys. The air felt refreshing and cool as it brushed over John.

They exited the lift and stepped out into a wide courtyard lined by stone barracks. Looking out, John could not only see the terraces of Vundomu spilling out beneath him, but the moonlit ribbon of the distant Samsira River.

A group of eighty or more men awaited them. Like Wah'roa, they looked hard and lean and carried rifles. All of them bore red Prayerscars on their brows. Scarlet moons decorated the cuffs and collars of their black uniforms, and when they called out a salutation to Wah'roa, John couldn't help but note the flash of so very many sharp white teeth.

Though, he also noted that these men, like the guards on the terraces below, addressed Wah'roa with the formal honorifics normally reserved for the holiest of the ushman'im.

Back in Rathal'pesha, Ushman Nuritam would not have been pleased with that. Yet the kahlirash'im presented such an intimidating presence that John couldn't imagine anyone reprimanding them in person.

"I'm afraid we have to part here," Alidas told John quietly.

"Where are you going?" John wished the words hadn't come out sounding so startled; there was something about all those polished guns and sharp teeth that unnerved him. Alidas grinned as he'd been paid a compliment.

"It's where you're going that matters," Alidas replied. "I'm not ordained, so sadly I can't enter the heart of the kahlirash'im sanctum along with you."

"Oh, I see." And he did, at least enough to realize that it pained Alidas not to be counted among the kahlirash'im. "Well, you'll just have to take some consolation at the feast that's taking place, I suppose."

"That I will." Alidas appeared to cheer up at the thought. "I'll see you tomorrow."

"Tomorrow," John agreed.

With that, Alidas stepped away and the kahlirash'im fell into two tight formations on either side of John.

He and the rank and file of the kahlirash'im marched after Wah'roa. They passed beneath a raised portcullis and followed a narrow, paved lane toward the black silhouette of a strangely bristling building. It reminded John of a huge spruce pinecone in the way its edged scales seemed to armor the graceful symmetry of its curves. As they drew closer John saw that torches illuminated the brilliant red tiles that encased the entire surface of the massive structure. The doors, too, were red, though the steps leading up to them shone like gold.

Their entire procession drew to a halt at the foot of the stairs.

Wah'roa quickly stepped between John and the door, then turned to face him. He raised his hands to his forehead, touching his Prayerscar, and then briefly placed one callused finger to John's brow.

"Attendant, this night you are one of us. Raise your voice with us, so that our revered Kahlil may journey through the Palace of the Day to the Kingdom of the Night and return to us the divine destroyer. Pray with us for the cleansing wrath that will at last free his house of corruption and make us once again deserving of his blessings." Wah'roa spoke sternly, all traces of ease and warmth drained from his countenance. He stared into John's face with expectant intensity. In the silence, John realized that he was expected to respond.

"The honor would be mine," John managed. "Ah, thank you."

John caught Wah'roa's brief look of amusement at his awkward reply. Then Wah'roa's harsh expression returned.

"Then come into the sanctum of the most holy incarnation and kneel with us in brotherhood." Wah'roa turned to the large doors and pushed them open.

The entryway was cramped and dark. Then Wah'roa pushed through another set of doors and led John into the vast central chamber of a wide, circular chapel. Except for a black statue at the altar, the chapel was completely empty. Only a few oil lamps hung from the ceiling, but the light reflected and gleamed off the gold-inlaid walls. Where the light caught, the sweeping curves of script blazed, as if the gold plating were turning molten. The floor had been tiled a deep, glassy red. It gleamed almost as if it were wet.

John followed Wah'roa across the chamber to the foot of the huge, black iron statue. Looking up, John expected to meet Parfir's benevolent gaze. Instead he found himself looking into wide eyes, an open screaming mouth, and barred black teeth.

The pose was wrong for Parfir as well.

This figure was arched forward, arms thrown out. The hair swirled out around the enraged face as if caught in a storm wind. At the statue's feet, the tiles were cracked with black seams.

"This is the Rifter," John whispered.

"Parfir's most holy incarnation," Wah'roa said softly. "The divine destroyer. God's will given form."

John could hear the other kahlirash'im filing into the chamber behind him. They filled the space with the scent of tanned leather, veru oil, and sweat. The warmth of their bodies added a living heat to the blaze of the golden walls.

Wah'roa bowed down and lowered his head in prayer. Slowly, John knelt down as well. He closed his eyes, listening to the prayers that whispered and rolled through the chamber. They called on the Rifter to lend them strength, to make them fearless, to defend their world. A pang shot through John as he realized that he was the god they so softly called upon and he could offer them nothing.

John bowed his head, mumbling empty prayers in his own temple.

Chapter Forty-Eight

They departed from Vundomu the next day, and after six more days of train travel, the trio finally reached Nurjima. The sun was just setting. Common men and women greeted their friends and relatives at the station. Work crews unloaded goods and animals. A party of Bousim rashan'im had arrived and one man waved through the crowd at Alidas. John found it odd, particularly after the huge display at Vundomu, that no one came to greet Ravishan. Not even a single lowly ushvun awaited his arrival.

Noting this, Alidas drew a simple map of the streets to take to reach the Black Tower. He assured them that the Black Tower could be seen from any point in the city, so they couldn't get too lost. But it was a long walk, so he suggested that they really ought to take a carriage. When Ravishan asked if carriage drivers preferred blessed stones or wooden coins as pay, Alidas seemed deeply concerned.

"Prayer stones won't get you anything in Nurjima," Alidas said. "Don't you have any money?"

"None," John said, so that Ravishan would not have to.

"Here, take this. It isn't much, but it will get you to the Black Tower." Alidas offered John his coin purse.

"We can't take your money," John objected, but Alidas simply thrust the leather purse into his hand.

"It's the least I can do. And I'll have pay waiting for me at the Bousim barrack. Please take it as my offering to your pilgrimage."

"Thank you," Ravishan said. "Bless you."

"It was an honor meeting you—both of you." He hefted his pack up onto his shoulder as two rashan'im in Bousim green came striding up. Noting their approach, he said, "Here's my escort."

John and Ravishan both wished him well. None of them spoke of meeting again. Alidas departed with his fellow rashan'im.

John hired a battered brown carriage, drawn by two surprisingly plump tahldi. The driver looked like he shared living quarters with his animals, but the interior of the carriage was clean, if cramped.

They rode through the winding twilit streets, now and then glimpsing streetlamps and catching snatches of wild music. John felt the Black Tower long before he saw it. His empty stomach tightened. When they stepped out of the carriage, John looked past the massive stone wall that surrounded the grounds up to the black, corded height of the tower. He felt a familiar repulsion, which he suppressed immediately.

Instead, he and Ravishan walked side by side to the massive, wrought iron gates of the entry. There, two ushvun'im, who had apparently been waiting for Ravishan to arrive, informed them that the Usho and several of his highest-ranking ushman'im had contracted some kind of sickness. Fai'daum witchcraft was suspected. The ushman'im throughout Nurjima were performing rituals of cleansing and healing as well as exorcisms. Whatever the cause, no one wanted to run the risk of exposing the future Kahlil to the illness.

The men explained that the Usho's greatest wish was for the Kahlil to remain in good health. They apologized profusely, bowing so low and for so long that their faces went red.

"For the sake of your safety, the Usho begs that you do not enter the Black Tower," the younger of the two ushvun'im mumbled into the knees of his cassock.

"Of course I'll do as His Holiness wishes," Ravishan replied. "Can you direct us to the nearest church hostel?"

The older of the two ushvun'im looked pained.

"I'm afraid that we must ask you to consider other accommodations. As we said, the Usho has fears that a Fai'daum witch has discovered that the Kahlil is making his pilgrimage. If she were to cast out a curse, it would likely be over a church hostel where the Kahlil would be expected to stay."

"I see," Ravishan said, frowning. John knew what was troubling him and also knew that Ravishan was too proud to bring up a subject like money.

"The Kahlil," John cut in quickly, "doesn't possess any secular monies, only blessed stones. How is he to pay for this accommodation?"

The younger of the ushvun'im seemed baffled. "You have no money at all?"

"None. We do not use it in Rathal'pesha," John replied firmly. He knew Ravishan had to be exhausted. He had spent half the night pacing through the train car, reciting his prayers and preparing to meet the Usho. Neither of them had eaten since early afternoon. John glowered down at the two ushvun'im. What did they imagine he and Ravishan were supposed to do for food and shelter for a week?

"We are obviously dressed in the clothes of priests from Rathal'pesha." John held out his arms so that the two ushvun'im could take in the rough wool of his coat and cassock. The only difference between his clothes and Ravishan's were the silver moons pinned to Ravishan's collar. Not even the lowest ushvun'im of Nurjima seemed to dress in such a rough, provincial fashion.

Even these two ushvun'im with novice braids wore cassocks of brushed silk and suede shoes.

"Turning the Kahlil out onto the street with no money and dressed in these clothes is hardly going to hide him from notice." John drew himself up to his full height. "If you're going to send him away, then at least you could provide us with money and clothes."

The two ushvun'im gaped at him. John stepped closer to the older of the two, forcing the other man to crane his neck to look up at him. "Don't you think that's the least you could do?"

The man blanched and retreated toward the gate.

"Yes, certainly," the ushvun said quickly. Then he turned to his younger companion. "Tell Ushman Serahn of the Kahlil's request at once."

The young ushvun bolted back inside the tower grounds. The older ushvun smiled faintly at John, his pale lips seeming to wilt with each passing minute.

"I'm sure it won't be long," the ushvun said.

John didn't respond. He simply stood his ground. Ravishan remained a little behind him, looking both displeased and aloof.

In truth, John guessed that he was simply exhausted and hungry.

At last the young ushvun returned. He brought an intricately embroidered moneybag and several pieces of paper. Immediately he offered the bag of coins to John.

"Ushman Serahn will make arrangements for his personal tailors and cobblers to clothe you." He handed John several papers. They had addresses written on them. "They should be able to see you tomorrow. He has also written the names of a number of lodgings, which would be appropriate for the Kahlil. He sent for a runner to summon a carriage."

John accepted the papers and scanned through the list of names and addresses. They meant next to nothing to him. He held them out to Ravishan, who only shook his head.

"Wherever you choose," Ravishan said. "Just so long as we get something to eat."

"How long will we have to wait for this carriage?" John demanded. He was a little surprised at himself. It wasn't like him to be such a bully. But Ravishan deserved to be treated better. At Vundomu a thousand priests had gathered at the train station to cheer him. Here, two underlings had been sent to the front gate to tell him to come back in a week.

"A carriage should arrive before the seventh bell." The younger of the two bowed his head down as if expecting John to strike him. A sheen of nervous sweat was beginning to show on the forehead of the older ushvun. They knew this was the wrong way to treat the Kahlil.

"In the meantime, don't you think that you ought to offer the Kahlil some food?" John asked.

"Yes, I'm sorry," the older ushvun replied. He bumped the younger ushvun's leg with his foot. "Go get something from the kitchen."

"Yes, sir." The young ushvun rushed off again.

John and Ravishan waited in silence. The ushvun didn't attempt to make any kind of conversation. He just stood in front of the gate with his head bowed as if caught up in a deep and sorrowful contemplation of his shoes.

When the young ushvun returned, it was with a tray of several meat-stuffed rolls. Surprisingly, Ushman Serahn's ornate private carriage arrived only a few moments later. It looked like something from a Victorian fairytale—all gold and white, endlessly embellished with motifs of glittering suns. Even the driver and the team of four tahldi wore curling gold ribbons. John wasn't sure if the adornments looked more out of place twined around the deadly sharp horns of the bucks or braided through the weathered driver's grizzled beard.

After a few words with the driver, John settled upon an accommodation worthy of Ravishan's status.

Then he and Ravishan climbed into the luxurious, perfumed interior of the carriage and sat opposite each other on the supple, overstuffed leather seats. Through the small window in the carriage door John could see the relief on the faces of the two acolytes. He let the silk curtain fall back.

Once they had pulled away from the gate of the Black Tower, Ravishan broke into a wide grin.

"Who knew you could be such a tyrant, Jahn? I thought that ushvun was going to soil himself."

"I just asked him his opinion," John replied.

"You have no idea how glad I am that you did." Ravishan tore a huge chunk from his stuffed roll and wolfed it down.

"What did they expect us to do, just wander the streets for a week?"

Ravishan shrugged, his mouth too full to speak.

John continued, "And if they were so worried about contamination, then why didn't they send word before you arrived? Why not have someone meet you at the train station?"

Ravishan finished off the last off his roll and flopped back against the leather seat. "It's probably politics. Hann'yu said that many of the gaun'im are unconvinced of the need to return the Rifter to Basawar."

John nodded. He had overheard a number of similar conversations between Hann'yu, Dayyid, and Nuritam. Apparently, many of the southern gaun'im strongly opposed the training of a Kahlil.

Who could blame them? The return of the Rifter could mean the utter destruction of their holdings. After all, the Fai'daum weren't agents of a foreign land. Their strongholds were bound to be on one or more of the gaun'im lands.

"Sending you away for a week isn't going to solve anything."

"It might give them a little time to silence the objectors or at least distract them from interfering with the ceremonies," Ravishan said. "I don't know. I'm just glad you got us somewhere to stay. I'm exhausted."

John ate his own rolls. The delicate, faint flavors of the refined flour and soft meat were lost on him, but at least it stopped the ache of his stomach. After he'd eaten, he found his mood had mellowed somewhat.

He glanced to Ravishan. The diffuse light of street lamps poured through the silk curtains of the carriage, softening the hard planes his face. Ravishan's head was bowed down, almost to his chest. His long legs drooped against John's. He seemed like he might drift off to sleep. As the carriage jostled over the brick streets, their legs swayed and brushed each other. John felt the heat of Ravishan's body, even through the wool of their cassocks. Ravishan looked up, smiling slyly at the contact. And then, flushing, he glanced away. Reflexively, John shifted away from Ravishan. They were playing with fire here and they both knew it.

They rode on in silence over the brick road for several minutes.

"Do you feel someone is…watching?" Ravishan asked in a whisper.

John hadn't sensed the slightest distortion in the air around them, but he'd grown deeply cautious. Some ushiri—usually Fikiri—always seemed to be skulking through the Gray Space. Of course, that had been in Rathal'pesha, not Nurjima.

And suddenly it dawned upon John that here the only ushiri capable of moving so far and so adeptly through the Gray Space was Ravishan.

"No, I don't think anyone is actually." John felt almost stunned by the thought—not quite able to trust it.

"We're alone?" Ravishan sounded uncertain even asking.

"Who would be watching?" John asked.

"Fikiri, perhaps." Distaste sounded in Ravishan's voice and showed in his expression.

"But why would he bother anymore? We agreed to his demands." And with Dayyid gone, who would Fikiri spy for? John didn't say as much; both he and Ravishan refrained from discussing Dayyid as much as possible.

Lamplight flickered through the intimate confines of the carriage, momentarily illuminating the longing in Ravishan's handsome smile.

John only leaned a little closer to Ravishan, and yet after restraining himself for so long, even so slight an overture felt dangerous.

Ravishan met John's gaze and flushed as John continued to look into his eyes. Streetlamps flared and faded as they drove past. The rhythm of the tahldi's hooves against the cobbled street pounded through the carriage like a racing heartbeat.

Ravishan tilted his head just slightly and John wondered if he should kiss him or wait. The way Ravishan was gazing at him, he didn't think he could wait all that long.

Then suddenly the carriage jerked to a halt.

Ravishan rocked forward, smacking foreheads with John. Despite himself, John laughed at the absurd disruption. Ravishan looked much less amused. They both jerked back into their seats at the sound of the driver unlatching the door.

"We have arrived at the Ivory Bower, sirs," the driver informed them.

Ravishan scrambled out of the carriage. John gathered up their packs and followed him. From the way the driver stood expectantly beside the open door, John surmised that tipping was expected in Nurjima just as much as in any cosmopolitan city.

He paid the driver and quickly followed Ravishan into the palatial grandeur of the Ivory Bower. Marble blossoms festooned the exterior of the towering hotel and inside sprays of exotic southern flowers perfumed the grand entry.

Throughout the process, Ravishan avoided John's gaze and seemed strangely nervous about standing near him.

As an impeccably dressed footman showed them up to their rooms and then walked them through, Ravishan hung back, absently shredding the petals of a red lily that he'd plucked from some vase.

John hadn't seen him snatch it, but Ravishan was fast and here flowers seemed to be abundant.

Beyond the ornate vases bursting with blooms, the rooms also boasted a silken master's bed with a servant's cot at the foot, a private tub, and an expansive view of the city streets all lit up and shining in the darkness like strings of jewels spilled across black velvet.

Once the footman—who had walked them through the amenities of their suite with the air of a sommelier handing a bottle of 1787 Chateau Lafite over to two hillbillies—had accepted his tip and departed, John locked the door and took a moment simply to observe Ravishan in these new surroundings.

He stood near the large window that overlooked the street but didn't show any real interest in the view. Instead, he lowered his gaze to his hands. Discarded lily petals lay abandoned at his feet. He stole a glance at John and flushed ever so slightly as he realized that John was regarding him in return.

"I think that footman suspected us of stealing the money to rent this suite."

"He accepted his tip readily enough," John replied and Ravishan gave a fleeting smile.

John moved to Ravishan's side. Ravishan watched him with dark, expectant eyes. John couldn't remember him seeming this nervous…except that first night they'd met in Candle Alley. Flower blossoms had perfumed the air then too.

Though now, John could hardly think of that narrow alley without immediately remembering the heat of Dayyid's blood on his hands—the dead body at his feet. John instantly pushed the memory from his thoughts.

He was alone with Ravishan. That was all that mattered right now.

"Come to bed with me?" John asked.

Ravishan lifted his dark eyes to John for just a moment and his entire face flushed.

"Yes," Ravishan whispered, but he seemed rooted to the spot where he stood. John caught his hand gently and drew him back from the window. Ravishan's hand trembled, just slightly.

He was probably as nervous as he was excited about this, John realized. What experiences Ravishan had had with sex had most likely been limited to furtive, anonymous groping in a dirty alley. And at least once it had ended with a murder. The thought tempered John's own desire a little.

He stopped at the bedside and kissed Ravishan once gently, reassuringly. Ravishan returned the kiss slowly, as if just awakening to the idea of pleasure.

"It's going to be all right," John whispered to him. "In fact, it'll be lovely. I promise."

"Even if I'm a clumsy oaf who nearly knocks you unconscious trying to kiss you?" Ravishan hid his face against the curve of John's neck.

"You didn't come close to knocking me out." John had to fight not to smile. "There aren't many ways I'd rather get a bruise."

"I don't know how…not with someone like you." Ravishan sounded almost miserable and John realized that he couldn't tease him about this.

"I want to show you." John kissed Ravishan deeply this time. Ravishan's hungry response coursed through John's whole body.

John only broke away to hurl his heavy coat aside, and Ravishan followed his example, throwing off his coat and rough cassock. John caressed Ravishan's hard, scarred chest, marveling at how he could be so beautiful, despite his history of so much hurt.

Ravishan flashed one of his broad, joyous smiles.

"You have the most handsome smile, you know that?" John told him.

"I can do more than smile though." Ravishan kissed him quickly but with an expression of sultry promise.

They both toppled back onto the big white bed.

Ravishan's hands slipped under John's clothes. His fingertips were like fire as they traced the muscles of John's stomach and slipped down past the waistband of his trousers. A mindless, desperate pleasure flooded John. He flipped open the buckle of Ravishan's belt. Ravishan gasped as John gently caressed and stroked him. They moved together, graceless passion building to an intimate rhythm that only broke in ecstasy.

☾☾☾

The next morning, John woke to feel soft sunlight pouring across his cheek. He rolled deeper into the down blankets, pressing his body against Ravishan's.

Ravishan's skin felt warm. John drew in a deep breath, smelling the low woody scent of his skin, their mixed sweat, and sex. Slowly, John opened his eyes. Ravishan still slept. His black hair spilled across the white bedding.

John smiled and gently lifted a lock of Ravishan's hair. Ravishan mumbled something in his sleep and rolled over. It was good to see him get some rest at last.

Careful not to jostle Ravishan, John propped himself up onto his side. Beyond the sheer bed curtains, he could see the scattered piles of their discarded clothes. His heavy wool coat flopped across a delicate writing table. Ravishan's gray cassock hung off one of the cherry red carved chairs. John thought he could see the crumpled pale shape of his own underpants lying near the foot of the bed.

They hadn't drawn the curtains completely closed last night. Now John gazed out the tall windows at the streets of Nurjima far below. At first glance it could have passed for a historic Victorian district of Seattle. Brick and stone houses curled out along circular lanes. Many were enclosed by ornate gates or surrounded by gold and red autumn gardens. A young man in brown trousers and a jacket zipped up the street on a bicycle. But after a few moments, the details of the scene below began to betray its alien nature. The leaves on the trees that lined the brick streets were strangely pale, almost translucent. A pair of dark green tahldi hitched to an exquisitely carved carriage pranced along the red brick street.

A glance to the north utterly destroyed the illusion of familiarity. The massive structure of the Black Tower soared impossibly up from the city. Its dark girders and cables twisted and coiled, converging in a single black spire. Even from this distance John felt the Black Tower's presence searing the sky. All around it John could feel the deep, ragged open wounds of the torn Gray Space. If he concentrated, he could hear the faint hiss and whisper of the issusha'im as they prophesized endlessly to their master in the tower. John sensed currents of wind that ripped down from the heights of Rathal'pesha.

The Black Tower formed the center point of an immense, open doorway between the northern monastery and the southern convent.

John's contemplation was interrupted by the sensation of Ravishan's hand against his bare back.

"Jahn." Ravishan gently pulled him back down into the blankets. "We don't have to get up yet."

John collapsed back into bed. Ravishan's hands slid down John's chest. Heat from Ravishan's fingers lingered as he traced the curves of John's muscles.

"We can stay in bed all day if we want to." Ravishan leaned forward and kissed John's shoulder and then the curve of his neck. The anxiety churning through John melted into a languid pleasure. He could worry about the Black Tower, the Issusha'im Oracles, and Rathal'pesha later.

Right now he didn't want to waste the privacy and freedom that had been granted to them.

He kissed Ravishan once on the mouth and then again much lower. Ravishan gave a soft, ecstatic gasp. But this morning they were both rested and John wanted more than a few minutes of glorious friction. He took great care as he taught Ravishan what he knew of giving pleasure and taking it from another man's body. After only a little instruction, Ravishan applied himself with all of his natural enthusiasm and physical prowess.

They rose from bed late and took their time washing together. At last hunger drove John to disturb their isolation. After their meal of poached doves had been served and then the sad remains cleared away, a flock of tailors descended upon both John and Ravishan in a flurry of supple leather and costly silks.

By the time he and Ravishan left the Ivory Bower to explore the streets of Nurjima the sun was setting. Gold and scarlet streaks of light burned against the twilit blue of the darkening sky. Like stars flickering to life, the pale flames of streetlights illuminated their own corners of the descending night.

"It's beautiful," Ravishan said. "I didn't expect it to be beautiful."

For a moment John thought Ravishan was only commenting on the city, but then something in his expression told John that he meant much more. He was talking about what had passed between them.

"It'll get even better," John assured him.

"I can't imagine how," Ravishan replied, though he looked a little embarrassed by his own wistful tone. "I've already gotten to sleep in and eat four entire doves."

John laughed at the sad truth of Ravishan's words.

They had both lived in deprivation so long that this simple day of pleasure and ease came to them like a gift. Standing next to Ravishan, feeling the warmth of his body and gazing at the open sky, John felt suddenly overwhelmed with happiness. He didn't know if he had ever appreciated a moment of his life more than this. He glanced to Ravishan.

"Thank you," John said quietly.

Ravishan smiled and asked, "For what?"

"For everything." John didn't know how to convey the feeling that rushed through him. He was certain that words would fail. Ravishan seemed to sense this as well. He brushed his fingers against John's hand.

"You're welcome," Ravishan said, at last.

They continued walking beneath the flickering streetlamps and dark architecture in a quiet communion.

Chapter Forty-Nine

They passed the next day exploring Nurjima, and they discovered that the city remained vibrant and fascinating even after dark. At last, late in the evening, they stopped in a teahouse to rest and refresh themselves.

Thick humid warmth hung through the packed tearoom. Polished brass kettles released clouds of steam as they were emptied over loose leaves of daru'sira and other fragrant herbs. The young men working the tables swiveled and swung past one another, their arms loaded with steaming pots and trays of porcelain dishes.

At the far end of the room, behind a high wooden counter, women mixed the dry ingredients for the teas. Three girls rushed up and down ladders, picking dried leaves, flowers, and roots from the towering sheves of jars. Two older women then took the ingredients and distributed them into wide white cups and then slid those back across the counter to the waiters. As quickly as they sent out filled cups waiters called out new orders.

John watched in fascination as the process repeated over and over, men sweeping past each other, girls bounding up rolling ladders, and old women scattering arcane herbs perfectly into porcelain cups. Constant practice had transformed what should have been utter chaos into a kind of fluid choreography.

Despite the late hour, more patrons filed in through the green-painted doors. Little rushes of winter air followed them, only to be enveloped by the heat and perfume of their surroundings. All around him, John could catch snatches of conversations. People complained and laughed about their long day at work. Intimate friends sat close at small tables whispering to each other, while crowds of white-robed students slumped and slouched over heaps of papers and tiny, leather-bound books.

John leaned back in his seat, stretching his legs under the table. His knee brushed Ravishan's. Ravishan smiled but didn't look up from the pamphlet in front of him. John studied the newspaper he'd found on the table when they had come in. It had been left open to what looked like a letters column. John skimmed over the words,'...the teeming ghettos of yellow aberrations must be cleared, for they represent not only a danger to the health of the city, (as your article indicated) but the gravest danger to the moral character of this entire country. If they choose to live like vermin, then let them do it where they cannot harm decent people...'

Yellow aberrations. A day ago John could have misunderstood that phrase, but he'd now seen enough of Nurjima to understand that the descendants of the Eastern Kingdom lived as an underclass in Basawar. He had only seen them employed as street sweepers in the city and as menial laborers at the river docks. He supposed there were more in the back kitchens washing dishes and in the night factories pouring molten metals.

He had caught people staring at his own bright blond hair more than once, and when anyone had needed to ask them a question, it was always addressed to Ravishan and not himself.

John recalled Lady Bousim speaking of the few blonds that she had seen. John guessed that, due to her rank, she would have known almost none. There were certainly none among the gaun'im or even the wealthier merchants. It was quite clear now why Fikiri and his mother had been banished to the north. Among the gaun'im, Fikiri's light hair would have been taken as a testament of his mother's adultery.

When John and Ravishan had gone walking along the docks, they had encountered entire city blocks teeming with light-haired men and women. Most had been filthy and underfed.

A slim young girl there had slipped a pamphlet to John and then disappeared into the tight crowds of wagons, fishmongers, and laborers. Ravishan had wanted to read it and John had given it to him.

"It says the Fai'daum are the only path to equity," Ravishan had commented. "They're really very bold about their support, aren't they?"

John had replied, "I guess they are." In Amura'taye no one would have dared to say such a thing, much less write it down and distribute it. "They probably don't have much to lose."

The two of them had paused a moment, simply taking in the overflowing sewers, crumbling buildings, coughing smokestacks, and ragged poverty of the crowds. In Amura'taye people had been poor, but they hadn't been forced to live in filth. They'd had fresh air and clean water.

But in the slums of Nurjima, there had been garbage in the streets, and the walls of buildings had been plastered inches thick with old peeling posters. Some had been calls for temporary workmen; others had offered rewards for wanted criminals. Here and there, he had seen simple line drawings of Payshmura priests dangling from nooses.

"It's a good thing that we aren't in our church robes," Ravishan had said as he'd gazed at one of the faded posters. John had agreed.

They had been, in fact, dressed in the perfectly tailored, glossy black coats and ornate vests of the moneyed upper class. John had never owned boots that fit so well or felt so good. But their appearance of wealth attracted more than a few glares from the surrounding populace. They hadn't lingered near the docks, but stayed just long enough to purchase the sheaves of dried river grass that Hann'yu had asked John to look for.

Now, in the steamy warmth of the teahouse, John flipped through the pages of the paper, skimming over reports of new milling machines, gaun'im alliances, and scandalous plays. Fine-lined engravings illustrated a few of the articles. John gazed at a detailed rendering of the twisting girders and cables of the Black Tower then started to absently peruse the article below. Immediately his wandering attention focused on the words. He read them quickly, then slid the worn newspaper across the table to Ravishan. "You should read this."

"Ushman Serahn denies that a Kahlil has been selected, much less trained," Ravishan read the first line aloud but then continued reading to himself. Finally, a derisive snort escaped him, and he continued reading aloud, "The Gaunsho'im Council would be informed if such a course were ever to be considered."

"Apparently the Gaunsho'im Council recesses at the end of the week."

"So, there'll be no council to inform. That's convenient." Ravishan pushed the newspaper aside and picked up his drink.

"What about yours?" John nodded at the pamphlet Ravishan had been reading so intently. "Anything interesting?"

"I don't know." Ravishan sipped his tea, then frowned at the porcelain cup. "What did I order?"

"Infusion of red blossoms."

"I should try to remember that. It's good. How's yours?"

"A little too subtle for me," John replied.

Ravishan drank a little more of his tea, then set the cup aside. "I don't know how to feel about it."

"I thought you liked it."

"This pamphlet," Ravishan clarified.

"I see." John poured more honey than he had intended into his own drink. He stirred it, watching the pale green fluid turn golden. Ravishan glanced at the smudgy pamphlet in front of him but didn't say anything more.

John didn't attempt to force the subject. He knew that Ravishan had to feel some conflict deep within himself. His parents had been Fai'daum. And while his achievements within the Payshmura were a source of pride, the church itself had been cruel to him.

"The Fai'daum are enemies of Parfir." Ravishan lowered his voice. "I'm the companion to his holiest incarnation. When I think of it that way it's all very clear. But other times…" He frowned down at his hands. "You probably think I'm such a weakling. It's just hard for me to hate them as I should."

"Why would I think that made you weak?"

Ravishan looked up at him. "Because I'm going to be Kahlil and I shouldn't be unsure. And it's not that I don't believe. Parfir's presence burns through me. I believe in him as I believe in life. But I know that men like this Ushman Serahn misuse their power. All of the ushman'im of Nurjima live like gaun'im while farmers in Amura'taye struggle to pay their tithes. And the conditions those people at the docks were living in…I don't know how that can be Parfir's will."

John picked up the pamphlet. He could feel the letter-press type through the back of the thin paper. The accusations enumerated against the Payshmura Church each rang true. They did demand huge tithes. They did rarely, if ever, pay a fair price for goods purchased. They did keep the common populace in fear of death. But nothing in the pamphlet mentioned the god Parfir.

"Just because they oppose the church doesn't mean that they oppose Parfir," John reasoned. "Things aren't always so clear cut."

"True," Ravishan agreed, but he didn't look happy about it. "I suppose it's because of uncertainties like this that a man simply has to have faith. He has to believe that Parfir's will shall be done in the end. I want to believe that, but sometimes I can't help but wonder..."

"What?" John asked.

"Nothing." Ravishan surveyed the crowd of strangers at the surrounding tables. "How many more people do you think they can fit inside here?"

More students were pouring in through the green doors, their faces pink from the cold and the hems of their white scholar's coats muddied. Most carried books, though a few seemed to have come along just for the company. They threw themselves into their chairs with a theatric air of nonchalance. John could tell when one of them thought he was being particularly clever, because his voice would rise just enough to carry his words over the general roar of the group conversations.

One or two of them peered at John in a curious manner. He guessed that they weren't used to seeing a blond man dressed so well. When he met their gazes, they looked quickly away.

Another cluster of students rushed in from the cold night outside. They crowded in around already full tables. They laughed among themselves, sharing seats and balancing on the arms of chairs.

"I'd say we're about fifteen past maximum occupancy already," John said.

He almost let the earlier conversation with Ravishan go at that. He was used to abandoning political discussions. Most of them would have no bearing on his life once he returned to Nayeshi. He was used to thinking of the philosophy and politics of Basawar as both ephemeral and inconsequential in that regard. The knowledge that he would return home saved him from having to concern himself too deeply.

But this was different. Ravishan would be with him in Nayeshi. What Ravishan felt about the Fai'daum would impact how he dealt with the Rifter and responded to the orders sent to him from Basawar.

"Do you know what I think?" John asked.

Ravishan regarded him with slight surprise. "I never know what you're thinking. You keep things so private, even from me."

"I know. It's one of my bad traits." John extended his leg, so that his calf stroked Ravishan's. Ravishan offered him a brief, secret smile.

"Are you thinking that you want to get back to our rooms?"

"I do, but not just yet."

"Then what is it?" Ravishan asked.

John sipped his tea. The honey had made it incredibly sweet. Ravishan waited as John poured a little more water from their kettle into his cup, diluting the honey. He sipped his tea again. It was better.

"You're not good at this, are you?" Ravishan asked.

"No, I'm not," John admitted.

"You don't have to tell me if you don't want to."

"I want to," John said. "It's important that we talk about this because someday they're going to send word to you in Nayeshi and you're going to have to decide whether to obey those orders or not."

Ravishan nodded. "So, tell me what you think."

"I think that you know the church is corrupt and what they're doing to common men and women is wrong. But they have your sister, so you can't afford to challenge them."

"That's what I think." Ravishan cocked his head slightly. "I thought you were going to tell me what you thought."

"That doesn't really matter. I'm not the one who will have to decide what to do."

"It matters to me." Ravishan leaned a little closer to him. "So, tell me."

John frowned. It had been so much more simple to reveal himself physically to Ravishan. He had not needed words.

Ravishan folded his arms across his chest and leaned back in his seat. John recognized the posture. Ravishan was willing to wait all night for his answer.

"I think that the Payshmura have to change," John said at last. "They can't just keep ripping the world apart every time the issusha'im warn them of a possible conflict."

Ravishan gave a silent nod, plainly waiting for him to continue.

John went on, "They claim that the land is Parfir's flesh and yet they summon the Rifter to destroy it for their own sakes. You can see the damage it's done. The Great Chasm hardly supports life now. But if you read back through the texts, that area used to support a huge diversity of—"

"Jahn," Ravishan interrupted, "I know how you feel about diversity and about the disruption of environs. What I want to know is how you feel about the church."

"They need to relinquish power and learn to compromise," John said.

Ravishan raised his brows.

"And it's not just the Fai'daum they're up against," John went on. "The gaun'im are obviously stoking the dissent against the church in hopes of grasping more power for themselves. And the kahlirash'im at Vundomu seemed pretty damn pissed off at the Payshmura ushman'im as well."

"Pissed off?" Ravishan asked.

"Angry," John clarified.

"About what?"

"The inequity of power within the church—the way the ushman'im are dealing with the Fai'daum. A lot of the kahlirash'im come from farming families and they know what the tithes are doing. I don't think it strikes them as Parfir's will so much as the greed of the ushman'im. When they talked about the Rifter, a lot of them seemed to think he would return to wipe out the corruption within the church."

"They told you that?" Ravishan asked.

"Not directly," John admitted. "I overheard it when they were speaking among themselves."

"Maybe you misunderstood them."

"Maybe, but I don't think so. And I don't think that you think so either."

"No?" Ravishan seemed amused by John's presumption.

"No," John said firmly. "I think that you might feel the same way, but you wouldn't dare to admit it because you have too much to lose if anyone ever found out."

"Maybe," Ravishan said softly. He gazed down at his hands. "I don't like the idea of the Rifter returning to destroy the church."

"It isn't as though he's selective. He rips apart entire landmasses. You can feel how injured the land is already. I don't know if Basawar could withstand another wave of destruction."

As John spoke, Ravishan's expression changed. He began to look almost sick. The color drained from his cheeks and mouth, making his dark eyes seem like black holes.

John suddenly realized that as Kahlil, Ravishan would consider himself directly responsible for that destruction. More than the corruption of the ushman'im, it was the thought of unleashing the Rifter and tearing the world to pieces that filled Ravishan with doubt in his faith. The Payshmura had already made him take responsibility for his own mother's death. They had forced him to burn women alive as a kind of precursor to his greater duty as Kahlil.

Ravishan looked quickly away from John's gaze. He caught hold of his cup and drained the last of his tea. "I don't want to think about that. I can't and still become Kahlil."

"It won't happen," John told him quietly. "The Rifter will not destroy Basawar."

"How can you know?"

John almost told him the truth then. But he stayed silent, thinking that it would be too much for Ravishan to have to accept. It was almost too much for John himself to accept.

"We won't let it happen."

Ravishan smiled wanly and repeated, "We won't let it happen… as if it were our choice."

"Maybe it is." Again the urge to confess rose in John, but he held back.

"I want to believe you so badly."

"Then believe me," John told him.

Ravishan pressed his eyes closed the way a child would before making a wish. "Tell me it's going to be all right."

"It's going to be all right."

"Promise?"

"I promise," John assured him.

Ravishan opened his eyes. He looked out at the tables of debating students and men caught up in private conversations. The influx of patrons had ebbed. A pair of waiters leaned against the wooden counter at the back of the room, drinking their own cups of tea.

"I couldn't do this without you, Jahn."

"You could. But you won't have to."

Ravishan smiled a little wryly. Then he studied John for several moments.

"You should finish your tea," Ravishan announced at last.

From under the table John felt Ravishan's leg brush against his thigh. A rush of desire pulsed through John's body. He glanced at his cup. It was still half full.

"I'm done," John decided.

Ravishan nodded. "We should probably get to bed then. We have a long week ahead of us."

Chapter Fifty

It didn't feel like it had been a week already. John shifted in the elegant velvet-backed chair. It was too small for his big frame. He stood up and slowly paced the ornately gilded hall.

He wanted more time. Another week. He and Ravishan had just begun to explore Nurjima. They had visited only a few of the brightly painted bookshops and raucous theaters that Hann'yu had recommended.

They'd spent the better part of an evening listening to loud political debates in one of the teahouses near Scholars' Park. Scattered between students' and teachers' orations, there had been a provocative speech from a red-veiled widow and one ferocious diatribe from a young blond man. The diversity of opinion had given John hope. Nurjima was far from a utopia, but people here were free enough to say as much.

After that, Ravishan and he had sampled a few of the sweet and spicy dishes that came from the southern holdings. They had heard beautiful new music played by a blond beggar and seen the brilliant gold uniforms worn by the priests in the city dress guard. John had caught glimpses of trees and animals he had never seen before, books he had never read. He had seen sculptures and paintings that made him wonder about the forgotten histories of Basawar. There was so much more than a week's time had allowed him to take in.

But most of all, John wanted more time to simply linger in bed with Ravishan. He could have spent a week doing just that and still have wanted more. John traced his thumb across the edge of his lower lip, remembering Ravishan's last hungry kiss.

He dropped his hand back to his side and scowled at the riot of intricate gold filigree that scrolled across the iridescent pearl-like walls. All along the length of the hall small portraits of past usho'im stared haughtily out from circular gold frames. John had imagined the interior of the Black Tower to be different than this. He supposed the dark exterior had led him to expect something more like the powerful utilitarian interiors of Vundomu.

Instead, little gold suns winked at him from the carpet beneath his feet. Two silk-clad acolytes strolled past him. They couldn't have been younger than John, but their soft faces and careless expressions made him think of children. If Ravishan had seen them, he would have joked that the ushman'im of Nurjima were allowing girls into the priesthood.

But Ravishan wasn't with him, so the two acolytes passed without comment.

John glanced to the arched white doors at the far end of the hall. He had no idea how long Ravishan would have to remain in the Usho's audience chamber. Ushman Serahn had told John that he could wait if he liked, but he hadn't thought that Ravishan would be released before nightfall.

John supposed he could have gone out and explored Nurjima alone. But he wanted to be there when Ravishan finally emerged. It would be the first of five days spent preparing for his blessings, and John imagined Ravishan would be exhausted and probably injured in some manner as well. The Payshmura reverence for ushiri'im blood seemed to ensure that it would be spilled for as many rituals as possible.

John stood and paced.

If Ravishan were released before it was too late in the evening, John intended to take him to a puppet theater. They had already been once, but Ravishan seemed to take an unusual delight in seeing glorified socks swear, carouse, and beat each other. The theater had been dark and few other people seemed to ever attend it. The last time they had gone Ravishan had traced his fingers over John's palm and wrist, communicating his own silent desires.

As John turned to close the circle of his pacing, a young red-haired acolyte came rushing up the adjoining corridor. He drew to a halt in front of John, taking in quick gulps of air with as much dignity as he could manage.

"You are Ushvun Jahn?" the acolyte asked.

"I am." John frowned at the young man. "Why?"

"Ushman Serahn needs you at once."

"What's happened?" John asked, his thoughts already flashing through myriad terrible possibilities. What if something had gone wrong with the rituals? If Ravishan had been badly hurt, they would need someone strong to bear his wounds.

"I don't know. The ushman said you must be brought at once. Please come with me."

John followed the acolyte at a fast pace down the corridor and up a winding staircase. John would have gone faster but the young acolyte couldn't keep up with him in a full-out run. Nor could the acolyte take the stairs with the speed that years of living in Rathal'pesha had imparted to John. Finally, the acolyte gave up and waved John ahead of him.

"Ushman Serahn's at the very top of the tower. Keep going up." The acolyte hunched over, trying to catch his breath. "The guards know that you've been summoned. They'll let you pass."

John bounded up the stairs without another word. He threw himself forward as hard and fast as he could. The first three flights were wide but also busy. John had to twist and bolt between clusters of priests going about their daily business. After the fourth floor the stairs became almost deserted.

Perfumed air burned through John's lungs as he raced ahead. On the landing of the eighth floor, armed priests stood guard. As John charged forward they parted, allowing him past to the next flight of stairs.

"The gold door," one of them called after him.

John's heart hammered in his chest and his muscles felt like they were burning against his bones. He took a sharp turn, almost leaping up onto the next landing, and then suddenly jerked to a halt.

The sick, torn sensation of open Gray Space washed over him. John paused briefly to fight his sense of violent nausea before continuing up. The winding staircase seemed to curl forever upwards in tighter and tighter turns. The walls on either side of him steadily shifted from pearly white to the same odd yellow color he'd found in the highest reaches of Rathal'pesha. They grew increasingly tight as John ascended higher and higher, until he found himself almost enclosed. Another man couldn't have passed him without them both flattening against the walls.

The feeling of the Gray Space increased and he caught the distant but distinct whispers of the issusha'im. He had to be well above the main building now, somewhere in the twisted column of the central spire.

He turned a corner and almost smacked into a dark yellow stone door. The stairs simply ended there. John couldn't imagine how the door could open out to anything but the empty air swirling around the narrow spire of the black tower. Still he opened it and stepped through.

The room inside was huge and elaborately gilded with flowing Basawar script as well as English. Two wide stone arches filled the center of the room. There were no other furnishings. Ushman Serahn stood near the right arch, a small book in his gloved hands. Surprise showed on his soft, southern features as he took John in.

"That was quite fast. Did you run the entire way?" Ushman Serahn seemed amused by the thought.

John could hardly manage a word. The sensation of sickness that poured out over him from the two arches almost brought him to his knees. He bent over and drew in sharp breaths through his gritted teeth. The issusha'im's cacophony of voices hissed and whispered desperately from the arch on the left.

"They puts him in the fire."

John caught one clear phrase from the hundreds of others.

"Catch your breath," Ushman Serahn said. "I don't think I've known anyone to run the whole way. Very blond of you." He flipped his long black braids back over his shoulder, opened his book, and began to read.

"Ravishan…" John panted.

"Pardon?"

"Ushiri Ravishan," John said, "where is he?"

"With the Usho." Ushman Serahn looked slightly puzzled. "Oh, you thought I summoned you on his behalf? No, nothing of the sort."

"What then?" John managed to straighten. A nauseous tension still played through his stomach. He tried not to look at the two sweeping arches. Their yellow stones made him think of rotting teeth and rancid butter. The issusha'im's voices scraped and whimpered at John.

"It comes to cuts us open and cracks our bones."

"It sucks our marrow. It burns us."

"They must not brings it to us. Must not brings it to us!"

"Hates it. Hates it. Hates it. Hates it."

"Get it out," a childlike voice was almost sobbing. "Get it out. It hurts."

John couldn't understand how Ushman Serahn could just stand there looking so bland, reading. Not unless the man couldn't hear the issusha'im.

"He kills us, one of the issusha'im suddenly howled. They puts him in the fire and he kills us all!"

"You are needed back in Rathal'pesha at once," Ushman Serahn informed him offhandedly. He flipped a page in his book.

"Rathal'pesha?" John asked. The issusha'im were growing more agitated, their words breaking down into hoarse screams and thin howls. He had to concentrate to hear Ushman Serahn over them.

"Yes, Rathal'pesha," Ushman Serahn replied with a self-amused expression. "It's the monastery that you came from, the one up in the mountains."

John ignored the ushman's patronizing reply. "What's happened?"

"Ushman Hann'yu only said that it was urgent and that you must be sent to him at once. He invoked the highest authority, so one imagines that it is rather important." Ushman Serahn snapped his book closed. He stepped away from the yellow arch that filled the right side of the room and waved John toward it.

John felt his stomach clench into a painful knot at the thought of touching the obvious Gray Space within the arch.

"I can't go through there," he said. "The Gray Space will tear me apart."

"Ushman Hann'yu seems to think otherwise. It's a gate after all. It will transport you on its own. All you have to do is step in. I wouldn't think that was too much for you." Ushman Serahn stepped past John and opened the door. "The choice is yours. You can cross through or you can return downstairs where the guards will place you under arrest for disobedience of your vows."

"NO. NO. NO. NO. NO. NO. NO. NO. NO. NO. NO. NO. NO. NO. NO", one of the issusha'im wailed above the noise of all the others.

"They puts him in the fire," another issusha hissed. "They puts him in the fire and he kills us all."

"As I said, it's your choice." Ushman Serahn leaned against the doorframe and opened his book once more. "I really don't have all day," he added without looking up.

John took in a deep breath. The air felt sick and weak in his lungs. It tasted of seared ozone. If Hann'yu had sent for him, it had to be important. John regarded Ushman Serahn. He didn't want to entrust the man with anything, but there was no one else.

"Will you tell Ushiri Ravishan what's happened?" John asked.

"I'll explain when I appoint a new attendant to take your place." Ushman Serahn barely glanced up at John. "It's not as if he needs anyone to carry his bags at this point anyway. He should be fine without you."

John couldn't bring himself to thank Ushman Serahn, so instead he stepped forward into the arch. Instantly, he regretted his choice.

The sensation was not pain. Pain, at least, would have assured him that he was still alive. This was an absence, a terrible numbness that felt as though it had ripped him from himself, as if the Gray Space had devoured and digested him.

This was like dying. No, it was like being dead already—as if he were wide awake in a dead body. John could sense his thoughts building toward panic.

It made him think of the desperate thrashing of a drowning man, his lungs consumed by the absence of air. It was a feeling like that. It was as if he couldn't breathe, couldn't see, couldn't hear, and couldn't move. It felt as if he had been swallowed by an utterly alien environment.

He wasn't dying, he told himself. It just felt like dying.

And he realized why. The Gray Space isolated him from the world that sustained him. No, sustained was too weak a word.

The world defined him. He felt the earth, air, water, and stones of Basawar as deeply as his own flesh. Without them he became some excised organ.

A severed limb. A terrified self-aware amputation. He was the head on the wrong side of a guillotine's blade. And he was dying. It didn't just feel like it, John realized.

He was dying. This was what killed a Rifter. This was how his death could be opened like a door. There was even a key to lock him in. He remembered that from the holy texts.

He had walked right into it.

John wanted to scream with anger and fear. He wanted to thrash and tear the enveloping Gray Space asunder. But he had nothing to grab, nothing to rip or beat against. The Gray Space was a vacuum offering no opposition and no sustenance. Its embrace was a slow suffocation.

This was how every Rifter before him had died, John thought. After poisoning and bleeding, this last slow suffocation had destroyed them. They had died like kittens in a sack, sinking to the bottom of a lake. Later the Payshmura priests dredged the space for the Rifters' bones and carved their keys to kill the next Rifter.

One Rifter after another would die, until the world of Basawar had been utterly bled to death. They would murder the whole world with these endless little amputations.

And John knew the shreds of his self-control were slipping away under waves of shock and horror.

He couldn't die now, not like this. But he had no way to fight it. He had nothing but a desperate, overwhelming refusal.

"NO!" The word tore from his throat. Bile and blood followed it up. John staggered forward and then spilled onto the cold stone floor at Hann'yu's feet. He had crossed through the Gray Space in just a matter of minutes.

Chapter Fifty-One

Outside the infirmary window, dark clouds hung at the edges of the pale sky. Only a small circle of luminous haze betrayed the presence of the winter sun.

"I'm never doing that again," John whispered hoarsely. He accepted the cup of daru'sira from Hann'yu and sipped it cautiously. His throat still felt raw. The deep, involuntary shuddering had mostly subsided. Earlier, he had been almost unable to make it down the stairs from the upper chamber of Rathal'pesha to the infirmary. John pulled the blankets closer around his shoulders. His body still felt as if his bones had turned to ice.

Hann'yu watched him in uncharacteristic silence. He looked terrible. His skin had a yellowish tone and the bags under his eyes were as black as bruises. Hann'yu seemed to have aged years in the month that John had been gone. He'd lost a great deal of weight. His once lithe, tanned arms looked desiccated and skeletal.

John sat his cup on the bedside table. "Why did you call me back? What's happened?"

"So much." Hann'yu shook his head. "I have nothing but bad news. It was like the whole world collapsed as soon as you and Ravishan left. I don't know how to tell you."

"Just tell me."

"Your brother-in-law, Behr, is dead," Hann'yu said quietly. "Rasho Tashtu murdered him. They were arguing and Tashtu shot him."

"No." The word came out like a reflex. John's chest tightened unbearably. They were only days from escaping Basawar.

"No," John repeated, feeling the terrible loss sweep through him. Distantly, he heard thunder crash through the sky. Droplets of freezing rain began to slap against the closed windows.

"I'm sorry, Jahn." Hann'yu gently pressed a kerchief into John's hand. As his fist clenched around the cloth, John realized that tears were slipping down his cheeks. He tried to wipe them away, but his hands were still clumsy and numb.

"There's more." Hann'yu's voice was strained. "Your sister was there when it happened."

Laurie, John thought suddenly, *God, what would this have done to Laurie?*

"She burned Tashtu to ash where he stood," Hann'yu said. "Half a city block went up in the fire as well. The thatch caught sparks and just…just went. Two children were killed."

John opened his mouth, but he could hardly make himself breathe, much less speak. This was like some kind of terrible nightmare. And he knew it had to get worse. He knew that Laurie's reaction wouldn't be defensible.

"They wanted to kill her right then and there," Hann'yu said, "the neighbors, you know. It was the middle of the day and they saw it all. They were going to beat her to death, but one of the rashan'im, a man named Pivan, stopped them and sent word here."

"Then she's alive?" John asked in a desperate whisper.

"I did what I could, but the city judges were hardly willing to hear me out," Hann'yu went on as if he hadn't heard John.

"Is she still alive?" John asked with more force.

"Yes, she was with child." Hann'yu looked up at John. "Did you know?"

John just nodded. Bill had been so happy. Laurie and he both had been. John wiped at his cheeks with Hann'yu's kerchief. He couldn't seem to stop crying.

"It saved her life," Hann'yu went on. "She's in Umbhra'ibaye now. We sent her through the gates. Once the child is born, she will be inducted into the issusha'im."

"No." John's body was still clumsy from the effects of the Gray Space, but he managed to pull himself to his feet. "We have to go there. Get her out—"

"There's nothing you can do for her now." Hann'yu caught John's hand. His fingers felt as cold and desiccated as dead leaves.

"I'm not going to let them flay her!" John swayed on his feet and Hann'yu's grip fell away.

"Your sister is safe for the moment," Hann'yu said with quiet urgency. "It's Ravishan that we have to worry about right now."

"What does Ravishan have to do with this?"

Hann'yu looked miserable. "You have to understand, things were such a mess. People in Amura'taye panicked and accused half the women in the city of witchcraft. It was like some kind of hysteria. After what had happened in the blood market, none of them wanted to be associated with an enemy of the priesthood. Accusations were made against everyone. No one up here knew what to do. If Dayyid had still been alive, he would have taken control of it, but…I honestly thought it might just die down on its own." Hann'yu closed his eyes and bowed his head in silence.

John sat back down on the edge of the bed. "You have to tell me what this has to do with Ravishan."

Hann'yu nodded. "It was after your sister was sent to Umbhra'ibaye. Suspicion immediately fell on other women in Lady Bousim's household. And on you as well."

"Me?" John asked.

"I told you people were coming forward with all manner of mad claims. Some old woman swore that she'd seen a blond man dancing naked with a circle of wild animals." Hann'yu rolled his eyes at the charge. "It turned out that she was blind as a stone and couldn't describe you in any detail, save the color of your hair. Most of the allegations were of similar merit. They could be dismissed almost at once. The only thing that you could really be considered guilty of was being fair-haired. But one of Lady Bousim's maids was not so lucky. They burned her on the Holy Road."

Horror rolled through John's gut at the thought.

Hann'yu took a deep drink of daru'sira. He turned the clay cup through his hands as if searching the surface to find out what his next words would be.

Behind Hann'yu, John watched the dark clouds growing and steadily enveloping the pale sun. A storm wind buffeted the highest branches of distant trees.

"It was after they burned the girl, Ohbi, that Fikiri began to act strangely. I tried to calm him, to reassure him that his mother would be safe. Not even the wealthiest merchant of Amura'taye would dare to lay an accusation against a woman of the gaun'im, certainly not without very solid proof, and his mother was blameless. But it did no good. He disappeared for days, came back torn up and fevered. He kept talking about your sister."

Hann'yu scowled down at the empty cup in his hands.

"I don't know why Fikiri did what he did. I've tried to figure it out but I can't. If he had come to me, I think I could have reasoned with him, but he went directly to Ushman Nuritam. He claimed that he had been there when Dayyid was murdered, that it hadn't been one of the Fai'daum that had killed him. He claimed that Ravishan had done it."

"Ravishan?" John couldn't believe it. This was some kind of nightmare. It didn't even make sense. What could Fikiri possibly gain by accusing Ravishan of Dayyid's murder? Then, sickeningly, an answer came to John.

"Fikiri wants to take Ravishan's place as Kahlil."

"I don't know," Hann'yu replied, but his expression made John think that he shared John's opinion. "He was so distraught. I thought he might have gone mad."

But John was sure Fikiri hadn't. With Laurie and Bill both gone, and John himself accused of witchcraft, that left no one to ensure that Ravishan would keep his promise to take Fikiri and his mother to Nayeshi. Fikiri and Ravishan had never gotten along. Without John or Laurie's pressure, Fikiri couldn't expect Ravishan to save him or his mother. He needed to take Ravishan's place as Kahlil.

"Ushman Nuritam has to know that Ravishan would never kill Dayyid," John insisted. But Hann'yu's desolate expression assured him that he was wrong.

"Ravishan does not come from a background that inspires much trust in Ushman Nuritam," Hann'yu said. "He ordered me to speak to Dayyid's wounds, to summon his spirit and find what I could."

"And?" John felt his hands clenching Hann'yu's kerchief as if he were holding onto it for his life. Knives of lightning split black clouds and thunder crashed so loudly that John had to strain to hear Hann'yu's response.

"From the wounds I realized that the blade used against him was one of our own, a curse knife. That lent a ring of truth to Fikiri's accusations. Nuritam wanted to summon Ravishan back from Nurjima immediately, but I argued that he should give me more time to find Dayyid's spirit. He agreed to a week. We asked the Usho to delay the rituals."

"We had wondered about that," John said numbly.

"I tried with all my strength to draw Dayyid's spirit back to the remains of his flesh." Hann'yu closed his eyes for a moment. "The curse blade that killed him must have consumed him utterly. I can't even imagine how much anger and power the man wielding it must have had. I couldn't rekindle a shred of Dayyid's soul from the darkness that had devoured it. It nearly killed me just trying."

"So there's no evidence against Ravishan?" John asked.

"There is Fikiri's word, the blade that was used, and where Dayyid's body was found. It was a place called Candle Alley. Dayyid had caught Ravishan there once already—a year before you arrived, I think."

That would have been why Ravishan's hair had been shorn when they first met. It was how Dayyid had known exactly where to look for Ravishan when he had gone missing at the Harvest Fair.

"If it weren't for Fikiri's accusation, it would seem suspicious but it wouldn't be enough. But as is…" Hann'yu trailed off.

"You can't be serious," John said. "You can't think Ravishan killed Dayyid."

"I…I don't know. My soul tells me that he didn't. Ravishan has always had willfulness about him but not the kind of pure malice that I felt in Dayyid's wounds. I have never in my life touched something so malevolent. It felt nothing like Ravishan." Hann'yu sighed heavily. "But I'm not the one that has to be convinced."

"So how do we convince Ushman Nuritam?"

"I don't know. I summoned you because you were with Ravishan most of the day of the murder. I thought that you might be able to account for Ravishan's whereabouts."

"He was with me until just before the Fai'daum attacked. I sent him to find you then," John said.

Hann'yu frowned. "He didn't find me until after the attack. He was in a bad state when he did. Drunk and very shaken. That won't convince Nuritam."

"If we can't convince him, then what happens to Ravishan?" John asked.

"Instead of the consecration wine he will be given poison to drink. It will be over quickly, at least." Hann'yu bowed his head.

"At the Black Tower?" John asked. "Right now?"

"Tonight," Hann'yu said. "He's too powerful to handle in any other way."

Outside the window John heard the wind screaming and he knew it was his fault. This was all his fault.

"He didn't kill Dayyid," John said slowly. "I…take me to Nuritam. I'll tell him."

"Tell him what?" Hann'yu asked.

John didn't want to confess to Hann'yu. He didn't want Hann'yu to know that the darkness, the malevolence, and hatred that had horrified him had been John's doing.

"I know Ravishan did not murder Dayyid," John said firmly.

"You were there?" Hann'yu asked.

"Yes," John replied.

"And you can swear that it wasn't Ravishan? Even after drinking fathi?" Hann'yu peered at him intensely.

John remembered the golden liqueur that Hann'yu had served to Dayyid and how even a small sip of the stuff had seemed to draw unwilling admissions from Dayyid's lips. A sick, trapped feeling crawled through him.

"Yes, I can," John answered.

Hann'yu regarded him for one long, silent moment. Outside, lightning flickered through the clouds and sheets of snow began to tumble down on the walls of Rathal'pesha.

John imagined it wouldn't let up for some time.

"You have to help my sister," he said at last.

"I'll do everything I can for her," Hann'yu replied in a whisper. He looked devastated.

"You'd better take me to Ushman Nuritam."

Hann'yu didn't move. Instead he studied John with a searching gaze as if trying to see the murderous hatred that he'd felt in Dayyid's fatal wound.

"Dayyid's body was found with his blade drawn," Hann'yu said at last.

"Yes," John replied.

"He didn't give you any choice, did he?"

"No," John replied. He knew that Hann'yu needed to know that. Otherwise he wouldn't have been able to even look John in the face.

Hann'yu leaned close, whispering, "Are you sure that you want to go before Nuritam?"

"I have to," John said. "Ravishan shouldn't suffer for something I did."

Hann'yu looked away and wiped something from his face. When he turned back to John, he forced a wan smile.

"Let's walk together then," Hann'yu offered.

They went in silence. John stared down at the stones beneath his feet. He couldn't stand to think any farther than that. He could hear thunder crashing far above in the heights of the clouds as the sudden storm worsened.

"I wish..." Hann'yu began and then he trailed off. There was nothing either of them could say.

They reached the chamber where Ushman Nuritam held audiences. John came to a halt at the foot of the raised stone dais, where the old man sat. He knelt in the same place he'd knelt before when Dayyid had tested him by laying two black-bladed knives down in front of him. John had chosen the knife he had later used to kill Dayyid. He wondered if it would have been any different if he had chosen the other blade.

A white arc of lightning illuminated the chamber, making the shadows of the columns jerk and twist as if they were shattering. The stones beneath John felt like blocks of ice.

Hann'yu approached Ushman Nuritam. The two of them spoke in soft whispers. Unlike Hann'yu, Nuritam looked exactly the same as John remembered: long white braids, skin so aged that it verged on translucence. Behind Ushman Nuritam the huge statue of Parfir arched up. His raised hands extended to the ceiling. John extended his awareness out to feel the weight and strength of the stones beneath Parfir's fingers. If he tried, John wondered, could he tear it all down?

If he did, what good would it do? John dropped his gaze. Ravishan would still be killed. And Laurie…John couldn't even think about that right now. He had to take consolation in what Hann'yu had said. Until her baby was born, she was safe.

Nuritam's dark eyes shifted from Hann'yu to John. His colorless mouth curved down into a deep frown.

"Do you know what you are claiming to have done, Ushvun?" Ushman Nuritam asked.

"I do."

"You will swear to it with fathi in your blood?"

"I will," John said.

Nuritam nodded to Hann'yu. John watched as Hann'yu walked back behind Ushman Nuritam to the small altar at Parfir's feet. He poured a golden, honey-like fluid from a dark glass bottle into a small white cup. Then, moving almost furtively, he selected a second bottle. He poured a clear liquid from it into his own flask and then slipped that into the pocket of his coat. John frowned but said nothing. He supposed Hann'yu had the right to sneak some holy narcotic after all he had been through.

Hann'yu turned back and carried the white cup of fathi back to Ushman Nuritam. To John's surprise, Nuritam took a sip from the cup. He closed his eyes for a moment and then nodded to Hann'yu. When Ushman Nuritam opened his eyes, his expression softened slightly. John remembered seeing Ushman Nuritam looking distant and unconcerned often. He guessed the fathi must be the source of the ushman's tranquility.

Hann'yu brought the cup of fathi down to John.

"You must drink it all," Hann'yu whispered to him.

"Is it going to make me sick?"

"No." Hann'yu placed the cup in John's hand. "It's quite pleasant, actually. You will feel relaxed and perfectly at ease. Don't fight it and you'll be fine."

John took the fathi like a shot. Apart from a slight sweetness, it had little flavor. Some of the thick fluid still clung to the sides of the cup. John guessed he'd only drunk about half the contents. Hann'yu took it back anyway.

John waited to feel some change. There was nothing. He gazed out the delicate mica panes of the windows. The storm outside churned and twisted. Then, from the north, a little beam of sun shot through the clouds. The shaft of light fell across John. Its warmth felt relieving after so much cold.

Suddenly John wondered if the fathi might not affect him. He was the Rifter, after all. He glanced to Hann'yu. He ought to have told him that.

"Hann'yu, I should tell you—" John just barely caught himself. What was he saying?

"Yes?" Hann'yu asked.

"I gave the book you bought me away," John substituted quickly. "Alidas loved the poems so much that I let him keep it."

"Don't worry about that now, Jahn," Hann'yu spoke gently to him, as if he were talking to a child. "You just need to answer Ushman Nuritam's questions."

"I really don't want to. I think I might get into trouble," John admitted.

"I know," Hann'yu replied. "But don't worry. Whatever you say will be the truth. There can be nothing wrong with telling the truth."

Hann'yu's words were so soothing, so reassuring. John smiled. Sunlight poured in through the windows. John turned his face into the light. Dark storm clouds hung back at the edges of the clearing sky, black and sorrowful. A shudder passed through him.

Suddenly he remembered that Bill was dead and Laurie was imprisoned. Ravishan was going to be killed. Those black clouds were the remains of that knowledge. They lingered, reminding him that this warmth and happiness was only an effect of the fathi. John forced himself to keep smiling.

He grinned up at Ushman Nuritam while fighting to keep his thoughts clear.

"You say you were there when Dayyid was killed?" Ushman

Nuritam asked the question gently. He smiled slightly at John and John felt as if it were an expression of genuine affection. Like a child, John found himself flushed with pleasure at the thought.

"Yes, I was there." John hardly recognized the chirpy tone of his own words.

"Who killed Dayyid?" Ushman Nuritam asked.

"I did." John beamed.

Hann'yu flinched, as if deeply pained, and John felt an ache of sympathy for all that Hann'yu had endured these past weeks.

"I'm sorry that it makes you sad," John said to Hann'yu. "I didn't want that."

"I know, Jahn." Hann'yu offered him another of his strained smiles.

"Why were you both in Candle Alley?" Ushman Nuritam reasserted himself.

"We were both looking for Ravishan." John had to choose his words carefully so as not to give too much away.

"And why did you kill Dayyid?"

"I thought he was going to kill Ravishan." John knew that if he left the response at that, then Ushman Nuritam would ask why he thought Dayyid would kill Ravishan. That could lead to a confession John did not want to make, so John continued on, "It was inevitable that one of us would kill the other. What it was over didn't really matter. He hated me and I hated him. If it hadn't happened at the Harvest Fair, it would have happened in the golden chamber."

"So you murdered him?" Ushman Nuritam asked.

"Yes." John was astonished at how easy it was to say. Why had he been so worried about it? John sighed. The sun felt so good, pouring in through the golden panes of the windows. Life should always feel like this.

"Ushvun Jahn?" Ushman Nuritam asked.

"Yes?" John yawned.

"Can you answer a few more questions?"

"Of course." A sloppy, wide grin spread across his face in response to Ushman Nuritam's fatherly regard of him.

"Why do you think Fikiri would accuse Ravishan of the crime?"

"Because he wants to take Ravishan's place as Kahlil and escape from Basawar." John shrugged. He had thought that would be obvious.

"Of course." Ushman Nuritam appeared very pleased with the answer. He leaned forward, observing John intently. "And do you know whether your sister practiced witchcraft?"

John snorted at the idea of his sister practicing witchcraft. His sister wouldn't let her daughter watch Sesame Street because it was full of the devil's work.

"Is that a yes or a no?" Ushman Nuritam asked.

"It's a stupid question," John replied. "My sister would never practice witchcraft. Never."

"I see." Ushman Nuritam nodded.

"Lady Bousim is the one you ought to be asking about."

A few feet away, John saw Hann'yu go pale. Then the horror of his own words struck John. What had he just done? How could he have said that?

"I see," Ushman Nuritam said again.

"No," John said quickly, "I didn't mean to say that."

"It's all right, Ushvun Jahn," Ushman Nuritam told him kindly. "You are only speaking the truth. There can be nothing wrong in speaking the truth."

John felt sick with himself, but Ushman Nuritam's words still soothed him. A moment later he couldn't remember what it was that had disturbed him.

Ushman Nuritam looked to Hann'yu. "I believe that is all that I needed to know. I will send word to the Usho. Have Ushvun Jahn prepared for the Holy Road."

"You're not going to let them kill Ravishan?" John demanded.

"No," Ushman Nuritam replied. "It seems that Ushiri Ravishan was quite surprisingly blameless."

"He was. He did nothing wrong," John said. Ravishan was safe. He could relax. Hann'yu walked to John and motioned him to his feet. John started to stand, but his legs buckled. He stumbled and barely caught himself, staring at the floor in confusion. He couldn't remember ever losing his balance before.

"Hann'yu," Ushman Nuritam added, "while you are in Amura'taye, see that the city guards call on the Bousim household."

"I will," Hann'yu replied. He moved close to steady John.

"Is it going to be all right now?" John asked. He swayed. The full heat of the afternoon sun seemed to disorient him. But it was so warm, so soothing. Caught in its blaze, John could hardly think at all.

"Yes, everything is going to be fine," Hann'yu said, but he looked like he was going to be sick.

John tried to give him a reassuring smile, but then his legs crumpled beneath him and he dropped to the floor. A dull pain washed through John's head and hip as he hit the stones. But then he forgot it. He grinned up at Hann'yu's worried face. He didn't know why he was lying on the floor. The sun felt good on his face. He laughed for several minutes before passing out.

Chapter Fifty-Two

For the first time in years John dreamed of Nayeshi.

In the dream, he sat at the kitchen table in his old apartment, listening to Bill surfing through television channels in the living room. Briefly, the theme song of some cartoon played, only to be cut off by a burst of static and then the cheap flat sound effects of some poorly dubbed kung fu movie. Bill laughed.

"Hey, Toffee," Bill called. "You gotta come see this."

"Just a minute." John picked up a letter and turned it over in his hands.

"You're gonna miss it," Bill shouted.

"I'll be right there." The letter was terribly familiar. John slid his thumb under the flap of the sealed edge. He started to tear it open but then stopped. Bill had turned up the volume of the television. The sounds of fists slamming into muscle were oddly authentic now.

"You're missing it," Bill yelled over the loud crash of splintering wood.

"Just a second," John said.

"No." Bill's voice had taken on a strained tone. "You have to come now."

John sighed, began to open his mouth to reply, and then there was an explosive boom. Instantly everything went silent. John bolted up from the table and ran to the living room. The television was shattered. Stuffing and pieces of fabric from the couch littered the floor. In the very center of the room there was a small pool of blood.

"Bill," John called.

There was no reply.

"Bill!" John shouted. "BILL!"

John woke up, sobbing on a dirt floor. The shackles locked around his wrists and ankles were cold. The heavy chains only allowed him to move a few feet. He curled his body in over his naked groin. His stomach rolled and his head was pounding as if he had spent the entire night drinking grain alcohol.

The smell of urine and sour sweat hung all around him. Even without light John could sense the cramped confines of the granite walls surrounding him. The dirt beneath him was the overworked soil of Amura'taye. He was in a prison somewhere in the city. Distantly, John thought he heard a scream. It was a woman's voice. John suddenly remembered Lady Bousim.

What had he done to her?

John pressed his eyes closed. Waves of sickness welled through him. He lay still, waiting for it to pass. Outside the door of his cell, he heard the steps of guards as they passed down a corridor. Briefly he caught a smell like that of roasting meat. From some cell far away there came more screams. Sharp wrenching cries tore through the air again and again until they broke into raw gasps.

John curled his arms over his head, pressing his hands over his ears. He needed to get out of this place. But he was still too sick to even stand. Instead he slipped from nauseous, pounding consciousness into dark, fevered dreams. He bolted awake an hour later, shrieks still ringing through his mind.

Faint yellow light seeped in from the edges of the cell door. The darkness of the cell had given way to soft gray shadows. The sun would be up soon. John knew he couldn't afford to waste more time. He had to find a way out.

He pulled himself up to his knees and ran his hand along the wall. All around him the solid crystalline structures of stone interlaced like twining fingers. Fissures of mortar spread between them. John concentrated, pushing his hand up against the wall. He needed it to break. He shoved his arm against the rough surface of the stone until it began to bite into his palm. His muscles strained as he pushed against countless tons of masonry.

"Break," John growled as anger and desperation burned through him. "Break, damn you!"

He felt the mortar crumbling under his fingers. Then, suddenly, the stone split. A violent crack shot out from John's hand. Splinters of stone exploded out of the rupture. A shard of rock tore into John's palm. He jerked his hand back.

Pain flared through John. He swore under his breath and the stone wall groaned. Cracks surged across its surface. Tiny seams split and spread out across the dirt floor, rushing toward John. Above him fine cracks raced over the ceiling. Dust and splinters of stone poured down on him. He coughed and tried to move back, but the destruction followed him. He came up short at the ends of his chains.

He was about to bring the entire prison down directly on top of himself. He had to stop it. He had to calm down.

John closed his eyes and took in a deep breath. He released the air from his lungs, feeling his pulse calm as he did. The cracks in the wall slowed their spread. John took another deep breath, concentrating on his even breathing and the steady rhythm of his heartbeat. Desperation drained from him and the erosion of the floor, wall, and ceiling stopped.

For a few minutes John simply sat there covered in dirt and dust, too shaken to move. He looked up at the huge, splintered stones above his head. If he hadn't been able to control himself, he could have been crushed.

He'd had no idea that it would be so difficult to stop. He had to be careful. But he couldn't afford to give up altogether. His memory was not clear, but he did recall Ushman Nuritam saying that he should be prepared for the Holy Road.

John caught hold of the chain that restrained his left arm. The links were forged from red iron, not black. The red metal oxidized much more quickly. Patches of rust already covered many of the links of the chain. When he closed his eyes and concentrated, John could feel the rust burning into the red iron like a slow fire.

John held his right hand over one of the most degraded links. Very carefully, he focused his will on the soft orange circles of corrosion. For several moments nothing happened. John held his breath, concentrating intensely. Nothing. He could feel the air going stale in his lungs. The slight discomfort of it spread through his chest.

Then John felt a spark. Not in the iron but in himself.

A surge of heat burst through his chest. His lungs expanded, drinking in desperation in place of oxygen. The searing sensation rushed through his bloodstream. His muscles tensed; his heart began hammering out a new, strange rhythm. The feeling was so overwhelming, so forceful, that John could have mistaken it for rage. But he knew he wasn't angry.

There was purity to the sensation that went beyond anger. It surged through John with a wild power and drive. It awoke every cell in his body with a raw will to live. He felt as if something deep and dormant within him had suddenly come awake. And it could do what he could not. As the full sensation of it rushed through him, he could almost hear it whispering from within him.

It would shatter stone, burn iron, ignite the air, and sear the oceans into smoke. It would devour mountains, split the earth, and tear the atmosphere to pieces. It would destroy worlds just to keep living. To survive, it would do anything. Destroy everything.

John heard the walls of his cell groan. The air felt like ice flowing over his hot flesh. He tasted frost and smelled traces of sweat and soot from the torches. Power churned through him, aching to be released in a riot of destruction.

John concentrated intensely. He didn't need to split the earth. He didn't need to tear down mountains or ignite the atmosphere. He just needed to break a single link of chain. The power within him hungered to do so much more. The scents on the air, the texture of the earth beneath him, they would each be so easy to rip apart in a riot of flame and force.

He glared at the chain in front of him. He focused his will on a single link of iron. It was all that he saw. A single circle of dull red metal, flecked with tiny orange and yellow flames of rust. John pushed at those fires, willing them to grow.

Instantly they spread over the iron link. The metal blackened and cracked. Smoke poured off it as the rust burned through. It was consumed in an instant and the burning continued. Link after link of the chain seared to vapor as John fought to regain control of the force surging through him. Charred, smoking hunks of iron cracked and dropped to the cell floor.

Again, John retreated into his own strong pulse and even breath until he felt the power within him recede. At last it slipped back into its slumber.

Red burns streaked out from the edges of the smoking shackle on John's left wrist. All that remained of the chain were piles of ash on the floor and a strong corrosive smell in the air. John's body was damp with sweat from the exertion of controlling the power within him.

That had been the Rifter, John realized. It was part of himself but nearly as involuntary as his heartbeat. It was an unthinking reflex for survival and destruction. Like an insanely over-armed immune system, it could as easily harm John as save him. And he could barely control it.

He sank back down to the floor of the cell. His right arm and both his legs were still chained to the wall. He didn't know if he could go through all of that three more times. But he had to get out of here.

John looked up at the cracks in the ceiling. If he called on his power as the Rifter again and he couldn't stop the destruction, would it kill him? If a piece of stone came loose above him, could he pulverize it as he had the cart in the blood market?

What about the other prisoners in their cells?

No, protecting them was out of the question. He didn't even know where they were. So how many of them would he be willing to kill to save himself? He knew the answer that the Rifter would have given: every one of them could die. Every living creature in Amura'taye could be sacrificed if it meant even a moment more life for himself.

"My id obviously has a scorched earth policy," he murmured to himself. It was something Bill might have said. The thought made John suddenly miserable. He pressed his face into his knees.

To escape he would have to kill at least some of the people in this prison. He knew it. He wasn't strong enough to make any other choice.

Outside, guards strode past the door of his cell. He heard the slap of their boots against the packed dirt floor. Then, without warning, there were noises from beyond his door. John pushed himself back into a corner, hoping the shadows would obscure his missing chain. The heavy stone door swung open. Two city guards stood in the bright hall outside. Between them, looking tired and holding a small tray of food, was Samsango.

"You have until the next bell," one of the guards told Samsango. He barely glanced at John. The other guard spat on the floor of the cell but said nothing.

"Thank you." Samsango entered the cell and the guards pulled the door closed again. John heard them sliding the heavy bolt back into place and securing the lock beneath it. Samsango said, "Jahn? Are you awake?"

John watched Samsango feeling his way along the wall.

"I'm here." He pulled himself to his feet.

Samsango slowly knelt down with his tray. His knees creaked and popped. "I brought a lamp."

A moment later Samsango had lit the simple little lamp. Its perfumed oil gave off a faint aroma of flowers. The old ushvun smiled as he caught sight of John and then his expression turned slowly sad. "Did they beat you?"

"No, I don't think so." Now that the room was illuminated John could see the deep black bruises marring the pale skin of his naked hip. "I fell. It looks worse than it feels. I hadn't even noticed it."

"I brought you food." Samsango beckoned him closer. "Sit down and eat with me."

"The chains don't reach that far," John said. He frowned at Samsango. "Does the prior know that you're here?"

"No, only Ushman Hann'yu knows and he will tell no one."

"If the prior notices that you're missing—"

"It's too late to worry about that now." Samsango moved closer with the tray.

"But if he takes your braids…" John couldn't imagine Samsango enduring a year of ostracizing and punishment. It would kill him.

"We don't have much time, Jahn. Certainly not enough to waste it arguing over what's already done." Samsango unwrapped a loaf of bread. He tore off a piece and held it out to John. "I'm already here so you might as well come and eat with me."

John sat down beside Samsango and took the bread. He ate a little, but he didn't have much of an appetite. Samsango didn't seem hungry either. He hardly ate more than a bite.

"You should get back to Rathal'pesha," John said softly.

Samsango shook his head. The lamplight glistened across the tracks of tears slipping along the deep wrinkles below Samsango's eyes.

"They're going to burn you on the Holy Road, Jahn," Samsango only whispered the words. "The rest of the ushvun'im think that you're staying in Nurjima. But Ushman Hann'yu told me."

"Did he tell you what I did?" John asked.

Samsango nodded. He wiped his eyes with the worn sleeve of his robe.

"There's daru'sira." Samsango picked up a clay bottle and handed it to John. "You should drink it before it gets bitter."

John accepted the bottle and drank from it. It tasted different from the daru'sira he had grown used to. This was more earthy, faintly chocolate tasting. He hadn't realized how thirsty he was until now. He took another deep drink and then passed the bottle back to Samsango. Samsango drank a little.

"Ushman Dayyid was never fair to you," Samsango said quietly.

"It doesn't matter now." John accepted the clay bottle from Samsango. He was past worrying about Dayyid.

Dayyid was dead. That made him the least of John's problems.

John leaned back against the wall and drank more of the tea. It left an almost numbing tingle on his tongue and throat. John closed his eyes. Now that he wasn't trying to crack apart the walls or break his chains he could feel how deeply tired he was.

"This tastes good. What is it?" John held up the bottle. He had nearly finished it all.

"Tumah'itam," Samsango replied softly. "Ushman Hann'yu gave it to me to bring to you. He did not want you to suffer."

"He didn't want me to suffer?" John's eyes popped open. "What's that supposed to mean?"

"Tumah'itam brings the blessing of a painless death." Samsango's voice was quiet as if he, too, were on the verge of falling asleep. "Normally only the ushiri'im and ushman'im are allowed its respite. But Ushman Hann'yu did not want you to suffer. He brought it to me last night and told me everything."

"It's poison?" John asked.

"Yes, but painless," Samsango replied.

"But you drank it as well."

"The guards wouldn't have allowed me in if I hadn't tasted and drank a little of what I had brought. They're young men and can't imagine anyone freely drinking poison." Samsango smiled almost slyly at John. "I've seen so many worse deaths, Jahn. Old men grow weak and sick, becoming burdens to everyone. I never wanted to be one of those."

"You didn't—"

"Jahn." Samsango placed his hand on John's arm. "I have already made my choice. And it is done. There's nothing left for you to argue against."

"But I don't want this…" John glared at the clay bottle in his hands. "I'm not ready to die."

"Ushman Dayyid did not want his death either. But all our actions have consequences. The quality of our souls lies in how we face those consequences." Samsango bowed his bald head. "You do not deserve to suffer. You should not have to burn. But you murdered a man, Jahn, and you must pay for that."

John's throat felt almost too tight for him to speak. "How can you tell me about the consequences of murder, when you've just poisoned me?"

Samsango glanced up at him. He looked a little startled by John's angry expression.

"I've already accepted the price for my actions. I did not come to you to harm you, Jahn. I came to save you from pain. It was never my wish to hurt you."

"No," John said. He wanted to be furious. But the strength simply wasn't there. The tumah'itam, like fathi, seemed to soothe his emotions. John didn't feel the radiant happiness that he had experienced with the fathi. He simply felt calm and strangely reasonable.

John gazed at Samsango. The old man had always been good to him, always cared for him. Samsango had no way of knowing that John had a chance at escape. Neither he nor Hann'yu would have ever guessed at what John could do. And it wasn't just that they couldn't have known that he was the Rifter. They didn't know what kind of man he was.

If their positions had been reversed, John knew Samsango would never have considered the sacrifice of dozens of other prisoners for his own sake. And John doubted his own courage would be great enough to swallow poison just to ensure that his friend did not suffer.

"You shouldn't have done it," John said. "I'm not the kind of man who deserves a sacrifice like this. I've done things—"

"I know." Samsango's voice was hardly a whisper now. "We have all done things, Jahn. I have made terrible mistakes. When I was young…you would not believe me. But our mistakes are not all that we are. To me, you have been a great kindness. I have been my happiest when I was with you. I tasted apples from Umbhra'ibaye. I sat among the most divine ushiri'im and spoke with them. You have brought me so much more than I…"

John waited for him to finish his sentence, but the end never came. Still smiling, Samsango slumped to the floor. John dropped the clay jar and pulled Samsango up into his arms.

"Don't," John whispered. "Please don't."

Samsango's skin was warm. He felt alive, but John couldn't find a pulse. Samsango's body began to grow cool in his arms. John's own breathing felt labored. He felt suddenly weak. Then a terrible sensation of absolute relaxation washed through him. His arms and legs crumpled. He slumped, half across Samsango's body, half on the dirt floor.

Briefly, his vision faded but then slowly it cleared. He gazed down at himself, his naked body sprawling over Samsango's frail form. Shattered pieces of the clay bottle spread out from beside them. He was filthy and bruised. Samsango looked almost as small as a child beneath him.

John desperately willed himself to rise, even if just to push himself off Samsango. But his flesh did not respond.

The city bell rang in the new hour. The guards would return soon. John didn't know what they would do when they discovered his and Samsango's bodies.

Get up, he thought desperately at his inert body. A slight tremor moved through his right hand but nothing more.

From above, John watched as the cell door swung open. Two guards came in. They were the same guards who had shown Samsango in earlier. The taller of the two carried a torch. The light cast a sick yellow hue over the dirty walls of the cell. John's bruised, pale skin looked jaundiced. Samsango's flesh looked like it had been sculpted from butter.

"Damn it!" The shorter guard crouched down beside John's and Samsango's bodies. He shoved John's body roughly off Samsango and felt for the old priest's pulse.

"Dead as a stone," the guard announced in disgust.

The taller guard cursed under his breath and quickly closed the cell door. "What about the other one?"

The shorter guard stepped over Samsango and hunched down next to John's body. He groped and prodded at John's throat. Despite the roughness of the man's touch, John felt nothing.

"He's warm. I think I can feel his heart, but it's weak."

"The bastard." The taller guard strode to John's body and kicked him hard. An involuntary groan escaped from his lips.

"He's not dead yet," the taller guard said with an angry smile.

"We'll be whipped through the street if the commander finds out we let the old priest in." The shorter guard glanced back to where Samsango lay. "What do we do?"

The taller guard kicked John again. This time John remained silent. The guard scowled.

"We can't just leave him here," the shorter guard said. The taller guard studied Samsango's body. "Any marks on him?"

"None that I could see." The shorter guard scowled at the clay shards on the floor. "I think they drank poison."

"Cowards," the taller guard said. "You take the old man. Throw him out into the street. It's cold enough for him to have frozen. Dump him near Candle Alley."

"What about the yellow bastard?" The shorter guard eyed John's body.

"I'll get him cracked and trussed for the Holy Road. The boys will just think he's another fainter." He prodded John's limp arm with the toe of his filthy boot.

"Right then." The shorter guard opened his heavy coat and unlaced a short tool from his belt. As he handed it to the taller guard, John realized it was some kind of hammer. There were blessings carved into the wooden handle.

"Good luck with those big bones of his."

"I'll do well enough." The taller guard shrugged. "Make sure no one sees you with the old priest."

"He'll be out in no time. Parfir forgive me." The shorter guard easily hefted Samsango's frail corpse over his shoulder. He opened the cell door a crack and then slipped out into the hall. The taller guard gave John's body an appraising look. He turned the hammer experimentally in his hands.

"Just speak up if I'm a little too rough." The guard smirked at John's sprawled body. Then he slammed the hammer down across John's shin. The skin went instantly red. With a second blow the flesh began to swell. The skin tore and bled. A third brutal blow cracked John's tibia. A shudder of pain moved through him and a gasp escaped his body.

"Still got a little life, don't you?" The taller guard grabbed John's left leg and jerked it straight. It took him four hard blows with the heavy hammer to break John's left shin. After that he brought the hammer down across John's hands, crushing his fingers.

When he was done, the guard was breathing heavily and sweating. He leaned back against the cell wall and wiped the blood from the head of the hammer on a corner of his stained coat. The cell door opened and the shorter guard came in. His nose and cheeks were pink from the cold. He carried a leather bag.

"All taken care of." He grinned at the taller guard. "How're things here?"

"Not bad. He's a lot less trouble than the bitch before him." The taller guard wiped the sweat from his face.

The shorter guard dropped the bag to the cell floor and opened it up. The strong smell of veru oil rolled off of the contents.

"Has the commander gotten in yet?" asked the taller guard.

"Just." The shorter guard lifted yellowed rolls of oil-soaked cloth from the bag. "Let's get him trussed, shall we?"

The taller guard took two of the rolls and began wrapping them around John's chest. He folded John's broken hands into fists and bound them to his torso with the oil-soaked cloth. Red pools of blood seeped up from John's hands. Droplets of oil glistened across the surface, giving his blood the iridescent sheen of gasoline. The smell of veru oil was overwhelming. Tremors passed through John's body but he couldn't offer any other resistance. He simply watched as the two men bound him from head to foot in the long strips of cloth. Then they left him lying on the cell floor.

Soon the door opened again and a group of teenage boys came in. They wore heavy leather aprons, which were streaked black from veru oil. Cursing his size, they hauled John's body out of the prison.

Outside, the air was frigid and still. Pale clouds filled the morning sky. Drifts of dirty snow lined the walls of the prison courtyard. But the middle of the grounds had melted into an icy wallow from the constant passage of wagons and tahldi.

The boys dragged John across the open grounds to a cart loaded with other bound men and women. They hurled John onto the pile. The people directly beneath John struggled as his dead weight crushed onto them. Next to him a woman was crying while another moaned and screamed. The sharp smell of urine mixed with the scents of blood and oil. There were sobs and muffled pleas from all around him.

Neither the boys nor the surrounding city guards seemed to take any note of the desperate whimpers and cries. They hitched a pair of tahldi to the cart. Two guards took the seat at the front of the cart. The boys piled into a second cart, talking quietly among themselves. Then they started out for the Holy Road.

As they traveled through the streets of Amura'taye, physical sensation crept back into John's consciousness. At first he only felt slight throbs of pain as the movement of the cart jarred his broken limbs. Then it grew more intense. The smell and taste of veru oil began to burn in his throat. The muscles of his thighs convulsed and jerked as the belated rush of shock washed through them. As the pain built into agony, John sensed his composure eroding.

The tumah'itam was wearing off. He should have known it would. It took more than poison to kill the Rifter. He had read as much in the holy texts. Nothing but suffocation in the Gray Space could kill him. He didn't even know if burning would destroy the Rifter. He was sure that it would awaken his fury first.

Already a hard, cold wind twisted and rushed over the cart. The clouds overhead darkened and churned. The cart jostled over the uneven cobbles of the Holy Road and a gasp of rending pain tore through John. Above him lightning writhed across the sky. The guards fought to control the tahldi as they jumped and reared nervously.

John heard the guards swearing. He couldn't see them anymore. The pain and shock coursing through him seemed to restrict his extended awareness. It pulled him back into his bound and blindfolded body. He hurt unbelievably, unbearably. All around him the choking stench of veru oil closed in. The cart came to a stop. John felt hands roughly grab him and jerk him off the other bodies on the cart. He hit the cobbled road hard. The impact sent agony stabbing through his legs and hands. He howled in pain, and above him, thunder exploded through the air.

"Witches," a boy hissed.

"The quicker they're burned, the better we'll all be," one of the guards replied. John heard the heavy clanking of chains and metal gears. Then he felt the chains being wrapped around his body. A pulley creaked and groaned as John was hoisted up onto one of the iron torch poles. He remembered the first time he had seen someone burn. It had been here. He remembered the way the bodies had thrashed as the flames rushed over the oil-soaked bindings.

He was shaking, not just in pain, but with terror. All it would take was a single flicker of a spark and he would burn.

He'd take them all with him, he thought. He'd tear the entire city to pieces, exactly as the issusha'im had prophesied.

They puts him in the fire and he kills us. He kills us all.

And John knew he would.

He heard the moans and pleas as other men and women were shackled to the torch poles. Lightning splintered and cracked through the sky, burning white tracers into John's eyes even through the swathes of cloth. Thunder sounded like an impact, sending a shudder though the ground. The guards swore and John heard one young boy whispering Parfir's name.

Not far from him a woman began shrieking wildly. Moments later, John smelled burning veru oil and flesh. He felt a rush of heat and rage surge through his body. The sky jerked and convulsed with tongues of lightning. Thunder sounded like cannons. The guards cursed and prayed, but they did not stop their work.

Hysterical, desperate screams pierced the bursts of thunder. John could feel the fires growing around him. He could taste walls of black smoke rising through the air. Power and fear churned through him. The ground shuddered. Stones beneath him cracked. Farther down, he felt miles of earth and stone tremble. Molten seams pushed up at the opening fissures.

He kills us all.

The horror of it came to John suddenly. The issusha'im had seen him destroy everything. Not just this length of the Holy Road. Not just Amura'taye, but everything from Rathal'pesha to Umbhra'ibaye. Ravishan, Laurie, Hann'yu, they would all die.

He couldn't let himself do that.

John fought to hold back the raw force of the Rifter. It tore through him like a molten brand—as if he were burning from the inside out. The more John hurt, the more desperate he was, the stronger the Rifter's force grew. He wished that he were strong enough, brave enough to face his death as Samsango had.

Above him, the wind howled as if it were being murdered. John could feel steam rising off his own hot flesh. He clenched his jaws and tried to think of prayers. Flames and torrents of searing ash filled his thoughts.

Then he felt a whisper that chilled him to his bones. The Gray Space tore. A guard made a startled noise and then was suddenly silent. John heard a boy give up a wet, choking gasp. Then John felt himself being lowered to the broken ground. His chains fell away. His bindings were cut loose with a gentle urgency.

Veru oil burned John's eyes as he opened them.

Ravishan's face was ashen, his dark eyes wide and desperate. Other men's blood flecked his cheeks and hands. He shoved the oil-soaked bindings aside and pulled John to him.

"Jahn." Ravishan's voice was low and rough. His hands bit into John's bare back as he held him.

"It's all right," John whispered. And suddenly the burning rage, his inhuman fury and unrestrained power dissipated. John sagged against Ravishan. All around them the bloody bodies of boys and guards lay sprawled across the snow and stones. Black smoke poured off the smoldering bodies hanging from the torch poles. John hung against Ravishan as if he were grasping the only salvation he had ever known.

Arc Six: The Haunted North

THE STORY SO FAR:

Unbeknownst to John, his roommate, Kahlil, follows him through the shattered gates in order to stop him from unleashing an apocalypse on his home. The passage back to Basawar leaves Kahlil badly injured and deeply changed. When he arrives he no longer possesses the Prayerscars that marked him as Kahlil, nor does he bear the ugly red scar that once disfigured his face. But most jarringly, his memories of his world's history and his own past are now all wrong. The Payshmura church had been utterly destroyed and the Fai'daum revolutionaries now rule most of the northlands.

Fortunately, Kahlil is taken in by Alidas, a captain of the Bousim rashan'im in the vibrant city of Nurjima. There, Kahlil spends two years as Alidas' secret weapon—an assassin who can walk through walls and kill with just a touch of his hand. Though Kahlil is plagued by uneasy memories, he takes comfort in his work and the certainty of his future.

But a final assignment from Alidas changes everything. Kahlil is deployed to stop an assassination against the leader of the Fai'daum—a powerful sorcerer called Jath'ibaye. While posing as a messenger in the house of the ambitious and seductive Ourath Lisam, Kahlil not only discovers that several of the ruling class of gaun'im are involved in a larger more deadly plot but that they are conspiring against a man Kahlil remembers from his shattered past—John.

Kahlil thwarts the assassination but in the chaos two noblemen are killed and Kahlil suffers of a mortal wound. Expecting to die, he instead finds himself rescued by Jath'ibaye and sailing with him into the northlands.

Chapter Fifty-Three

Kahlil watched the dark waters of the vast Samsira River twist and break beneath the bow of Jath'ibaye's sleek clipper. Normally the river flowed from the north to the south and its current should have carried the ship back toward Nurjima, not away. Yet the waters directly beneath them surged in the opposite direction. Confused fish darted between the two currents.

Overhead the single mast stood bare. Kahlil doubted that the wind rushing over the river would have aided any sailing ship. He felt it twisting and spiraling as it brushed through his loose dark hair. If the sail had been up the wind would have spun the boat like a toy top. All along the shore, fishermen glanced up from their nets and then stared as the ship raced past them. Some held up their hands as if receiving blessings.

Three days before, when they had sailed past the city of Shaye'hahlir, the fishermen and sailors had averted their eyes or placed their palms against their mouths to ward off curses. Now, in the north, groups of children and women rushed to the river's edge and sprinkled themselves with water. Some even knelt in supplication as Jath'ibaye's clipper swept by.

Both the people of the north and the south seemed to recognize the extraordinary nature of Jath'ibaye's mere presence. But whether he was a harbinger of destruction or a force of salvation seemed to be a matter of geography.

Either way, they were right to recognize his power, though the form it took surprised even Kahlil.

He studied the swirling eddies foaming up in the wake of the clipper and pondered the subtle control required to reverse a single current of this huge river. He wouldn't have thought the Rifter capable of something so precise. The holy books had only spoken of him burning seas to vapor, rending open mountains, and destroying kingdoms. The Rifter's power was always synonymous with divine judgment and destruction. Yet here Jath'ibaye was proving himself capable of so much more.

Kahlil brushed a fine spray of river water from his cheeks. Honestly, he didn't know what to make of the man John had become during his time in Basawar. He looked so similar that, at a glance, Kahlil could imagine him to be the same young ecology student he'd roomed with. Yet hearing him speak in flawless Basawar and seeing him command his people, Kahlil suspected that much had changed since John had become Jath'ibaye'in'Vundomu.

Though, he could only guess just how much the man had altered over the years because so far he'd seen surprisingly little of Jath'ibaye. And considering the ship's small size, Kahlil found that a little suspicious. Only a dozen ship hands manned the clipper, and yet Jath'ibaye always managed to disappear among them. Kahlil tried not to feel slighted. Jath'ibaye had reason to be annoyed with him.

He knew all too well what part Kahlil had played in the collapse of relations between the Fai'daum and the gaun'im lords. Though Kahlil himself had only discovered the extent of the trouble last night.

He'd woken from restless dreams to the sounds of odd, tinny voices in the adjacent cabin. After listening for a little while, he had recognized the buzz of witches' stones as they transmitted their creators' messages in tones reminiscent of old radio dramas. Words had skipped and fizzed, cutting out for instants, but the stones had steadily relayed reports from Jath'ibaye's agents.

Looters had assaulted the glass palace, forcing the evacuation of all Fai'daum from Nurjima. Kahlil's stomach had twisted when he'd caught the names of gaunsho'im and the numbers of armed men they commanded. Armies were mustering. With Nanvess' death, the Bousim house was in an uproar. Already warships mobilized for the journey to Vundomu.

Kahlil gazed back down at the spinning, swirling fish and felt something of their haplessness.

Just two days after being well enough to rise from his bunk, he'd already grown restless. He had been trained for conflict, for stealth and battle. Even when he had worked as a runner in the

Lisam household, there had been a greater purpose for him. Now he had nothing. No orders, no duty, no mission. He was utterly free of responsibility and it did not suit him.

Kahlil didn't hear anyone approach. He only noticed the shadow that fell across him. He turned back from his study of the water and distant shore. Jath'ibaye stood only a few feet behind him. His hair had been tied back from his face, but a wild curl already worked free. His rust-colored coat hung open and the shirt beneath appeared unusually crisp and white. He almost seemed dressed up.

Or maybe he just looked healthy. The effect of Fikiri's poison was clearly fading. Over the last few days Jath'ibaye's pallid complexion had returned to its natural golden tan. The deep shadows beneath his eyes had lifted. The wounds around Jath'ibaye's throat had healed to a few faint pink marks. Kahlil doubted that there was much left of the bullet wound in his chest either.

"I'm sorry if I'm interrupting." Jath'ibaye's low voice just carried over the noise of rushing water.

Kahlil shrugged. "I wasn't doing anything important."

"You looked happy."

"Did I? I was just thinking about the water." Kahlil glanced back down at the contrary current. "It's you, isn't it?"

"Me?" Jath'ibaye stepped closer and followed Kahlil's gaze down to the churning surface of the river.

"Creating the northward current," Kahlil clarified.

"I felt it would be wise to put a good distance between us and Nurjima as quickly as possible," Jath'ibaye said.

A somewhat evasive answer, but Kahlil let it go. Certain characteristics of John's obviously remained the same even after all this time. Kahlil wondered if it was possible to find secretiveness charming. Perhaps it was simply nostalgia.

A speckled turtle plunged out from the current beside the ship and snapped up an unsuspecting fish. A moment later the turtle dived back into the wake of the ship.

"So, is the truce at an end?" Kahlil asked.

"Truce?" Jath'ibaye frowned for just a moment. "You mean between the gaunsho'im and me?"

"You had others?" Kahlil asked.

"I thought you might have meant the truce between you and me." Jath'ibaye's gaze lingered on him, then shifted to something in the water. Kahlil tried to see what had merited such a concerned expression, but all he made out were the waves.

"There's no need for a truce between us," Kahlil said. "I never thought of you as my enemy. Not even in Nayeshi. I just had a duty to do. But that's all over now. It's been over for decades, hasn't it?"

Jath'ibaye nodded. Kahlil gazed north to the sharp ridge of mountains ahead of them. He didn't remember the mountains surrounding Vundomu looking like that. They were steeper and more jagged. Had they changed during the cataclysm that had destroyed Rathal'pesha? Or had they, like the river current, been altered through careful control?

He stole a quick glance to Jath'ibaye. He seemed so human. And yet the rushing water beneath them and the jutting mountains ahead of them were all testaments to his divine nature.

"You can't have been in Basawar that long. I would have known…" Jath'ibaye's expression remained firm, almost stern, but there was something like concern in his tone.

"What?" Kahlil asked. Then he remembered his own mention of the two decades that had passed. "No, just two years. When I followed you from Nayeshi, I skipped years ahead. I couldn't control the Great Gate so I just had to focus on the bond I have to you. It pulled me through to Nurjima two years ago."

"I wonder why there and not Vundomu?" Jath'ibaye asked.

"You must have been in Nurjima when I came through," Kahlil said. "It would have been close to the time for the Gaunsho'im Council's opening sessions. If you'd been upset or angry, I probably would have been drawn to the strong emotion."

Jath'ibaye nodded. Kahlil didn't know if the gesture meant that he had, indeed, been upset then or if Jath'ibaye was simply acknowledging that his physical location had been accurate.

"Then you've only been home a little while." Jath'ibaye didn't look at Kahlil. Instead his blue eyes were narrowed, watching the waters below them. "A great deal must have changed since you left."

"More than I can know, most likely," Kahlil replied, but he wasn't about to let Jath'ibaye pull him into a reverie of days gone by. The world of his past was long dead. "What about you? How long have you lived here now?"

"Longer," Jath'ibaye answered, as if that was all there could be to say on the subject.

"Much longer? Three weeks? Or more like a hundred years?" Kahlil raised his brows and for just a moment he caught the hint of a teasing smile on Jath'ibaye's lips.

"Somewhere between the two."

"You must have been here for at least twenty-seven years now," Kahlil informed him. "But I think longer than that, because you were already established in the Fai'daum by then."

Jath'ibaye gave a nod, though the playfulness had fled his expression.

"Thirty-one years," Jath'ibaye said. His tone did not imply that they had been kind years.

"That's more time than I've spent in Basawar in all my life," Kahlil commented. "I think you must be more of a native now than I am."

Kahlil wanted to ask Jath'ibaye about his arrival here and the destruction of Rathal'pesha. But he felt afraid of what Jath'ibaye might tell him. There was no way that it could be a pleasant reminiscence. He knew what it took to awaken a Rifter. Jath'ibaye had to have endured terrible pain.

"You still haven't answered my question about whether the peace treaty with the gaunsho'im is broken." Kahlil decided that the future was probably a better subject than the past.

"No, I haven't," Jath'ibaye replied.

Kahlil waited, but Jath'ibaye said nothing more. Wringing conversations out of him had never been easy, even on Nayeshi. Life in Basawar seemed to have made Jath'ibaye into an unassailable fortress of noncommittal silence. Kahlil frowned at him and Jath'ibaye gave a slight laugh.

"What?" Kahlil demanded.

"You just look so obviously annoyed." Again, his playful smile faded. "You reminded me of someone else, that's all."

"Oh."

"I can't answer your question because I don't know yet if our truce is broken or still salvageable. The gaun'im will have to decide that."

Kahlil leaned against the side of the ship. The sky above them was a washed-out blue. Faint, streaky clouds rolled slowly past.

"I'm not good at this," Kahlil said at last. He glanced back to Jath'ibaye. His eyes seemed a brilliant blue, so much brighter than the sky. "I'm no good at standing around doing nothing."

"If you'd rather be alone…" Jath'ibaye began to move away, but Kahlil caught him by the arm. Jath'ibaye's muscles were as tense as iron cords. Kahlil released him immediately, wondering what reflex could have inspired such a presumptuous action. Even in Nayeshi, he'd never been physically free with John. He had never dared to allow himself that. The only time they'd ever touched was to shake hands once upon meeting.

"I didn't mean you should go," Kahlil said. "I'm thinking more generally of my life. I need some purpose to serve."

"Such as?"

Kahlil straightened. "I was hoping you would tell me."

"Me?" Jath'ibaye gazed at Kahlil.

"Why not? I have skills. I'm well trained. You have enemies. If there's going to be a war, you could use a man like me."

"If there is going to be a war, then yes, you would make an invaluable weapon," Jath'ibaye said. "But are you sure that you want to be a weapon?"

"What else would I do? I am your Kahlil and so long as I am bound to you, you might as well use me."

"You have other options," Jath'ibaye replied. "The Payshmura can no longer force you to live that way."

"What options?" Kahlil asked.

"Anything you like."

Kahlil rolled his eyes. "It's not as though I have the skills to take up farm life, do I?"

"I don't know. Perhaps you do," Jath'ibaye replied. But Kahlil could see that even Jath'ibaye didn't put much faith in the idea of Kahlil scratching out his living in the dirt. For a panicked moment,

Kahlil thought Jath'ibaye meant to brush him off, give him a train ticket and send him on his way as Alidas had done.

"Don't you want me? I am well trained and no one could be more loyal to you in a fight." Kahlil's tone grew emphatic.

"It's not a matter of what I want," Jath'ibaye said. "The question is, what do you want? For yourself?"

Frustration flared up in Kahlil at the obtuseness of Jath'ibaye's thinking. In Nayeshi, men chose their profession. Not here. Could he truly not understand that after all these years?

"I want to be your Kahlil. It's all I've ever wanted and you know that. In Candle Alley, you told me yourself that I couldn't run away to another life. And you were right. I—" Kahlil stopped as he realized that his memory had to be wrong.

"I told you that?" Jath'ibaye's voice was oddly soft.

"I thought it was you, but it couldn't have been, could it? You were never in Amura'taye with me. It must have been another ushvun."

"Who?" Jath'ibaye asked. "Do you remember?"

"I don't know." Kahlil tried to call up the memory again, but it eluded him. He had thought it had been John. He had thought that there had been blood on the man's hands. Kahlil shook his head. "Since I came through the Great Gate my memories have been…"

Jath'ibaye waited, watching him with a strange, intense expression. Kahlil turned away in embarrassment. He felt suddenly like a sideshow oddity.

"They've been a mess, that's all. I was injured during the crossing. Badly injured." To avoid the discomfort of Jath'ibaye's fierce scrutiny, Kahlil chose to observe the sky. White clouds twisted and turned in the wind and for a moment Kahlil could have imagined that they were circling above him. "I remember things that could never have happened. I've forgotten things that I know I had to have done. Even my body isn't right. There should be Prayerscars on my eyelids and across the backs of my hands. You remember that I had them, don't you?"

Jath'ibaye's face had gone pale. Perhaps he was not as completely recovered from the poison as Kahlil had first assumed.

"It was a long time ago," Jath'ibaye said slowly. "But yes, I remember. In Nayeshi, you bore the black Prayerscars of the ordained Kahlil."

"There was something else. Two red scars across my mouth, but now they're hardly there at all." Kahlil traced the surface of his cheek where the scars should have been.

"And you don't know why the scars are missing?" Jath'ibaye asked.

"I have no idea," Kahlil admitted. He fought to keep his frustration from sounding in his voice. "I don't understand where they've gone, but I know they were there. I remember the afternoon it..." Kahlil couldn't bring himself to admit how the scars had come about. He glanced to Jath'ibaye.

There was a strange tension to Jath'ibaye's expression, as if he were suppressing some violent pain. He really wasn't well yet, Kahlil realized. He should let him go and rest. Kahlil nearly said as much, but Jath'ibaye spoke first.

"Do you have any idea of what affected you?" Jath'ibaye asked the question carefully, but Kahlil just shook his head.

"I understand that the world I left behind when I traveled to Nayeshi isn't the same one I've returned to...But I shouldn't have been changed...I don't know. Perhaps the issusha'im did something before Umbhra'ibaye was destroyed," Kahlil offered, though he had no idea what they could have done that would have changed him like this.

"I don't think so...I don't know," Jath'ibaye said quickly, without meeting Kahlil's gaze. "There's something Ji asked me to take care of below deck. I'd better deal with it while I'm still thinking of it. Will you excuse me?"

"Sure," Kahlil said. The announcement came so abruptly that Kahlil doubted its validity.

"We'll talk again later." Jath'ibaye disappeared below decks.

Kahlil wondered which of the things that he had said had disturbed Jath'ibaye so much. Perhaps Jath'ibaye had simply grown tired of the whole rambling discussion. It certainly hadn't gone the way Kahlil had intended.

He looked back down at the two currents slipping past one another. The waters looked rougher than before. Tiny white crests churned and crashed.

Perhaps Jath'ibaye's sudden departure had nothing to do with him at all. He had looked so unwell. Kahlil wondered how difficult it was for Jath'ibaye to restrain his power. Did it hurt him to hold back that immense destructive force in order to turn a single current in the river?

It was more than a little egotistical to assume that Jath'ibaye's every reaction had to do with him. The man had the entire Gaunsho'im Council to contend with. He had a river to master and enemies like Fikiri to consider. Jath'ibaye's thoughts had probably been miles away throughout most of their conversation.

Kahlil himself worried about the armies currently on the move. He scowled at the jagged mountains looming on the northern horizon. Distantly, he remembered the vast, walled garrison of Vundomu. That would have been decades ago. How well fortified was it now? How well could it withstand the onslaught of the gaunsho'im's unified forces?

He considered moving through the Gray Space and seeing Vundomu for himself. But his sudden appearance would probably cause alarm. It was wiser to wait and arrive with Jath'ibaye, assuming Jath'ibaye still wanted his services.

The idea of Jath'ibaye refusing him felt both absurd and terrifying—and he couldn't quite understand why except that he had endured so much and come so far to reach this point that he couldn't bear the prospect of it all having been for nothing. He'd crossed two worlds and nearly died just to find John. And now that they were together, it felt as though he had at last found his place.

And yet when they'd stood speaking there'd been something so uneasy about Jath'ibaye's manner that it shook Kahlil's confidence.

He scowled at the dark, disorienting waters swirling in the wake of Jath'ibaye's ship.

Better not to brood about what he couldn't understand, Kahlil decided.

Instead, Kahlil turned his attention to the three ship hands working on deck. One of them was a young woman; the other two, men in their twenties. All wore knit caps, dull red coats, and thick pants cut from oiled leather. Despite the chill in the air, none of them seemed displeased to be out in the open. While they worked, mending fishing nets, they talked among themselves.

It took Kahlil a moment to recall their names. Ji had introduced the entire crew to him two days ago, but he'd been dazed and exhausted at the time. Still, when the young woman glanced up at him and smiled, he recalled that her name was Besh'anya. Her curvaceous figure and thick black hair reminded him of one of the cooks he'd met in the Lisam house, though her expression struck him as far more inquisitive. The man beside her was Piam—the earlier introductions were coming back to him now. Piam couldn't have been much past twenty, but his thick black beard made him look older. The second man bore the light hair and skin of an Eastern ancestry and Kahlil's gaze lingered upon him the longest for that. He was called Chyemon. Despite the difference in their coloring, Chyemon's fine features resembled Besh'anya's closely enough that Kahlil couldn't help but think that they were siblings.

They had all seemed friendly enough when they had been introduced. He supposed it wouldn't hurt to sound them out. At the very least he might learn more about Vundomu.

As he approached the group, Besh'anya waved. The other two looked up to him and offered friendly smiles. He caught the smell of oil from their coats and wool from the clothes beneath. Their cheeks, noses, and ears had gone red from the wind and cold.

"It's chilly today, isn't it?" Kahlil asked.

Piam nodded. "It'll get colder still. We'll be seeing snow by tomorrow morning."

"The worst of the winter's passed though, even in Vundomu." Chyemon shifted the netting through his callused hands, looking for frayed fibers. The sharp smell of fish drifted up. "You shouldn't have to get much colder."

"That's good," he said a little absently. Across both worlds the discussion of the weather seem a universal opener into wider-ranging conversations. He supposed it was because even complete strangers at least shared the surrounding temperatures and winds.

"Ji says you're from the fallen church," Besh'anya remarked.

"I was trained by the Payshmura priests at Rathal'pesha." Kahlil still felt strange admitting that. He'd hidden his identity for so many years. Now there was no point. The Payshmura had been destroyed twenty-seven years before. These ship hands wouldn't have even been born when Kahlil had crossed through the Great Gate into Nayeshi.

"You don't look that old." Besh'anya studied Kahlil's face.

"No, I suppose I don't," Kahlil replied. He was, in fact, only in his early thirties. He simply hadn't lived through all the years that had passed here in Basawar since the time he had been born and now. He doubted that the ship hands would understand that. So, he didn't attempt an explanation. "I imagine the northlands have changed quite a lot in the last thirty years."

"Since the fall of the old church?" Piam ran his hand over his beard. The motion wasn't quite natural. Kahlil thought that it was probably a gesture that Piam was attempting to cultivate into a habit.

"My grandmother traveled to Amura'taye when she was a girl—before the fall, you know," Piam went on. "She said that everything was different then. You could take a train almost all the way there. The great chasm hadn't expanded from the east yet. And you didn't have to watch for hungry bones, either. The dead stayed down back then."

"So they say," Besh'anya commented. "The old church raised the bones even back then, didn't they?" She addressed her question to Kahlil. Her brother Chyemon glanced to him as well but said nothing.

"The issusha'im, you mean?" Kahlil asked. He couldn't imagine what else they could be talking about. He had never heard of them being called 'hungry bones' though.

"Yes, the women they flayed and kept alive," Besh'anya said. "Ji was one of them, you know."

"No, I didn't," Kahlil said, though he thought that perhaps he had known that.

"She escaped and had to hide in the body of a dog to keep the priests from finding her. That was in the early days of the revolution, when the Fai'daum were still without a homeland."

The other two men nodded. This was obviously something they expected everyone to know. Kahlil's own knowledge of the Fai'daum's early history was limited to the monasteries they had burned and the tithes they had stolen from caravans.

"That was a little before even my time," Kahlil said.

"It was terrible back then," Besh'anya told him. "They burned people alive."

Kahlil just nodded. He was far more familiar with that than he would have wanted any of these three to know.

"Were you at the Battle of Vundomu?" Chyemon asked with boyish shyness. Kahlil couldn't help but like how easily his fair skin betrayed a faint blush. It reminded him just a little of John when he'd been quite young.

"Yes," Kahlil answered automatically, though he immediately realized that he couldn't have been there. By the time Vundomu had fallen he would have already been in Nayeshi. And yet he could almost see it in his mind. The huge black walls tore themselves open. Steam and flames burst up as tracks of machinery twisted apart. Metal screamed and the heat of raging fires distorted the sky. His heart raced as he thought of it, as he remembered Jahn's pale form against the rolling walls of black smoke.

"Jath'ibaye conquered an army in a day," Chyemon said. "I wish I could have seen it."

"There was too much smoke for anyone to see anything, really." Kahlil didn't want to say any more about it. Hundreds of men had been killed. Crushed, burned, suffocated bodies had littered the shattered rubble of every street. The fires had burned for days. In the midst of the memory, Kahlil suddenly wondered how he could know all this. Had Alidas told him about it? Had he read it in a history book? Had he just imagined it in some fever dream?

Already the memories receded from him.

"Ji always says that battles are in the moment and not in the retelling," Besh'anya said.

Piam nodded. Chyemon seemed disappointed at the turn of the conversation. Clearly he had been hoping to hear a detailed account of the conquest.

"Is it true you can walk through walls like the devil Fikiri?" Chyemon asked.

"A little better than Fikiri, I think." Kahlil couldn't suppress the arrogance in his tone.

Chyemon grinned at this. "Are you going to kill him?"

"That would depend on what Jath'ibaye wishes." Kahlil shoved his hands into his pockets.

"But you could?" Chyemon asked.

Kahlil considered the brutal force Fikiri had wielded as he tore through the Gray Space. Noise and flames had burst through the air. He had used Eastern sorcery as well, manipulating fluid as if it were his own flesh. Fikiri was no drunken clumsy murderer; he possessed skills that matched or perhaps even exceeded Kahlil's own.

And yet some deep part of him revolted against the thought of Fikiri ever besting him in battle. He was the Kahlil. Fikiri was just a treacherous coward.

"If he needs killing, then I'll kill him," Kahlil stated.

Chyemon gazed at him with open awe. Piam and Besh'anya, however, looked simultaneously troubled and hopeful.

"Ji says that you were nearly made the Kahlil, the Payshmura's god slayer," Chyemon added, as if Kahlil could not have known what the word meant.

"Yes," Kahlil replied. One of Chyemon's words lingered with him: nearly. Why would Ji say that he had 'nearly' been made Kahlil? He was Kahlil. Even without the Prayerscars, he knew that he had been.

He still was.

"I bet you know battle forms that no one can beat," Chyemon went on. "Ancient attacks that were lost with the Payshmura—you probably know them all."

Chyemon's obvious eagerness to worship him struck Kahlil as both flattering and discomfiting. Who knew what kind of stories had cropped up about the ushiri'im and the Kahlil since the fall of the Payshmura Church? He didn't want Chyemon, or anyone here, to take him for more than he was.

"No matter how well I might have been trained," Kahlil said, "it would still just take one well-placed bullet outside of the Gray Space to take me out."

"But you said you could kill Fikiri." Chyemon's smile suddenly faded.

"I can. He's as human as I am. For every man it just takes one bullet."

"But it has to hit him." Besh'anya's young face was grim. "Plenty of guards and kahlirash'im have tried."

"He's like a ghost, passing through walls and locked doors. He takes whomever he pleases, kills anyone he wants." Piam lowered his voice as if just talking about Fikiri might summon him. "Nothing touches him."

Kahlil plainly saw the fear written in all three of their faces and he regretted his earlier insistence on realism. These three young people wanted a hero who would inspire them to keep fighting against the monster that Fikiri had become. Chyemon, at least, had apparently hoped that Kahlil would be that hero. Kahlil's disdain for Fikiri returned to him like an instinct and with it came a strange feeling of audacity.

"Anything Fikiri can do, I can do to him," Kahlil said. Then, to prove it, Kahlil flicked his fingers apart and sliced open the Gray Space. He stepped through Piam and emerged just behind Chyemon.

"And I'm much quieter than he is," Kahlil added.

All three of the ship hands spun around to look at Kahlil. This time the awe and admiration on all their faces was evident. A breathless laugh escaped from Besh'anya. Piam stared at Kahlil wide eyed while Chyemon grinned like a delighted child.

"You did it," Chyemon gasped. "Just like that."

"Just like that," Kahlil agreed.

"You were silent." Besh'anya smiled. "The devil won't even hear you coming."

"Can you do it again?" Piam asked.

"Yes, can you?" Chyemon chimed in.

"Sure, but I think it might disturb Jath'ibaye if I move too many times." Kahlil belatedly recalled how he had first been ripped from the Gray Space when Jath'ibaye had mistaken his movements for Fikiri's. Only an instant later Jath'ibaye bounded up from below decks. His expression was one of utter fury. He pivoted, searching the deck, and then stopped, catching sight of Kahlil's guilty expression.

"Sorry," Kahlil called. "That was me."

Jath'ibaye frowned at him, but the anger was already fading from his expression. When he had burst up from the stairs, he had looked ready to kill. Now he just appeared vaguely annoyed. He crossed the deck to meet Kahlil and the three ship hands.

"You should probably warn me if you're going to be opening the Gray Space," Jath'ibaye informed him somewhat tersely.

"I'll remember that in the future."

Jath'ibaye glanced between the ship hands, their netting and Kahlil curiously.

"So, what exactly were you doing?" Jath'ibaye asked.

Apparently, he expected Kahlil to have a good reason for opening the Gray Space. Kahlil doubted that Jath'ibaye considered improving morale by showing off to be adequate cause. Kahlil leaned against the ship's railing and gave a rebellious shrug.

"Just killing time until you give me something useful to do. Assuming that you want to accept a man with my unique skills into your household, that is."

"I see." Jath'ibaye's bright blue eyes narrowed. A feeling of deep familiarity washed through Kahlil as he smiled into Jath'ibaye's rising vexation. All three of Kahlil's new acquaintances immediately made themselves very busy with their nets. He couldn't blame them, but he couldn't resist riling Jath'ibaye either.

"I told you I was bored," Kahlil added.

"Yes, you did."

"Idle hands, devil's workshop," Kahlil repeated the saying from Nayeshi. Jath'ibaye gave him a slightly puzzled look, then just shook his head.

"Come on, then. As it happens I do have a use for a man of your unique skills." Jath'ibaye turned sharply and strode toward the ship's stern. Kahlil gave the astonished ship hands a brief wave and then hurried after. He half expected Jath'ibaye to lead him below deck and hand him over to the ship's cook for scullery duty. But anything was better than just pacing the deck, letting directionless anxiety fill him.

Jath'ibaye led Kahlil back to the cabins above deck in the quarter gallery. He unlocked a heavy black door and held it open for Kahlil. After they were both inside, Jath'ibaye allowed the door to fall closed behind them.

The cabin was small, particularly with both himself and Jath'ibaye in it. Kahlil stepped back and felt his leg bump into the edge of a bed. A desk, locked cabinets, and a simple bed had been bolted to the floor. Between the bars of the cabinet doors Kahlil could see glass cases of soil and seedling plants. A large book sat on the desk along with several rolls of bandages. Loose pages of another book lay on the bed. Rumpled white blankets were thrown across the mattress without any regard for appearance. Despite the cramped space and disheveled state of the room, the air smelled rich and sweet, like a garden.

Kahlil knew at once that this had to be Jath'ibaye's private cabin.

"Have a seat," Jath'ibaye told him. "The bed or the chair. It doesn't matter."

Kahlil sat back on the bed. Jath'ibaye took the chair, turned it around backward, and sat straddling it with his arms crossed over the chair back. It was an assured, modern position and the very first Kahlil had observed that betrayed Jath'ibaye's early life in Nayeshi.

"Are you serious about serving me?" Jath'ibaye asked.

"I wouldn't be here if I wasn't, would I?" Kahlil replied. "It's not as though I couldn't leave this ship under my own power."

Jath'ibaye simply responded with an unconvinced expression.

"I chose to stop the assassination at the Bell Dance against my commander's direct orders so that I could protect you and recover the yasi'halaun." Kahlil saw Jath'ibaye was about to make a reply. He went on quickly, "I followed you across the worlds, twice. I am bound to you. I have known since I was a boy that I would be with you. So there's no point in denying me. And please don't try offering me some new existence on a taye farm. I know what kind of man I am and what kind of life I'm made for. I was chosen and consecrated to be the guardian of a god, not a goat herder!" The words came out with more force than Kahlil had expected. Jath'ibaye seemed as taken aback as Kahlil was by his outburst.

"All right," he said at last. "But if you are going to serve me, you have to understand that things beyond Vundomu are not like they are in the rest of the world. It's dangerous."

"Well, my life up to this point has been nothing but gentility and peace, but I'll try to adapt the best I can," Kahlil commented.

Jath'ibaye frowned at his sarcasm and Kahlil didn't continue.

"Your life and the lives of others may depend on absolute obedience." Jath'ibaye gave him a hard, direct stare. "That has never been your strong point."

"I'm obedient!" Kahlil protested, but he immediately realized that he was lying and they both knew it. If he had been obedient, he wouldn't have disobeyed Alidas. When Umbhra'ibaye had been about to fall, he wouldn't have secretly crossed back to Basawar to rescue his sister. In his youth, he wouldn't have gone to Candle Alley again and again.

"I can be obedient when required," Kahlil amended.

"You will have to be." Jath'ibaye leaned slightly forward, still staring straight into Kahlil's eyes. "I need you to swear that you will obey me, no matter what. When I give you an order, you must obey it."

Kahlil didn't think he had ever seen a man look so serious. The air felt electrified by Jath'ibaye's will. And Kahlil thought he could understand why his compliance would matter so much.

Unlike himself, Jath'ibaye had led armies to war. He had had to order men to their deaths. The freedom of all the Fai'daum had depended on those orders being carried out. If there was another war, Jath'ibaye would have no use for a rogue agent, no matter how talented.

"I swear," Kahlil said.

Jath'ibaye slouched back and sighed. Kahlil wondered if he had been holding his breath.

"Good," Jath'ibaye said. "Then I have work for you."

"Just give me a name and I will give you a corpse." Kahlil prepared himself to hear the name: Fikiri.

"This book." Jath'ibaye pointed to the two volumes on the desk.

Kahlil carefully lifted the ancient, brittle tome. Cautiously he opened the cover. The writing inside was Payshmura script but in an archaic form. It took him a while to read the page. It appeared to be an old botanical guide.

"You want me to get rid of this book? I guess I can see why. I can't stand this old-fashioned writing either."

"I want you to translate it. It's written in a dialect I can barely understand," Jath'ibaye said. "Ji doesn't know how to read it either. We think it's an archaic style of writing. I need you to go through and keep a list of the unfamiliar or new plants mentioned in it."

"You're joking," Kahlil said. "Anyone could do this. Don't you want me to go after—"

"Obedience. Remember?" Jath'ibaye gave him a hard smile, but there was an amused tone to his voice.

Kahlil scowled sullenly down at the book. He couldn't have devised a more appropriate punishment for his own insolence if he had tried.

"And this isn't work just anyone could do." Jath'ibaye's tone softened slightly. "There's almost no one left who can read Payshmura writings. Even those of us who can read them often can't understand the dialectical ones." Jath'ibaye stood and walked to the door. "Feel free to make yourself at home in here."

"Is this some kind of a test?"

"You can think of it that way if you like. But the information in those books really is of great importance to me." As Jath'ibaye spoke, a shadow of sorrow drifted across his expression. "You'll be in harm's way soon enough, Kyle. There's no need to rush into it."

"I know, I know." Kahlil bowed his head over the book. "I just don't want all my life to have been for nothing."

"None of us do," Jath'ibaye said. "But that's no reason to throw yourself away."

A strange cold breeze whipped through the room and Kahlil's head came up in alarm, but it was only a draft from the open door. Jath'ibaye stepped out and the door fell closed behind him.

Kahlil gazed at the door for several moments. He could easily pass through it. If he wanted, he could be in Vundomu in a matter of seconds or even travel beyond that to find Fikiri. Kahlil felt the temptation strongly, but he hadn't yet recovered his full strength and more importantly he'd given his word. In any case, Jath'ibaye was probably right about opportunities for future battles. With the gaun'im raising armies he'd soon have more than his share.

Kahlil stretched out on the bed and opened the book. He only made it through three pages before he was dozing, doodling, and absently wondering how Jath'ibaye had come to know him so well.

Chapter Fifty-Four

For three days Kahlil did little other than translate the botanical guide. He rarely left the cabin and he fell asleep often, lulled into unconsciousness by seemingly endless lists of small to middling seeds as well as detailed descriptions of countless earthworms.

Ji called on him twice, inquiring about his health. He assured her that he felt fully mended and she offered him a gaze that was as skeptical as her canine countenance allowed. Strangely, Kahlil found her company deeply soothing. He knew he should have been suspicious of the witch, but some inexplicable instinct made him trust her.

Jath'ibaye returned infrequently, most often to change his bandages. He certainly wasn't a good conversationalist, but often during their brief exchanges, Kahlil sensed Jath'ibaye making an effort for his sake.

If Jath'ibaye slept, it wasn't in his own bed. Kahlil soon came to suspect that Jath'ibaye's bed, like Alidas' chairs, were only maintained for the comfort of guests.

They at last reached Vundomu just before dawn. Jath'ibaye woke him where he'd passed out, face down in the botanical tome. Embarrassed and still groggy, Kahlil packed up the book and the yasi'halaun, making haste to join Jath'ibaye and the ship hands on the deck as they cleared the last of the locks in the river city of Mahn'illev and made for Vundomu's port.

The vast fortress straddled the river's mouth the way that Kahlil remembered it once looming over railroad tracks. In sheer scale it rivaled the jagged mountains surrounding it, but where the cliffs abounded with vegetation, the seven stepped terraces of Vundomu bristled with heavy artillery and godhammers.

For a sleepy instant Kahlil wondered how it could remind him so strongly of both a Nayeshi wedding cake and a warship. Then their clipper passed through the cavernous port entry and was moored among the dozens of other ships in the heavily guarded harbor.

On the dock a small entourage of men and women waited to greet the ship. As Jath'ibaye stepped off the gangway, they crowded around, full of questions and urgency. Kahlil watched Jath'ibaye disappear into their midst, not knowing what to do with himself. Then Ji brushed up against his leg.

"Jath'ibaye has asked me to look after you while he sees to his duties." Ji gave a slightly annoyed sniff in the direction of the crowd engulfing Jath'ibaye. "More than likely we'll get to his holdings long before he does. Come, I'll show you the way."

They walked together from the docks up through the predawn streets. Kahlil took in the sights illuminated by flickering gas lamps: carved shop signs advertising tailors, coopers, smiths, weavers, and a bounty of other skilled tradesmen. He smelled roasting taye and yeast drifting from bakeries just opening for business and from brewpubs that were perhaps just closing. As they continued up the cobbled street past neat rows of private residences and the odd public bathhouse, Kahlil realized that behind its imposing, fortified walls Vundomu sheltered a thriving little city.

Certainly, it was not the squalid, ignorant mire that so many of the southern newspapers would have led him to believe Vundomu to be.

If he wasn't mistaken, he thought he even spotted the sign for a public toilet.

"You've used a lift before, haven't you?" Ji asked. She came to a stop in front of a wrought iron grate set into the face of a stone wall. The young girl standing guard in a patched russet coat and dress stifled a yawn at the sight of them. After offering Ji a warm welcome back home, she cranked the grate open to expose the interior of an elevator.

"I think…" Kahlil felt as if his memory stumbled, but then he assured himself that he'd been up numerous escalators and elevators in Nayeshi.

"Yes, several," he replied belatedly.

"Good. This one will take us straight up to the heights. It should be light enough for you to enjoy the view from the watchtowers in

Jath'ibaye's holdings. We have telescopes, you know."

She showed her teeth and Kahlil thought it was meant as a smile.

"It seems you have about everything here," Kahlil commented.

"Indeed," Ji agreed. "Perhaps that's why the gaun'im resent us so."

Ji padded into the elevator and Kahlil followed. The girl cranked the grate back closed.

Though it smelled of veru oil, the lift reminded Kahlil strongly of a service elevator from Nayeshi—large, functional, and filled with redundant safety measures. They rose quickly and Kahlil's ears popped. Beside him Ji flicked her golden ears.

When they stepped out of the lift, the air felt of frost and smelled like gunpowder. The first golden rays of morning gleamed on the eastern horizon but hadn't yet reached the very peak of Vundomu where they stood. Unlike the quaint village they'd left on the third terrace, the seventh terrace betrayed Vundomu's military origins. Here stood archaic-looking barracks, heavily guarded armories, and tahldi stables.

As he and Ji passed four stern-faced young men in red uniforms, Kahlil thought he heard a woman calling drills to troops inside a large courtyard. And above a wall, he glimpsed the sharp, dark silhouette of the Temple of the Rifter. He almost expected them to go there. But instead Ji led him farther up along the cracked cobbled street to a large but unassuming three-story stone building.

Two massive watchtowers jutted up from its shingled roof, but otherwise it looked like it could have served as a common hostel. Tahldi snorted and called from the stables, and the aroma of roasting meat drifted from the smokestacks of the kitchens.

Inside, an unadorned entryway opened into a large, common room where the only decorative flair seemed to be a pair of staircases that led up to an overhanging balcony and the upper floors. But Kahlil's strongest impression came not from the spartan surroundings but the flurry of excited servants and runners, who rushed past like flocks of red swallows.

A pretty young woman called out a warm greeting to Ji, but a moment later she disappeared up a staircase.

Apparently their ship had arrived earlier than expected and the house steward had rallied Jath'ibaye's entire household to make all ready for his imminent return.

Ji winked at Kahlil as two footmen bustled past them, speculating as to who Jath'ibaye's mysterious guest could be.

Despite the chaos, Ji easily caught the attention of a young, blond kitchen servant and arranged for him to send taye cakes and warm goat stew up to the western watchtower.

"It'll be quiet up there," Ji informed Kahlil as they mounted the staircase. "We can enjoy our meal and the view in peace."

The small chamber of the watchtower was packed with rolled maps and shelves of finely ground lenses. Two beautifully polished telescopes stood on brass stands near the thick windows. Kahlil sat at the desk, sampling his stew and trying not to stare as Ji lapped hers up from a gilded plate on the floor. She ate surprisingly daintily considering her form.

Despite the lure of the warm meal, Kahlil couldn't keep himself from the telescopes. Soon he stood behind one, surveying all the surrounding lands.

Snow still capped the dark mountains that rose all around. The air felt cold and thin, the way Kahlil had remembered it being in Rathal'pesha. But the similarity between the two locations ended there.

The mountains spreading out from the massive fortress of Vundomu were almost as straight as walls. Neither wind nor weather had yet eroded their sharp peaks. Their sheer cliff faces circled north, forming an immense ring around the huge lake, which lay across much of the valley below. From the mouth of the lake flowed a deep river.

And when Kahlil briefly turned the telescope south, he realized the river rolled directly beneath Vundomu's black iron walls, heavy guns and godhammers, to feed into the headwaters of the great Samsira River.

Kahlil hadn't remembered the river reaching so far north. He had been almost certain that it had required railways to reach Vundomu from Nurjima. When he said as much, Ji nodded her gray and gold head.

"During the Seven Years' War we destroyed their trains." She briefly flashed her yellowed teeth. "Jath'ibaye brought the river up over their stations and tracks. Now if they want a war they have to swim upstream."

A shudder shivered down Kahlil's spine at the thought of the Rifter unleashing such force. His memory flickered with the images of crumbling mountains and shattered kingdoms that had filled so many holy books. Just how far would Jath'ibaye go to protect his Fai'daum?

Kahlil turned his attention back to the kingdom that Jath'ibaye had forged from the ruins of the northlands. Gazing down, Kahlil could make out the traces of the Vundomu he remembered. The original walls curved like ribs around new domes and towers of red stone and glittering glass. From the steep southern walls, the structures of Vundomu cascaded in gentle avenues of shops, cottages, clock towers, and raised walkways down to the vast lake at its feet.

The three verdant islands that rose from the lake reminded Kahlil of gigantic shells in their perfect symmetry. Stately white buildings dominated what appeared to be a village occupying the largest island. The other two seemed lush and wild, even this early in the northern spring. Hundreds of small boats darted across the lake's glassy surface, sailing between the islands.

Carefully, Kahlil adjusted the lenses of the telescope, focusing in on one bright blue boat. The women on board seemed to be line fishing. Kahlil watched as a blond girl hauled a tiny fish up from the water. An older woman held the fish up to a caliper, then shook her head and tossed the fish back into the lake.

"What are they doing?" Kahlil asked.

Ji looked up at him from where she had curled up near a heating pipe. She yawned, showing her yellowed teeth.

"Where?" Ji's voice sounded soft and still half asleep.

"Out on the lake. They're throwing fish back."

"Probably featherfin." Ji lowered her head back down to her foreleg. "They have to be as long as a hand, otherwise they aren't old enough to have bred yet and there won't be any left next year."

"You have fishing regulations now?" Kahlil asked. He supposed he should have expected as much. After all, John had been an ecologist. Briefly, Kahlil wondered how differently the Fai'daum homeland would have turned out if the Rifter had been a different man, a theater arts professor, for instance. People's clothes certainly could have been a bit flashier.

"We only introduced the featherfin six years ago, but they have established themselves well enough," Ji said. "They give the blue eel something to eat other than little moonfish. They seem to be attracting crown geese as well."

"Right." Kahlil's knowledge of fish was limited to what he had experienced in Nayeshi and that, for the most part, had come in the form of breaded sticks. Or perhaps that had been chicken. He wasn't sure anymore.

"It bores me too," Ji sighed, "but it matters to him, you know. The fish, the plants, the animals, the stone, and soil, it all matters to him."

"Jath'ibaye, you mean?"

Ji nodded. "After the fall of Rathal'pesha, all these lands were in ruins. Just miles of mud, ash, and shattered rock. He brought it all back. It took years, but he did it." Ji cocked her head. "He brought you back as well. I never would have thought he could have done that, but here you are."

"Yes, here I am." Kahlil frowned, thinking how odd it was that he should be so comfortable with this woman and that she should seem so at ease with him as well. "Did you know me, Ji? I mean, before now. I think I remember you from some other time."

"I knew you and have known you many times over," Ji replied. "Once, you were meant to kill me. I saw it when I was still a captive within the issusha'im. It was the price I was to pay for the destruction of the Great Gate."

Inside Kahlil, a distant memory stirred. The shattered yellow stones. The broken blade.

"I was to lead an assault into Umbhra'ibaye, send a false message to the Kahlil in Nayeshi, and then destroy everything."

"I think I remember. My sister was there." Kahlil closed his eyes, trying to pull the faint memories into focus. He recalled a weight against his back. Something whispering words softly into his ear.

He thought there had been flowers and then the smell of a cigarette. Each impression faded even as he tried to concentrate on it.

"But that never happened," Ji said gently.

"That's not true. Umbhra'ibaye did fall." That, Kahlil was sure of. All of the Payshmura strongholds had fallen.

"Not as I had seen it and not as you saw it either. Years before then," Ji replied. "Jath'ibaye destroyed it."

"But I remember—" Kahlil stopped himself. He wasn't sure what he remembered.

"You remember what never happened." Ji shifted to scratch at her side with her back leg. Kahlil fought to keep a sense of reality. It was disorienting to be having this conversation with a dog. Even knowing that Ji was an escaped Issusha Oracle speaking from inside an animal form didn't keep all this from seeming like it should have been a dream.

"It's the same thing that drove so many issusha'im mad. They saw what happened and what never happened—lives, kingdoms, endless histories that the Payshmura altered and destroyed before they could come into being. Only the issusha'im lived them, knew them, and at the same time, knew that they had never come to pass." Ji shook her head. "To cling to what is lost, no matter how real it once seemed or once was, will lead only to madness."

"But I do remember you," Kahlil said. "Not just from Umbhra'ibaye."

Ji's gaze lifted and she studied him for a few moments. Kahlil thought she might be weighing her response, but just the fact that she took pause told him he was right.

"Yes," Ji admitted. "When you were a child, before the Payshmura came and took you and Rousma, I lived with your family for a while. Eventually, I left to join the Fai'daum. But when you were just a tiny baby, I talked to you. I used to play with you."

"Oh," Kahlil said. That was not at all what he'd expected. As a child he'd been cared for by a large dog? It seemed utterly strange and yet there was a deep warmth, an almost soothing reassurance that he felt when he looked into her big brown eyes.

"But that isn't what you remember, is it?" Ji asked.

"No," Kahlil said. "I remember…" The heat of her blood on his hands. His black blade driven into her body. He realized that he didn't want to tell her these things. In Nurjima she had helped to save his life.

"You remember killing me," Ji put in smoothly. "In the rain, beneath the apple blossoms, we fought. You won. But what you did afterwards, what you did in Nayeshi, changed all of that. Our battle never occurred. That entire history was written over by a new one."

Kahlil knew this, and yet hearing Ji say as much disturbed him. For the first time he allowed himself to consider the full implication of the changes he'd wrought by allowing the Rifter to enter Basawar unguarded and unrecognized.

"And I'm not part of this new history, am I?" Kahlil asked. "That's why my memories are all wrong."

Ji only nodded.

"I was in Nayeshi and then lost between the worlds. I missed the changes."

"Maybe you did. Maybe you didn't." Ji lowered her head onto her paws again. "Tell me, are there things that you recall, but you know couldn't have happened?"

"Yes," Kahlil said, but he didn't elaborate.

"I had them as well." Ji nodded. "Dreams, thoughts, brief flashes. Visions of another life. I imagine that you resist them. I imagine that you suppress them as much as you can." She paused, but Kahlil offered no confirmation. Ji went on, "You are carrying two lives. One belongs to this history and another does not. You may not want to know the life you lived here. You may not want to be the man you were, but let me tell you that there is danger in not knowing. There are mistakes that you could avoid if you would just allow yourself to know."

Kahlil scowled at Ji. She sounded very much the Issusha Oracle now.

"Or not." Ji closed her eyes. Kahlil turned back to the telescope. He focused out past the farthest mountains, out to the very brink of the telescope's limit. A churning cauldron of white clouds and mist filled his vision. Faint gray shadows seemed to move just behind the swaths of vapor like bones beneath translucent skin.

"I died, didn't I?" Kahlil asked at last. "I mean Ravishan—he died."

Ji didn't immediately respond. Kahlil thought that she had fallen asleep again. Then he heard her voice.

"There is no difference between you and Ushiri Ravishan. You are one and the same. But yes, you died when Rathal'pesha fell."

He'd had dreams of this death. The fire and confusion of battle, and then agony. Jath'ibaye had been there—holding him and shaking with desperation. Kahlil felt cold and sick.

"You died," Ji said gently. "But now he's brought you back. And he needs you more than you can know—"

Kahlil cut her off with a shake of his head. He wasn't the man Jath'ibaye needed—not the one who had rescued him on the Holy Road, not the one who had fought an army here at Vundomu. Not the one who had died like a hero.

He was the man who'd lurked in shadows and silence. He was the assassin.

"Kyle?" Ji asked softly. "Is something wrong?"

He almost laughed at that. Something was very wrong and it was him. Here.

"No. I…I just need to be alone for a little while," Kahlil said. "I need to go somewhere and think."

"What should I tell Jath'ibaye?" Ji asked.

"He told me I was free to do as I pleased." Kahlil could see from Ji's expression that she would try to persuade him to stay if she could. She would want him to talk to her and to Jath'ibaye. But Kahlil didn't want to talk. He needed to be alone.

He brought his hand up and split open the Gray Space.

"Be careful," Ji called to him. She might have said more, but Kahlil was already far away.

Chapter Fifty-Five

Kahlil went north, as far north as he could before the Gray Space turned treacherous and contorted with distortions. Unconsciously, he supposed, he was searching for Rathal'pesha, the place where he had grown up, been tested, trained, and died. But Rathal'pesha had long since crashed into the sea. He dropped out of the Gray Space on the northern edge of the chasm.

He knelt down and touched the pale soil. It was dry and cold, each distinct pebble looking like some broken bit of shell or eroded bone. It felt nothing like the rich soil surrounding Vundomu. He opened his hand and the grains fell through his fingers like fine sand. The desolate white plateau stretched out to the very edge of the land and then dropped straight down to the ocean below.

Kahlil couldn't see the waters. Mist and fog rose up from the ocean in thick, swirling walls. Distantly, he could hear the crash of waves more than a mile below. Only the utter silence allowed him to notice them at all. He had never seen the ocean of his own world, and briefly, he wondered if the waters were as emerald and fertile as the northern Pacific of Nayeshi. Or were they as dull and gray as the lands above them?

He shifted the weight of the yasi'halaun against his back. He had not wanted to leave it in Vundomu. Not after he had almost died to retrieve it in Nurjima. He had almost died so many times—come so close to it so often that he supposed that it shouldn't have been a surprise to discover that in another life he had died.

Kahlil scowled out at the rolling fog. Rathal'pesha once stood out there, somewhere. Perhaps the remains of his body were out there as well. It would have been nearly thirty years. There would just be skeletal remains, if anything.

What would it be like to touch his own bones?

Kahlil glanced down at his hands. Whatever remains that might lie out beyond the mist weren't his. They were Ravishan's. Though Ji had said that there was no difference, Kahlil knew otherwise. Ravishan had died. Kahlil was still here, the vestigial remnant of a history that never existed.

He supposed he could do as Ji wished. He could usurp Ravishan's life. If he wanted to, he could lay claim to everything Ravishan had known and felt, to Ravishan's entire existence.

Kahlil closed his eyes. Already he could summon memories that could not have been his own.

Ravishan had rejected the Payshmura. He had turned away from his initiation as Kahlil to save the man he loved. He had abdicated his entire upbringing, his training, his church. For a moment, Kahlil reveled in Ravishan's memories. They were filled with assurance and belonging. He had been happy and he had been loved. Ravishan had won friends, comrades, a lover, a home. He had known that he belonged to this world.

Kahlil's own history was one of solitude, deception, displacement, murder, and failure.

But he was not Ravishan. They might have been one at some point in the past, but they were no longer one and the same. He had not possessed the same brilliant faith that emboldened Ravishan nor had he made the sacrifices that Ravishan had. He'd done nothing to earn the joy and assurance that suffused Ravishan's memories.

The idea of claiming Ravishan's identity felt like theft or something worse. A wave of repulsion rolled through him as he realized how jealous and envious he was of Ravishan. Of course Kahlil wanted Ravishan's life. He wanted it so much that it came as a relief to know that Ravishan had not lived to claim his own history.

But he knew down to his very bones that he neither deserved to claim Ravishan's identity nor could he live up to it if he tried. The only decent course of action for him to take was to leave. Let the people who had befriended and loved Ravishan keep their memories of him intact.

That would be the right thing to do.

Kahlil kicked at the pebbled white sand in frustration at his own selfishness. For all his reasoning and ranting at himself, he remained where he was. He simply couldn't bring himself to abandon the promise of a home. He couldn't stop yearning for even a shred of the belonging that Ravishan had claimed here.

Kahlil lifted his gaze and glared out at the distant roiling mists.

He wasn't Ravishan—he never would be—but there was still something he could offer. Even if he'd never become more than a lurking assassin, that was still what Jath'ibaye needed if he wanted to be free of Fikiri.

That was something. Maybe not noble, but useful nonetheless.

The faint call of a voice interrupted Kahlil's thoughts. He turned and scanned the rolling white dunes behind him. He couldn't see far through the haze of fog and mist. But the voice came again, closer and louder.

"Kyle!" It was Jath'ibaye, searching for him. But not really for him. For Ravishan.

Jath'ibaye had, apparently, been able to find him without much trouble. It had to be their bond. Jath'ibaye had probably learned to use the connection to find Ravishan. It annoyed Kahlil to think that he would never be able to hide from Jath'ibaye outside of the Gray Space.

"Kyle!" Jath'ibaye called again, this time from even closer. Kahlil didn't reply. As he watched, a tall gray shadow appeared through the fog. Jath'ibaye strode forward as if he could already see Kahlil.

Condensation from the mist made Jath'ibaye's heavy leather coat look black. Droplets of water clung to his hair. There was an easiness in the way he held his rifle that unnerved Kahlil. Jath'ibaye caught sight of him immediately but paused a moment before he said anything.

A dim memory flickered to life in Kahlil, a scene from his other life. Jath'ibaye had found him like this before, but that time he had been high in the cliffs above Rathal'pesha. Jath'ibaye had not carried a rifle then or even gone by the same name, but his expression had been the same. That time Jahn had wrapped his arms around Ravishan and promised to be his lover. This time he kept his distance.

"You shouldn't be here," Jath'ibaye said. His eyes only focused briefly on Kahlil before roving out to where the land plummeted away.

"I just wanted some time to think. Somewhere that wasn't so busy," Kahlil said. "I told Ji. I assumed that she told you—"

"Not here," Jath'ibaye cut him off. "You can go anywhere else that you like, but not here. It's not safe this close to the chasm."

"I wanted to see where I—where Ravishan died," Kahlil said.

Jath'ibaye's mouth compressed into a hard line. When he spoke, his words came out clipped and cold. "It didn't happen here. It was farther north, in Rathal'pesha. There's no way you could go there now. And there's no point. It was all ruined."

Kahlil nodded. The lands had been so utterly torn asunder that even the Gray Spaces were disrupted.

"Once in Nurjima, when I was following Fikiri, I crossed into a twisted, contorted area of the Gray Space. That's where the ruins are. Rathal'pesha didn't fall into the ocean, did it?" Kahlil asked.

"No, it didn't. The ruins of Rathal'pesha, the Black Tower, and Umbhra'ibaye form an island out there." Jath'ibaye pointed the barrel of his rifle out into the clouds of mist. "In the summer, when the fog thins, you can see it from the Greenhills watchtowers. The hungry bones come from there. Though, some sleep in these cliffs as well. We should get moving."

Jath'ibaye turned and Kahlil stepped up beside him. If Jath'ibaye didn't feel safe, then Kahlil was pretty certain he wasn't safe either. There weren't many things that could threaten the Rifter.

"So what are these hungry bones?" Kahlil asked as they walked. "Issusha'im?"

"Some used to be." Jath'ibaye moved quickly.

Kahlil had to work to keep up with him. The sand slid away under his feet.

"What the rest of them used to be, I don't know. I think they might be attempts at making issusha'im. Or maybe just punishments." Jath'ibaye grimaced. "They feed on blood. Scavenge corpses for more bones. In the winter, when food is scarce, they sleep. But the weather is getting warmer and some of them have to have already been feeding on birds and weasels."

"Can't you destroy them?" Kahlil asked.

"She makes more." Jath'ibaye glanced back over his shoulder. Kahlil was about to ask who, when Jath'ibaye held his hand up for silence. He froze, listening. Kahlil strained to hear what Jath'ibaye heard. There was only the sound of the distant waves, a soft rolling hiss.

Kahlil frowned. He shouldn't have been hearing the ocean from directly below him while he stood on solid ground.

"They're digging through the sand beneath us," Jath'ibaye said. "Come on."

Jath'ibaye swung his rifle across his back and broke into a run. Kahlil followed.

"You should go through the Gray Space," Jath'ibaye yelled back over his shoulder.

Kahlil could have done as he was told. It would have been easy. But he didn't. He didn't want to leave Jath'ibaye. Kahlil continued to run. The sand was sliding from under him much more rapidly now, as if the ground was being pulled out from below him.

Jath'ibaye had no such trouble. Every step he took was sure. He moved quickly and Kahlil suspected that Jath'ibaye could move even faster if he needed to. As Kahlil fell a few more steps behind, Jath'ibaye turned.

"Go through the Gray Space!" Jath'ibaye bellowed at him.

"I don't want to leave you alone!" Kahlil shouted back. His voice was almost drowned out by an explosive, dry roar. Sand and smooth white pebbles spewed up from the ground like a geyser. Kahlil covered his head as the spray of sand and stone pelted down around him.

When he looked up he saw a long serpentine form rearing up from the sand. Thousands of bones, human and animal, hung together on iron hooks and red cables. Sharp ribs bristled out from the body; some curved down, like the legs of a centipede; others jutted out as gigantic talons. Between the ribs, Kahlil caught sight of hundreds of toothy jaws. Other broken bones shot up like spears all along the length of the creature's immense spine. Some were already stained with the blood of recently killed animals. Hissing, whispering voices filled the air with a hum like a multitude of flies.

The sand under Kahlil swept downward toward a set of gaping jaws. Kahlil crouched to keep his balance, but slid with the sand toward the bloodied bones.

Immediately his hands went to the yasi'halaun. Its hilt was hot against his fingers, almost alive.

"Get out of here now!" Jath'ibaye shouted.

Kahlil heard the loud crack of a rifle shot. The jawbone ahead of Kahlil shattered as Jath'ibaye's bullet blasted through it. Broken bits of bone and tooth showered across the sands. The creature swung its body back, rising up over both Kahlil and Jath'ibaye.

Kahlil swung the yasi'halaun up as the creature came hurtling down upon him. The blade split bone and cables. Splinters of rib cut Kahlil's bare hands and slashed his cheek. As the first bones snapped and broke, others swung into their place, churning up like shark teeth.

The yasi'halaun burned in Kahlil's hands as it drank in the twisted, desperate souls that were bound to the bones. Kahlil heard them shrieking. But the creature as a whole hardly seemed affected. It curled around Kahlil and flexed its hundreds of jaws toward him. He swung the yasi'halaun through two animal skulls and then felt a blunt thigh bone hammer into his shoulder.

Instantly the bone was jerked back. At his back, Jath'ibaye snapped the bone in half. With his bare hands he caught hold of one of the massive ribs and ripped it from the rest of its body. Blood poured down Jath'ibaye's arms and there was a deep gash in his throat. He snarled in unrestrained fury as he punched into the creature's vertebrae.

Kahlil could feel the ground beneath them shuddering as Jath'ibaye cracked bones and ripped through iron cables. The sky flashed with gathering lightning.

"Get out of my way," Jath'ibaye growled to Kahlil, "so I can kill this thing!"

Still, Kahlil hesitated. He couldn't abandon John like this. But then he realized that this wasn't John or at least not the John he had known. This wasn't the gentle man who Kahlil had spent years guarding. The man with him now had killed thousands in battles. He had brought down mountains. The only thing stopping him from crushing this creature and all the land surrounding it was Kahlil's presence. It would kill Kahlil to be caught up in such force.

"That's an order, damn it!" Jath'ibaye shouted.

Kahlil snapped open the Gray Space and stepped into its cool silence. Miles of land stretched out before him, instantly obtainable. But Kahlil didn't go. He watched as Jath'ibaye rent bone from bone. The ground rolled up in waves, twisting and crushing ribs, skulls, hips, and leg bones into grit and pebbles. Jath'ibaye threw himself into the coils of the creature with a reckless fury. Bones speared through his body and he wrenched them out. From above, lightning split through the bones, shattering them. In minutes, the creature was torn to pieces and ground to swathes of fine white sand and pebbles.

From the Gray Space, Jath'ibaye's blood looked black as it poured down his face and body. Where it fell on the sands, it remained only a few moments before the shards of bone drank it in.

Kahlil remembered how dry the sand had felt in his hands despite the surrounding mist. He hadn't thought about it at the time, but now he realized that all of these thousands of white pebbles were drinking in the moisture just like they drank up Jath'ibaye's blood. They weren't hungry so much as thirsty bones. Their broken remains blanketed the ground for miles.

Jath'ibaye swayed on his feet, then straightened himself upright. He kicked through the sand for a few moments and then located his discarded rifle. He held it in his hands, not like a weapon, but like some unwanted consolation. He turned, staring out at the rolling clouds in the north. Kahlil didn't think that he had ever seen a man look so unguarded and desolate before in his life.

A moment later, Jath'ibaye's attention whipped back to where Kahlil stood, hidden in the Gray Space. Jath'ibaye's gaze narrowed and Kahlil knew he shouldn't have spied on such a private moment. Jath'ibaye brought his right fist up and flicked his fingers through three Fai'daum hand signs.

"Vundomu. Go. Now."

What feeling was missing from the motions alone was incredibly clear from Jath'ibaye's displeased expression. It had been less than a week since he had sworn obedience to Jath'ibaye and already he had wandered off on his own, disregarded an order, and lingered where he was not wanted.

This time Kahlil obeyed at once. He reached Vundomu even before the black clouds and flashes of lightning had cleared from the northern sky.

Chapter Fifty-Six

The sun had set nearly an hour ago. From his window, Kahlil watched the gas lamps being lit all along the main road far below him. Inside his room, the lamps burned pale green mashaye oil and perfumed the air faintly with the scent of almonds.

Kahlil sat on the wide window ledge, holding the tome that Jath'ibaye had given him to translate. He closed it and set it down beside his stacks of papers, ink bottle, and pen case. It amazed him that a windowsill could accommodate so much. It was nearly the size of an entire desk. But then, everything about his room was big. The doors were high and heavy. The bed loomed up like an iron cathedral. The shower seemed like it would accommodate a half barrack of rashan'im.

Kahlil supposed that if he had owned anything the spaces would have seemed smaller. He remembered how the shelves of books had filled Alidas' rooms. They had lent the unremarkable architecture a sense of presence. They had made it seem almost as if Alidas was there even when he wasn't. Kahlil's three magnificently inlaid and detailed chambers felt empty even when he occupied them.

Outside, people gathered in the streets—far more than there should have been at this hour. Kahlil peered down. The huge iron gates that separated the wide, new streets at the base of Vundomu from the old iron avenues on the terraces above were being cranked open. Kahlil heard someone give a cheer. Then more voices joined in. The crowd washed around the riders coming up the main street.

Kahlil suddenly felt a rush of anxiety. He picked up the heavy book again, opened it, and tried to read. His concentration slipped across the words. He put the book back down and suddenly wished that he'd bothered to buy some of the new clothes he'd noticed down at the market. At the time he'd been worried about the money.

He'd only discovered this morning that Jath'ibaye had provided him with a salary. Eriki'yu, the slim blond house steward for Jath'ibaye's massive holdings, had brought the Fai'daum coins to Kahlil. He had apologized for the delay and then explained what deductions had been taken from Kahlil's pay and what his employment within Jath'ibaye's household entitled him to.

His rooms were provided free so long as he chose to live in the household. A new coat and one change of clothes were allotted to him twice a year, as was a pair of boots. The tailor and cobblers would be up to see him within the week. He was welcome to eat in the common hall or, if he arranged it beforehand, his meals could be brought up to his rooms.

Kahlil had been pleased to know that he got paid. In Nayeshi, he'd had to steal every single dollar he'd needed. It had grated on him to make himself a thief, and whenever possible, he'd committed his crimes against large institutions like banks or mints, where the loss could be afforded.

"As for your duties…" Eriki'yu had paused and glanced down at the red leather-bound book in his hands. He had frowned. "They have not been fully described as of yet, but I imagine that you will be reporting directly to Jath'ibaye. His apartments are just south of these. Almost directly across from yours, in fact."

"Across the walkway?"

"Yes. You can see them out your window."

Kahlil had looked across at the facing windows. Somehow he'd expected Jath'ibaye's apartments to be an entire palace or temple, not just a few rooms next to a watchtower.

"The first thing tomorrow you'll want to report to him there. We're expecting him back later tonight."

"I'll do that." Anxiety had clenched Kahlil's stomach into a hard knot. Jath'ibaye's orders in the morning could very well be to get out of Vundomu.

"Don't look so worried. He's really quite kind. I'm sure you'll get along just fine." Eriki'yu had given Kahlil one of those brief, professional smiles that all house stewards seemed to cultivate.

Obviously, Eriki'yu had not seen the expression on Jath'ibaye's face at the edge of the northern chasm two days prior. He'd been furious. In the interim, Kahlil had gone back to translating to get his mind off Jath'ibaye's return.

But now that Jath'ibaye had arrived, the entire fortress of Vundomu seemed to be lighting up. Shouts, cheers, and even strains of music rose from the street below.

Kahlil sighed. There was no point in putting it off. He stood and started for the door. He might as well go down and just get it over with. Then he stopped. He wasn't sure he wanted to join an adoring throng. And if Jath'ibaye was still furious, the last place he wanted to be reprimanded was in front of a crowd.

It would be better to just wait for Jath'ibaye to come to him. He sat back in the window. The riders, Kahlil counted twenty, had already made their way up to the courtyard. Grooms rushed out to take the tahldi. Jath'ibaye was easy to pick out. Even at a distance his long frame was noticeable. Ji trotted along beside him.

More people poured out from the circle of buildings that made up Jath'ibaye's household. Kahlil thought he recognized the slender figure of the house steward as well as the almost emaciated form of the ancient kahlirash commander. Probably every person in this entire three-story complex had something to tell Jath'ibaye. It wasn't as if he was Kahlil's private deity anymore.

It could be hours before Jath'ibaye got around to him. That was if he came to see Kahlil at all. He might just want a bath, a meal, and some sleep. Not that Kahlil thought Jath'ibaye would be allowed much rest. The last two days he'd overheard many of the Fai'daum anxiously discussing the peril of their friends and families in Nurjima. They all seemed to expect Jath'ibaye to arrive and answer their prayers. Doubtless, he'd be busy long into the night.

Kahlil gathered the loose pages of his translation and tried to read through them. He read a page and then had to read it again. He couldn't concentrate on worm castings or soil content. His thoughts just kept circling back to what he would say to Jath'ibaye. He needed to explain himself, to ensure that Jath'ibaye didn't think that he was undependable. Or worse, disloyal.

He looked down at the paper in his hands. He still had no idea of what he'd just read.

He wasn't going to be able to think about anything until he'd seen Jath'ibaye and settled things. He laid the papers aside and headed for the door. As he reached for the handle, there was a light knock. Kahlil yanked the door open.

Jath'ibaye stood in the hallway, his hand still raised to the door. He looked tired and dirty from traveling. The cuts across his forehead, throat, and hands had faded to thin scratches. Kahlil's own injuries looked far worse. His hands were peppered with scabs and the cut across his cheek looked ugly. The deep bruise on his shoulder was still darkening to black.

Jath'ibaye lowered his hand to his side. Kahlil's heart began hammering in his chest. Suddenly the silence between them seemed unbearable. Words came rushing out of him.

"Look, I just wanted to tell you that I realize that it was stupid of me to go off on my own when I didn't know anything about this place." Kahlil's grip on the doorknob was far too hard. The tendons were standing up on his hand. "I did tell Ji that I was leaving for a while and I couldn't have known that the northern chasm was dangerous. So I don't feel that I was completely to blame there." Kahlil rushed on before Jath'ibaye could get a word in. "But, when you came to get me and you ordered me to leave, I should have just left. I was in the wrong on that point. I'll admit that right out. It won't happen again. You don't need to send me away."

Jath'ibaye made no reply at all and Kahlil could read nothing in his expression.

Kahlil suddenly felt slightly sick. Why was he jabbering his jaw off? This wasn't like him—he was assured and knew how to handle men and the conflict they brought. He'd been more collected when he'd killed Nanvess Bousim than he felt now, with Jath'ibaye just standing in his doorway. But then, he hadn't cared if Nanvess had liked him. Jath'ibaye mattered to him enough to make him nervous, to make him feel like a nineteen-year-old idiot hanging back in the shadows of Candle Alley.

"I translated more of that book you gave to me." Kahlil tried to sound casual. "I'm almost done with the chapter on loam."

Jath'ibaye regarded Kahlil with an uncertain expression.

"How many pages have you translated?" he finally asked.

"Sixty."

"And to think I was about to give you a long dull speech." Jath'ibaye smiled just a little.

"Long and dull," Kahlil said. "I am way ahead of you."

"So it would seem," Jath'ibaye remarked. "And the next time I tell you to go, you'll go?"

"Absolutely," Kahlil said, though he suspected that it would depend on the situation.

"Really?" Jath'ibaye's eyes narrowed.

"Well, probably," Kahlil admitted.

"Probably? That's quite an oath of loyalty. You swear that you will probably do as I say." Jath'ibaye shook his head.

"It's not a matter of loyalty. I am loyal," Kahlil insisted. "It's just that sometimes someone ought to be there to keep you from getting yourself hurt. I know it's hard for you to grasp, but in Nayeshi I guarded you for over a decade—even if you didn't know I was there. It's difficult for me to leave you when it seems like you don't care what happens to you. You let Ourath Lisam lure you into an assassination attempt. You let some monster impale you. You gave up your blood to save me. You'd have let them burn you alive in Amura'taye if I hadn't come for you—I mean, if Ravishan hadn't..." Kahlil trailed off in frustration. Every time he talked to Jath'ibaye he had to struggle to keep his memory straight.

"You remember that?" Jath'ibaye stepped into the doorway.

"It would be hard to forget a day like that," Kahlil replied. The low scents of Jath'ibaye's sweat and his leather coat floated over Kahlil.

"Yes, but before you said that you weren't certain of your memories," Jath'ibaye contended.

"I wasn't. I'm still not. But I've been thinking about some things Ji told me."

"Yes, well, sometimes she can say a little too much too soon." Jath'ibaye's expression softened slightly. "She told me what the two of you had been discussing just before you took your outing to the wastes."

"My death—" Kahlil caught himself. "Ravishan's death. I'm still here, still alive."

Jath'ibaye glanced back down the hall. Kahlil could hear rushed, serious voices rising up the stairs. More than once Jath'ibaye's name was called; it sounded as though his would be the final say on some unstated disagreement.

"May I come in?" Jath'ibaye asked quickly.

"What? Oh. Yes, of course." Kahlil stepped back to allow Jath'ibaye to enter. "Sorry. I didn't realize you were waiting for an invitation."

"I just don't want to get caught up with a lot of other people right now." Jath'ibaye stepped in and pushed the door shut behind him. He surveyed the empty room. "Have you told Eriki'yu that you don't have any chairs?"

"No, I…I hadn't thought to," Kahlil said. "He'll get me chairs?"

"Yes." Jath'ibaye smiled. "What have you been sitting on? The floor?"

"The windowsill. It has a nice view." Kahlil returned to his previous position. "It's not so bad. Try it."

Jath'ibaye joined him on the sill. He picked up a page of Kahlil's translation. Kahlil leaned in slightly, following Jath'ibaye's reading.

He felt relieved that they had left the previous conversation behind. After witnessing the pain in Jath'ibaye's face at the subject of Ravishan's death, discussing a dry botanical text seemed like a relief.

"I didn't know exactly how to translate some of the words," Kahlil commented. "There's one long contracted phrase in particular. It means something like 'fine hairs knotting roots.'"

"They're probably trying to describe mycorrhizae." Jath'ibaye leaned back against the window.

"I have no idea how to write that in Basawar script," Kahlil said.

"Just use English. I'll know what it means." Jath'ibaye picked up Kahlil's pen. He held it for a moment, thinking, and then very carefully printed the word on the margin of the page. Kahlil wondered how long it had been since Jath'ibaye had even thought of his native language.

"Mycorrhizae are fungal filaments," Jath'ibaye said. "They entwine around plant roots and aid in the uptake and transfer of nutrients between root systems. Many newly germinated plants can't get enough nourishment without them."

"I had no idea," Kahlil admitted.

"I can't imagine you cared to know," Jath'ibaye replied and again Kahlil caught that flicker of a teasing smile. He must have joked like this often with Ravishan.

"I don't know…It seems like it could be important," Kahlil answered. "It could affect people's lives."

"True enough," Jath'ibaye agreed, though he seemed a little surprised that Kahlil had said as much.

As Jath'ibaye read, Kahlil observed his expression. It was so serious and at the same time almost tender. All at once, Kahlil felt that mycorrhizae had to be important. It mattered that he had translated those dozens of tedious pages for Jath'ibaye. He recalled Ji's comments about the introduction of featherfin to the lake. This is what she had meant when she said that it mattered to her because it mattered to Jath'ibaye.

Jath'ibaye finished reading the page and set it aside. He looked to Kahlil and his expression changed. The intensity was still there in his bright blue eyes, but he also seemed troubled, as if he were contemplating a difficult equation.

"Will you tell me," Jath'ibaye asked, "why you talk about Ravishan as if he were someone else?"

"He was." Kahlil frowned down at his hands. "I may carry his memories, but I didn't live his life. I didn't make the choices he did."

"But you remember his life? You remember…" Jath'ibaye didn't seem able to say anything more. His jaw clenched and he shook his head.

"If I don't think about it, then Ravishan's memories come to me as if they were my own," Kahlil admitted. "But then I realize that they can't be. When I try to straighten out what's mine and what's his, it all gets garbled and confused. Everything I know about myself is suddenly contradicted by this other life I didn't live. It's like my memory is haunted."

"How do you get through the day like that?" Jath'ibaye lifted his hand and for a moment Kahlil thought he might reach out to touch his cheek, but then Jath'ibaye caught himself and dropped his calloused hand back to the book in front of him.

"I try not to think about the past too much." Kahlil shrugged. "You'd be surprised by how little you have to know about yourself to just get through the day."

"Sounds like hell," Jath'ibaye replied.

"When I first arrived it was, but lately…" Kahlil sighed. "I don't know. Either I'm getting used to it or my memories are beginning to settle out."

"Settle out?" Jath'ibaye asked.

"I can think about the past a little more easily. There are still two histories, but instead of just crashing into each other, it's more like…" Kahlil tried to think of a way to describe the interplay of the two sets of memories in his mind.

"You know when you look out this window," Kahlil said at last, "there's the view outside but there's also your reflection in the glass. You can watch everything going on outside, but the reflection is always there. And every now and then you notice it, and the entire view outside goes out of focus. But if you shift your focus, the view comes back. That's kind of how it is for me."

Kahlil noticed Jath'ibaye's gaze flick to the window. He nodded. "So which life is it that you plan to focus on?"

"I don't know," Kahlil replied. "This entire world is Ravishan's. His history is consistent with everything that has happened here. But this is also the world that killed him. His place in this history ended twenty-seven years ago, didn't it?"

"It shouldn't have," Jath'ibaye said. He didn't meet Kahlil's gaze but instead stared out the window to the courtyard below.

"But it did." Kahlil shrugged to cover the edge of disappointment that moved through him. He knew that Jath'ibaye would prefer him to become Ravishan, his brave heroic dead lover, resurrected. But as much as Kahlil wanted Ravishan's life, he couldn't be any man but who he was. "The way I see it, neither he nor I belong to this world anymore. But I'm the one who lived and he—for better or for worse—died. I can't change that…Not even you can change that."

Jath'ibaye averted his bright gaze from Kahlil's face down to the stack of pages Kahlil had translated. "There are people here who knew him—people who were his friends. When they see you, they're not going to know what to do. They're going to want you to be him."

"I know," Kahlil said.

"They'll make mistakes. They'll want you—" Jath'ibaye cut himself short, and swallowed before continuing, "They'll want you to remember them the way they remember you. What will you tell them?"

"I'll just have to tell them that I'm not Ravishan."

"But you are fundamentally the same man. Not only are you the same flesh and blood, but you also had the same parents, the same upbringing—"

"No. When I prayed to Parfir to send me a new teacher, a man better than Dayyid, I got no one. He got you. It changed his life forever." Seeing the way Jath'ibaye's jaw clenched just slightly, Kahlil felt bad for disappointing him and also more jealous of Ravishan than he had imagined possible. "I can't be Ushiri Ravishan'in'Rathal'pesha any more than you can be John Matthew Toffler from Arlington, Washington."

Jath'ibaye looked truly surprised at the mention of his own name. Kahlil wondered if he had somehow managed to forget it. He supposed that it had been decades since anyone had called him by his real name.

At first, Jath'ibaye seemed like he might offer some further argument. The muscles of his jaw clenched and flexed but he remained silent. At last he simply said, "It's getting late."

Kahlil nodded. The hour would have been early in Nurjima but Vundomu didn't seem to support the same wild nightlife.

Jath'ibaye gathered the pages Kahlil had translated and then stood. "I should let you get some rest. Tomorrow we'll talk more about your duties and your disciplinary problems." He smiled almost ruefully as he said those last words and Kahlil couldn't help but smile back at him.

"Until then, good night." Jath'ibaye moved quickly to the door.

Kahlil tried to think of something to say, some other topic to introduce so that Jath'ibaye would not leave. But Jath'ibaye was already at the door. He glanced back at Kahlil once, just briefly. He was dirty and tired and there was an emptiness to his gaze that struck Kahlil as utterly defeated.

"Take care," Kahlil called out, but Jath'ibaye had already gone. The door closed on Kahlil's last words.

Chapter Fifty-Seven

Kahlil slept badly and only for a few hours. In his dreams, the walls of Vundomu collapsed around him. A desperate voice called to him. As he searched through the crumbling ruins, arcs of flames exploded through the halls. Out of the corner of his eye he noticed something white stalking him. With insectile speed, it skittered between the jumping shadows. As he watched he noticed more and more of the sudden flashes of motion. Bones, he realized, hundreds of hungry bones were crawling up through the wreckage.

He startled awake. Despite the cold night air, his body was damp with sweat. He heard people rushing through the hall outside his room. The sun hadn't even risen. He kicked the sheep skins and quilted blankets off his body and sat up in his massive bed, feeling disoriented and unsure of where he was or why he was here.

Then he remembered.

Vundomu.

After his dream of stalking bones, the sound of people running outside his rooms disturbed him. He got out of bed and wandered out into the empty greeting room.

He glanced out his window to Jath'ibaye's chambers. The rooms blazed with the bright green light of mashaye lamps. The silhouettes of a half-dozen people jumped and shifted as the light flickered across the white curtains.

Kahlil went to the bathroom. When he returned, the noise in the hall had stopped but Jath'ibaye's chambers looked packed. Kahlil guessed that there were at least twenty people gathered there.

He wondered what was going on. Had something gone wrong? It certainly looked that way. Did it have to do with the gaun'im in the south or with the hungry bones in the north? Or something else that he didn't even know about yet? There were too many possibilities for Kahlil to guess what had happened. But he wanted to know.

He pulled on his dark wool pants and then found the cleaner of his two shirts. His socks were getting a little ripe even by his low standards. Absently, he wondered where he was supposed to go to get his clothes laundered.

The thought slipped from his mind as he continued watching the people gathered in Jath'ibaye's chambers. He easily recognized the unique shadow cast by Ji's canine body. She was up on something—a chair or a table—shaking her head as she spoke. Her back arched slightly, hackles up.

Kahlil reached to unlatch his window, with the idea that he might be able to overhear them. Just as he slipped the latch open there came a loud knock at his door.

When he opened it, he found the young woman he's spoken with aboard Jath'ibaye's ship standing on the other side. She was no longer dressed in sailing gear, but now wore the heavy russet coat and black pants that seemed standard issue for Vundomu.

"Besh'anya?" Kahlil was almost certain that was the dark-haired girl's name.

"I didn't know if you'd remember." She smiled charmingly.

"How could I forget?" Kahlil supposed he looked a wreck, but then it was the middle of the night. Her expectations probably hadn't run too high.

"I'm going to guess from the late hour that this isn't a social call?" Kahlil hoped it wasn't a social call at least. Especially not a private one.

"I'm sorry. It's not," Besh'anya replied. "The Five Districts Council has asked for you. They're holding a meeting in Jath'ibaye's apartments right now."

"I noticed the commotion out the window," Kahlil remarked.

Besh'anya nodded. "I think everyone in the fortress has been called up in front of them. Ji sent me to get you."

"Let me get my boots." Kahlil stepped back from the door, allowing it to swing open. Hesitantly, Besh'anya followed him into his rooms.

"I'd offer you a seat, but I don't have any chairs yet." Kahlil went to the bedroom and found his boots.

"So tell me," he called from the bedroom as he laced his boots up, "what is this Five Districts Council that I'm being called before?"

"You don't know?" Besh'anya asked.

"Not yet," Kahlil replied.

"They're an elected council that makes decisions concerning the five districts of Vundomu. Wah'roa represents all of us here in the Fortress District. Tai'yu speaks for the Greenhills District. Hirran represents the Iron Heights in the east, and Gin'yu speaks for the Silverlake Islands."

"That's only four," Kahlil remarked.

"Litivi supposedly represents the Westcliff District, but really he's just his mother's proxy—Gin'yu, I mean."

"Jath'ibaye isn't a member?" Kahlil asked. He grabbed his leather coat as well as the yasi'halaun, which he strapped across his back.

"No." Besh'anya smiled at him in a shy manner that assured Kahlil that he couldn't be looking all that bad. "Jath'ibaye acts as a representative for the council when he visits the gaun'im in Nurjima."

"Really?" Kahlil went to the door and Besh'anya followed him. "I don't think the gaun'im know that."

"No," Besh'anya replied, "the gaun'im fear Jath'ibaye. So it's better if he presents the council's decisions."

"And no one is worried that he might just be presenting his own decisions?" Kahlil couldn't help but ask. He was honestly much more comfortable with the idea of Jath'ibaye as a solitary ruler than as a representative to some council. An elected council could not claim any divinity. Its members were only human and likely to fall prey to the rivalry, bribery, ambition, and short-sightedness of all mortal men.

"Of course not. Jath'ibaye is beyond reproach." Besh'anya gave Kahlil a rebuking look, but then went on, "On the few occasions that Jath'ibaye has gone ahead with a decision without the council's approval, they have always agreed that it was the right choice afterwards."

"Then, when it comes down to it, Jath'ibaye is in charge," Kahlil said, grinning.

Besh'anya studied Kahlil briefly, then hesitantly she nodded. "If Jath'ibaye wished, he could overthrow the council, but he never would."

"No," Kahlil said, "that wouldn't be like him." Doubtless, government by an elected council had been Jath'ibaye's idea in the first place. It was the kind of idealistic system that a native of Nayeshi might implement.

"Ji says he just doesn't like to be involved in politicking," Besh'anya admitted.

"Why are they meeting in his chambers then?" Kahlil asked.

"The council originally called on him to discuss the withdrawal of our people from Nurjima. But now—" Besh'anya lowered her voice and said, "—they're asking about the death of Nanvess Bousim. Ji sounded pretty frustrated when she sent me to get you."

"That doesn't sound too promising," Kahlil remarked. He had been the one to kill Nanvess, but only he and Jath'ibaye knew that—or perhaps not, if Jath'ibaye really did report to this council. It was difficult for Kahlil to imagine Jath'ibaye reporting anything to anyone. He just wasn't naturally forthcoming—at least he hadn't been when Kahlil had known him.

"Tell me as much about this council as you can, will you?" Kyle asked, and Besh'anya did her best to inform him and keep up with his fast, agitated strides.

Outside Jath'ibaye's apartments, they were greeted by several guards dressed in russet coats with the red Prayerscars of the kahlirash'im marking their brows. To his surprise, Kahlil noticed that two of the five were women. Doubtless, this was another of Jath'ibaye's progressive ideas.

Outside the heavy door Kahlil caught the tones of raised voices, but when he and Besh'anya entered the expansive greeting chamber, the crowd of some twenty people gathered around the huge marble table went quiet. All their attention turned to Kahlil.

He refused to feel intimidated. He'd faced greater audiences than this in far more unsettling surroundings. Kahlil allowed himself to take in Jath'ibaye's private suite. It appeared to be laid out much like Kahlil's own, with high ceilings and wide, deep window casings. But where the red marble inlay of Kahlil's walls stood bare, Jath'ibaye's were lined with tall wooden pharmacy shelves.

Dozens of glass terrariums filled shelf after shelf as if displaying an inventory of summer's verdancy. Beyond the gawking group of men and women gathered around Jath'ibaye's table, Kahlil noted several large Wardian cases reaching nearly to the ceiling. Dwarf apple trees, scarlet-mouthed blossoms, and huge delicate ferns filled them. Kahlil thought he caught the flash of a butterfly's wings.

He didn't know why, but he half expected to see Jath'ibaye standing there beside all that contained wilderness. But Jath'ibaye didn't appear to be in his rooms at all.

Kahlil's attention snapped back to the representatives who had summoned him. Aside from Ji, they were the only people actually seated. The rest—their secretaries, pages, and runners stood in clusters beside and behind their chairs.

Kahlil was glad for Besh'anya's descriptions of them as it allowed him to identify each of them in an instant.

The aged but still surprisingly powerfully built woman seated on the far right was Gin'yu, representative of the Silverlake District. The bland, brown-haired thirty-something with his mouth hanging half open was obviously her son, Litivi, whose filial obedience apparently granted Gin'yu power over the humble shepherds of the Westcliff District as well as her own island populations.

Looking past Litivi, Kahlil's gaze fell upon an older man with graying red hair, dark eyes, and a nose as hooked as an eagle's beak. This had to be Tai'yu, the Fai'daum war hero who represented the vast taye-producing northlands, called the Greenhills. Besh'anya had claimed that he possessed a charming sense of humor, but the expression he wore as he regarded Kahlil seemed far from amused.

In sharp contrast to Tai'yu was his daughter, Hirran. She was young and startlingly beautiful. Kahlil could only assume that she'd inherited her graceful figure, long black hair, and pixie nose from her mother. She represented the Iron Heights, where the vast seams of iron that so many gaun'im craved were located. Hirran was also Besh'anya's favorite cousin, apparently.

Last among them was Wah'roa, the commander of the kahlirash'im as well as the representative of the entire city of Vundomu. His slim build and slight stature could have been a boy's, but the deep wrinkles lining his gaunt face bore testament to the tumultuous seventy-three years he'd lived through. Thin war braids held his fine white hair back against his skull. The red Prayerscar that Kahlil remembered blazing like a brand upon his brow had now faded to a dull garnet. He alone of the representatives gazed at Kahlil with an expression of open welcome.

And Kahlil realized that Jath'ibaye and Ji weren't the only ones who wanted Ravishan to have been brought back to them. He had to look away from the old man's warm regard.

Two toned young women dressed in uniforms of the kahlirash'im stood behind Wah'roa's chair. Both sported black tattoos of wedding bands across their fingers. Neither wore marriage chains. Kahlil had yet to see a woman in the Fai'daum northlands who did.

Beside Wah'roa, Ji crouched on a red, overstuffed chair. Against the full velvety curves of the chair, she looked faded and scruffy, like a hunting trophy that had been badly stuffed. Besh'anya's brother Chyemon stood behind her.

"Members of the council," Ji addressed the room in a low soft voice, "this is Kyle'insira."

Wah'roa stood, with surprising grace for a man of his age. He held up his red, knotted fingers in the Payshmura sign of blessing. Instinctively, Kahlil returned the gesture. Their exchange caused an unnatural, sudden hush. Wah'roa slumped back down into his seat.

"Kyle'insira was responsible for stopping the assassination attempt," Ji continued.

"Our thanks go out to you," Gin'yu told him.

Kahlil inclined his head to her. She smiled, and the expression seemed to lighten her otherwise dour countenance.

"Ji advises the council," Besh'anya whispered to Kahlil. "We're with her."

She led him to Ji's chair, beside Wah'roa's. Everyone in the room watched his movement. All the while, Kahlil scanned the gathering for Jath'ibaye as if he could have somehow overlooked his blond, towering figure between two of the mousy secretaries or behind the cluster of scrawny, yawning runners. It seemed wrong that he shouldn't be in his own chambers when so many other people were.

"*...and in the hour of darkness, the Kahlil shall return, and in his wake, divine wrath shall fall upon our enemy and he will be no more...*" Wah'roa quoted the scripture so softly that Kahlil doubted even he was meant to hear it. Certainly, none of the other representatives seemed to take notice.

"Now that Kyle'insira has arrived, we should continue." Gin'yu rose from her seat and gave Kahlil a severe glare. "There are questions that the council would like to put to you, Kyle'insira. We hope that you will be forthcoming and honest in your answers."

"I will do my best," Kahlil responded.

"Ji will sense it if you are not," Litivi informed him with what he probably felt was a menacing glower. If the circumstances had been different, Kahlil might have taken the time to knock that sneer off Litivi's face before answering. But instead he chose to behave civilly.

"I understand," Kahlil replied. "Ask what you will."

"Tell us how you came to know of the assassination planned against Jath'ibaye," Gin'yu commanded.

"A Bousim spy in the Lisam gaunsho's house reported it to my commander." Kahlil could see that the council members were not pleased with his answer.

"And what happened after your commander was informed of this plot?" Gin'yu asked.

"He sent me out to stop it." Kahlil shrugged.

"And why didn't you or your commander simply inform Jath'ibaye of the danger he was in?" Gin'yu asked.

Kahlil almost laughed at the suggestion. What self-respecting gaun commander did she imagine would go running to the leader of the Fai'daum at the first sign of trouble?

"It was hoped that the problem could be handled within the gaun'im."

"The Bousim family wanted to protect Jath'ibaye?" Tai'yu asked. His tone was soft, but his expression was concerned. Hirran, too, seemed intent upon this specific question. At least the pair of pretty girls gathered around her were taking rapid notes.

"Yes," Kahlil replied. "Their holdings border your lands. Of all the gaun'im, the Bousim family would be most likely to suffer the worst losses if there were another war." Kahlil couldn't help but think of Alidas. He had wanted so deeply to avoid another war.

"And yet Nanvess Bousim was one of the conspirators in the assassination plot?" Tai'yu asked.

"Yes." Kahlil nodded.

"If the Bousim gaun'im are as anxious to maintain the peace as you claim, then why would the heir to their household do such a thing?" Gin'yu demanded.

"I don't know," Kahlil replied. He didn't like where these questions seemed to be leading.

"You couldn't guess?" Gin'yu asked. "You couldn't offer even one reason why we should believe that the first heir to the Bousim house would risk so much?"

"He might have been promised lands." Kahlil did not want to mention Nayeshi without first consulting Jath'ibaye.

"Which lands?" Gin'yu demanded before Kahlil could gather his thoughts.

"I don't know," Kahlil replied.

"Did they discuss the Iron Heights?" Litivi suggested. "Or control of the Samsira River?"

"I don't know," Kahlil repeated. The memory was clear in his mind. He could see Fikiri, weathered and scarred, smiling as he spoke of feeding the yasi'halaun on Jath'ibaye's blood. The blade would become powerful enough to tear open the space between the worlds. That was where they had hoped to find their new kingdom. Fikiri and his Lady had promised them Nayeshi.

The impossibility of such a conquest still stunned Kahlil. Nayeshi was vast, more than twice Basawar's landmass. The militaries there possessed weapons that none of the gaun'im could have even imagined. Jets, tanks, napalm, hydrogen bombs. And that was assuming an invasion force could even survive the passage through a Great Gate. He was the Kahlil, but even he had nearly died in his last passage.

"Are they after Vundomu itself?" Litivi's voice cut into Kahlil's thoughts. Kahlil scowled at the man, unsure of how many more times he would have to state ignorance before Litivi moved on with the questioning.

"I don't know," Kahlil told him. "But maybe if you ask another five or six times I'll have made something up—"

"Certainly you can hazard a guess—"

"If he doesn't know, he doesn't know." Ji barred her yellowed teeth as she spoke.

"This is not an interrogation!" Wah'roa called out. "Rav—Kyle'insira has come to us as an ally and we must remember that!"

"No one is saying otherwise, Wah'roa," Gin'yu replied coolly, soothingly. "But you know as well as I do that these events have put us on the brink of another war with the gaun'im. Right now the Bousim's demand for justice for the murder of their heir is the driving force behind the aggression. If we are to answer their demands, then we must know exactly what happened and why."

"Jath'ibaye has already told you what happened," Ji answered.

"He has." Gin'yu bowed her head slightly at the mention of Jath'ibaye's name, but then she pressed on, "But he cannot know why these things occurred. A confessed agent of the Bousim house might be expected to possess a little more insight."

"Don't forget, Ji," Litivi took up the instant Gin'yu paused, "if your son or anyone else was harmed in the riot against the glass palace in Nurjima, it will have been because of Nanvess Bousim's death."

"Nanvess' death was due to his own treachery," Ji growled.

"Yes, Nanvess obviously deserved his death." It was the first time that Hirran spoke since her introduction. "We all know that. But, if we are to keep peace with the gaun'im, we must convince them of that. Right now we have little to support our claim that Jath'ibaye was defending himself against assassins. And it appears that Ourath Lisam has led the rest of the gaun'im to believe that Jath'ibaye killed Nanvess in a brawl. So we need Kyle'insira to provide us with as much information as possible." She offered Kahlil a warm smile. If he'd been a different man, he suspected he would have been very flattered, but as was, he couldn't help but notice the calculation in her gaze.

"As I said, I'll answer as well as I can," Kahlil replied.

"Let us leave the question of Nanvess' motive aside for the moment then," Gin'yu decided. "Tell us exactly what your instructions were concerning the assassination."

"Originally, I was ordered to stop it—"

"Originally?" Gin'yu cut into Kahlil's answer. "Were your orders changed?"

"Yes." Kahlil frowned. "After I reported back that Nanvess was one of the conspirators, I was told not to interfere with the assassination."

"Why?" This time the question came from Tai'yu. The deep furrow of his red brows over his sharp nose gave him a predatory appearance, but his tone was polite.

"Nanvess was the heir. If a Bousim agent were discovered to have sabotaged him, then it would have destabilized the family. So I was ordered to cease my work."

"But you didn't?" Tai'yu asked.

"No," Kahlil replied.

"Why not?" Tai'yu cocked his head slightly. The gesture did nothing to dispel his resemblance to a large bird of prey.

"Because it would have been wrong," Kahlil replied.

"That's quite morally upstanding for a gaun's agent, isn't it?" Litivi asked.

Kahlil narrowed his gaze at the thickset man. "You make it sound as if I should have allowed them to kill Jath'ibaye."

Litivi's face flushed furious red. "How dare you—" he began, but Hirran cut him off.

"Let's not get off track in our questions. We are all glad that Jath'ibaye is well and protecting us." She gazed sweetly at Litivi for a moment, then glanced to Kahlil. "Kyle'insira could not have known that Jath'ibaye did not need his aid."

But Jath'ibaye had needed his protection that night. Nanvess had wielded the yasi'halaun, the blade created to destroy the

Rifter. Kahlil refused to reveal that information to these people, though. The fewer people who knew of the yasi'halaun, the fewer there would be who would think to use it. He really needed to ask Jath'ibaye what his council knew and what they did not.

"Speaking of Jath'ibaye, shouldn't he be here?" Kahlil addressed his question to Ji, but Hirran answered.

"Jath'ibaye is securing the safe return of our people from Nurjima. He asked that we proceed without him." There was the slightest flicker of her thick lashes, but it made Kahlil suspect that she was not being entirely honest about Jath'ibaye's request. Kahlil had lied enough in his life to recognize the signs in others.

"Let me speak frankly, Kyle'insira." Tai'yu leaned forward. "The only thing we really need to know about the assassination is who actually killed Nanvess."

It went against Kahlil's better judgment to answer the question honestly. But these people had already spoken to Jath'ibaye. They likely knew the answer.

"I killed him. I cut his throat."

Hirran broke into a wide, beautiful smile. Kahlil found it slightly sinister that she looked so happy about a murder.

"So, Nanvess Bousim was killed by an agent of the Bousim gaunsho? Then this entire conflict need not involve the Fai'daum at all," Hirran pronounced.

"I wasn't acting under the gaunsho's orders," Kahlil said.

"All the better." Gin'yu looked around the table at the other members of the council. "I believe that we may now cast our votes. All in favor of returning Kyle'insira to the Bousim to stand trial for his crimes, show your hands."

Kahlil's stomach lurched at Gin'yu's words.

"This is an inexcusable injustice!" Ji growled. Gin'yu shrugged in response. She glanced around the table, giving a hard little smile to the three other council members who, like herself, held up their hands. Only Wah'roa failed to cast his vote with theirs.

"Are you abstaining, Wah'roa, or did you fall asleep again?" Litivi asked.

"The kahlirash'im do not repay a man's loyalty with betrayal," Wah'roa replied. "I will not surrender him to the Bousim."

"Your objection is noted," Gin'yu said, "but four to one still passes the motion. Kyle'insira will be sent to the Bousim first thing in the morning."

"No, he won't."

Kahlil jumped at the sound of Jath'ibaye's voice. Clearly, he had just entered the room. His heavy coat was flecked with snow. His cheeks looked red from the cold outside. His gaze moved over the assembly of men and women. Immediately, the council members dropped their hands. Hirran lowered her head as if she were embarrassed. For a moment Jath'ibaye's full attention rested on Kahlil. He straightened slightly and Jath'ibaye smiled. Then he glanced to Ji.

"Our people have arrived from Nurjima," Jath'ibaye told her. "I had to flood the river to get them here ahead of the gaun'im, but their ship just cleared the locks."

"Saimura?" Ji asked.

"He's fine," Jath'ibaye assured her. Then he turned his attention back to the gathered crowd. "As for Kyle'insira, he is under my protection. Any act against him is an offense to me."

"Certainly, we meant no offense, Jath'ibaye." Gin'yu kept her head bowed as she addressed him. "But if we can avert a war by sending this man back to his masters, then surely you must see the necessity of our decision." Her voice changed as she spoke, softening and rising almost like a child's.

"None of us want a war," Jath'ibaye replied, "but an act of desperate appeasement will not secure peace. It will only tempt the Bousim house to make further demands."

"A treaty might be drawn up to ensure…" Hirran's voice was little more than a whisper. She went silent as she saw Jath'ibaye's deepening scowl.

"None of you know what you would be sacrificing if you turned this man over to the Bousim house," Jath'ibaye stated.

"Our honor and pride as a nation!" Wah'roa's deep voice was far too loud for the perfect hush of the room. If the situation had not been so serious, Kahlil might have found Wah'roa's sudden bellow amusing.

"Yes, on moral grounds it would certainly put us at an all-time low." Jath'ibaye glared at Gin'yu and Litivi with particular force.

"But aside from that, there is a very real and powerful force that we would lose if we lost Kyle. Most of you are too young to know of the Kahlil. But you have seen the power of a man trained to claim that title. When Fikiri comes and slaughters our guards, when he steals our children, he is misusing the skills of a Kahlil. This man, Kyle, is also a Kahlil. And he, too, can move in the Gray Space."

Instantly, the focus of every gaze in the room shifted from Jath'ibaye to Kahlil. The expressions were a mix of surprise, shock, and fear.

"Can you give them a demonstration?" Jath'ibaye spoke as if he were asking for the time.

"Certainly." Kahlil had been preparing to give them a demonstration in any case. If they had attempted to seize him so that they could turn him over to the Bousim house, he would have slipped away. As it was, Kahlil flicked his fingers apart and stepped into the cold, gray silence. He moved through the wide-eyed crowd. Litivi's mouth hung open. Gin'yu seemed terrified. Hirran clasped one hand to her chest and the other over her mouth. The assistants and secretaries stared in awe at the empty space where Kahlil had been standing.

Only a second later Kahlil stepped out of the Gray Space, just beside Hirran's seat. She screamed as he appeared beside her. Other women and men in the room cried out and shouted in surprise. Several assistants dropped their papers. Wah'roa let out a raucous laugh.

Kahlil glanced to Jath'ibaye. There was just the slightest hint of a smug smile at the corners of his mouth. He said, "I think that it's no exaggeration to say that we will need Kyle's help if we ever hope to stop Fikiri."

"How…how did you do that?" Hirran was still breathing a little raggedly.

"Years of training," Kahlil replied.

"Are there other ushiri'im in the Bousim house?" Tai'yu asked. Now that he had left the colorless Gray Space, Kahlil could see how the blood had drained from Tai'yu's features. He looked like he was carved from chalk. Kahlil didn't miss his use of the Payshmura title. Tai'yu was old enough to have fought ushiri'im before.

"No," Kahlil assured him, "only Fikiri and I are left of the ushiri'im. The rest died when Rathal'pesha fell."

"That was nearly thirty years ago," Gin'yu said.

"I'm older than I look," Kahlil replied. He wasn't about to offer her any further information.

"This still doesn't solve the problem of the gaun'im," Litivi announced. "What are we going to do about them?"

"Right now," Jath'ibaye said, "there is nothing we can do but wait. It will be another week before the river is traversable. That should give them a little more time to cool down before they can reach us."

"It doesn't need to come to actual battle, though, does it?" Litivi asked. "Jath'ibaye could just destroy the lands or overflow the river."

Jath'ibaye looked pained by the suggestion. "If I had to, yes. But either action would destroy the river villages as well the cities of Shaye'hahlir and Mahn'illev."

"We have trading partners in those cities," Hirran objected.

"And families!" Tai'yu glared at Hirran. "We can't destroy Mahn'illev."

"I'm not planning to," Jath'ibaye said.

"Then what are we going to do?" Litivi demanded.

"Right now?" Jath'ibaye said. "We're going to dismiss this meeting and go welcome our people back from Nurjima."

"But—" Litivi didn't seem to know when to give up.

"Jath'ibaye is right," Gin'yu cut him off. "We've all been at this table arguing too long." She asked for another show of hands regarding the fate of Kyle'insira. This time the vote was unanimous. He could stay.

Gin'yu nodded. "With that decided, let us dismiss this council." She looked to Jath'ibaye and inclined her head. "Thank you for your patience and efforts on the council's behalf."

"Thank you for considering my opinions," Jath'ibaye replied.

As the council members and their assistants quickly departed, Kahlil drifted back toward Ji. He noted that Wah'roa had risen from his seat only to linger.

"Thank you both for speaking for me," Kahlil said.

"I'm just glad to have seen you again," Wah'roa said. "The last time it was hardly a meeting at all."

Kahlil couldn't really remember the old man but he felt certain that Ravishan would have. As with Ji, an instinctive feeling of trust came to him when he regarded Wah'roa.

"You should come to the training field later. You could show my young kahlirash'im a trick or two." Wah'roa grinned. Kahlil was surprised that even at his advanced age he retained so many of his teeth and that the filed points were still so sharp. He smiled back at Wah'roa and promised to visit soon.

Wah'roa started for the door and Ji jumped down from her seat. She glanced to where Jath'ibaye stood, holding the door for Wah'roa, and cocked her head to look up at Kahlil.

"He hasn't slept in days," Ji whispered. "Make him go to bed."

"Make him?" Kahlil raised an eyebrow. "I don't think anyone makes him do anything."

Ji fixed Kahlil with a meaningful stare. "Don't underestimate your influence over him."

"It's not what you think. He and I, we aren't—"

"Forget about what you aren't," Ji replied. "Just remember what you are—his friend, his guardian. Make him rest."

"But I don't think he wants me—"

Ji yawned, cutting off Kahlil's objection. "I need to go see my son. So, like it or not, I'm leaving Jath'ibaye in your care."

She flashed him a toothy smile, then padded out behind Wah'roa. The door fell closed behind her and he was alone with Jath'ibaye.

Chapter Fifty-Eight

Kahlil was suddenly very aware of the subtle green fragrance that hung in the air of Jath'ibaye's rooms. The richness of the atmosphere reminded him of Nayeshi. It made him think of the Sunday mornings in the summer when he had woken up to the smell of fresh-cut grass. John had always been out in the yard, pushing his old manual mower.

Kahlil remembered watching the muscles of John's bare back and listening to the sound of the whirling steel blades as they sheared through the grass. The grass was always too long, always an effort to mow. It was John's presence that stimulated its growth, but John couldn't have known that. He had simply labored under the bright Nayeshi sun, his muscles flexing and shining with sweat. Often, he would pause, studying some weed or passing insect with a gentle appreciation.

Recalling that, Kahlil could now see how Jath'ibaye's face had changed since they had lived in Nayeshi. He bore neither wrinkles nor scars as testaments to the hardship of his decades in Basawar; physically, he remained handsome and young. It was not a matter of what Jath'ibaye had gained, but what he had lost.

In Nayeshi, Kahlil had loved to watch John smiling, lost in some daydream. There had been something beautiful and touching in John's unconcerned expression, in the way he would lie under the open sky, his eyes almost closed. Both languid and exposed, he had seemed so at ease, utterly assured of the world around him.

All of that was gone now. The tension in Jath'ibaye's body remained even as he leaned back against the edge of the table. He held his shoulders too straight. His hand always rested close to his holstered pistol. Even as his gaze moved through the empty space of his room, it was focused, searching. Jath'ibaye seemed always to be looking at something just out of sight, always watching as if he were calculating the speed and distance of some impending attack. As far as Kahlil could tell, Jath'ibaye's gaze never softened or drifted into carelessness anymore.

How long had been it since Jath'ibaye had indulged in a pointless daydream? Years, probably. He couldn't command Jath'ibaye to relax, but he might be able to make him go to bed. Maybe. If he used just the right approach.

"You look like hell," Kahlil commented. Jath'ibaye shot him an exasperated look, but he went on undeterred, "I think you need to get some sleep."

"I will later." Jath'ibaye waved the idea aside.

"Really?" Kahlil asked. Jath'ibaye had made no move to remove even his heavy coat. "Because you don't seem like you're planning to go to bed anytime soon."

"I don't need to sleep," Jath'ibaye replied. "I can go weeks without it."

"Sure you can, but that's no reason to avoid it," Kahlil said. "I could survive in the Gray Space for days at a time. It doesn't mean that I should."

"That's hardly the same thing. The Gray Space would grind you apart," Jath'ibaye said.

"And what's happening to you?" Kahlil asked. "I know you could keep going. Physically, you could survive without ever sleeping or eating or even breathing. So long as you are in this world, you will live. But that's just your body. It's not your mind. Certainly not your spirit."

"Did Ji put you up to this?" Jath'ibaye asked.

"She told me you hadn't slept in days, but frankly anyone looking at you could see that." Kahlil frowned at him. "When was the last time you even had a bath?"

"I have been a little busy," Jath'ibaye responded tersely. "I did just evacuate my people out of Nurjima, after riding all the way from the northern chasm, and before that, I was occupied with saving your ass."

"My ass could have taken care of itself." Kahlil couldn't quite keep a straight face at his own words. He caught the flicker of a smile on Jath'ibaye's lips as well, so he continued, "My ass is highly trained."

"Your ass—" Jath'ibaye began and then cut himself off, face flushed. "I'm sorry. I'm obviously too tired to do my best talking."

"Obviously," Kahlil agreed.

Standing together like this, bickering without any real anger, it was easy to forget that they were not lovers. It was even harder to remember that they never had been. He knew the heat of John's naked skin against his own body. He knew the feel of his lips and the taste of his sweat. Kahlil's skin warmed at the memory.

He had to stop thinking of making love with Jath'ibaye or he would never make it though this conversation.

To distract himself Kahlil made a study of the jungle of terrariums filling the shelves along the walls. The flash of a yellow moth's wings momentarily caught his attention. He watched the small insect flit from one white bell-like flower to another. He wondered what Jath'ibaye would tell him if he asked about this creature.

Probably too much. He always concerned himself about such small things. Microscopic things. Ever since he'd been a little boy.

Kahlil said, "If you won't take care of yourself for your own sake, you ought to do it for the population living here in Vundomu."

"I can't possibly look that bad." Jath'ibaye finally took off his coat. He tossed it across one of the chairs. "I might smell that bad but—"

"The people here look to you for their protection," Kahlil said. "They don't want to see you looking haggard and filthy when they're facing the threat of a war."

"You realize you're advocating for the same people who just tried to sacrifice you to the Bousim house?" Jath'ibaye asked.

"They're just scared," Kahlil replied. "And they don't know me. As far as they were concerned, I was a Bousim spy who went against his own masters. Why not sacrifice me to save their own people?"

"Maybe that was what they were thinking," Jath'ibaye said. He frowned at the table. "But if it's Hirran we're talking about, then the whole thing probably just struck her as an opportunity to reopen trade negotiations."

At the time of the meeting, Kahlil hadn't gotten much of an impression of Hirran. She had been pretty and soft spoken. But Kahlil trusted Jath'ibaye's opinion. Oddly, Jath'ibaye seemed to sense that and he shook his head.

"I shouldn't say that. Hirran's a good girl, when it comes right down to it. She's just very driven, very focused on building relations with the gaun'im."

"A war might make that difficult."

"It might, but I'd bet my teeth that if anyone could come up with a way to trade with the gaun'im while fighting them it would be Hirran." Despite his disapproving words, affection carried through Jath'ibaye's tone.

Kahlil pulled out one of the chairs and sat down. He had to shift a little to accommodate the length of the yasi'halaun.

Jath'ibaye dropped back into the chair opposite him. Against the dark red upholstery Jath'ibaye's skin looked deathly pale and the shadows beneath his eyes appeared almost blue. He leaned back and closed his eyes.

"I know the people here count on me," Jath'ibaye said.

Studying him, Kahlil thought that perhaps too many people counted on Jath'ibaye for too much. He turned rivers, defeated hungry bones. He represented them in Nurjima and protected their lands. He was their first defense as well as their last hope. It was too much to expect of one man, no matter how powerful he was. Kahlil knew from his own experience how crushing such responsibility could be.

"Well, you're no good to anyone like this." Kahlil caught hold of Jath'ibaye's hand. His skin was warm and dry. "You need to have a bath and get some sleep."

"I should go down to the forges—" Jath'ibaye murmured but Kahlil cut him off.

"Is your bath on the left? Mine is. The layout of our apartments seems pretty similar."

"They're identical," Jath'ibaye said.

"Let's go then."

"Fine," Jath'ibaye said at last. He stood and allowed Kahlil to pull him into the tiled bathroom. The tub was much larger than the one in Kahlil's rooms, apparently specially made to accommodate Jath'ibaye's long limbs.

Kahlil pumped the first rush of cold water down the drain and then closed the trap to catch the hot water that followed. Wisps of steam curled up to fog the mirror mounted on the wall.

"You'd better get in while it's still hot," Kahlil told Jath'ibaye.

Jath'ibaye began, clumsily, to undress. Kahlil stepped out of the room but didn't close the door. He heard Jath'ibaye's filthy clothes fall heavily to the floor. Then came the quiet whisper of the water breaking as Jath'ibaye eased himself into the tub.

Kahlil went to the table and dragged one of the chairs over and sat with his back to the bathroom door to give Jath'ibaye his privacy. He gazed again at the huge glass case in front of him. A thick vine twined its woody stem between the planes of glass, using them to support its canopy of green and gold leaves. Tiny red mushrooms and velvety green moss covered the soil.

"So, why all the plants?" Kahlil called back to Jath'ibaye.

"What do you mean?" Jath'ibaye countered. Kahlil could hear him unscrewing a soap tin.

"You've got this huge collection. What's it for?" Kahlil asked.

"Does it have to be for something?"

"They don't have to be for anything, but knowing you, they are."

Jath'ibaye gave a soft, low laugh. Kahlil smiled to himself.

"So?" Kahlil prompted.

"Just a minute. I have to rinse my hair."

Kahlil waited, rocking his chair back against the wall, while Jath'ibaye dunked his head under the water.

"I'm trying to rebuild the natural diversity of these lands," Jath'ibaye said at last. "Every time the Payshmura opened the Great Gates it placed an incredible strain on the land. The soil weakened; the air lost much of its nitrogen and oxygen content. The plants and animals that I've been gathering were all once native to this area. I'm trying to reintroduce them."

“I didn’t know that the Great Gates damaged the lands,” Kahlil remarked.

“When they’re opened, living force drains from Basawar to Nayeshi. The Eastern sorceresses knew about it, but they couldn’t convince the Payshmura to destroy the gates.”

“Really?”

“I don’t think the Payshmura widely publicized their dissent. But even when I first arrived I felt something was wrong with the land. It felt weak, almost sick. I had no idea why, of course.” The water sloshed as Jath’ibaye rose from the tub. “Ji told me about the rest.”

Kahlil glanced back, catching a glimpse of Jath’ibaye’s naked body. He was as strong and lean as Kahlil remembered. Tiny rivulets of water traced the curves of his muscles. The fine blond hairs on his chest, arms, and legs glistened with droplets of water. He reached for a towel.

Kahlil whipped his eyes back around to the front.

“So where did you find them, the plants, I mean? If there weren’t any left here?” Kahlil asked, though he was only half prepared to listen to Jath’ibaye’s reply. The image of Jath’ibaye’s body still played through his mind.

“Some are common, just growing farther south. Others, like the moonvines, were propagated from one sickly plant that managed to survive at the edge of its natural range.” Jath’ibaye’s voice was slightly muffled as he toweled his hair. “I think a few species might have survived on some of the islands, east of the great rift, but so much has become extinct.”

Jath’ibaye came to the door. He’d wrapped the towel around his hips. His skin was still pink from the heat of the bath.

“Sometimes when I’m looking through the old bestiaries and botanical books this sense of loss overwhelms me…”

“You do what you can with what remains.” Kahlil wasn’t sure if he was talking about his own life or Basawar’s mass extinctions. “It’s a beautiful plant. I’m glad you could save it.”

“So am I.” Jath’ibaye crouched down beside Kahlil’s chair. He pointed to the tiny red mushrooms dotting the soil in the glass case in front of them. “Before we discovered that mushroom we couldn’t get any of the moonvine’s seeds to germinate. But once we brought the two together they started sprouting right and left. And not just moonvine, frond trees as well.”

“Because of the mycorrhizae?”

Jath’ibaye smiled, beautifully. “Yes. I’m amazed you remembered.”

“I’m a little amazed myself,” Kahlil admitted. The scent of soap lingered on Jath’ibaye’s skin. Already, his hair was beginning to curl into disordered locks.

“What we see above the ground are just the mushrooms’ fruiting bodies. Many of them only fruit every ten or twenty years. The rest of the time they lead existences that are invisible to us, but they are integral to entire forests.” Jath’ibaye gazed at the glossy red mushrooms almost affectionately. “Sometimes they remind me of you.”

“Mushrooms?” Kahlil laughed.

“It’s not a bad thing,” Jath’ibaye protested.

“I know,” Kahlil said. “You’re probably the only man who would compare me to a fungus and mean it as a compliment.”

“It’s just the hidden nature of what you both do.” A hint of red crept up Jath’ibaye’s face. “I shouldn’t be trying to talk. Everything is coming out wrong.”

“Sleep might help that problem,” Kahlil suggested.

“I know. I should just go to bed.” Jath’ibaye stood as if to bid him good night and see him out but then hesitated at Kahlil’s side. He said, “If you aren’t too tired, I would like to show you one last thing.”

“I’m not the one who’s asleep on his feet,” Kahlil replied. “Sure. Show me what you’ve got.”

Jath’ibaye gave a short laugh at that and then shook his head before Kahlil could ask why. He said, “Come back to my bedroom and have a look.”

As Kahlil followed Jath’ibaye into his bedroom, his heartbeat quickened irrationally.

Here too, the several Wardian cases and glass terrariums brimming with lush botanical specimens lent the cold stone walls the illusion of summer. Earthy scents permeated the atmosphere. Worn leather tomes littered the few shelves not overflowing with vegetation. A wooden writing desk and chair stood beside a larger table—the top of which appeared to be entirely engulfed by mosses and ground covers. It took Kahlil a moment to notice Jath'ibaye's simple bed and dresser pushed back into a far corner, as if they were necessary inconveniences.

Jath'ibaye went to one of the large terrariums that filled his deep windowsill. Kahlil followed, though he paused as he took in the display of mosses, stones, and tiny flowers that dominated Jath'ibaye's table.

It was a scale model, Kahlil realized. He easily recognized the mountains surrounding Vundomu, though they were carved from black granite. He followed the stream of blue quartz pebbles that represented the Samsira River down through the emerald, moss-covered hills and valleys to Nurjima. Farther south, the rolling hills of the Du'yura lands flattened into the fields of tiny white flowers and the clover meadows of the Lisam lands. At every point where a major city, town or fortress would have stood, clusters of polished stones gleamed.

Kahlil frowned at the fine white sand that covered the northern tip of the display. Kahlil recalled Fikiri speaking of stones that Jath'ibaye used as wards.

"What is this?" Kahlil asked.

"A model," Jath'ibaye replied without much interest. "The soil and stones are linked to the real lands. Ji built it to keep track of things outside of Vundomu. I just use it to grow varieties of winter moss."

A dim red light flickered through the blue quartz of the Samsira River. Very slowly it moved northward toward Vundomu.

"You can see the gaun'im's forces approaching with this, can't you?"

"Yes," Jath'ibaye said. "But that's not what I wanted to show you right this moment. Will you come over here?" Jath'ibaye beckoned Kahlil to where he stood.

Reluctantly, Kahlil left the model to join Jath'ibaye beside a terrarium filled with low-growing plants. Splashes of scarlet colored the dark green leaves and red runners spread from one plant to another. A few had produced small white flowers, while others sheltered dark red fruit beneath their leaves.

"Are these Nayeshi strawberries?" Kahlil asked in amazement.

Jath'ibaye nodded. "Fragaria ananassa. I think they crossed to Basawar with me. I had all kinds of seeds and pollens on me and in my pack." He shook his head. "I have no idea how these, out of everything, survived, but they did. I came across them in the Iron Heights three years ago. Would you like one?"

Kahlil nodded.

Jath'ibaye lifted the lid of one of the glass cases, picked several plump red berries, and then closed the case again. The sweet fragrance of the berries floated in the air. Jath'ibaye carefully placed the strawberries in Kahlil's cupped hand.

"Don't you want any?"

"No, I glutted myself a while back. You go ahead." Jath'ibaye flipped back the blankets of his bed. Kahlil watched as Jath'ibaye reached under his pillow and fished out a pair of russet long johns. Kahlil nibbled at the first strawberry while trying not to be caught ogling Jath'ibaye's nakedness as he tossed the towel aside and pulled on the long johns. The fabric clung to the muscles of his thighs.

The berry was intensely sweet and tangy. He closed his eyes, and for the briefest moment, it seemed that he was back on Nayeshi. He remembered the first time he'd eaten a strawberry there. Unprepared for the brilliant taste, he'd been shocked at the way other people could simply toss them into their mouths and chew.

"These are so good." He looked to Jath'ibaye, who had settled on the simple bed. "You could make a fortune selling these to the gaun'im, you know."

"Actually, they seem to be something of an acquired taste, at least in Basawar. A lot of people think they're too strong." He stifled a yawn. "The fruit burns their mouths, apparently."

"Pineapple would probably kill them." Kahlil sat down in Jath'ibaye's desk chair. He knew he should leave, but it seemed so natural to remain beside him. Kahlil shifted the yasi'halaun so that he could lean back into the chair more comfortably. He stretched out his legs in front of him.

"If I had just one jalapeño pepper I could bring them all to their knees," Jath'ibaye muttered.

"Yeah, I'm sure that's all that's holding you back." Kahlil closed his eyes and let his head drop back against the chair.

"Are you going to sleep there?" Jath'ibaye asked.

Kahlil's eyes popped open and he straightened. "No, I was just resting my eyes for a few minutes before I left."

"There's room on the bed," Jath'ibaye said. "You can stay."

"Things are already so complicated…" Kahlil said. "I should go back to my own room." But he didn't move.

"Stay," Jath'ibaye said. His eyes were almost closed, his hands curled up close to his chest. He seemed disarmingly young, vulnerable, and human. He looked the way Kahlil remembered John looking years ago. "It doesn't have to be anything you don't want. Just lie beside me, so that I can know you're safe."

"I'm the one who's supposed to keep you safe," Kahlil told him.

"All right," Jath'ibaye agreed easily. "Stay and keep me safe. But just stay with me."

Neither of them was the man the other remembered. They couldn't be. Kahlil knew that. But gazing at Jath'ibaye now, he felt that they weren't so different either.

Kahlil slung the yasi'halaun down off his back and laid it across Jath'ibaye's desk. He removed his boots and coat, aware of Jath'ibaye watching his every move. He stripped to his underwear and guttered the lamps. Then he slid under the blankets, careful to keep to his side of the bed.

He lay there, staring up at the ceiling, every part of his body aware that Jath'ibaye rested just a few inches away.

It was torture. But he couldn't bring himself to get up and leave.

It was strangely touching to think that Jath'ibaye could know him so well and still trust him so completely. There had been a time when one of Kahlil's duties would have been to kill him. They both knew that but it didn't seem to matter anymore.

That knowledge had kept Kahlil from ever becoming too close to John while they had lived together in Nayeshi. The inhibition remained with him even now, as memories of Ravishan and Jahn's first night together in Nurjima flooded back to him. The smell of Jahn's sweat, the heat of his hard, naked body and the taste of his skin churned through Kahlil's thoughts. An aching desire pulsed through him. He yearned to reach across those few inches and touch John the way he had never allowed himself to while they lived together in their rented house on Indian Street.

Kahlil slid his hand across the bedding and lightly traced the line of Jath'ibaye's shoulder. His fingers skimmed the thick mass of Jath'ibaye's bicep. Hard muscle flexed beneath hot, delicate skin. Kahlil started to pull his hand back, but Jath'ibaye caught him in a firm grip. A moment later his soft mouth covered Kahlil's.

Kahlil curled his hand around the back of Jath'ibaye's neck, pulling him into a deeper, more desperate kiss. Desire eclipsed all other thought. They tore aside what little clothing they each wore and took their pleasure in the drive and rhythm that their bodies had never forgotten. And when they were done, exhausted and breathless, they slept in each other's arms.

Chapter Fifty-Nine

Kahlil didn't want to wake up. He pressed his face deeper into the warm darkness of the blankets. Distantly, someone called to him. The voice broke and cut out like a bad radio signal. It was thin and desperate. Something white skittered through his sleeping mind.

Bones wired together with copper.

Kahlil awakened suddenly, tense and searching. Next to him, Jath'ibaye shifted.

"Don't go," Jath'ibaye whispered without quite waking up, his hand curled protectively over Kahlil's stomach. Kahlil relaxed back into the bed. The first rays of morning sun streamed through the windows, filling the room with soft gold radiance. A restful quiet still reigned over the household and the courtyards below.

Kahlil ran his hand over Jath'ibaye's.

Jath'ibaye's fingers were callused and strong. The sprinkling of freckles beneath his fine blond body hair evoked summers long since past. Kahlil traced the line of Jath'ibaye's sinewy muscles up from his tanned forearm and bicep to the curve of his pale shoulder.

Lying so close to him, Kahlil could see the faint blue shadows of veins and the kick of Jath'ibaye's pulse in his throat. Gently, Kahlil ran his hand down over Jath'ibaye's chest. The fine blond hairs tickled his palm. The raw, pink scars remaining from his fight with the hungry bones looked ugly—and reminded Kahlil of how readily Jath'ibaye threw himself into danger.

Kahlil pressed his palm against Jath'ibaye's chest, feeling the reassuring beat of his heart.

Jath'ibaye sighed and curled his arm around Kahlil's back. A brief smile lingered on his lips and then faded into an expression of serenity as he settled back into a doze.

As Kahlil watched, the scars marring Jath'ibaye's chest faded away.

Kahlil slipped his hand beneath the blankets. His fingers brushed over the ridges of Jath'ibaye's ribs. He felt the rise and fall of Jath'ibaye's breath and the smooth hardness of his abdomen. The muscles curved down into a deep cleft. Kahlil followed it to Jath'ibaye's belly button. His fingertip slid around the small circular indentation.

"Belly button," Kahlil whispered the Nayeshi words. It sounded so absurd, almost childishly cute. A belly button had to be the absolute antithesis of the world-crushing Rifter. And yet he had one.

"That tickles," Jath'ibaye murmured.

Kahlil glanced to Jath'ibaye's face. His eyes were open now. Kahlil could feel the languid torpor of Jath'ibaye's body giving way to attentive awareness. His skin felt just a little cooler. Kahlil wondered if he should pull away. Then Jath'ibaye smiled at him.

The expression was neither brilliant nor breathtaking. Kahlil doubted that many people would have found it alluring. Jath'ibaye's smile was simply too pure. He radiated an innocent, unguarded happiness.

Kahlil bowed his head to kiss Jath'ibaye's chest and felt the heat flush instantly through Jath'ibaye's body. There was an exhilarating flattery in seeing how easily he could affect him.

Last night Kahlil had been too desperate to notice little things. He had mindlessly and ravenously taken his pleasure. But now in bright morning light he could see how Jath'ibaye watched him with open desire and devotion. Again the edge of jealously touched him. This adoration rightfully belonged to Ravishan, not to him. But then, Ravishan wasn't here to claim Jath'ibaye. It was Kahlil's turn to have a lover. This lover.

He brushed his lips over Jath'ibaye's abdomen, taking in the tiny shivers of excitement that his attentions aroused. Then he kissed Jath'ibaye long and low—exalting in Jath'ibaye's surprise and breathless joy. He took a private, almost profane pleasure in witnessing how just the flick of his tongue could move a god. After the taste of ecstasy spilled over his lips, Kahlil drew back expecting nothing. But Jath'ibaye drew him close and returned Kahlil's attentions with a tenderness that left Kahlil dazed and sticky with spent pleasure.

For the first time he felt truly happy that he'd come back to this broken history—that he had survived to at last reach this moment.

Jath'ibaye settled down beside him.

"You know," Jath'ibaye said softly, "you have the most beautiful smile I've ever seen."

Kahlil suddenly realized that he was smiling, grinning, in fact. He attempted to school his features into an expression of a little less arrogance but he doubted that he succeeded.

"It's my Colgate smile," he said.

Jath'ibaye's expression went completely blank. Then he said, "That was from a toothpaste ad, right? God, I'd completely forgotten about the toothpastes of Nayeshi."

"Not me. I have to admit I miss my minty-fresh gel."

"Not so fond of our Basawar gum-scouring grit?" Jath'ibaye teased.

"Not so much."

Beside him Jath'ibaye stretched, his expression thoughtful but for once not concerned.

"It's been so long since I even thought of those days. It's strange to have someone here who can remember it all—ramen noodles, BBC nature documentaries, The Cubs, cats."

"I know," Kahlil said. "You're the only one who could possibly understand what I meant if I admitted to missing cheap gas station nachos."

"I miss salsa," Jath'ibaye said. "About four years back I just couldn't stop thinking about it. I even tried to breed a hot pepper from blister-blossom."

"I can't imagine that went well," Kahlil said. Not only did the plant's flowers cause a rash of blisters, it stank.

"All the pain, none of the flavor. Ji finally forced me to stop. She thought I was trying to kill myself." Jath'ibaye paused for a long moment, then said, "It must have been lonely for you. In Nayeshi, I mean."

Kahlil smoothed a hand down Jath'ibaye's chest, not wanting to answer his implicit question. Of course he had been lonely. But he'd always had John to watch over. He had always felt the connection of their bond.

Aloud he said, "Not really. I used to come out of the Gray Space and sit in your mother's sewing room to eavesdrop on your family's dinner conversations. Sometimes I'd sleep under your bed."

"Really?" Jath'ibaye asked. "That's a little creepy, isn't it?"

"Just during the day when you were gone," Kahlil said quickly. "Your baby brother saw me once though. I told him I was a ghost."

Jath'ibaye laughed.

"I was the mysterious cereal eater as well," Kahlil confessed.

"I knew we didn't have rats. There were never any droppings." Jath'ibaye absently stroked Kahlil's hair. "I don't believe you weren't lonely, though. You love to talk, even to strangers."

"Oh, I talked to plenty of strangers." Kahlil kept his tone light. He rarely allowed himself to think back on the isolation of those first years watching John. "But I'll admit that it was hard for me not be able to talk to you. Especially after your family disowned you. I wanted to find a way tell you that I was proud of you but I couldn't. You didn't know me. Then, about a week after that, you kicked Bill out and placed that ad for a new roommate. I took it as a sign from Parfir and I answered."

"I remember…" Jath'ibaye squinted up at the ceiling. "I think you were the only person who did."

"Well…" Sudden guilt moved through Kahlil, and he said, "That's not exactly true. A lot of other people wanted the room, so I erased their messages and emails and then showed up with cash in hand on the day rent was due."

"You erased my messages?" Jath'ibaye raised his brows.

"I knew you wouldn't choose a knife-wielding freak if you had other options," Kahlil admitted sheepishly. "Are you angry?"

"What? Now? No, I'm actually impressed with your ingenuity. It's not like you to leave anything important to chance," Jath'ibaye said, then added, "I'm sorry I described you as knife-wielding freak."

"It's not like I wasn't one," Kahlil said, laughing.

"I was an ignorant ass." Jath'ibaye shook his head. "I should have been better to you."

"You were plenty good to me. You have no idea." Kahlil curled a little closer to Jath'ibaye. "You hardly knew me, but you still made me feel so…human. Nothing we did probably seemed special to you but just hanging out with you, watching baseball games, and listening to the thunder during all those power outages—those were great times for me."

Jath'ibaye's expression went strangely tender. He said, "I wish I could offer you a life here that was as peaceful as that one."

"I don't need peace as much as somewhere that I belong," Kahlil told him, because he felt certain that Jath'ibaye's values were just the opposite. "If I have a purpose and a place, I'm not afraid to fight for them."

"As far as I can remember," Jath'ibaye responded dryly, "you've never been afraid to fight for anything."

"I'm wounded by your implications," Kahlil said, grinning. "I'll have you know that I picked up numerous conflict resolution skills in Nayeshi."

"Such as?"

"For one, I've learned to listen closely to an opposing point of view before delivering a rebuttal punch in the mouth." Kahlil tried to keep a straight face but failed.

Jath'ibaye just shook his head.

"I didn't smack the smirk off Representative Litivi's face last night. I think that counts for something." Kahlil ran his hand over Jath'ibaye's thick forearm, feeling the tickle of fine, golden hair beneath his palm. "But overall I suppose you're right. I'd certainly be the first to admit that my greatest skills are pretty much wasted on translation."

"Yes, as I recall, you were the first to point that out," Jath'ibaye agreed. He leaned forward and kissed Kahlil's brow softly, almost absently.

Distantly, Kahlil heard the noise of someone working a waterpump. The first smoky scents of cooking fires drifted up from the stories below them. Soon Jath'ibaye would be inundated with people needing his attention, and Kahlil would be left with nothing but that moldering tome.

Kahlil sat up a little in the bed. Jath'ibaye propped himself up on an elbow. He met Kahlil's gaze with an expression of curiosity.

"I'm thinking about the invitation Wah'roa offered me last night," Kahlil volunteered. "He asked me to visit the kahlirash'im's barracks. I think he wants me to demonstrate battle stances, probably some hard contact maneuvers as well."

"Yeah, I think that would be a dream come true for Wah'roa," Jath'ibaye replied. "Do you want to take him up on it?"

"I'd like to give it a try. But Eriki'yu mentioned that you have duties for me. If there's something you need done, I'll do that instead."

Jath'ibaye started to say something but then just released a heavy sigh. He gazed at Kahlil and then looked past him to the model of Basawar spread across his table.

"No, nothing urgent. Just—" He cut himself off and then said, "Try not to show off too much, all right?"

"I won't," Kahlil replied offhandedly. Jath'ibaye's expression told him that they both knew he was lying.

Chapter Sixty

Just as Kahlil belted his trousers, Wah'roa arrived to call upon Jath'ibaye in his private suite. Jath'ibaye stood beside Kahlil, dressed in only the bottom half of his russet long johns; his right hand brushed down Kahlil's spine in a pleasant, sleepy caress.

But the moment Wah'roa stepped into the room Kahlil felt as aware of Jath'ibaye's fingertips against his bare back as if hot brands stroked his skin. He jerked away, despite the fact that he knew it only made the two of them look all the more guilty.

Oddly, Wah'roa seemed utterly unconcerned to discover Kahlil and Jath'ibaye standing so close and only half dressed. While Kahlil reflexively scoured his mind for any explanation—other than the obvious—for his nearly nude presence in Jath'ibaye's rooms, Jath'ibaye displayed no furtive behavior whatsoever.

He yawned and absently scratched his belly.

"You're not taking any chances on missing him, are you?" Jath'ibaye inquired of Wah'roa.

"I suspected that he might be more interested in visiting the kahlirash compound than listening to you work out the taye seeding schedule." The kahlirash commander offered Jath'ibaye a smug smile. "Oh, and I saw Gin'yu's runners behind me on my way up."

Jath'ibaye sighed heavily but then gave Kahlil a rueful smile. "You two might as well make your break for it. I'm probably going to end up spending most of the day discussing fish stocks on the Silverlake Islands."

Kahlil quickly finished dressing and then swung the yasi'halaun over his shoulder. Minutes later, runners from the Silverlake District appeared at Jath'ibaye's door. A group of taye millers from Greenhills followed them. Jath'ibaye offered Kahlil a quick goodbye before returning his attention to the demands of his early-morning callers. Kahlil slipped out with Wah'roa.

After taking in the hearty offerings of the kahlirash'im's mess hall, Kahlil followed Wah'roa past the high wall surrounding the compound's training grounds. The crisp, cold air smelled of tahldi feed and gun oil. Captains called out fast commands and their troops responded with varying degrees of perfection. In the courtyards just below Kahlil, uniformed ranks of kahlirash'im performed their morning drills. Experienced riders raced through a maze of obstacles, taking out targets with precise shots, while in another courtyard young kahlirash'im practiced loading and firing their rifles in fast succession. Others charged straw dummies with bayonets or gathered around a heavy cannon to observe its maintenance.

Wah'roa pointed out a troop of first-year artillery women. Most of them were young, not even wearing braids yet; their Prayerscars shone like fresh blood on their brows. Their uniforms appeared to be secondhand and faded, but their rifles gleamed as beautifully as the finest gaun'im's firearms. Despite the all-male training of his own upbringing, Kahlil had to admit that these women handled their weapons with professional speed and determination.

He told Wah'roa as much and the commander looked truly pleased.

"I'd bet my teeth on any one of my girls against those soft, spoiled gaun bastards," Wah'roa stated. Kahlil nodded. With their filed teeth and toned bodies, these women seemed an entirely different breed from the demure, sheltered girls who inhabited so many noble drawing rooms and parlors.

"I'm not sure that I could teach them anything that you haven't already," Kahlil admitted. His breath came out white as steam in the frigid morning air.

"About guns and riding, probably not," Wah'roa allowed. "But no matter how much they train at battle forms, no matter how fast they can ride or sharp they are with those rifles, it won't be enough." Wah'roa's lip curled up into a snarl, showing his small sharp teeth. "Not if they have to go up against a man like Fikiri."

Wah'roa pointed across the ranks to where an angular girl stood at attention with her rifle. Even from the distance of the wall, Kahlil noticed the red scar that carved a deep furrow from her hairline down through her right eyebrow and just past her eye. She didn't appear to be more than fifteen, but something about the resolve in her expression resonated through Kahlil. He had no doubt that he'd worn a similar, hard look in Rathal'pesha.

"That's Pesha," Wah'roa informed him. "She lost her mother and both her brothers to Fikiri. Nearly lost her own life as well."

"She's just a child." Kahlil couldn't imagine how Fikiri could justify such an act. He'd been a cheat and a snitch, but assaulting a gawky teenage girl seemed low even for him.

"A child is all potential," Wah'roa stated, "and Fikiri seems set on ensuring that Pesha and others like her never fulfill their potential."

"What—" But even as Kahlil formed the question, he sensed the air around Pesha shudder and nearly split. Kahlil's jaw almost dropped in shock. "She's an ushiri?"

"She could be. That's certainly what Fikiri fears she will become," Wah'roa replied. "But right now she has no one to teach her or train her." His gaze settled on Kahlil meaningfully.

"I'm not a teacher." He hadn't even been a particularly good student.

"There are only two of you remaining who travel through the Gray Space, and can bend it to your wills. You and Fikiri." Wah'roa crossed his arms over his chest. "If Fikiri gets his hands on Pesha again, he'll end her—her and every other child like her."

"No, he won't. As soon as Jath'ibaye gives me the order, I'm going deal with Fikiri," Kahlil replied.

"And if you fail?" Wah'roa asked coolly.

"I won't." He couldn't imagine any way that Fikiri could defeat him.

"He's clever and he's grown stronger since you've been gone. You shouldn't underestimate how very devious he can be."

A distant memory fluttered through Kahlil. He'd underestimated Fikiri once before and it had cost him. For a moment he concentrated, trying to capture the details of the memory. It had been here at Vundomu, but long ago. Fikiri had begged him to help rescue his mother and Kahlil's sister from Umbhra'ibaye before the Fai'daum attacked the convent. Kahlil remembered agreeing to help. Then the thread of memory escaped him again, degenerating into confused images of bones, blood, and smoke.

"What happens when you're no longer here, then?" Wah'roa's question snapped Kahlil back to his present surroundings.

"What do you mean?" Kahlil asked. "I'm not going anywhere."

"When you die," Wah'roa said flatly. "We all die, don't we? All of us but him." Wah'roa's eyes briefly lifted to the Temple of the Rifter. Its black-tiled walls gleamed in the cold morning sunlight. "He'll survive us all. It is our duty to see that another generation arises to serve him after we are dust in his shadow."

Kahlil was more than familiar with his own mortality. And he knew that in principle the Rifter would live as long as the world of Basawar itself. But he'd always been so focused on the way that a Rifter could be killed—bled by the yasi'halaun and then sealed within a Great Gate by the deathlock key—that he hadn't considered the implications of the Rifter's survival. He hadn't thought of the passage of years or decades, much less eons. Mountains lasted for thousands of years, didn't they? And worlds?

Jath'ibaye would live as long as the world. But Kahlil himself certainly wouldn't. More than likely he wouldn't outlive those saplings planted beside the barrack guardtowers. Someday someone else would have to take his title and his place as Jath'ibaye's guardian.

He glared down at the neat lines of young kahlirash'im parading across the nearest courtyard.

"So, you asked me here because you want me to train the next Kahlil," Kahlil said.

"It has to be more interesting than translating that book," Wah'roa replied, and apparently reading Kahlil's surprised expression correctly, he added, "Ji mentioned it to me."

"I'll think about it," Kahlil said at last. But he already knew that Wah'roa was right. There would have to be another Kahlil to guard the yasi'halaun after he was gone.

Besides, he did need something to do aside from translate that dull botany tome.

"Why don't you introduce me to Pesha."

☾☾☾

He soon discovered that despite her often hunched posture and lanky limbs, Pesha was quick and coordinated. In the company of other, prettier, girls, she brushed her ragged black bangs over her scarred right eye, but she wasn't too shy to ask a question or even offer an argument under her breath—all of which reminded him just a little of his sister Rousma.

But most importantly, despite—or perhaps because of—Fikiri's assault, she was driven to master her innate skill. Only her panicked flight into the Gray Space had saved her the night Fikiri had butchered the rest of her family. Now, she habitually attempted to access the Gray Space. The countless fresh scars and ugly scabs on her hands attested to her relentless efforts.

Kahlil remembered the discomfort of those same injuries from his first years under Dayyid's instruction. He decided that if nothing else he could teach Pesha to avoid such pointless pain.

He brought her heavy leather gloves on the second day of their lessons. Then he spent several hours describing and demonstrating how to sense the right point from which to seamlessly split open the Gray Space. Pesha imitated him enthusiastically, though as the morning stretched into the afternoon, her strength and concentration waned. In a momentary lapse of attention, she nearly slit her own throat when she unintentionally wrenched open an Unseen Edge.

Kahlil lunged forward, knocking Pesha back and blocking the advance of the Unseen Edge with his left forearm. An instant later the edge collapsed on itself.

The thin gash across Kahlil's forearm looked worse than it felt, though he had to repeat that fact multiple times to Pesha and later to Jath'ibaye before either of them seemed to believe him. In truth, he'd suffered worse injuries while bicycling as a runner for the Lisam house. Though he did take an amused pleasure in the additional attention Jath'ibaye paid him that night.

The next day Besh'anya met Kahlil outside the gates of the kahlirash compound with a medical bag.

"Ji wants me to ensure that neither of you loses an arm," she informed Kahlil.

"Good to know I inspire such confidence."

Besh'anya flushed and protested that she had the utmost belief in his skills. "It's just—well, it's wiser to be safe, isn't it? The kahlirash'im infirmary is all the way across the compound and you might need help sooner—not that I think you'd need help..."

Kahlil tried not to laugh as Besh'anya followed him past the busy smithies and across the training grounds to the cobbled area where Pesha waited with her patched coat draped over her lanky arms.

Kahlil, too, carried his coat. The morning felt unseasonably warm. Drifts of snow that had gathered in the corners of the kahlirash training courtyards melted away, exposing pale green mosses and young shoots of frostgrass. Warm shafts of sun glittered over the black iron tiles of the roofs.

Most of the young men at the front of the courtyard had stripped to their waists to practice hand-to-hand combat. Another group of young kahlirash'im lounged in the sun, surreptitiously placing wagers on the men wrestling in front of them. The few who noticed Kahlil watched him pass with expressions of uncertainty. Over the past three days he'd overheard many of the kahlirash'im whispering about him, the Kahlil who supposedly had returned from death. Not all of them had sounded certain that his presence was auspicious. He, like Fikiri, was a remnant of the old church.

But Pesha beamed at the sight of him. Her expression only faltered slightly when she noticed Besh'anya and the medical bag she carried.

"Is your arm healing right, Kyle'insira?" Pesha asked.

"It's fine," Kahlil told her. "Besh'anya's really just here to spy on us for Ji."

"I am not!" Besh'anya protested.

"She's also amusing to tease," Kahlil added and Pesha grinned. Besh'anya flounced down onto a bench and gave an annoyed huff that sounded exactly like the snort of an exasperated tahldi. Kahlil didn't laugh at her, but it wasn't easy. He laid his coat down on the bench but kept the yasi'halaun strapped across his back. Then he turned to survey their training grounds.

He'd chosen this particular courtyard because old incantations lingered in some of the cracked flagstones, locking the Gray

Space away from even him. He didn't enjoy the sensation of those incantations, as they stirred boyhood memories of his own training, when Dayyid had trapped him in the darkest chambers of Rathal'pesha and done all he could to break him.

Even as weak and worn as the incantations were, Kahlil would have avoided this place under most circumstances. But he'd discovered that, for Pesha, nothing helped her define the presence of the Gray Space like briefly feeling its absence.

"All right, Pesha, let's warm up by locating a few more of those locked spots we talked about yesterday," Kahlil decided. He'd already sighted a few of the flagstones bearing the telltale scratches of Payshmura script.

"Yes, sir." Pesha laid her coat on the far end of the bench next to Besh'anya. As she did so, Kahlil noticed the look of infatuation that crossed her face and the glances she stole at Besh'anya from beneath her dark bangs. A pang of sympathetic dread shot through Kahlil when he saw Pesha's emotions so clearly written in her expression.

"That dress looks very nice on you, Lamiri Besh'anya," Pesha commented.

"Thank you, Kahlirash Pesha—or should I call you Ushiri Pesha?"

"I-I'm not—"

"Ushiri Pesha," Kahlil confirmed and Pesha's angular face lit with pride.

"Well, Ushiri Pesha, allow me to return the compliment and say that your uniform suits you very well, I think." Besh'anya smiled as indulgently at Pesha as she had at the fumbling adolescent boys who'd flirted with her when they'd walked past the smithies that morning.

"This is just a hand-me-down…but thank you…I washed it yesterday…" A flush colored Pesha's cheeks as she grinned and nervously brushed her bangs over her scarred right eye.

Kahlil wondered if he'd ever flirted that awkwardly in his life. Then the memory of a halting confession amid the filth and flowers of Candle Alley came to him. It hadn't been him but

Ravishan who had stood there with his heart hammering and his hands shaking with both longing and fear. Yet he still felt a pang of sympathy for Pesha.

Though, it would have been stronger if he hadn't seen her flirting just as excitedly with one of the kahlirash artillery women a day ago.

Kahlil cleared his throat loudly and Pesha quickly turned to him. She schooled her grin back to serious attention as she met Kahlil's gaze.

"Locked spots," Pesha repeated his earlier order and then she got to work.

She located the breaks in the Gray Space quite quickly once she had stopped peering over her shoulder to where Besh'anya sat reading a slim volume of poetry. After a half hour or so, Kahlil beckoned Pesha to a stretch of incantations covering five flagstones. Here it would be easiest for Pesha to sense the texture of Gray Space as it broke to flow around the line laid down by the incantations.

"Here, try to feel the direction that the Gray Space opens most easily."

Pesha hurried to his side. She closed her eyes and held up her gloved hands the way Kahlil had taught her. He felt the air around her shivering as her fingers twitched and turned. Then she stopped and flicked her fingers apart. Yellow sparks lit the edge of the Gray Space as it tore open with a low, scraping moan.

"Good. Now hold it, if you can," Kahlil instructed her. He extended his own hands above Pesha's, safeguarding her, though she couldn't see it. Pesha's arms trembled but she held the Gray Space open.

"You're doing very well. Now we're both going to step inside and let the Gray Space close around us. I'm right behind you, so there's nothing to worry about, all right?"

Pesha nodded and stepped forward. Kahlil followed her into the colorless, frigid silence.

Kahlil had not been trained this way himself. The ushman'im at Rathal'pesha would have thought nothing of hurling an ushiri into the grinding depths of the Gray Space and simply praying that Parfir would lend him the strength to fight his way free.

Kahlil had been among the few who had risen to the challenge. Many others had died—needlessly, he was now beginning to suspect—because in the mere two days that he'd shadowed Pesha in her training and protected her from the worst injuries the Gray Space could inflict, she had improved remarkably.

Now she only glanced back at him once and then moved ahead, negotiating the ropy, cutting texture of the Gray Space. She ducked and sidestepped her way across the courtyard, weaving between the impenetrable, glassy distortions that the Payshmura incantations threw up from the flagstones. At last she lifted her hands and, flicking her fingers apart, wrenched open an escape from the Gray Space. Kahlil followed her out, feeling the rush of mountain air like a summer wind after the deathly cold of the Gray Space.

Only an instant had passed but they now stood together halfway across the courtyard. The notes of birdsong sounded loud and sweet, but the gathered kahlirash'im went momentarily quiet as they stared at Pesha and Kahlil. Awe showed in their faces. Then their captain called them back to their own practice.

Pesha hugged herself, shivering with cold but beaming with pride. Kahlil couldn't keep himself from returning her smile. Many of the ushiri'im he'd known in Rathal'pesha had struggled for years before ever mastering such a controlled passage.

"Uh, I can't believe how cold it is in there." Pesha rubbed her gloved hands over her arms. "I feel like my bones are made of ice."

"You'll get used to it," Kahlil assured her. "But why don't we cross back to Besh'anya and retrieve our coats?"

Pesha shuddered but then raised her hands and again tore open a passage into the Gray Space. An arc of flames seared along the edge and the scent of burned ozone filled the air, but Pesha held the Gray Space open. Kahlil sensed her fatigue in the stiff motion of her arms but knew that only constant practice would build her endurance.

As they crossed the courtyard the second time, Kahlil noted an odd, new distortion—a moving shadow, like a ripple passing through water, warped his view of the surrounding courtyard and its busy occupants. Someone very near them was tearing his own passage through the Gray Space.

Fikiri. Kahlil could almost feel his presence in the way he powered ahead with complete disregard to the grain and resistance of the Gray Space.

Pesha was far too focused on crossing the courtyard cleanly to take note of Fikiri's shadow closing in. She wheeled her way between cutting expanses and impenetrable planes with an expression of strained intensity. Kahlil didn't attempt to break her concentration; fear wouldn't help her right now.

His hand went to his knife as he watched Fikiri draw nearer. For an instant he thought that Fikiri might attempt to rip through the membranous walls of the Gray Space to make his attack in the cold silence. But instead, Fikiri went still and Kahlil realized he was waiting to ambush Pesha when she re-entered the open air near Besh'anya.

As Pesha rallied her strength to drop out of the Gray Space, Kahlil took careful aim between her and Fikiri's shadow.

Pesha broke free and Kahlil felt Fikiri explode from the Gray Space just to her right. White flames hung over his gaunt face. Terror contorted Pesha's features and sudden shock showed on Besh'anya's face. The surrounding kahlirash'im hardly had time to register anything beyond flames outlining Fikiri's black-robed figure before Kahlil bounded out from the Gray Space to block Fikiri's black blade as he thrust for Pesha's throat.

Fikiri stumbled back a step, his eyes wide.

"You can't be..." Fikiri gaped.

"But I am." Kahlil punched his knife into Fikiri's chest, only to feel the blade skid across the hard armor hidden beneath his tattered black robes.

"Damn it," Kahlil swore.

With his curse blade, Fikiri slashed for Kahlil's extended arm. Kahlil bounded back. Fikiri took a second swing, but this time Kahlil charged into the thrust, blocking Fikiri's blade with his own and using his free left hand to plunge a Silence Knife into Fikiri's heart. Pain rocked up Kahlil's arm as Fikiri's armor held against his assault. After second fast blow, Kahlil felt something crack. The wailing screech of some dying creature rose from Fikiri's chest and he suddenly went pale.

Instantly, Fikiri dropped into the Gray Space and was gone. Kahlil nearly followed after, but then he remembered the tangled chaos of the Gray Space in the far north. He couldn't afford to lose his bearings while he carried the yasi'halaun. He had to keep it out of Fikiri's hands.

Suddenly a roar of cheers erupted from across the courtyard. All around him half-dressed kahlirash'im hooted and clapped. Alarmed guards came sprinting into the courtyard with their rifles at the ready. As their fellow kahlirash'im described the fight, their stricken expressions transformed into joy. Besh'anya quickly regained her feet from where she'd toppled off the bench.

"Everything is fine—" Kahlil began, but to his surprise, Pesha suddenly threw herself at him, gripping him in a fierce hug. She buried her head against his chest and squeezed so hard that Kahlil had to fight to breathe.

"You fought the devil," Pesha mumbled into his shirtfront. "You beat him!"

Her raw gratitude touched Kahlil but made him uncomfortable at the same time. He wasn't a hero. It would be unwise for these people to take him for one. Still, he patted Pesha's head and allowed her to crush his ribs for a few moments more.

"I can't breathe, Pesha."

"Oh! Sorry." Pesha released him immediately. The red scar over her eye stood out vividly against her deathly pale skin.

"Those are some strong arms you've got." Kahlil made a show of drawing in a breath and Pesha flushed. It was good to see a little color return to her pallid face.

Then Kahlil took in the kahlirash'im gathered in the courtyard and those peering out from their barrack windows.

"Sorry for the disturbance. Everything's fine now," Kahlil called out.

He saw Wah'roa's emaciated figure appear atop the training grounds' wall. Wah'roa surveyed the gathering and then gave a hand sign for dispersal. Immediately the kahlirash guards returned to their duties and the troops in the courtyard made a show of taking up their battle stances again. Several of them grappled but more gossiped in soft whispers.

"Kyle, your hand is bleeding." Besh'anya snatched up her medical bag and hurried to Kahlil's side.

He glanced down and was annoyed to see a bloody gash across the back of his hand. It wasn't wide or too deep. Much of the blood was already congealing.

Kahlil started to wave Besh'anya aside. But then he remembered Pesha, standing there watching him. He didn't want her to get the idea that she should just shrug off injuries from the Gray Space or, worse yet, cursed weapons. Many of the wounds could be internal or feel nearly painless but too quickly turn deadly.

"It doesn't look bad, but it's hard to be sure. I'd appreciate your opinion, Besh'anya." Kahlil almost laughed at how unlike himself he sounded, but no one else seemed to be aware of it.

He rolled up the cuff of his new white shirt—now stained red, damn it. Besh'anya took his arm in her hands almost reverently. As she caught sight of his forearm a little gasp escaped her. Immediately, Pesha drew closer.

"There are so many scars," Besh'anya breathed.

Kahlil was so used to the masses of white scars that crisscrossed the muscles of his arms that he hadn't given a thought as to how they might look to others. Most of them were remnants from Payshmura bloodletting practices.

"Ji says that the Payshmura priests tortured the boys they trained." Besh'anya held Kahlil's arm as if it were a dying animal in her care. "Did they torture you?"

That was the last thing Kahlil wanted to talk about, especially in front of Pesha. But Besh'anya clearly couldn't see the alarmed expression on Pesha's face; as far as Pesha knew, Kahlil was training her in the same way he had been instructed.

"No," Kahlil replied lightly, "they just punished me a lot for swearing."

"Oh." Besh'anya seemed disappointed by his answer, but Pesha gave a little, nervous laugh.

"So, it's just a scratch?" Kahlil prompted.

"What?" Besh'anya started slightly. She had been staring at the scars on Kahlil's arm again. "Yes, it looks fine. I should probably clean it, just to be safe."

Besh'anya opened her leather bag and brought out a red bottle of some kind of liquid. A sharp metallic tang rose from it, and as she poured the stinging fluid over his hand, it turned acid yellow.

"I can make you a bandage as well," Besh'anya offered.

"No, I—" His reply was cut off by a blast of unexpected wind that cut through the courtyard. Looking to its source, Kahlil saw a tall, blond figure striding toward them from the barracks. He should have known that the violent disturbance in the Gray Space would bring Jath'ibaye.

He quickly retrieved his discarded coat and started toward Jath'ibaye.

"Your bandage," Besh'anya called after him. She held the roll of white cloth as if it were an enticement.

"I'm fine." Kahlil rolled his sleeve down quickly. The last thing he wanted Jath'ibaye to see was him wandering around swathed in bandages.

"But…" Besh'anya seemed to give up before she even began.

As, Kahlil started for Jath'ibaye, Pesha hurried to his side.

"Can you do me a favor?" Kahlil asked.

"Of course," Pesha replied.

Kahlil dug several coins from his coat pocket and handed them to Pesha. "Buy Besh'anya and yourself a nice meal on me."

Pesha took the coins but looked uncertain.

"What if the devil comes back?" Her voice dropped to a whisper.

"He won't." Not while his armor was cracked, Kahlil felt certain. "Not today, at least. Go on. Have a little fun. I'll be putting you through hard training again soon enough."

"Yes, sir." Pesha gave him a quick salute and then dashed back to join Besh'anya.

Kahlil smiled at her from over his shoulder, then quickened his own pace to meet Jath'ibaye.

"I thought you went out to the Silverlake Islands," Kahlil called as they drew close.

"I did," Jath'ibaye said. His gaze roved over Kahlil. "Is everything all right here?"

"Just fine." He adopted what he thought was a confident stance.

"I felt the Gray Space tear and burn," Jath'ibaye commented. "It felt like Fikiri."

"It was Fikiri," Kahlil replied, in as casual a manner as he could muster. "I spanked him and sent him crying back to his Lady."

Jath'ibaye gave him a long, silent look. All around the courtyard, the kahlirash'im stood furtively watching for Jath'ibaye's response. Finally, he said, "Were you hurt?"

"Just a scratch. My new shirt got the worst of it."

"Let me see it."

Kahlil held out his hand. Jath'ibaye took in the small gash and the deep concern in his expression faded away. Then he pulled Kahlil into his arms and held him. Kahlil felt his entire face flush red. Two troops of kahlirash'im as well as Pesha and Besh'anya stood only a few yards away, and who knew how many of the kahlirash'im were gaping at them from the barracks?

And yet it was so reassuring to feel Jath'ibaye's arms around him. It was so pleasant to return Jath'ibaye's embrace, and to savor the warmth and strength of his body.

A moment later Kahlil drew back.

"We should be more careful in public," Kahlil said quietly.

"The kahlirash'im are faithful to me," Jath'ibaye said. Still, he stepped back from Kahlil slightly. "If any of them start grousing, I have no doubt that Wah'roa will pound the Sixty-Six Fai'daum Edicts of Equality into them before treating them to a truly tedious speech concerning the sacred bond between the Rifter and his Kahlil. He doesn't tolerate bigotry." He glanced up to the wall and exchanged a wave with Wah'roa.

"But is it wise?" Kahlil couldn't keep himself from lowering his voice further. "I mean, to acknowledge anything so…intimate between us?"

"It's honest," Jath'ibaye replied. "And it isn't as if my persuasion is a secret here. Everyone in my holdings and on the council already knows about me. Ji, Wah'roa, all of my friends know." Jath'ibaye studied Kahlil for a few moments and then went on, "Even if some asshole doesn't like it, here in the Fai'daum lands our laws protect gay relationships."

Kahlil should have suspected as much, he supposed, but the idea still surprised him.

Jath'ibaye smiled wryly at his startled expression, and said, "You know, I did have a little something to do with codifying the laws here. What did you expect?"

Hazy memories flickered through Kahlil's mind as he studied Jath'ibaye. He remembered feeling this same sense of pride and anxiety the day he had watched from the Gray Space as John came out to his father. The steely major general had not taken his son's revelation well, but John had not wavered. He'd held his head high, even when the old man had cuffed him across the face and ordered him to leave and never come back.

Of course, Jath'ibaye would not bow in the face of other men's bigotry. Kahlil longed to be that confident, but his history was nothing like Jath'ibaye's.

"I…It's so hard to imagine lovers living openly here in Basawar." Kahlil shook his head. "Dayyid executed men for having sex with each other. He would have killed me twice over if he'd had even a single other ushiri as strong as me."

Kahlil lifted his hand to the corner of his mouth, where Dayyid's knife had torn through his flesh. The scars had vanished with another lifetime, but Kahlil still remembered the humiliation and agony of that punishment. Every one of the other ushiri'im had known why Dayyid had mutilated him. None of them had been kind. Only the sad, drunken ushman who ran the infirmary had even spoken to him after that. Something inside of him had broken then. He'd never touched another man again, not even in Nayeshi.

Not until now.

Suddenly, he remembered Dayyid's blood covering Jahn's hands. All at once he knew what had become of the scars he so clearly remembered disfiguring his face. Ravishan had never borne them. Jahn had stopped Dayyid.

"It was different in Nayeshi," Kahlil said.

"Yes, it was."

"I was amazed by the parades and seeing men marching in each other's arms. You can't imagine how shocked I felt when I discovered that men openly declared themselves lovers there, that they had lives together." Kahlil understood that people were not always kind to them, but they chose not to live like frauds and criminals. He'd envied their honesty and pride.

"I don't want to make a liar of you," Kahlil said at last. "And I'm not ashamed of what's between us."

"I'm glad." A subtle pleasure showed in Jath'ibaye's expression.

"But this is still Basawar and not everyone is your friend or governed by Fai'daum laws," Kahlil went on. "Right now you are facing two very dangerous enemies, and if either knows that I'm your lover, then they won't hesitate to attempt to harm you through me. I don't want to become a tool to be used against you." As Kahlil spoke he felt a chill pass through him. What he once would have thought was some kind of premonition, he now recognized as recollection. He'd been used against Jath'ibaye before; he wouldn't let it happen again. "For now we need to be discreet."

For an instant Jath'ibaye looked like he might argue, but then his expression turned grim and he simply nodded his assent. He shoved his hands into the pockets of his heavy coat.

Kahlil hated to see him withdraw in this manner but he knew his decision was the wisest.

"Does this mean that I shouldn't invite you out to a romantic lunch with me?" Jath'ibaye's tone was only half teasing.

"Of course not," Kahlil replied. "Just don't bring anyone else along."

Jath'ibaye gave a dry laugh.

"Between the two of us there wouldn't be enough food for anyone else."

☾☾☾

They walked through the barrack gates and crossed a small paved courtyard to the walkway leading up to Jath'ibaye's holdings. A few men and women with goods from the lakeside market passed them on the way. Small carts and stalls offering hot food crowded the alleys between the shops and residences that had been built into the walls. A strong smell of seared fish and hot oil drifted by on clouds of steam and smoke.

No one seemed to take much note of the two of them beyond a first glance to Jath'ibaye. He offered a friendly smile to a pair of boys hauling a cartload of raw wool down the narrow street.

"Do you think we'll ever have cars or trucks here?" Kahlil asked.

"I hope not too soon. Right now the environment just isn't strong enough to withstand the kind of explosive industrial development that comes with automobiles," Jath'ibaye replied. "But maybe someday."

"I can't imagine you ever wanting that time to come," Kahlil commented.

"I don't," Jath'ibaye admitted. "But I can't stop technology from moving forward."

"You could," Kahlil said. "If you wanted to, you could wipe everything clean. No trolleys, trains, roads. You have the power to destroy all of that."

"I could." Sadness crossed Jath'ibaye's features and Kahlil knew he shouldn't have brought the subject up. "I don't think I'd feel too good about myself afterwards. I've already razed enough of Basawar to keep me busy rebuilding for decades. Last time thousands of people died. I don't want to go through that ever again."

"I'm sorry. I shouldn't have—"

"No, it's all right," Jath'ibaye assured him. "It's not something I'm particularly proud of, but you shouldn't think that you can't speak of it."

They crossed the wide walkway to a narrow, gated staircase. Intricate braids of iron leaves and branches decorated the gate. Jath'ibaye took a ring of keys from his coat pocket and quickly flipped through them. A moment later he pushed the gate open and led Kahlil up the stairs.

Like much of Vundomu, the stairs were a mix of the old black iron tiling and organic swaths of stone. Ancient urns embossed with the kahlirash symbol of crescent moons hung from the walls of the staircase. Despite the winter conditions, woody vines cascaded down from the urns.

As he walked, Jath'ibaye absently ran his hands over the dark leaves. The plants seemed to lift slightly, reaching for his touch as they might reach toward sunlight. Jath'ibaye didn't take any note of it. If he had, no doubt he would have stopped immediately.

Jath'ibaye seemed to go out of his way to downplay the immense power that he wielded. He used keys when no natural lock could bar him. He walked at a natural pace, even allowing common men and women to outdistance him when he could cross miles in seconds if he wished. Across a short distance he could even keep pace with an ushiri moving through the Gray Space.

He restrained his power and seemed to take steps to mitigate the impact of his immense physical prowess. He was a god who dressed in the rough, ugly clothes of a laborer and who walked among fishmongers and street traders almost invisibly.

If their positions had been reversed, Kahlil knew he wouldn't have been so self-effacing. He'd always liked beauty and ceremony. He supposed it was a holdover from his Payshmura upbringing. Even in the supposed austerity of Rathal'pesha, the walls had been inlaid with gold and ivory. The books had been gilded; the curse blades intricately carved.

Unlike Jath'ibaye, Kahlil took great pride in his power and sacred title. The two years he had spent unable to remember who or what he was had been the most disconcerting of his life. Living bereft of identity and purpose, he had simply given himself over to the first man who could use him. He needed the knowledge that he was the Kahlil. It resonated through his sense of himself.

But he suspected that Jath'ibaye could never feel the same way about being the Rifter. It simply wasn't in his nature to take pride in sheer destruction. He did not glory in the thousands who had died at his hands. Another man might have relished being the Rifter. A man who enjoyed the power it gave him over all other life would have exploited every opportunity to terrify and punish those around him. A man like Ourath would have crushed the world on a whim—just because he had one bad day. Kahlil himself would have demanded temples and palaces. He would have expected and taken dominion over all of Basawar.

Jath'ibaye had done none of that. He suppressed the devastating forces within himself with a constant, almost reflexive self-restraint.

So many years spent with John lent Kahlil an insight into Jath'ibaye's nature. Doubtless his restraint was in part concern. Jath'ibaye did not want to cause another cataclysm. But there was extremism to Jath'ibaye's self-deprivation—his rough clothes, tough food, constant exertions and injuries—that bordered on punishment for the thousands he'd killed. He would not allow himself to forget or forgive. Kahlil wondered if he ever would.

Kahlil realized that there might have been more behind Ji's insistence that he watch over Jath'ibaye than just a little sleep deprivation. Kahlil himself had been shocked to discover that Jath'ibaye had known Ourath was planning to kill him. He had known and still followed Ourath anyway.

On a sudden impulse, Kahlil caught Jath'ibaye's hand. Jath'ibaye looked at him, slightly startled.

"Stop worrying so much," Kahlil told him.

"I..." Jath'ibaye began, but then he cut himself short. "Was it that obvious?"

"I can't think of any other reason you'd miss this opportunity to describe the unique attributes of this oddly winter-hardy vine," Kahlil replied.

Jath'ibaye laughed.

"You're right," he admitted. "I must have been distracted. The vine is called frostbraid. It's notable for its very high content of glycerol, which aside from being a natural anti-freeze, also comes in handy in the production of smokeless gunpowder."

"A very useful botanical then," Kahlil commented, and Jath'ibaye nodded a little absently. Kahlil squeezed his hand.

"Whatever's bothering you, let it go. If trouble comes, I'll handle it."

Jath'ibaye seemed amused and Kahlil knew it was because Jath'ibaye found his arrogant statement charming. He interlaced his fingers with Jath'ibaye's.

"So, how are you going to avoid a war for me?" Jath'ibaye asked.

"The older gaun'im will remember the last wars. They won't want another," Kahlil replied.

"Let's hope so," Jath'ibaye said. "But I wasn't just thinking of the gaun'im."

"You mean Fikiri?" Kahlil asked. "I think I handled him pretty well."

Jath'ibaye nodded gravely, then said, "You did, but he came alone this time."

"Does he have the forces to mount a large offensive?" Kahlil felt slightly cold at the thought of a battle on two fronts. How could a country as small as Vundomu fight the gaun'im in the south and Fikiri in the north at the same time?

"Every year there are more hungry bones. And they get bigger. He's bringing up creatures from the ocean, using their bones." Jath'ibaye frowned at the clear blue northern sky.

"I could go now and take him out," Kahlil said.

"No." Jath'ibaye suddenly returned his grip with force. "I need you here when the gaun'im arrive. Fikiri will come to us again. He always does."

"It might take him off guard if I went—"

"No." Jath'ibaye didn't raise his voice, but Kahlil couldn't miss the finality of his expression. "Right now I need you here, with me."

"All right," Kahlil agreed. "I just want to do something to help you."

"You can. You have," Jath'ibaye replied. He pulled Kahlil close and kissed him. Kahlil guessed that it had been meant to be a brief, mollifying gesture. But he returned the kiss with passion. It wasn't in his nature to accept a chaste peck and quiet down—especially not after winning a fight. Instantly, he felt the response in Jath'ibaye's body.

Jath'ibaye's hands slid inside Kahlil's coat. The chill of Jath'ibaye's fingertips traced the line of Kahlil's back. Jath'ibaye's hands were warming up quickly. He touched and held Kahlil as they kissed. Kahlil pressed closer, slipping his hand into the front pocket of Jath'ibaye's pants. A brief gasp escaped Jath'ibaye. His arms tensed around Kahlil's body.

From above them, there suddenly came a soft cough. They bolted apart and turned. Ji stood on the steps ahead of them.

"Eriki'yu asked me to tell you that your meal is ready," Ji said to Jath'ibaye. She glanced to Kahlil, and for an instant, he thought that she might have been grinning.

Chapter Sixty-One

Over the next five days Fikiri stayed away, but the gaun'im drew nearer. Jath'ibaye hardly ate or slept but seemed occupied every moment by either preparations or evacuations now necessitated by the threat of a gaun'im attack against the southern border. Kahlil occupied himself by honing Pesha's skills and training with the kahlirash'im.

Though, late in the afternoon, he found himself trailing along beside Ji as she surveyed the incantations etched into the flagstones of the kahlirash training grounds. Kahlil hoped that she could adapt them in some manner to secure the grounds so that Fikiri could not breach them. At the very least he wanted to offer Pesha some security when he was called away to deal with the gaun'im.

"Yes," Ji murmured. "Yes, these will do."

Kahlil leaned against one of the black pillars of the kahlirash'im's barrack. Overhead, the sky was growing dark. The faint disc of the moon shone overhead like a luminous drop of wax. Kahlil lowered his gaze and studied the distant white line of the northern horizon. Somewhere out there beyond his sight was an army. Fikiri and his Lady were waiting, amassing thousands of hungry bones.

Much closer and more immediately visible were the gaun'im's armies that had converged just south of Vundomu at the mouth of the river in the city Mahn'illev.

Through Jath'ibaye's telescope he'd seen the banners of all seven families flying over battalion after battalion of troops. But they did not disturb Kahlil quite as much as the possibility of an attack from the north. He could count the numbers of men assembled in the south. He could see riders and foot soldiers clashing while their commanders argued among themselves.

Compared to the perfect order of the kahlirash'im, the untried gaun'im's armies presented an undisciplined, chaotic force. They had obviously been thrown together to create the illusion of a vast, unified military—as if ages of rivalries could be miraculously forgotten in a few days. Kahlil had lived with Bousim rashan'im. He knew how strongly they disdained the Lisam riders. Naye'ro rashan'im constantly brawled with those from Du'yura. Such animosities were common among the gaun'im's rashan'im.

It reassured Kahlil to discover, at a glance, a weakness to exploit.

Their sheer numbers certainly constituted a genuine threat, but they did not present him with a vision of doom.

The enemies hidden within the northern mist were different. Kahlil had only glimpsed their power in the fear that gripped the people of Vundomu, in Jath'ibaye's troubled silences, and in the constant flashes of white bones that hunted him in his dreams. None of which offered him anything real to observe, beyond one brief clash with Fikiri. He could not assess the strength or weakness of shadows moving through distant mists.

Ji's low voice murmured Eastern words that Kahlil didn't recognize. She paused every few feet and scraped her claws against the flagstones surrounding the kahlirash courtyard. Each time she dragged her claws against a stone, a soft pulse shuddered through the stones at Kahlil's feet. Beside him, Ji staggered but then steadied herself and moved to the next flagstone.

The dark red blood staining her paws and claws was Jath'ibaye's. No other blood could offer her more power. Though Kahlil had found the amount Jath'ibaye had readily sacrificed disconcerting.

From the stones behind Ji, thin trails of steam rose like vapor rising from dry ice. The blood burned and bubbled, revealing incantations that must have been carved there years before. Kahlil could feel the difference in the air of the courtyard. It was tighter, almost acrid in his lungs. His tension increased as the sensations of open air and cool wind faded from the courtyard and its resemblance to those dark chambers where Dayyid had confined and beaten him grew.

Ji finished the last stone, creating a wall around the grounds. Fikiri would have to leave the Gray Space if he wanted to cross the barrier and enter the courtyard. Outside of the Gray Space he would be vulnerable. The ritual was obviously a powerful defense, but it demanded immense effort and a god's blood just to secure a few yards. It also grew weaker the larger the area it was used to protect. This courtyard was probably the limit. But at least Pesha would be safe during their practices.

Ji limped to Kahlil's side and lay down at his feet as if she were dying. She smelled of blood and sweat. "It's done," she said quietly.

Kahlil crouched down beside her. "Are you all right?"

"I'll be better in a while," Ji answered. "What about you?"

"Me? I'm fine." Kahlil arched a brow. "Why do you ask?"

"I just wanted to hear you say so," Ji replied.

"I'm very good." Without thinking, Kahlil reached out to stroke Ji's shoulder as if she were a familiar pet. He stopped himself, horrified at his gaffe. Ji glanced up at him and laughed.

"Go ahead," Ji said. "It's one of the few advantages of this body. It's easier for people to give and receive affection from an animal. A woman as old as I am living in her natural body would never be fortunate enough to be touched and hugged as often as I am."

Kahlil gently petted Ji's shoulders and back. Her hair was coarse and shedding. He could feel her bones just under her thin skin. She felt too frail to even be alive. She closed her eyes, but Kahlil could tell from her breathing that she wasn't asleep.

"How old are you, Ji?"

"Oh, I've probably stayed in this worn out body too long. Sixty years is a long time for dog-flesh to last, even with a witch wearing it." Her tone struck Kahlil as fond, as though she were speaking of a favorite dress and not her own body. Ji's tail flopped softly against the flagstones. "I suppose I should change, but I've grown so familiar with this body…I love being able to smell so much."

Kahlil scratched behind her ears and Ji leaned into his hand.

"Saimura wants me to take a human body again," she confided. "But I can't bring myself to steal another woman's flesh. Not even a criminal's. I remember too well how I suffered when mine was stripped from me."

"That must have been long ago." Even when he'd still been a child, Ji Shir'korud, the demoness in animal flesh, had been famous in the heights of Rathal'pesha.

"Yes, long ago. Though time changes when you become an issusha," she replied. "I turned fifty the summer the Eastern kingdom fell into the sea and I felt ancient then. I don't know how long the Payshmura kept my bones at Umbhra'ibaye after that. I saw kingdoms rise and fall, histories play out, and then alter, and run their course again. I couldn't say how long I remained imprisoned before your mother took pity on me and freed me." Ji sighed. "She was quite brave, you know. Though, impulsive as well. You take after her."

"I don't remember much about either of my parents," Kahlil admitted. What he could remember he did not like to think about. Ji seemed to recognize as much and let the subject rest.

Kahlil studied the north horizon. A luminous glow lit the pale sky, as if a second sun hung in the north. He thought he saw a flicker of lightning jump through the walls of clouds and mist.

"Ji, do you know anything about the forces in the north?" Kahlil asked.

She opened her dark eyes. "What has Jath'ibaye told you?"

"Just that he's worried. And that he doesn't want me going there."

"Well, it is worrying and you shouldn't go there," Ji told him. "Out past the edge of the chasm, there is an island where the monastery of Rathal'pesha once stood. You died there." Ji paused, studying Kahlil. The last time she had told him of his death he'd fled. Now Kahlil merely waited for her to continue.

"That island is where Fikiri and his Lady make their home." Ji shifted a little under Kahlil's hand and he realized that she wanted him to scratch lower on her skinny back. Kahlil complied.

"When Jath'ibaye destroyed the northlands, he crushed the Black Tower and Umbhra'ibaye as well. Do you know how?" Ji asked.

"No, I don't remember that."

"All three of the great Payshmura centers were linked," Ji said. "There was an open gateway connecting them. Jath'ibaye collapsed that gateway, pulling all three into one ruin. The priests, nuns, acolytes, servants, animals, all living flesh died. But one of the issusha'im survived intact."

Kahlil suddenly thought of his sister. His hands went still on Ji's hide. There was such a slim chance that his sister, of all the issusha'im, would have survived. He knew it was foolish to even hope. Still, he couldn't keep from asking, "Do you know what her name was?"

"Loshai," Ji whispered. "But we do not speak her name too often for fear of summoning her."

"Oh," Kahlil said. He hardly took the name in. It was not his sister's. It wasn't Rousma. Kahlil closed his eyes and tried to lay memories of her back to rest as they had been before that momentary flash of hope.

"I don't know if you can imagine what it was like after the northlands fell," Ji went on. "Storms of ash and mud, then week after week of earth tremors, mudslides, and always rain. Even with the stores of food at Vundomu, hundreds of people starved. And Jath'ibaye was nowhere to be found.

"At last the land calmed enough for me to go and search for him. I found him out where the Greenhills are now. He was half buried in stone and mud. After I dug him out, he hardly seemed alive. He didn't notice food or warmth, not even pain. He was emaciated and unresponsive. He wanted to be left to die. But of course he couldn't die and I couldn't afford to leave him.

"By that time the Bousim family had already sent word to us that we should surrender Vundomu to their forces. They had an army marching toward us. We were all half starved and sick from fouled water supplies. We needed Jath'ibaye if we were to stand against the Bousim.

"And that was when Loshai arrived, looking for Jath'ibaye. She knew him. She railed at him, shouting and cursing him in a language I had never heard. At last that seemed to rouse him. They both returned to Vundomu with me and the Bousim forces were defeated in less than a week. After that Jath'ibaye dedicated himself to protecting Vundomu and to healing the lands.

"For a while that seemed to be Loshai's wish as well. But then she began visiting the island in the north. Sometimes she returned with Payshmura books, ancient scrolls, even cursed relics. She was not interested in what I could teach her. She wanted Payshmura teachings about raising the Great Gate, creating issusha'im, and altering the past. I heard her arguing with Jath'ibaye more and more. After three years it seemed to be all they ever did in each other's company."

"What did they fight about?" Kahlil asked.

"I couldn't say. But I do know that Loshai had been deeply wronged, as were all the women who were forced to become issusha'im." Ji sighed heavily. "There is always the temptation, once you have seen what the issusha'im see, to reach back and somehow save yourself. It is nearly impossible not to think of altering history for your own sake. Other lives, joyful existences, haunt your dreams and drive you nearly mad because you know they aren't just whimsy, not just fantasy. They are the lives the Payshmura stole, the histories they destroyed. Everything you dream of could have been real once." Ji paused and lowered her head.

Kahlil understood what it was to be haunted by another life. He wondered what lost histories haunted Ji. But he didn't ask. It seemed too personal.

"I don't know if that was what drove Loshai. But I remember her screaming a word at Jath'ibaye with such loss and anger that he could say nothing in response. He looked like he had been shot. I've thought about the word since then, but I've never been able to decide what it meant."

"What was it?" Kahlil asked.

"Bill," Ji said quietly. "It's a small word, but it meant something important to Loshai. And to Jath'ibaye as well. After that last argument, Loshai went out to the north island and did not return. A few months later the first of the hungry bones arose and after that Fikiri began killing and stealing our children."

"Where was Fikiri before then?" Kahlil asked.

"Who knows? None of us had seen him earlier. He was probably hiding on the island. From what I've heard, he and Loshai knew each other before she was taken to Umbhra'ibaye. Jath'ibaye hated him, but I don't think Loshai ever did."

"I never liked him," Kahlil commented, but he wasn't thinking about that. He was remembering the countless souls trapped in the white sands at the chasm's edge. "Why would they create hungry bones?"

"Because she is making issusha'im. Not all attempts succeed. Some only create hungry bones."

"But—" Kahlil began, but then he remembered Fikiri's promises of a gateway to Nayeshi. If Loshai were really creating a new gateway, then she would need issusha'im to control the moment in history that her gateway opened into.

"We've never managed to infiltrate the island. The hungry bones guard it too well," Ji told him. "But we all know there is little use for issusha'im unless one is reconstructing the Great Gate."

"Yes." With all the remnants of the Payshmura holy places that littered her island, there was a good chance that she could build a Great Gate. It would depend greatly on the kind of power she could wield.

"Loshai," he said the name quietly. It was familiar, as Fikiri's name had been when Kahlil had first heard it.

"You knew her?" Ji asked.

"When I was a youth," Kahlil said, frowning. Distant memories washed over him. The image of a slender woman came to him. Her hair was long and white blond; her eyes were large and blue like John's. And then he remembered her dressed in weasel skins. Snow swirled around her as she carefully fed twigs into a cooking fire. Her thin husband, Bill, leaned against a bare tree fighting for breath. And John had been there as well. He had said she was his sister.

But Kahlil knew she wasn't. She was his childhood friend, Laurie. She had been the one to give John the nickname of Toffee. She had been with John the day he intercepted the golden key. She was the witch whose powers had stirred even in Nayeshi's atmosphere.

"Loshai was one of Fikiri's mother's attendants," Kahlil said at last. "Bill was called Behr. He was her husband. He was murdered, I think. I don't remember exactly, but it led to the Payshmura discovering that she had witches' blood."

"And then they made her an issusha," Ji stated sadly. Kahlil felt a shudder creep down her spine.

"I think so."

"She must have been with child," Ji said. "Otherwise they would have burned her."

"I don't know…I guess so." Sentimental warmth lingered in Kahlil's memories of Loshai and Behr. He couldn't help but feel sympathy for all that Loshai must have lost and endured. But he also knew that he had to crush those feelings. If Loshai had rebuilt the Great Gate to return her to her past in Nayeshi, then she would need an immense source of power to awaken it. She would need to feed the stones with a god's blood and bones. She would need to kill Jath'ibaye.

"And Jath'ibaye knows all this?" Kahlil asked.

Ji nodded.

It was getting too cold and dark to stay outside. Kahlil stood up. Ji watched him. After a slow yawn, she drew herself up to her feet.

"Why doesn't he destroy the island?" Kahlil asked.

"He says he can't," Ji replied.

"Of course he can." Kahlil scowled at the absurdity of that idea. "There is nothing in this world that he cannot destroy if he wishes."

Ji shifted, letting out a slight groan as she resettled herself. "But if he doesn't wish it, then the power may not come to him."

"What do you mean?"

"She was his friend," Ji said. "She gave him something to live for when he had nothing else. Even now, when he knows that he must destroy her or she will keep killing our children, that friendship still lives deep within him. It won't allow him to destroy the island."

"Someone should just tell him to do it," Kahlil said.

"We have. He's tried." Ji shook her head. "It's not so simple."

"But it is," Kahlil replied. "He's the Rifter. He is Destruction Embodied—"

"No," Ji interrupted Kahlil, before he could launch into a recitation of the hundreds of names of the Rifter. "He is Jath'ibaye."

"Yes, but—"

Ji snapped her yellow teeth, startling Kahlil into silence. "No matter how powerful he might be, he's still a human being. He has already accepted responsibility for thousands of lives. If he can't bring himself to murder a friend, then I am willing to accept that. I would not force him to be responsible for that death as well."

Kahlil almost snapped out an aggravated response, but then he stopped himself. Only days before, he had admired Jath'ibaye for never losing his humanity despite his power. Surely it was that very same trait which Kahlil now found so exasperating.

He knew that he wouldn't want Jath'ibaye to become the kind of man who easily murdered a friend. He took a deep breath of the cold air and released it. The living heat of his breath formed a pale wisp against the dark sky.

"Jath'ibaye can't do it, but I could," Kahlil said. He glanced to Ji. "That's why everyone here is so relieved that I'm going to kill Fikiri. You're all hoping I'll take out Loshai as well."

"We're counting on it."

"If that's what I have to do, then that's what I'll do." Kahlil shrugged. But he wondered how Jath'ibaye would respond. Would he be sickened or relieved after Kahlil had killed Loshai? Jath'ibaye probably didn't know himself. He probably dreaded finding out. Perhaps that was why he insisted that Kahlil remain here in Vundomu instead of leaving to hunt Fikiri down.

"We should get back to Jath'ibaye's holdings before he comes to find us," Ji said.

Kahlil glanced to the barracks just in time to see Jath'ibaye striding toward them across the courtyard.

"Too late," Kahlil replied.

Ji squinted across the courtyard. Kahlil noticed that her tail began to wag just slightly at the sight of Jath'ibaye. He wondered if she knew that she was doing it.

Even in the dark, Jath'ibaye walked straight to them, never missing his footing. Kahlil enjoyed watching Jath'ibaye move. He seemed so at ease in his physical prowess. Despite his size, he hardly left prints in the soft earth.

"I thought I'd come and see what was taking the two of you so long," Jath'ibaye said.

"We were just about to leave," Kahlil replied. Briefly, he caught Jath'ibaye's hand. Their fingers touched and parted.

"I'll walk you back up then," Jath'ibaye said.

"Do you know what Eriki'yu has planned for dinner?" Ji asked. "I hope not dog. I never feel right eating dog."

"It was fish this afternoon," Jath'ibaye replied. He clearly hadn't paid much attention to the dinner preparations.

"Fish might be worth the walk," Ji said. "Buttered bird would definitely be worth it, but there aren't too many birds this time of year. Not big juicy ones. Fish, though…I don't know."

"Shall I carry you?" Jath'ibaye offered.

Kahlil saw Ji's teeth flash, but he wasn't sure if it was meant to be a smile or threat. Ji's expressions and gestures were an odd blur of both animal and human. He recalled that his sister had become deeply animalistic when she had worn that same body. He supposed that living in the flesh of a dog had to have an effect on Ji as well, especially after so many years.

Jath'ibaye understood Ji. He knelt and picked her up. She relaxed against him. Her head hung over his shoulder. Her paws curled in against his chest. In Jath'ibaye's arms, she looked like a strange, exhausted child.

Kahlil walked beside Jath'ibaye, matching his fast pace. They walked close. From time to time their shoulders brushed. They exchanged smiles in the darkness.

In the silence, Kahlil contemplated both Ji and Jath'ibaye. Neither was quite natural and yet they both clung to their humanity.

Kahlil supposed that he struggled far less than either of them. He did not resist his abilities or the nature of his body. Both Ji and Jath'ibaye would have been more careful, but then perhaps that was why they needed him.

For the first time since he'd crossed from Nayeshi, Kahlil felt a glimmer of old pride and even a little of his old faith returning. He'd wondered why Parfir had allowed him to cross through the broken Great Gate and return to Basawar. The answer now coalesced within him: he still had a purpose. Loshai hunted Jath'ibaye, and only Kahlil had the skill and the will to protect him.

As they strode through the courtyard of Jath'ibaye's household, a succulent roasting scent floated over them. Ji's eyes opened slightly. She smiled, an almost perfectly human smile, and said, "Roasting doves."

Chapter Sixty-Two

After dinner Kahlil followed Jath'ibaye back up to the watchtowers. He peered down through the telescope at the gaun'im's armies. Campfires blazed and torches burned bright yellow against the dull night sky. The armies' camps spread like flickering constellations around the river city of Mahn'illev.

Kahlil carefully adjusted the lens. He could see the gray shadows of rashan'im riding through the city streets. Groups of them rode from building to building, searching.

"Are they looking for food?" Kahlil guessed. Marching as quickly as they had, they couldn't have transported many rations. The men were probably sick of what they had brought.

"Probably." Jath'ibaye frowned out at the tiny fires. "I think some of them have taken women as well."

Kahlil almost asked why but then realized that he didn't need to. He had spent enough time among rashan'im to know what uses they had for their enemies' women. Kahlil felt slightly sick. The only consolation he could think of was that there weren't many women left in Mahn'illev. In the last three days a majority of the inhabitants had fled the city and taken refuge within Vundomu.

"Can you see the crests?" Jath'ibaye asked.

"Of the looters in the city?" Kahlil studied the packs of rashan'im through the fine lenses of the telescope. He focused in close on a group of three men. Their tahldi were loaded with sacks of grain, bolts of cloth, and glittering baubles. Kahlil recognized the Lisam bull on their coats easily. Its golden form flashed in the light of the streetlamps.

But there were other crests as well. The white lily of the Anyyd clearly decorated the saddles of several riders near the city stables. There weren't many animals left in there, but the rashan'im seemed to be willing to take anything they found.

Closer to the river, Kahlil noticed a flurry of movement. A young girl struggled free from the two men holding her. She ran and the men rode after her. As they pursued her across a small stone bridge, Kahlil made out the crests on their coats. They wore the swans of the Naye'ro family. One of the men knocked the girl to the ground with the butt of his rifle. The man dismounted and strode to the girl's prone body. Kahlil lifted his head from the telescope, unwilling to witness any more.

"Lisam, Anyyd, and Naye'ro," Kahlil told Jath'ibaye. "There aren't many of them, and I didn't see any captains among them. They might just be a few men raiding without leave."

"None of the Bousim, though?" Jath'ibaye asked.

"No." Kahlil shook his head. "Why?"

"I thought that perhaps this was a ploy to provoke an attack," Jath'ibaye said. He glowered down at the city, and for a few moments, the rage in his expression reminded Kahlil of the snarling images he had seen in the Temple of the Rifter. The air in the watchtower grew cold as a frigid wind began to stir. Then Jath'ibaye turned away. The air stilled.

"Do you really think the Bousim family wants a war?" Kahlil asked.

"The family? No. But Nanvess' father, Nivoun, probably does. Most of the Bousim troops gathered here are from his lands," Jath'ibaye said.

Kahlil waited for Jath'ibaye to say something more, but he was quiet. He ran his fingers over the stones of the wall as if soothing an animal.

"I wish…" Jath'ibaye began but didn't go on.

"Wish what?" Kahlil asked. If Jath'ibaye told him to go and kill the looting rashan'im, he would do it in a heartbeat.

"I wish I could crush them all," Jath'ibaye growled. He closed his eyes and was silent for several moments again, running his fingers over the stones. "But obviously I would destroy Mahn'illev along with the gaun'im's armies if I lashed out right now. I'd kill the people I wanted to save. So, I suppose I'm going to have to do what I keep telling everyone else to do. I'm going to have to wait.

The gaun'im will send runners tomorrow with their demands." Jath'ibaye's tone turned contemptuous on the last word.

"You should get some rest then," Kahlil said. Though he couldn't imagine going to sleep at a time like this. But Jath'ibaye would need to be rested. He might not get another chance until after matters were settled with the gaun'im. That could take weeks, even months.

"I can't. Tai'yu's called another council meeting. Wah'roa's asked me to attend."

"What more could they need to talk about?" Kahlil asked, exasperated. "The gaun'im haven't even issued any demands. They should just let you get some rest."

"The planting season," Jath'ibaye replied.

"What?" Planting seasons were so removed from the train of Kahlil's thoughts that it took him a moment to really understand what Jath'ibaye had said.

"Taye," Jath'ibaye replied. "The seeds have to be sown soon or the crop won't be ripe by harvest. They need to know when the winter weather in the north will break."

"Couldn't it wait until later?"

"The meeting can't go much past the tenth bell," Jath'ibaye said. "Will I see you after that?"

"I'll be there," Kahlil promised. They had spent every night of the past week together. He had no idea what might happen in the coming days. Despite his bravado, there was a chance that if he fought Fikiri again he might not win. He didn't want to waste what might be their last peaceful night together.

Jath'ibaye nodded and then left. Kahlil glanced to the telescope again and thought of the girl and of the rashan'im. Someone, he thought, should help her. Another look down at Mahn'illev assured him that no rescuer had appeared.

Kahlil listened to the sound of Jath'ibaye's footsteps receding down the stairs. During the time that Kahlil had been training Pesha, Jath'ibaye had grown less sensitive to individual openings in the Gray Space, particularly if they were smooth. But Kahlil still thought it best to make sure Jath'ibaye had put some distance between them.

Kahlil imagined that by now Jath'ibaye had reached the landing. Doubtless Ji, Saimura, or Eriki'yu would be nearby, waiting for him. It would only be a matter of moments before Jath'ibaye was occupied with rationing grain stores for refugees or discussing news from Nurjima.

He'd said he'd be back at the tenth bell. That gave Kahlil just under three hours. He waited just a moment longer than he wanted to. Then, silently, he opened the Gray Space. An instant later he stepped out onto the streets of Mahn'illev.

A cold wind rolled off the river. It blew through the pale flames of the street lamps, washing the oily scent of smoke down to Kahlil. Rows of empty single-story houses slouched on either side of the cobbled street.

He slipped back into the colorless cold of the Gray Space. He crossed the small stone bridge. He could see the girl still struggling against the Naye'ro rashan on top of her. The second rashan grabbed her arms and pinned them above her head, while his companion finished cutting the girl's clothes open.

Kahlil drew his own knife. A pistol would have been faster but it also would have drawn the attention of the other rashan'im looting the city. He stepped out of the Gray Space only inches from the rashan who hunched over the girl's body. With a fast thrust, Kahlil drove his knife deep into the man's back. He felt the blade slide easily between ribs as it sank into the man's heart.

Releasing the knife, Kahlil shoved the man's body aside. The rashan holding the girl's arms stared at Kahlil in shock. He opened his mouth to speak. Kahlil brought his hand up, opening an Unseen Edge. He thrust the edge forward. Blood burst from the rashan's throat as the Unseen Edge tore through the muscle and bone of his neck. The rashan's head fell and his body toppled backwards to the ground behind it.

The girl stared up at Kahlil. She couldn't have been much older than sixteen. Her face was bruised and spattered with blood. Her clothes were in tatters. She sat up immediately. Her hands shook as she attempted to pull the remains of her shirt closed over her bare breasts.

"Here." Kahlil slid his newly mended coat off and held it out to her. She took the coat silently and put it on.

"I'm from Vundomu," Kahlil said. "I've come to help you."

The girl said nothing. Her eyes darted from the body of one rashan to the other and then back to Kahlil.

"Can you walk?" Kahlil asked.

The girl nodded.

Kahlil glanced to where the tahldi stood, tethered beside the bridge.

"Do you think you could ride?" Kahlil asked.

The girl's lips trembled, and for an instant, Kahlil feared that she would burst into tears. Instead she nodded and then forced herself up to her feet. Kahlil led her to the tahldi. He chose the smaller of the two animals and held its reins as the girl pulled herself up into the saddle.

"You know how to handle a tahldi?" Kahlil asked her.

"Yes," she whispered.

"Good." Kahlil turned and surveyed the layout of the streets. "The main road leads out of the city to Vundomu's gates, doesn't it?"

"No." The girl shook her head.

Kahlil frowned. He clearly remembered the wide main road. He had followed it as he moved through the Gray Space.

"My family is east from here, in Yep'pasa." She seemed to almost choke, then recovered herself. "I came here with my husband but those men, they killed…" Her mouth trembled as if unable to shape the words she needed. Kahlil saw tears dribbling down her cheeks. She wiped her face.

"I want to go home," she whispered.

"Then you should go home."

"There are more of those men in the city. I heard them," the girl said.

"I'll take care of them," Kahlil assured her. He didn't miss the way her eyes darted fearfully back to where the two rashan'im's bodies lay.

"If I can get you out of Mahn'illev, will you be able to find your way to Yep'pasa?" Kahlil asked.

The girl nodded.

"Don't keep the tahldi once you've gotten home," Kahlil said. "It's got a rashan's brand."

Again the girl nodded.

"Go on then," Kahlil told her. "Ride as fast as you can."

"But those men—"

"You just ride. Leave the men to me." Kahlil smiled at her. She nodded in return and then urged the tahldi forward. She didn't look back to see Kahlil. This, Kahlil thought, was just as well since she wouldn't have seen anything.

He slipped back into the silent, cold Gray Space and raced along beside her. The rashan'im in the streets heard her. More than one tried to overtake her. Kahlil descended upon them, dropping from the Gray Space only long enough to rend their bodies. In the instant that he appeared, Kahlil flicked open an Unseen Edge, severing heads or bisecting torsos. The rashan'im's blood gushed across the backs of their tahldi. Swathes of the cobbled road were black and slick with it. Hidden within the Gray Space, Kahlil remained perfectly clean.

The girl rode without a single backward glance while Kahlil tore rashan'im apart, one after another. Block after block of houses and shops blurred into a haze of repetition. Each time Kahlil burst out of the Gray Space, the city sounded a little quieter. The air felt a little hotter. Kahlil's arms began to ache. Little pangs of fatigue played through his thighs and back.

Then suddenly the rows of buildings were gone. There was nothing but the open road, empty fields, and the thousands of tents of the Bousim army.

Kahlil saw the girl shudder as she caught sight of the armed soldiers standing guard beside the road. Kahlil's stomach clenched. If they had gone north as he had planned this wouldn't have happened. But it was too late to turn the girl around. Light from raised iron lamps had already illuminated the girl far too clearly. For an instant she stared at the dozen men standing guard. Then she urged her tahldi forward.

Kahlil threw himself ahead of her, praying that he could shatter a dozen rifles before one opened fire. He knew he was too late.

The men had already taken aim. Then all twelve of them lowered their rifles. The girl raced past them. They simply watched her go.

Kahlil stared at the soldiers. He heard nothing, but he could see the rashan'im's commander shouting orders. All along the length of the road Bousim soldiers lowered their rifles. Kahlil watched the girl disappear into the distance.

He turned his attention back to the Bousim commander.

Small but not slight, his build reminded Kahlil of those Nayeshi greyhounds—all bone and muscle. His hair and eyes were dark, his features rather delicate. Thick black brows dominated what would have otherwise been an almost girlish face.

He hardly looked thirty. Kahlil frowned at the insignia the man wore: commander of an entire Bousim territory. That was a very high rank for someone so young. Then Kahlil took in the insignia at the collar of his coat. He was one of the Bousim gaun'im.

The young commander shouted something more and several captains came running.

Kahlil moved back from the group of guards and their commander. He crouched down under a heavy munitions wagon. Hidden in the deep shadows, Kahlil slid out of the Gray Space. He wanted to know what it was that the commander was saying.

"—are not to be harmed in any way. We have not yet declared war and until that time you are to treat the civilians here as we would our own people. I want that made perfectly clear to all the men!" The commander's words seemed jarringly loud after the utter silence of the Gray Space. It was a deep, powerful voice with a strong northern accent.

Kahlil peered out through the wooden spokes of the wagon wheel. Four rashan captains stood alongside their commander. They were older men, well into their forties and fifties.

"No rashan'im, of this or any other army, are to be allowed to pursue or harass any citizen of these lands. I don't care if they are beggars or whores. They will be treated with respect. Am I understood?"

"Yes sir," the captains answered in unison.

"Good," the Bousim commander said. "Dismissed."

All but one of the captains withdrew. The one remaining stepped closer to the commander.

"That was a Naye'ro tahldi she was riding, Joulen," the captain said.

"Good for her," Commander Joulen replied.

"If the rashan comes looking for his mount?" the captain asked.

"Have him brought to me and I will personally flog him for looting," Commander Joulen said. The captain seemed to appreciate this response. He grinned wickedly.

Kahlil knew the name Joulen Bousim. He'd never met the man personally, but Alidas had spoken of him on several occasions. He was the youngest son of the Bousim gaunsho. This made him a possible, if unlikely, candidate for Bousim leadership.

He had been sent into military service when he was only a boy. Despite his youth, he had risen quickly through the ranks. The harsh mountainous lands between the eastern chasm and the Iron Heights had apparently brought out the best in him. Now, as high commander for the Bousim Mountain Forces, Joulen answered only to his uncle Nivoun, the governor of the Northern Territories.

Out of uniform, Joulen probably could have passed as a new recruit. His mere physical presence didn't radiate power the way Jath'ibaye's did. Still, Kahlil found himself watching closely as Joulen stiffened slightly and then turned on his heel back toward the open road.

The captain, too, followed Joulen's sudden motion. His expression was expectant, like a hunter who waited to catch sight of the game his hound had already sensed. Joulen's eyes narrowed.

"Another tahldi!" Joulen called out to the men guarding the road. "Catch its reins!"

Following Joulen's gaze, Kahlil could see why the commander looked so troubled. The animal was covered in blood. The lower portion of its rider's body hung from the saddle; the upper portion lay on the road miles away, but only Kahlil knew that. The tahldi pranced and shied nervously. The Bousim soldiers approached it cautiously, speaking in calm, low tones. At last one of them caught the animal's reins. The tahldi quieted somewhat.

"Don't touch the rider's remains," Joulen called. "Leave that for the Anyyd captains to see. Take the animal back to their camp."

The men scrambled to follow their commander's orders. Joulen and the captain moved away from them.

"It's turning out to be quite a night," the captain said.

"And this is only Jath'ibaye's doorstep," Joulen replied. "If those southern asses think they can raid and rape in Vundomu they're going to get us all killed."

"The Milaun men are keeping behind their lines," the captain said.

Joulen nodded. "The Du'yura and Tushoya as well, but three lesser houses aren't enough. All the commanders have to control their men or we're going to end up fighting every single northern villager before we even get to the kahlirash'im."

"Shall we send men into Mahn'illev to stop the raiding?" the captain asked.

Joulen shook his head. "No Lisam rashan is going to answer to any but his own commander. The same for the Anyyd. After the tahldi has been delivered to the Anyyd camp, I'll call on their commander and see if he wants to hear me out now."

Again the captain flashed a quick cruel smile in response to Joulen's words.

The two of them walked back closer to where Kahlil crouched beneath the wagon. Remembering how sharp Joulen's eyes were, Kahlil slid deeper into the shadows.

"Do you think it was a natural creature that cut that rashan in half?" the captain asked, his voice a low hush.

"It didn't look like the work of bones, but who knows what other monstrosities Jath'ibaye breeds in Vundomu." Joulen's voice was almost a whisper. "Parfir protect us if this really does come to a war."

"Indeed." The captain's voice was a whisper as well. "There have been reports of yellow fire in the far northern skies again. Do you think he's creating more of those bones?"

"If he is, then we'd better pray for snow. It's the only thing that will slow them down." Joulen stopped a few feet from the wagon.

"The Anyyd and Lisam and Naye'ro will be riding south the first time they catch a glimpse of one of those things."

"Leaving us to fight, no doubt," the captain grumbled.

"No doubt," Joulen replied. He sounded tired.

"Do you think it'll come down to that? To another war?" the captain asked.

"I don't know," Joulen replied. "Ask me again tomorrow night."

"Your uncle hasn't said anything?" the captain asked.

"He's said plenty. Ourath and Gethlam have too. But it's easy to talk when you aren't actually facing Vundomu's godhammers."

Both men were quiet for a time. Then Kahlil heard a quick scratch and hiss. The familiar scent of cigarette smoke spread through the air. Joulen gave a quiet laugh.

"There's a munitions wagon right behind you, Shira," he said.

"Shit." Kahlil heard the captain jump away from the wagon. "All this worry about monsters and I get blown up by our own mortars. My wife would never forgive me."

"If there was anything left to forgive—" The rest of Joulen's response was cut short by a distant but terrible screaming noise, like metal rending open.

"What the hell is Ourath keeping in his camp?" Joulen growled.

"Doesn't sound good," Captain Shira responded.

It wasn't, Kahlil knew. It was Fikiri.

☾☾☾

Seconds later Kahlil was moving through the Lisam camp. He raced through tents and tahldi enclosures, searching for traces of Fikiri's passage. If he were Jath'ibaye, he could have easily picked out the heavy scars Fikiri left in his wake. Then again, if he were Jath'ibaye, he wouldn't have been down here at all.

Kahlil swore as a rough area of the Gray Space scraped against his forearm. He stopped, staring at the tiny distortion that had bitten into his skin. It hung in front of Kahlil like a fine scratch on a glass pane. Against the gray forms of the Lisam tents and patrolling guards, the disturbance was tiny.

He only managed to follow it a few yards before it faded out completely. But it led him far enough to guess where Fikiri had gone. Even at a distance Kahlil recognized Ourath's private accommodations. Huge bulls charged across the tent walls. Pale banners billowed from the steepled tent top. Rashan'im in dress uniforms stood guard all around the walls and at the entrance.

Kahlil walked through one of the guards and into the tent. Both Ourath and Fikiri were there. Dressed in ragged, dark robes and nearly motionless, Fikiri resembled an old drop cloth that had been hurled across a finely carved chair. His eyes moved, not following Ourath's motions but searching the empty air. Ourath stood several feet away, drinking from a goblet. A large table stretched between the two of them. Platters of roasted birds, fish, and dog crowded the table. There were several different loaves of bread, and Kahlil imagined that the dark liquid steaming in a little decorative pot was some kind of mulled wine.

Ourath was obviously not a man to deprive himself, not even on the battlefield. A servant entered, and Fikiri's head snapped to where the cold night wind blew in at the boy's entrance.

Kahlil briefly considered attacking Fikiri right here and now. But appearing in the middle of the gaun'im's camp wouldn't be particularly wise. And if Fikiri escaped him, then Kahlil would have caused an uproar for nothing. Doubtless, Jath'ibaye would be blamed for any foreign attack within the gaun'im's camps. He was already being blamed for the hungry bones.

But if Kahlil could find out what Fikiri and Ourath were planning, then it might aid Jath'ibaye greatly. The only trouble was that he couldn't hear a thing while he was in the Gray Space. Leaving the Gray Space would require making an opening and releasing one of those cold whispers. And Fikiri would definitely notice that.

There was also the problem of finding a place to hide. Unlike the underside of the Bousim munitions wagon, Ourath's tent was very well lit. Several perfumed lamps hung from its supports. Their light blazed as it was caught and reflected by the full-length mirrors that had been placed in the corners. Fikiri had seated himself in the darkest corner of the tent. What space remained all seemed to be illuminated to an afternoon glow.

Ourath briefly glanced into one of the mirrors, watching the serving boy as he added fresh cutlets of dog to the meat platters.

As the boy stepped back from the table and began bowing his way out of the tent, Kahlil made his choice. He rushed behind the far mirror. When the boy opened the tent flaps, Kahlil stepped out of the Gray Space.

Fikiri straightened. His eyes darted from the corner of the tent to the flaps as they fell closed. Kahlil caught his breath as if Fikiri could sense even that small of a movement in the air. Slowly Fikiri slumped back in his chair. He continued to watch the folds and shadows of the tent walls suspiciously.

"A little jumpy, aren't you?" Ourath commented to Fikiri. His voice was so smooth and low that Kahlil had to strain to hear him. "Are you certain it was the same man? We hardly glimpsed him."

"It was Ravishan. I would know that arrogant face anywhere. He should be dead twice over now. I saw to that myself," Fikiri replied. "Still, somehow, he returns."

"But you said yourself that the yasi'halaun is fatal. It devours the very soul of a man." Ourath's eyes lingered on the mirror and for a moment Kahlil was afraid that Ourath had caught a glimpse of him. Then Kahlil realized that Ourath was studying his own reflection. Ourath flicked a bright copper curl of his hair back from his face.

"It does," Fikiri replied. He frowned, deepening the heavy lines that etched his weathered face. "But it is crafted from a Rifter's bones. Deep in its essence it is always his to command."

"I have no idea nor frankly do I have any wish to find out what any of that meant." Ourath, at last, turned his attention from his reflection to Fikiri. "What do you need me to do tomorrow?"

"You must delay any settlement," Fikiri replied. "You need to keep the armies here until the weather breaks in the north."

"That could take months," Ourath protested. "Not even Gethlam Anyyd can be played for that long."

"Not true." Fikiri started as the breeze outside moved the tent wall. "Jath'ibaye can't afford to wait that long. His people have to plant their taye soon or starve, which means that he must allow the thaw come by the end of this week. Our forces in the north should be ready for an assault within days of the thaw."

"And the armies here?" Ourath asked.

"I will tell you when to commence your attack," Fikiri replied. "We need only to capture Jath'ibaye in order to bring down the entirety of Vundomu."

"And to open your gateway, yes?" Ourath asked.

"Yes." Fikiri nodded. "The Kingdom of the Night and the Palace of the Day will be ours then."

Ourath smiled.

"You should eat," he said to Fikiri. He filled a plate with slices of meat and drizzled a fragrant red sauce over it. "Have you tried the doves?"

Fikiri took the food and ate quickly. Ourath refilled his glass with mulled wine.

"Your plan still puts me in a difficult position," Ourath said. "The gaun'im want this all settled as expeditiously as possible."

"What about Gaunsho Bousim?"

"He's angry, but he's willing to claim an exclusive contract for Vundomu's iron as compensation for the loss of Nanvess. After all, he was Nivoun's son, not the gaunsho's. And this opens the way for the gaunsho to name one of his own children as heir."

Fikiri scowled as he chewed his cutlet. "Too easy. They might just agree to that. There must be something else you can do."

"Perhaps. Nanvess wasn't the only one killed." Ourath paused to sip his wine. "If Gethlam Anyyd got it into his head that he had as much right to demand iron for Esh'illan's death as the Bousim have for Nanvess', then perhaps that would keep things delayed."

"Why shouldn't he claim reparations for his brother's death?" Fikiri demanded.

"Esh'illan wasn't well liked. Most of the Anyyd family are relieved that he's dead." Ourath glanced over the heaps of roast dog but didn't take any. "Still, he was a gaun and that alone makes his death worth something. Yes, I think that might keep things tied up for a while."

Fikiri studied Ourath. "Have you any influence over Gethlam?"

"Only a little," Ourath admitted. "But he and Joulen Bousim have been butting heads for days now. Gethlam might make the claim just to spite Joulen at this point."

"If the idea occurred to him," Fikiri said.

"Just so," Ourath replied.

"Would you need anything from me?"

"Not to stoke Gethlam's avarice, but Jath'ibaye…I doubt that I'll be able to enthrall him again, not after the Bell Dance. He'll probably try to kill me the moment he lays eyes on me. That might get your war started a little too soon, don't you think?"

"Much too soon." Fikiri looked as if he'd swallowed something bitter. "If Jath'ibaye destroys the gaun'im armies before our northern forces are roused, there will be no way to take him by surprise."

"So, am I to just throw myself into the beast's bed again and hope he doesn't kill me?" Ourath asked.

The contempt that Kahlil had felt for Ourath suddenly exploded into rage at the suggestion that he ever could throw himself into Jath'ibaye's bed again. The urge to spring through the Gray Space and tear the lying whore apart surged through Kahlil. Only the sheer stupidity of the impulse stopped him. Fikiri was sitting only a few feet away.

"If you must," Fikiri replied. Kahlil noticed the faint sneer of disgust that Fikiri gave Ourath when his back was turned. Kahlil wondered if Ourath also saw it as he watched Fikiri in one of his mirrors.

"There are poisons that dull his anger and wear him down. But I no longer have any way of feeding them to him," Ourath said.

"My Lady has sent you this." Fikiri drew a thick glass vial from the pocket of his robe. The surface of the vial was scratched and dull as if it had been sandblasted. Still, Kahlil could see a faint golden glow emanating from its contents.

Ourath took the vial and studied it.

"Wear just a little on your skin where it won't be seen," Fikiri said.

"What does it do?" Ourath asked.

Fikiri smiled, but not kindly. "It will do what you need it to do. Though, for your own safety, don't wear too much or go too close to the bucks while you've got it on."

Ourath observed the vial, then very carefully peeled back the stopper. A soft gold light radiated up from the mouth.

"Wait until I'm gone to use it," Fikiri put in.

Ourath frowned at Fikiri as if the mere thought that he would do otherwise was distasteful to him. Ourath drew in a slow breath, though he kept his nose far above the vial.

"Niru'mohim," Ourath said. "Nanvess used to make it. It irritates the skin and leaves welts."

Fikiri nodded. "Don't wear it where it will be seen."

"So not in a large splash across my forehead?" Ourath asked sarcastically.

"This is stronger than any of Nanvess' potions could have been." Fikiri gave Ourath a hard look as if he were chastising a child. "It will burn you and it will leave a scar."

"But it will affect Jath'ibaye?" Ourath asked.

Fikiri nodded. "Assuredly. Once he senses it, he'll probably try to keep clear of you, which will keep you safe."

"In the meantime, will I have to fight off every man in Vundomu?" Ourath asked.

"They'll notice you, but this was made with Jath'ibaye's blood. It will affect him far more than any other man." Fikiri's eyes darted to a movement up in the top of the tent. A cream-colored moth flittered close to one of the lamps.

"So then that only leaves us with the question of the yasi'halaun." Ourath pushed the stopper back into the vial and slipped it into his coat pocket.

"That is my concern, not yours," Fikiri replied. He slid his empty plate onto the table.

"But you will need it—" Ourath went quiet as the servant boy darted in.

"Forgive me, my lord, but Commander Joulen Bousim wishes to speak with you." The boy bowed deeply to Ourath.

"Right now?" Ourath asked.

"He is waiting outside, as is Commander Gethlam Anyyd, my lord." The boy kept his head down. Ourath looked to Fikiri.

"Perhaps it would be best if I took my leave," Fikiri said.

"Perhaps it would," Ourath agreed.

Fikiri rose to his feet.

Ourath turned back to his servant. “You may show the commanders in.”

“Yes, my lord.” The servant boy straightened and then retreated. Fikiri followed the boy out of the tent. It surprised Kahlil to see Fikiri just walk away. Then he realized that the noise and flames Fikiri caused when he opened the Gray Space were far too extravagant. They had already attracted Joulen’s attention. And Ourath would have particular difficulty explaining them if they occurred right inside his tent.

Soon the servant boy reappeared, followed by Joulen Bousim who was flanked by a second commander wearing the silver lily of the Anyyd House.

“Joulen. Gethlam.” Ourath inclined his head only a little to both men. “How is it that I can help you?”

An oddly voracious look came into Gethlam Anyyd’s eyes. For a moment Kahlil thought that Ourath might have used a little of the potion Fikiri had given him. Then Kahlil realized that Gethlam was staring at the food on Ourath’s table.

“Feel free to help yourselves to my table while you are here,” Ourath said.

“Very generous of you, Gaunsho.” Gethlam took a plate and began heaping meat onto it. His thick neck and square chest gave him more than a passing resemblance to the Lisam bulls that decorated Ourath’s tent. Though his dark brown hair was shot through with gray, there was a roundness to his chin and cheeks that made his face look almost like a child’s. Kahlil remembered thinking the same thing of Esh’illan Anyyd.

“We’ve come to discuss the discipline of our united troops.” Joulen scowled at Gethlam.

Gethlam avoided Joulen’s gaze, chewing his meat as if it took all of his concentration.

“Discipline?” Ourath inquired.

“Yes,” Joulen said, but then he paused. “May I ask who that man was that just left? I don’t recall seeing him before.”

“He was one of the residents of Mahn’illev,” Ourath replied smoothly. “Apparently he was quite concerned about our rashan’im.

He told me that his shop was destroyed by riders wearing Bousim colors—"

Gethlam grinned and rounded on Joulen.

"Bousim colors!" Gethlam crowed. "And you have the gall to tell me how I should handle my men."

Joulen's face flushed. "Every one of my men is accounted for in our camp."

"Yes, of course they are," Ourath said soothingly. "It's dark after all and it's easy to mistake one rashan for another. Still, we must not allow our men to run wild." Ourath filled a plate with cutlets of meat and sauce and then handed it to Joulen just as he had offered food to Fikiri earlier.

"Eat something, Commander," Ourath said. "I think you'll find it helps your mood."

Joulen took the food and wine that Ourath offered him. His expression was one of slight confusion, as if he wasn't sure how the dishes had ended up in his hands.

"Please, both of you," Ourath said, "sit and tell me what's bothering you."

"Joulen's bothering me." Gethlam took the chair that Fikiri had just vacated. Joulen seated himself across from Gethlam. He looked like he was about to respond to Gethlam's words; then he frowned. He narrowed his eyes, gazing past Gethlam to the mirror in the corner of the tent. He didn't look at the reflection but at Kahlil. He stared with an expression of uncertainty, as if not quite sure of what he was seeing. Then his gaze met Kahlil's directly and his eyes widened.

Instantly, Kahlil dropped back into the Gray Space. Joulen blinked and narrowed his gaze but there was no longer anything to be seen. Ourath said something and Joulen's attention turned back to the meats piled on his plate.

Kahlil didn't trust in his luck enough to push it much further this evening. He already had news enough to tell Jath'ibaye. And he knew he should get back to Vundomu before he was missed. He moved quickly through the Gray Space, returning to the watchtower at Vundomu just in time to hear the eleventh bell ring out.

Chapter Sixty-Three

At the heights of Vundomu, gusts of warm wind rose, twisting through the cool air. The warmth and moisture reminded Kahlil of a summer storm. The idea of summer was troubling. Heat was all that Fikiri was waiting for. Jath'ibaye had to be warned. Kahlil rushed from the watchtower down to Jath'ibaye's chambers.

As he came through the door, the lush green scent of flowers and vines washed over Kahlil. Breezes swirled and raced through the leaves and blossoms. The air churned as if a thunderstorm were trapped in the room.

Jath'ibaye sat at his table. Books and planting charts were stacked to his right. Polished stones were scattered across the papers, weighing them down in the face of the rushing gusts. Jath'ibaye looked up as Kahlil walked in. Without saying a word, he kicked one of the chairs out for Kahlil to take a seat.

"Sorry I'm so late." Kahlil walked to the chair but was hesitant to sit down. He studied Jath'ibaye and Jath'ibaye returned his gaze with a closed expression. The muscles in his jaw flexed and worked against each other. Jath'ibaye rolled a pale stone in his hand. As Kahlil watched, bits of the rock crumbled beneath Jath'ibaye's fingers.

"I went—"

"I know where you went." Jath'ibaye cut him off as if he couldn't stand to even hear Kahlil say it.

Jath'ibaye glared down at the book in front of him. Kahlil recognized it. It was the ancient tome he had been slowly translating. Despite his attentive expression, Jath'ibaye did not seem to be reading. His gaze focused on one spot as if pinning the words down. He continued worrying the stone in his hand.

Kahlil was silent. He had known that his excursion would annoy Jath'ibaye, but he hadn't thought it would warrant this kind of anger. He wasn't sure how apologetic he could bring himself to act.

"Are you all right?" Jath'ibaye's tone was flat.

"Fine," Kahlil assured him.

"Good. I'm glad that you weren't hurt." Again the muscles in his jaw flexed as if fighting for control of his words. "You could have been killed."

"No one even saw me," Kahlil said, grinning. He had thought to play the entire matter off as inconsequential. Immediately, he realized that he'd made a mistake. Jath'ibaye snapped the stone in half.

"You could have been killed!" Jath'ibaye shouted, abandoning the pretense of repose. He bolted to his feet, sending his chair skittering back behind him.

Kahlil stepped back.

"You could have died! You…you are so frustrating." He didn't seem to trust himself to go on. Several moments of silence passed. Kahlil waited, unsure of what to say.

"I know I can't expect you to follow my orders, but don't you think that you ought to tell me when you go into enemy territory?" His words came out with an unnaturally measured precision.

"Yes," Kahlil allowed. "But if I'm planning on doing something that you don't like, then you'll argue with me."

"If you're planning something stupid, it is my right to argue, but that doesn't mean you shouldn't tell me," Jath'ibaye said.

"I wasn't doing anything stupid. I saved a girl. You would have done the same thing, if you could have." Kahlil tried to keep his own temper from flaring. He wasn't sorry he'd done it and couldn't even pretend to be.

Jath'ibaye's jaw clenched against an immediate response.

"It was possible for me to go down there and stop those rashan'im when no one else could," Kahlil said. "It was the right thing to do and I don't regret going."

"Of course you don't," Jath'ibaye replied. "And I didn't say that what you did was wrong. I was glad to see those rashan'im die. I'm angry because you didn't tell me that you were going to do it."

"Oh." The righteous argument that Kahlil had been preparing to launch was suddenly pointless. "Well, you obviously found out what I was doing."

"I don't want to find out after the fact," Jath'ibaye growled. "We are on the brink of war. I need to know where you are."

"All right. I'm sorry. I just wasn't thinking about it." Kahlil held up his hands in the Payshmura sign of peace. "At least no harm was done."

"Not this time," Jath'ibaye snapped. "But you have to remember that I can't protect you if I don't know where you are."

"You can't always protect me no matter what," Kahlil replied, a spark of annoyance flaring through him. He had traveled between two worlds and survived in both of them for years without Jath'ibaye's protection. "And I'm not defenseless on my own, you know!"

"You're not invulnerable either," Jath'ibaye said.

"The rashan'im couldn't lay a finger on me."

"I wasn't thinking of rashan'im," Jath'ibaye said. "What do you think would have happened to you if I had crushed the gaun'im's armies while you were out there?"

"You wouldn't have," Kahlil replied.

"What if I had?" Jath'ibaye insisted.

"But you wouldn't—"

"I could have. And I would have killed you. I wouldn't have known you were there and I would have killed you accidentally." There was such cold certainty in Jath'ibaye's tone that it startled Kahlil. Jath'ibaye's expression was a strange mix of sickness and conviction. Kahlil knew he wasn't talking about a hypothetical situation, but something that had already happened.

In an instant Kahlil realized that he even knew when. When Rathal'pesha fell, Ravishan had been there. He must have gone without telling Jath'ibaye, just as he had done tonight.

And Jath'ibaye had killed him.

A chill shuddered down Kahlil's spine. He felt slightly sick at the idea. Reflexively, he wanted to escape the thought of it. But he couldn't, not with Jath'ibaye standing in front of him in such empty silence.

All at once, Kahlil understood Jath'ibaye's clenched jaw and balled fists. The emotion that he restrained was not anger at all, but heartbreaking loss and fear. It was an expression that as a young man in Nayeshi, John had shown to no one. But Kahlil, watching from the Gray Space, had seen. He knew that Jath'ibaye wouldn't speak now because the tremor in his voice would reveal him to be on the edge of tears.

He would have to be the one to make this right.

"I didn't think of that," Kahlil said. His own voice sounded dull. He had been an idiot. He, of all people, knew what kind of destruction Jath'ibaye was capable of unleashing and yet he hadn't even considered what Jath'ibaye might have done in his absence. He hadn't given the slightest thought to the idea that Jath'ibaye might take his own action.

This was what Ji had been trying to tell him about—the mistake that he could avoid if he only allowed himself to remember his other life. And what had he done? The same thing twice.

He would have thought that the knowledge that Jath'ibaye had killed him would make him angry or at least feel unsafe. But all he felt was embarrassment for having been so shortsighted and stupid.

"I'm sorry," Kahlil managed to say. He offered Jath'ibaye his open hands. It was all he had to give.

Jath'ibaye caught hold of Kahlil and pulled him into his arms. He hugged Kahlil to him with desperate strength.

"Just tell me where you're going," Jath'ibaye said. "Just tell me, all right?"

Kahlil nodded numbly. The scents of leaves and green wood that clung to Jath'ibaye's body curled around him. Kahlil leaned into Jath'ibaye's embrace.

"I didn't think…I'm not used to having anyone to tell." Kahlil didn't go on. There was no point in making excuses. "It won't happen again, I swear."

"All right." Jath'ibaye's grip loosened, but he didn't release Kahlil. He bowed his head slightly and kissed Kahlil's neck. A rush of relieved pleasure throbbed over Kahlil's skin. The air in the chamber stilled.

"I'm still not sorry that I killed those rashan'im," Kahlil said.

"To be honest, neither am I." Jath'ibaye kissed Kahlil again. The sensation of Jath'ibaye's lips against his throat pleased Kahlil deeply. He wanted to touch more of Jath'ibaye, to taste the expanses of his chest and thighs. He needed to smooth over that moment of fear and horror. Kahlil ran his hands down the curve of Jath'ibaye's buttocks.

"None of them saw you?" Jath'ibaye asked.

"None that survived." Kahlil couldn't keep himself from smiling proudly.

"I can't imagine the gaun'im are going to be happy about it though," Jath'ibaye said wryly.

"They can't blame anyone but their own men. The rashan'im shouldn't have been looting Mahn'illev in the first place."

Kahlil frowned. This wasn't the direction that he had wanted this conversation to go. Just seconds before he had been hoping that their reconciliation would lead the two of them to Jath'ibaye's bed.

But he knew that there were too many other things that he had to tell Jath'ibaye first. Disappointed but resigned, he drew his hands back and said, "I overheard things while I was down there."

"I suppose it can't wait?" Jath'ibaye removed his hands from Kahlil, seeming to already know the answer to his question.

"Fikiri was there with Ourath," Kahlil said.

Jath'ibaye's expression was grim but not at all surprised. "Tell me about it."

Kahlil did. Though halfway through he had to wait while Jath'ibaye called for Eriki'yu and gave orders to send for Ji and the members of the council.

None of them were going to get much sleep tonight.

Chapter Sixty-Four

Wah'roa and two kahlirash captains came first, followed by a waxy, haggard Gin'yu a few minutes later. Her gray hair hung in limp strands around her face. Numerous bleary-eyed attendants and secretaries trailed in behind her. Litivi hurried in just behind his mother. His clothes were rumpled and the distinct scents of wine and women's perfume clung to him. He looked deeply embarrassed when his mother glared at him.

Hirran appeared soon after Litivi. Her lovely, dark hair stuck up from her head at an unbecoming angle and would not lie flat, no matter how often she attempted to smooth it back. Tai'yu had evidently been at the advanced stages of sleep when the summons had come for him. The texture of his pillow had left an impression across his cheek and one side of his long, hawkish nose. His shirt wasn't even properly buttoned. The secretary accompanying him looked like he'd dressed in the dark.

Remembering the cold dignity of the council members when they had summoned him before, Kahlil found this contrasting vision of unkempt clothes, disarrayed hair, and hazy gazes somewhat pleasing. The members of the council were obviously not people well accustomed to sudden awakenings in the dead of night. Of all of them, Wah'roa presented the least ruffled appearance. His uniform was as clean and crisp as always. His black boots gleamed as if they had just been polished. But even he dozed off between the arrivals of the rest of the council.

Ji arrived at last. Saimura and Besh'anya accompanied her. Kahlil offered Besh'anya a friendly smile as she sat down, still pulling the curlers out of her hair. One of the kahlirash captains seemed to know Besh'anya well enough to tease her about wearing a nightshirt to a council summons. Besh'anya glowered at him.

Saimura, oddly, arrived better dressed than usual. His auburn hair hung loose and looked like it had been brushed to a deep luster.

Bright gold buttons adorned his russet coat. Fine silk threads gleamed across the deep garnet fabric of his vest and pants. A large ruby ring flashed on his smallest finger, and instead of his usual work boots, he wore leather shoes with polished brass buckles.

"You're dressed for an occasion," Jath'ibaye commented. "Not this one, I imagine?"

"Du'rai offered me a private recital," Saimura said. He shook his head ruefully.

Kahlil didn't know who Du'rai was, but Jath'ibaye clearly did. He looked impressed.

"That was quick," Jath'ibaye remarked.

"Apparently, I am not without a certain charm." Saimura's smug expression faded as he surveyed the gathering council members. "I'm not getting back there tonight, am I?"

"Probably not," Jath'ibaye said.

Saimura sighed and settled down into the seat next to Ji's. He fished into his coat pocket and, finding a ribbon, tied his hair back from his face. Ji sat in her chair and, like Wah'roa, dozed, still exhausted from the rituals she had performed at the kahlirash grounds. Her tail wagged sleepily when Saimura gently stroked her head.

Once all were assembled, Jath'ibaye told them what Kahlil had seen and heard. He left out most of the choice obscenities that Kahlil had used when discussing Ourath. And he was evasive as to the kind of potion that Fikiri had given to Ourath. Jath'ibaye simply referred to it as a poison. Kahlil realized that the council did not know what kind of relationship had existed between Ourath and Jath'ibaye. Doubtless Jath'ibaye did not want them to find out.

The subject moved instead to the gaun'im's intentions.

"They sent men in to raid Mahn'illev?" Hirran seemed deeply troubled by the idea.

"They weren't sent in," Kahlil repeated. "Some of the rashan'im went in against orders."

"Certainly none of the Bousim." Hirran spoke as though this were a statement of fact rather than a question.

"No," Kahlil answered. He wondered how Hirran could be so sure. "None of the men were from the Du'yura, Tushoya, or

Milaun houses either. In all, there were probably fewer than thirty men who raided the city."

"Then the raiding wasn't an act of aggression from the gaun'im so much as a lack of discipline among their rashan'im," Hirran said.

"Yes, but arriving with armies is certainly aggressive enough." Litivi gave Hirran a hard look.

"They have always brought forces as a show of strength," Hirran replied. "The gaun'im aren't just going to come alone to our stronghold. Certainly not after two of their own have just been killed."

"But to have armies and Fikiri aiding them?" Gin'yu's expression was bitter. "This is different. They think that they can take our lands this time."

"We must destroy them," Wah'roa said firmly.

Kahlil saw the way Jath'ibaye's body tensed at the suggestion and yet Jath'ibaye said nothing. He remained impassive, standing back from the table. His expression remained a mask of studied indifference.

"If we destroy them, then what about Mahn'illev?" Hirran demanded. With her tangled hair and red-rimmed eyes she resembled nothing more than a woman in mourning.

"We must not allow the gaun'im to coordinate their armies' attacks with those of the devil Fikiri. The wisest course is to crush them now, while they are unprepared." Wah'roa's expression was set. His dark eyes looked like chips of coal. "Mahn'illev can always be rebuilt."

A thin, cold breeze stirred, sending tremors through the leaves of the plants on the shelves behind Jath'ibaye. No one but Kahlil seemed to take any note of it. Catching Kahlil's concerned glance, Jath'ibaye shook his head silently.

"Attacking the gaun'im could mean war with all seven houses!" Hirran protested.

"Yes, it means war!" Wah'roa snapped. Kahlil didn't think he'd ever seen the old man looking so excited and alive. "War has been inevitable from the beginning. The gaun'im have denied the true god for too long. They have defaced his temples and defied his commands. They have dared to raise arms against him—to mock him! They have brought their own destruction with their vain greed. It is their own fault if their lands must be broken. Their armies will fall; their cities will burn. And they will bow down before his divine wrath!" Wah'roa thrust his bony arm out, pointing triumphantly to Jath'ibaye.

Jath'ibaye's hand clenched around something in his palm, but otherwise he gave no reaction.

Kahlil stared at Wah'roa, stunned by his fervor and his fury. Kahlil felt his faith in Parfir and Jath'ibaye quite strongly, but he had never thought of punishing those who didn't.

Wah'roa slumped back into his chair, looking tired and pleased. The entire room was silent for a few moments.

"There may be a complication." Jath'ibaye's voice was soft but it carried easily through the quiet of the room. "There are fault lines that run from beneath Mahn'illev to the south. If I disturb them too much, it could trigger extensive earthquakes."

"Extensive?" Hirran asked.

"Nurjima would certainly be destroyed." Jath'ibaye's tone remained even, as if he were announcing the possibility of rain. "The faults could spread much further. Most of the lands south of the Samsira River would probably collapse."

"But that could destroy all of the gaun'im." Hirran's face drained of all color.

Revulsion washed through Kahlil. All the lands south of the Samsira River. That was more than half of Basawar. It would mean the destruction of hundreds of beautiful cities and thousands of miles of verdant, fertile lands. Millions of lives would be lost. People he knew and liked would die: Yu'mir, Fensal, and Alidas.

Kahlil glanced to Jath'ibaye, expecting him to say that he wouldn't commit such an act. Jath'ibaye stayed as silent as a stone. He lowered his gaze to the floor, keeping his hands close to his sides.

"Still, it may be our only option." Gin'yu's voice held none of the enthusiasm that Wah'roa's had. She looked angry and miserable and heartbroken. "If they have made an ally of a monster like Fikiri, we cannot allow their plans to be carried out. Better to destroy them all than let them take Vundomu."

"But not all of the gaun'im have allied with Fikiri!" Again it was Hirran who protested. She looked suddenly to Kahlil. "Only Ourath Lisam was involved, yes?"

Kahlil shook his head. "Both Nanvess Bousim and Esh'illan Anyyd were plotting with Fikiri before they were killed. I don't know which other gaun'im might be involved." Kahlil realized immediately that he had to say something more, or his words would seem to condemn of all the gaun'im. "None of the gaun'im involved with Fikiri were speaking for their entire houses. Most of the gaun families want peace. When I was sent to stop the assassination it was because the Bousim gaunsho wanted to ensure peace with Vundomu."

"But you said yourself that your orders were changed when it was discovered that one of their own was involved," Gin'yu countered. "None of the gaun'im can be trusted."

"But the gaun'im's lands are not populated by the noble families alone," Saimura protested. "There are far more common men and women than there are gaun'im. Many of the people in Nurjima are sympathetic to Vundomu and the Fai'daum. It would be nothing short of an atrocity to kill them all." Saimura glanced to Jath'ibaye.

Jath'ibaye didn't meet Saimura's gaze. Kahlil realized that this was not a decision Jath'ibaye wanted to make. He desperately did not want to bear the responsibility.

"It may not come to that," Litivi said, despite his mother's scowl. "If Jath'ibaye destroys Nurjima and a few of the other gaun'im's cities, then perhaps the surviving gaun'im will submit to our rule."

"How can you even speak of such a thing?" Hirran demanded. "Only three months ago we were discussing trade with the gaun'im. We were considering opening our borders to their scholars and teachers and now you want to kill them all? This is insane!"

"You would not say so if you were older," Gin'yu snapped. "You are too young to remember the wars they waged against us. The gaun'im have never wanted peace as much as wealth. Only their fear of us kept them at bay, but now they have Fikiri to aid them against us. They will betray any promise they make to us."

"They have not all sided with Fikiri," Kahlil reminded Gin'yu.

"But you do not know how many have," Gin'yu said.

"Not so many that they dared to meet openly with him," Kahlil spoke quickly. "Ourath wouldn't want too many others involved. He wouldn't want to share his spoils."

"That's right." Hirran offered Kahlil a look of solidarity. "Fikiri would have next to nothing to offer all the gaun'im. Vundomu is simply too small to be divided among so many. This alliance can only involve a few of them at the most."

Gin'yu silently considered this. Wah'roa shook his head but made no response.

"Even if it is only Ourath Lisam, we are still caught between a mortar and a pestle," Tai'yu, who had been silent up until now, finally spoke. "We cannot fight an army of hungry bones in the north and the gaun'im's forces in the south. Not both at once. Even if they are not all allied with Fikiri, we may have to destroy them to protect ourselves."

"There has to be another way. We could make an alliance of our own, offer them iron—" Hirran began.

"What is wrong with you, Hirran?" Gin'yu demanded. "When will you stop thinking of the money you could make trading iron to the gaun'im and start thinking of your people!"

"I am thinking of my people!" Hirran's face flushed scarlet. "I am thinking of the families they have in Mahn'illev and Nurjima. I'm thinking of the books and theaters and art and music that none of us will ever see because we've ruined it all!"

"Hirran has a point—" Saimura began.

"Shut up, Saimura," Gin'yu cut in. "You just don't want to lose all that southern silk you've gotten used to wearing in Nurjima."

"Yes, and so what?" Saimura replied. "You'd like the silk as well. We all would. I think that's what Hirran was trying to say. If we destroy the gaun'im, then we lose everything they might have offered us."

"What other options do we have?" Tai'yu's question barely carried over the disgusted obscenity that Gin'yu growled at Saimura.

"That was uncalled for, you old hag," Hirran hissed. At this, Litivi launched string of curses at Hirran. Kahlil looked to Jath'ibaye, expecting him to intervene, but he didn't. He rolled something between his fingers. It was another stone. He slowly crushed it to dust.

A loud bark rang out through the cacophony of shouts and insults. Everyone fell silent and then all heads turned to Ji. She blinked and yawned.

"Sorry," Ji said. "I was trying to answer Tai'yu's question."

Even Tai'yu didn't seem to remember what his question had been.

"There is one other option which I think we should consider." Ji looked to Kahlil. "The gaun'im's forces must wait for the bones to rise, correct?"

"According to Fikiri's plan, yes," Kahlil said.

"So then, we won't have to worry about repelling the gaun'im's forces if we can deal with the bones first."

"We can't afford to extend the freeze. The refugees from Mahn'illev are already draining our taye stores too low to last through another winter," Tai'yu began to protest.

"I don't mean slowing the bones," Ji said. "I mean destroying them."

Even Jath'ibaye seemed to take interest in this.

"You said that it couldn't be done," Jath'ibaye said.

"That was before you brought Kyle'insira to us," Ji replied. "Or more accurately, before Kyle'insira brought the yasi'halaun."

Both Besh'anya and Saimura immediately looked to the sword hilt that jutted up over Kahlil's shoulder. Their eyes went wide in realization. Wah'roa nodded as if enjoying a confirmation of a private suspicion.

"Yasi'halaun?" Hirran asked, glancing between Ji and Kahlil. "What is it? What does it do?"

"It devours all life—blood, bone, the very soul of a creature." Ji didn't have to raise her voice now. Everyone in the room was silent, listening to what she had to say. "It is a curse blade carved from the bone of a Rifter. Only he can withstand it or bear a wound it inflicts." Briefly Ji's gaze flickered to Kahlil, but she said nothing of the wound he had received and survived. He had been lucky that Jath'ibaye had been there to bear it, otherwise he would have been killed.

"So it could destroy the hungry bones?" Tai'yu asked.

"Easily," Ji replied. "But the problem is finding a way to allow it to destroy many of them at once. As it is now, the yasi'halaun exists in the form of a sword. We don't have the leisure to stab every individual bone fragment."

"Then what do we do?" Tai'yu leaned forward. His lands were those in the north and his people would be the first ones to face Fikiri's army.

"Give me time to work with the yasi'halaun," Ji said.

"How long will you need?" Jath'ibaye asked.

"I can't say," Ji replied, "but if it takes me more than a week I would say that we shouldn't wait any longer. We will have to destroy the gaun'im's armies."

"And in the meantime?" Hirran asked.

"We prepare for war," Wah'roa replied.

Hirran scowled at the old man. "When the gaun'im's runners come to us with their lords' demands tomorrow, what are we going to tell them? Come back next week, we're making ready for war? What are we supposed to do in the meantime?"

"Perhaps we can stall them, keep them waiting outside," Litivi suggested.

"Couldn't we just once try to settle things diplomatically?" Hirran's eyes gleamed with tears, but it was frustration that carried through in her voice. "Ourath Lisam has to have enemies among the gaun'im. If we could find them—"

"It will make no difference when it comes to war," Wah'roa growled. "The gaun'im will always side with their own."

Gin'yu nodded her agreement.

"But what if it doesn't come to war?" Hirran asked. "What if Ji succeeds in destroying the hungry bones? Then we will still need to settle matters with the gaun'im. We should be using this one week to prepare for that."

Silently, Kahlil agreed with her. Wah'roa could prepare his troops for Ji's failure, but Vundomu also had to be prepared for success. He didn't know how his opinion would be taken. Gin'yu referred to him as a Bousim agent. She would probably disregard his opinion as lingering loyalty.

"It couldn't hurt to try and win allies," Tai'yu spoke up softly. Gin'yu frowned at him. Wah'roa shook his head.

"If we could build relations," Hirran went on quickly, "we might find a way to undermine Ourath Lisam's treachery. If we could make allies among the Du'yura, or the Milaun, or even the Bousim, it could help us. Not just now, but in the future."

"I wouldn't bet on it," Gin'yu commented.

"It couldn't hurt," Saimura said. "And in any case, if we seem earnestly invested in negotiations, it would keep them from suspecting that we're planning an attack."

"Exactly," Hirran said.

"So, what do you propose that we do, Hirran? Invite them in? Let them count our forces and assess our provisions? Offer them a tour of our lands? Throw them a feast?" Gin'yu asked.

"Yes, actually," Hirran replied. "I think that we should treat them like guests. If only for one week, we should try to offer them something other than malevolence. The only way we're going to make any lasting alliances is to show a little trust."

"Even to Ourath Lisam?" Litivi demanded. "You think we should just allow him in here where he can use his poison against Jath'ibaye?"

Hirran plainly had not been prepared for that question. Litivi indulged in a smug smile at Hirran's silence.

"Any poison he can conjure, Ji can counter!" It was the first thing Besh'anya had said all night. She flushed with embarrassment as the council members all looked at her. "Vundomu is Ji's stronghold. No one could challenge her sorcery here. No one!"

"Your loyalty to Ji is commendable," Gin'yu responded, "but she will need to concentrate on destroying the hungry bones. Ourath's presence would only distract her."

"That is true," Ji said. "I doubt I'll have the time or the strength to deal with Ourath. But between them, Saimura and Besh'anya have the skill to repel anything Fikiri could have supplied."

"I do not like the idea of allowing any of them inside Vundomu," Wah'roa said flatly. "There will be too many opportunities for them to observe our fortifications. We should crush them all. Now."

Kahlil gazed at Wah'roa. A vague loyalty to their shared religion tugged at him. And Wah'roa had always treated him with kindness and respect. He wanted to be able to support the old man. But he knew that Wah'roa's desire to punish the gaun'im for their lack of faith was wrong.

He spoke of bringing divine wrath to the gaun'im and all their lands almost flippantly. He had lost sight of the values of his own faith. Parfir, the living earth, was sacred. Life was sacred. To unleash the Rifter's power was to sacrifice both land and lives. It was meant to be a desperate last resort, never a glib first choice. During his initiation, with the sting of his new Prayerscars fresh on his skin, Kahlil had read the most sacred texts written by previous Kahlil'im, which had been kept in the Black Tower. There he had learned not only the method by which to unleash and kill a Rifter but understood that the possibility of ending the entire world existed with each new Rifter incarnation. No one else knew this, he realized.

He knew he must speak. Even if no one in this room would listen to him, he must speak.

"The worst crime of the Payshmura Church was its misuse and systematic defilement of the Rifter," Kahlil spoke suddenly before his nerve failed him. "You and I both know that, Wah'roa."

All eyes turned toward Kahlil.

He continued, "He is our most holy lord, not some inanimate machine created to serve the whims of men. For the Payshmura, the Rifter became nothing but a weapon used by corrupt priests to hold dominion over Basawar. For that blasphemy the ushman'im of the Black Tower and Rathal'pesha were rightly condemned to die. But if we demand that Jath'ibaye crush the gaun'im just so that we can hold Vundomu, we would be no better than the fallen Payshmura. Only he has the power to call down divine judgment, but it must be according to his own will and conscience."

Wah'roa looked utterly taken aback by Kahlil's words. Kahlil didn't know if it was because of what he had said or because it had been so long since he had been challenged by another priest of the old religion.

"No one should ever speak so lightly of so much destruction," Kahlil said. But it wasn't Wah'roa that he needed to say this to. He turned to Jath'ibaye.

"This isn't something a church or a council should decide." Kahlil stared into Jath'ibaye's face. "None of us have that right or that responsibility but you."

Jath'ibaye's blue eyes flickered to him briefly. "I abide by the council's decisions."

"You are the incarnation of Parfir, not the lackey of this or any other council!" Though his words were quiet, Kahlil felt his face flush with conviction. "Your flesh is my earth. Your blood is my river. Your breath is my sky. Your body is my world. Only you know how much destruction this world can endure. You can feel it as none of us can. This council, Ji, me, none of us know that. Only you can make this decision, no matter what you might like to pretend."

Kahlil expected to be shouted down or at least argued against. Instead, the council members kept their peace, watching Jath'ibaye. Kahlil studied their silent expressions. Despite their overtures at governance over Jath'ibaye, it was clear that they were awed by him. He was a god. Unlike any of them, he could comprehend the enormity of this decision personally and physically. His life and flesh was bound to the world around them. He had caused and endured a previous cataclysm.

Wah'roa silently nodded his head as if agreeing with Kahlil's thoughts. He bowed his head.

"It is as the Kahlil says. This is a matter for divinity alone," Wah'roa conceded.

Jath'ibaye's expression seemed almost blank, but Kahlil recognized the way his gaze seemed to focus just beyond the walls enclosing them all. He was watching them and at the same time sensing the far reaches of the world all around them. At last, Jath'ibaye met Kahlil's gaze. He knew it pained Jath'ibaye to have to make this decision, but no one else was qualified. Kahlil returned Jath'ibaye's gaze with a look that he hoped conveyed his confidence and affection. Jath'ibaye sighed.

"I will not allow Vundomu to fall," Jath'ibaye said at last, and Kahlil felt as if Jath'ibaye was speaking only to him, "but I do not want to destroy Basawar. I don't know if anyone but me would survive another great rift so soon after the last."

"Then what will we do?" Kahlil asked.

"Make the most of this week. Find a way to destroy the hungry bones. Try to make peace with the gaun'im," Jath'ibaye said. "If that fails, then I will crush the armies here in the north and we will have to see what comes of that."

Kahlil watched the muscles flex in Jath'ibaye's jaw. He remembered Jath'ibaye's expression only a few days ago when they had discussed the destruction of Rathal'pesha. He had said he never wanted to endure that again.

"Then we have to allow the gaun'im into Vundomu," Kahlil said.

Jath'ibaye nodded.

"What if they aren't interested in coming in?" Litivi asked. "What if they want a war?"

"They don't want a war." Kahlil scowled at Litivi. They had already argued this point and Kahlil didn't want to waste the entire night having the same discussion over and over.

"Ourath will see to it that they come," Jath'ibaye said, though he didn't look happy about it. "He needs to keep the gaun'im and their armies occupied here while he waits for the hungry bones to awaken."

"You're sure he will be able to convince all the gaun'im?" Litivi asked.

"Ourath can be incredibly persuasive when he needs to be," Jath'ibaye replied. Litivi opened his mouth to ask another question but then seemed to think better of it, seeing Jath'ibaye's deep frown.

"Then we need to make plans for their stay here," Hirran said, her tone bright despite her exhausted appearance.

Jath'ibaye simply nodded.

The council fell immediately to work, figuring out how it would be done. They still argued, but not heatedly. They decided who would host which of gaun'im and how they would keep them occupied. They discussed exhibitions and entertainments that would naturally divide the gaun'im. Steadily, they worked out the details and minutiae that Kahlil would never have suspected could be planned. Working together they had energy and a kind of genius that surprised Kahlil. He had only witnessed them in discord, rather than unity. He had not expected them to impress him.

Not that Kahlil liked all the decisions that the council made. He particularly disliked the idea of Ourath Lisam being invited to stay in Jath'ibaye's household.

"The last person Ourath should be close to is Jath'ibaye." Kahlil hadn't been able to keep from objecting to the suggestion. "The poison Fikiri gave him is made specifically to affect Jath'ibaye."

Ji lifted her head and gazed at Kahlil.

"Did Fikiri say what the poison was, exactly?" Ji asked.

Kahlil choked. He didn't want to reveal Jath'ibaye's secrets and he didn't know how much the name of the potion might give away.

"Niru'mohim," Jath'ibaye supplied the name for him.

Kahlil noticed the way both Besh'anya and Saimura started at the word. Clearly, they knew the potion's intended effect. Ji nodded.

"Jath'ibaye is in no danger from niru'mohim," Ji said. "And Saimura should be quite capable of dispelling its effects if it becomes necessary."

"But—" Kahlil began.

"It is far more important to make sure that Fikiri does not contact Ourath. The less he knows about what we are doing here the better." Ji's tone remained firm. "Fikiri will not dare appear so close to Jath'ibaye."

Jath'ibaye concurred with another silent nod.

"You will have to be moved though," Ji said to Kahlil.

"What? Why?" Kahlil demanded.

"Because we can't afford to have Ourath recognize you," Ji said.

"Kyle'insira is welcome among the kahlirash'im." Wah'roa tentatively met Kahlil's gaze and Kahlil offered him the Payshmura hand sign of peace. "There is an empty room near Pesha's."

"Thank you," Kahlil responded automatically.

"Then it's decided," Ji pronounced.

Kahlil wanted to argue. He had a right to stay beside Jath'ibaye. He did not want Ourath attempting to seduce his lover. And yet none of those were things he wanted to say in front of the council members and all their attendants. He glanced briefly to Jath'ibaye. Jath'ibaye sighed heavily but said nothing. Kahlil bowed his head.

Everyone agreed that Kahlil was to avoid detection, hidden away among the kahlirash'im. The council meeting continued on. Kahlil wanted them all to leave so that he could at least have a last night with Jath'ibaye. But by the time the meeting disbanded, both he and Jath'ibaye were too exhausted to do more than fall asleep next to each other.

In his dreams, white forms flickered at the edges of Kahlil's sight. Something hunted him in the darkness. A desperate, distant voice screamed his name.

He bolted upright, almost falling out of the bed. Instantly, Jath'ibaye caught his arm and steadied him. Jath'ibaye's eyes were hardly open but his grip was surprisingly strong.

"Are you all right?"

"Fine," Kahlil said. "Just a bad dream. Someone kept shouting for me." He settled back down beside Jath'ibaye.

"Who was it?" Jath'ibaye asked.

"I don't know." Kahlil shifted the blankets. He must have been thrashing in his sleep because they had become hopelessly tangled.

"I hate those kinds of dreams," Jath'ibaye murmured.

"Me too." Kahlil watched the faint shadows of leaves and vines that the pale morning light cast across the walls. These last few hours of morning were all that were left to them. Kahlil would have to leave soon. If it came to war, there would be no telling how long they could be parted. The sweet smell of strawberries drifted over him.

He said, "I wish I could dream of Nayeshi more often. I really enjoy those dreams. The smells and feel of everything is so vibrant. I always feel like I've briefly escaped from life, you know?"

Jath'ibaye nodded. "I feel like that when I dream of the islands across the East Ocean."

"You mentioned them before," Kahlil said. It had been on the same night that they had first slept together. "But you never said where the islands are."

"I don't know exactly," Jath'ibaye replied. "I feel them sometimes, when my thoughts are drifting across the water. I see sheer white cliffs of limestone rising from the ocean and miles of lush forests. There are plants and animals there that I've never seen anywhere else."

"I've never tried to travel to the east," Kahlil said. "I wonder how far away the islands are?" He had crossed greater distances through the Gray Space, but only while knowing where he was going. Attempting to find an island in the midst of a vast ocean intrigued him.

"I don't know," Jath'ibaye said. "With everything here, I haven't had much time to really look for them. I just dream of them now and then."

"Last night?" Kahlil asked.

"No," Jath'ibaye said, scowling. "I dreamed that we were still in the council meeting, arguing. It was a nightmare really."

Kahlil rolled closer to Jath'ibaye.

"Do you think that a ship could sail to the Eastern Islands?" he asked.

"Maybe," Jath'ibaye said. "Why?"

"I'd like to see them with you someday."

Jath'ibaye smiled at him.

"That would be nice," Jath'ibaye said quietly. He gathered Kahlil closer to him, then let out a quiet laugh.

"What?"

"I can't believe that you said that prayer last night." He chuckled again. "I suppose I forgot how religious you are."

Kahlil grinned. "Just because I'm a bad priest doesn't mean I can't remember my prayers."

He bent to kiss Jath'ibaye's shoulder, whispering, "With my body I worship you…"

He slid his hands under the blankets and over Jath'ibaye's bare skin. Jath'ibaye moved closer, returning Kahlil's caresses with a desperate, hungry kiss. The pretense of conversation fell aside as their bodies moved in a common rhythm.

Three hours later, Pesha arrived at Jath'ibaye's door to escort Kahlil to the kahlirash'im's barrack. She looked freshly scrubbed and proud when she announced herself as Ushiri Pesha. Kahlil slung the yasi'halaun onto his back, glanced to Jath'ibaye, and said, "Good luck."

"You as well." Jath'ibaye stood, silent as always when in the grip of strong emotion, hands at his sides. Kahlil thought that Jath'ibaye might embrace him, but he didn't. In the presence of Pesha, he kept his distance, honoring Kahlil's request for discretion.

Kahlil wanted to be able to leave without a backward glance, but dread welled up in him and he knew that he'd left Jath'ibaye once before, in another life, and they had not seen each other again. They couldn't part like that again. He spun back and pulled Jath'ibaye into his arms for one last, deep kiss.

Jath'ibaye embraced him with tender ferocity; his whole body almost trembled with the effort of restraining himself. His mouth tasted sweet and felt too good.

Kahlil pulled himself back while he still retained the willpower. Jath'ibaye released him.

"Tell me you won't forget me," Kahlil whispered.

Jath'ibaye smiled and murmured, "I won't forget you. I never could."

Kahlil turned back to Pesha, who stood goggling at their display. He said, "Let's be on our way, Ushiri. We shouldn't be here when Jath'ibaye's guests arrive."

Chapter Sixty-Five

Kahlil scowled at the entourage of attendants and guards as they filed, all dressed in the tawny gold Lisam colors, through the gates of Jath'ibaye's household. He wanted to be up there watching for treachery. Most of all, he wanted to be there so he could have the pleasure of driving his fist into Ourath Lisam's far too handsome face.

Instead, he attempted to content himself with glaring out from an observation tower in the kahlirash'im's barracks. It didn't offer him the vast, expansive views that Jath'ibaye's watchtowers had. He could only see the comings and goings on the grounds below and those of the nearest buildings. Not even using the telescopes could he observe what transpired within the walls of Jath'ibaye's household.

"Those are meant for watching the stars, aren't they?" Pesha asked shyly. She had taken her assignment as Kahlil's personal attendant rather seriously. Kahlil hadn't been alone since early this morning.

"I think so." Kahlil placed the telescope back in its delicate cradle of tiny gears and clasps. He wasn't used to being so closely observed. He leaned back against the stone wall. Pesha gazed at him expectantly. Kahlil realized that the day was going to be something of a disappointment for her. She probably expected that the life of the Kahlil would be much more exciting.

She had no idea how much of his life had been spent in silent observation. He'd tried to make the first part of the day interesting, demonstrating the battle forms for the Unseen Edge and the Silence Knife. He'd even acquiesced to attending midafternoon prayers in the Temple of the Rifter with the rest of the kahlilrash'im. But once the gaun'im began to arrive, he could not fight the irresistible urge toward surveillance.

He still hadn't spotted Ourath, though Kahlil was now very familiar with the faces of the Lisam porters, having spent the better part of an hour observing them toting luggage up and down Vundomu's many staircases.

Kahlil went back to the window to view the grounds below. The elite kahlirash'im were gathered for battle practice. Unlike the rashan'im of the gaun families, most of the kahlirash'im rode small, fast does instead of massive bucks. Their maneuvers exploited the speed and lightness of both female animals and riders. Targets splintered as the kahlirash'im fired their rifles from the backs of their bounding mounts.

Kahlil had never been much of a rider. He'd never needed to be. It was strange and fascinating to watch the precision of both the riders' movements and their tahldi's responses. Pesha moved a little closer to Kahlil, following his gaze out to the kahlirash riders. They both watched as a slender rider swung down to grasp a new rifle from a kahlirash kneeling on the ground. The rider came back up in an instant and fired. Another target cracked apart.

"Incredible," Pesha whispered. That was probably the kind of activity that Pesha had been hoping to engage in today.

"Very impressive," Kahlil agreed.

"Wah'roa said that Jath'ibaye had work that he needed you to complete." Pesha's dark eyes flicked quickly from the riders to Kahlil.

Kahlil nodded. Translating an archaic botanical tome was probably the last thing that Pesha would want to do all afternoon. And he didn't find it all that appealing either.

"Could I ask what it is?" Pesha clearly expected something secret and dangerous.

"You don't want to know," Kahlil said.

Pesha frowned and returned to watching the kahlirash riders. For a moment Kahlil felt the urge to offer Pesha some exciting lie. Perhaps he could claim that they were supposed to spy on Ourath from the silence of the Gray Space. He smirked at his own absurd desire to impress a teenage girl. Of course, there was also the fact that he wanted any excuse to return to Jath'ibaye's household and watch Ourath. But if he did that, then Jath'ibaye would feel his presence and know that Kahlil was, yet again, disobeying his orders and being where he should not be.

Once more Kahlil found himself staring at the walls surrounding Jath'ibaye's holdings. The stone faces and black iron gates gave him no consolation. Ourath was probably already inside, posing in Jath'ibaye's doorway and offering lurid apologies in his low, velvety voice.

Jath'ibaye would turn Ourath away, Kahlil told himself.

Still, the thought of the niru'mohim nagged at him. Ji had assured him that the niru'mohim wouldn't harm Jath'ibaye but she hadn't said it wouldn't affect him. Both Fikiri and Ourath had been willing to stake their futures on the potion's power. What if they were right? What if Jath'ibaye couldn't resist it? What if, at this very moment, Ourath was lying back in the bed that Kahlil had left this morning? The idea seared through Kahlil. He would kill Ourath if he found him in Jath'ibaye's bedroom.

He brought his hand up to split open the Gray Space, then stopped himself. He couldn't just go storming into Jath'ibaye's rooms, and he definitely couldn't murder Ourath. It would start a war. Kahlil shoved his hands back into his coat pockets. He just had to trust Jath'ibaye. He had to believe that Jath'ibaye could and would resist Ourath's advances.

For distraction, he tried to rekindle his interest in the riders and tahldi below. Steadily, his gaze began to rise again to Jath'ibaye's holdings. If only he could know what was happening up there.

He turned and strode to the windows on the opposite wall of the room. Here, the only view was of the kitchen gardens and the storehouses. The barracks of the kahlirash'im surrounded the small, open square with heavy black walls. The furrows of dark soil and rows of hardy green herbs drew Kahlil's thoughts back to Jath'ibaye. And to Ourath. The first time he had seen them together it had been in a garden. That night Kahlil himself had unknowingly brought Ourath's poison—a gift of niru'mohim—to Jath'ibaye.

He should have killed Ourath at the Bell Dance.

Kahlil hated this train of thought. He needed to find something else to occupy his mind or otherwise he was just going to spend the entire day planning executions for Ourath Lisam.

"Is something wrong?" Pesha followed him to the window and stared down expectantly at the clumps of winter herbs in the garden.

"No, I'm just restless," Kahlil said. He cocked his head slightly as a slender figure strode out of the kahlirash'im's barrack and crossed the open courtyard coming toward the observation tower. The woman's red coat and dress were unusually bright for the fabrics of Vundomu. Her black hair was pulled back in three thick braids. Two attendants hurried after her.

"Hirran?" Kahlil wondered aloud. It certainly looked like her.

"Representative Hirran?" Pesha stared down at her with an appreciative expression. Her eyes moved over Hirran's voluptuous figure in curious fascination.

"I think she's coming up here," Kahlil commented. A moment later she disappeared through the doors below them.

"To us?" Pesha flushed a little.

Really, Kahlil thought, Pesha was very lucky to have been born in Vundomu. Otherwise, her blatant attraction to her own sex would have gotten her into real trouble.

Aloud he said, "It could be her."

Kahlil eyed the door hopefully. Perhaps she had something for him to do. At this point, Kahlil thought he might welcome almost any task that would take his mind off Ourath.

Kahlil listened to the sound of footsteps mounting the stone stairs. Seconds later there was a soft rap at the door. Kahlil opened the door and beckoned Hirran in. She looked much more composed than she had the previous night, but there were still signs of exhaustion in her face. Kahlil guessed that she had slept as little or less than he had.

"Kyle'insira," Hirran inclined her head to him, "I've been looking for you."

"What do you need?" Kahlil asked. But Hirran didn't answer right away.

Hirran's two attendants reached the top of the stairs and hurried to their places behind her. They were both young women who resembled Hirran. Kahlil imagined that they might have been her younger sisters. They, like Hirran, wore low-cut flaring coats that emphasized the curves of their bodies. Pesha regarded them with a kind of awe. Few of the kahlirash women ever dressed so flatteringly. The younger of Hirran's attendants offered Pesha a flirtatious smile, which caused Pesha to flush to the roots of her hair. Then the attendant pulled the door closed.

"The matter might require a little discretion." Hirran glanced to Pesha, then returned her attention to Kahlil meaningfully.

"Pesha has sworn loyalty to me as my ushiri and attendant. She can be trusted," Kahlil replied. Out of the corner of his eye Kahlil caught the look of pride that his words gave Pesha. Kahlil guessed it was the least he could do to make up for the tedious day. Hirran accepted his statement with a nod.

"Last night," Hirran said, "I had the impression that you were not utterly hostile toward all of the gaun'im."

"I wouldn't support them against Jath'ibaye," Kahlil replied, "but I certainly don't despise them all."

"You've had an association with the Bousim house," Hirran said.

"True." Kahlil wasn't ready to commit to anything more at this point. But it seemed to be enough because Hirran went on.

"I also have an association with the Bousims—not as a servant of theirs. Nothing like that. But because of the shared border, there have been times when my forces have encountered those of the Bousim commander. My people and his are somewhat familiar with each other. So, over the last few years, he and I have exchanged a few letters…" Hirran trailed off.

"You're in correspondence with Commander Joulen Bousim?" That might benefit them, though common knowledge of it wouldn't make Hirran terribly popular among her fellow representatives.

"Yes, I had hoped that it would help pave the way for future trade relations," Hirran admitted. "But now I just want—well, you know what I want. I believe we share that goal."

"So, what would you like me to do?" Kahlil asked.

"I want to meet with him," Hirran said. "I think I might convince him to aid us against Ourath Lisam."

"He and his uncle are guests in Gin'yu's house. You could call on him there, couldn't you?" Kahlil asked.

"I would rather not be seen doing so by Gin'yu." Hirran lowered her voice slightly. "You may have noticed how little warmth the old woman has for me. And this is not the time that I would choose to reveal my relations with a gaunan. I'm sure that Commander Bousim is in much the same situation."

"So, you need to arrange a private meeting with him?" Kahlil asked.

"Not private," Hirran corrected. "Don't misunderstand me. I don't know him so well that I want to be alone with him. My idea is to propose a meeting with him later this evening in the Silverlake Gardens. You could be present and at the same time remain unseen, couldn't you?" Hirran gave him a speculative glance.

"I certainly could." Now it was all quite clear to him why Hirran had searched him out.

"And you could pass through Gin'yu's household to deliver a letter to Commander Bousim without anyone noticing?" Hirran asked.

"It would be simple." Kahlil was well ahead of her. He would need to have Pesha pretend to be practicing with the Gray Space in case Jath'ibaye noticed the disturbance. Hirran's letter would have to be wrapped in heavy leather, or better yet, a metal case to keep it from being torn to shreds.

"Will you help me?" Hirran asked.

"How could I say no?" Kahlil smiled at her.

Hirran looked almost startled and then smiled back at him as if he'd just saved her life. Beside him, he saw Pesha stand a little straighter, perhaps realizing that someday she might also be asked for such a favor by a beautiful woman.

"Thank you," Hirran said.

☾☾☾

By the time Kahlil slipped through the walls surrounding the Silverlake Garden, it was nearly dusk. From within the Gray Space the lush braids of trellised vines and clusters of tiny snow blossoms looked like they had been cut from newspaper. None of the humid scents that filled the huge greenhouse reached him. The massive iron supports of the building and its countless panes of glass resembled Jath'ibaye's glass palace in Nurjima. But Jath'ibaye's garden had been much more diverse. It had seemed natural in its random bursts of foliage and flowers.

The plants in the Silverlake Garden reminded Kahlil of the industrial agriculture he had seen in Nayeshi. It was not nearly so advanced, but the same aspiration for control and production seemed to underlie the Silverlake Garden's design. Huge beds of single crops stretched out in long rows. Between them, cobblestone avenues stretched like city streets. There was a mechanical precision to the distances between the beds, the rows in the beds, and even to the spacing of the plants themselves.

Most of the young starts poking up from the ground seemed to be tender vegetables. Older, hardy herbs loomed up in the beds beyond those. And far to the west were the enclosed orchards, his destination.

Kahlil hurried back toward the trees. He passed a few young couples lingering at the edges of the herb gardens. A few solitary individuals seemed to be sketching or taking botanical notes. Now and then Kahlil noticed a Silverlake insignia decorating the sleeve of a guard or a gardener. But most of the people seemed to have been drawn to the gardens just to take in the sight and scent of the first blossoms.

Later in the year, the orchards would be more popular. But now, at the end of winter, they were too cool and shadowed to appeal to many people. At least that was what Hirran had told him. From within the Gray Space, the orchards didn't seem much different from the rest of the garden. Kahlil was aware of faint beams of light filtering down between the slender branches of fruit trees. Many seemed to be blossoming, but the flowers and leaves were all the same dull gray to him. If it was colder under the expanses of branches, he didn't feel it. Everything was cold in the Gray Space.

As Kahlil strode through the orchards, he saw that Hirran had been right about their overall attractiveness. The only people who seemed drawn to the avenues that lined the orchards were Bousim militia. Kahlil discovered two captains waiting in the deep shadows near a wall. Three more rashan'im strolled along an avenue and then turned back, patrolling a stretch of trees near the west wall of the garden. None of the men were in uniform but Kahlil recognized the captains from his night in the Bousim camp. The rashan'im gave themselves away in the precision of their movements. No laborer in Vundomu squared his shoulders so stiffly or held his head so perfectly upright.

Hirran had not arrived, but Joulen was already waiting. He didn't look older out of his uniform, but stripped of the insignias of his rank, his boyish face didn't seem so surprising. He leaned against a railing that surrounded a stand of trees, absently drumming his fingers on the black wrought iron.

Kahlil walked past Joulen, easily brushing through the railing. It would be simple enough to remain in the Gray Space and watch over Hirran. But he wouldn't be able to hear anything. He contemplated the stand of trees for a moment. They weren't big, but their branches seemed strong enough to take his weight and the blossoms would hide him.

Kahlil shifted his direction within the Gray Space, rising with each step, until he crouched up in the tree branches. He braced himself and then dropped out of the Gray Space. Humid heat rushed over him. The fragrance of flowers and freshly tilled earth engulfed him. For just an instant, the texture of the tree bark seemed to bite painfully into his palms. Then his senses adjusted. The pain and heat receded. The smell of flowers saturated the air. All around Kahlil, slim branches bowed with the weight of their white blossoms. A low hum pulsed through the air as dozens of pale yellow bees buzzed between the heavily clustered flowers.

Kahlil watched Joulen take a cigarette from the case in his coat pocket, toy with it, and then put it back. Beyond Joulen, Kahlil recognized Hirran's graceful figure. She walked slowly. One of her attendants lagged behind her, taking notes. Hirran paused at a bed of firebloom, her long red coat and dress seeming to rise up from the scarlet flowers. Her black hair was startlingly dark by contrast and her skin looked like porcelain.

Joulen stared at her, the cigarette case forgotten in his hand. Kahlil wondered if Hirran had known she would be so eye-catching. He guessed that she did. She hadn't struck Kahlil as the kind of woman who wouldn't use her beauty to an advantage.

As Hirran came closer, Joulen frowned slightly. He glanced past Hirran as if expecting to see someone else on the avenue. Hirran stopped at the iron railing near Joulen and gazed at the white blooms that hung down close to her.

Joulen's frown tightened. He continued to watch the cobblestone avenue. Absently, he opened his cigarette case, then snapped it closed, and put it away in his pocket. Hirran watched him. After a few moments, she turned and looked down the avenue as well. Kahlil followed both their gazes. There was no one.

Hirran took a half step closer to Joulen.

"Was someone following me?" Hirran said, undervoiced.

Joulen started in surprise. "I beg your pardon, madam?"

"Have I been followed?" Hirran repeated.

"Not that I can see," Joulen replied. He seemed strangely awkward, as if almost unwilling to acknowledge Hirran's presence. She scanned the rows of trees and cobblestone avenues surrounding them. Catching sight of the two rashan'im, Hirran moved even closer to Joulen.

"Have you been followed?" Hirran whispered urgently.

Joulen sighed and at last turned to face her.

"Madam," Joulen said, "I'm sorry, but I'm expecting to meet with a businessman. Though I find you quite charming, quite lovely in fact, I haven't the time to dally. Perhaps another day?"

Hirran appeared to be flabbergasted and Kahlil almost laughed out loud. Joulen didn't know who she was. In typical gaun fashion, he had mistaken Hirran's assurance and interest for the advance of some prostitute.

"Dally?" Hirran demanded. Then she looked suddenly worried. "You are Joulen Bousim, are you not?"

"Yes," Joulen replied, "but I assure you that I am not so rich as people say. There are other men from the gaun'im who would be more worthy of your interest."

Hirran's brows knit together in consternation as Joulen continued to watch the empty avenue.

"You don't know who I am," Hirran said suddenly.

"No." Joulen glanced to her. He seemed amused by the idea that he would know of her. "Should I?"

"Yes, you should." Hirran's voice carried an edge of indignation. "I am Hirran of the Iron Heights."

Joulen gaped at her as if she'd claimed to be Gaunsho Bousim himself.

"I wrote that I would be wearing a red coat and my hair would be in three braids." Hirran pointed to her head. "I wrote that you were to meet me at the iron railing surrounding the snow pears at the fifth bell."

"Yes. But you can't be…" Joulen continued to stare at Hirran. A slight flush began to color his cheeks. "You didn't say you were…I had imagined that you would be a man."

"I never said I was a man."

"No, you never did," Joulen admitted, after a thoughtful silence. "I assumed…" Joulen glanced to the single attendant who hung far back behind Hirran. "Are you sure that this is safe for you?"

"The Five Districts Council could call me up for questioning, but technically I have not done anything wrong. So long as we are discreet, I think that can be avoided," Hirran assured him. "What about you?"

"Fine," Joulen replied, though he hardly seemed to have heard the question.

Kahlil realized that Joulen was not worried for Hirran's political career. No woman of the gaun'im would have met a man in a secluded garden with only a little attendant girl to protect her. Even in Nurjima, women traveled in large groups or were accompanied by fathers, husbands, or brothers. To Joulen, Hirran would seem to be at the mercy of any man who crossed her path.

"It's getting dark," Joulen commented.

"I know. They'll be clearing the garden soon," Hirran spoke quickly and softly, "but I couldn't meet with you any sooner. I suppose we should be as expeditious about this as we can."

"Yes, we should," Joulen agreed. "So why did you send for me?"

"Because this entire matter has gotten out of hand," Hirran replied. "You have to know that Jath'ibaye did not kill Nanvess."

"Do I?" Joulen asked, his dark brows rising. "Why did he flee from the Bell Dance then?"

Kahlil tensed, hoping that Hirran had the good sense not to mention him. Telling Joulen about Kahlil's part in the debacle would only make Hirran's story seem more implausible.

"Because he went in pursuit of the real murderer," Hirran answered and Kahlil was impressed by how easily she made it sound like the truth.

"And who was that?" Joulen asked.

"His name would mean nothing to you." Hirran dismissed Joulen's question with a wave of her hand.

"That's unfortunate, since you're trying to convince me of his existence," he replied.

"The murderer is called Fikiri. He is a devil who steals our children for their bones." The anger in Hirran's tone carried despite her lowered voice. "He is in league with Ourath Lisam to destroy Vundomu and the gaun'im as well. He wants us to kill each other in a war."

"In league with Ourath Lisam?" A spark of hope lit Joulen's face. "You have proof of this?"

"None that would convince you or the rest of the gaun'im," Hirran admitted. "But you have to know that the gaun'im would not survive a war against Vundomu."

Joulen stiffened slightly at her words.

"I'm not attempting to threaten you, Commander," Hirran went on, seeing Joulen's reaction. "I don't think either of our nations would survive a war. That's why it's imperative that our nations find a way to make peace. You're the only gaun that I would trust to approach like this."

For the first time Joulen offered Hirran a kind smile. No doubt his exaggerated sense of the danger that Hirran had braved to see him lent a deeper ring of desperation to her words. If it hadn't been a matter of war that they were discussing, Kahlil thought he might have found the two of them amusing.

"So, what are you willing to do to keep the peace?" Joulen asked.

"Anything," Hirran replied and Joulen flushed deep red.

"I meant as the representative of your holdings," Joulen said quickly.

"Yes," Hirran said, nodding, "anything that I can. But it isn't up to me."

"It might be," Joulen said. "My uncle plans to demand exclusive trade rights with the Iron Heights as compensation for Nanvess' murder. If you would submit to that, then the Bousim house will be satisfied."

"It's impossible." Hirran shook her head.

"Not even to prevent a war?" Joulen asked.

"No, you misunderstand me." Hirran stepped closer to Joulen and gazed up at him. "To save our two nations, I would give everything I possessed, but I can't give it twice. Gethlam Anyyd plans to demand exclusive trade rights to all of my lands as payment for Esh'illan's death."

"That's absurd. Esh'illan was a drunk and a wastrel." Despite his words, Joulen appeared to be troubled.

"Ourath Lisam has convinced Gethlam that he has as much right to make his claim as your uncle has," Hirran said.

"How do you know this?" Joulen asked.

"We had a spy watching Ourath." Hirran bowed her head as if embarrassed. She looked quite pretty in the pose and Kahlil could see that she was having some effect on Joulen. The young guan lifted his hand as if to reassure her but then caught himself.

"I imagine that you have spies in every gaunsho's camp," Joulen said.

"No." Hirran glanced up at him earnestly. "It's only because of Ourath's alliance with Fikiri that we sent out a spy."

Joulen's expression softened as he gazed down at Hirran. She really knew what she was doing, Kahlil thought.

"I had been worried that Gethlam might do something like this," Joulen said. "But we Bousim have the stronger house. The Anyyd will back down eventually."

"There won't be time," Hirran informed him. "In one week Fikiri's forces in the north will be gathered. He and Ourath Lisam plan to attack then."

"This Fikiri has forces in the north?" Joulen asked.

"An army of hungry bones," Hirran said. This time there was nothing appealing about her expression. Joulen paled.

"I thought the bones were Jath'ibaye's creations," Joulen said.

"If you've seen him among them, it was as an enemy," Hirran said. "The hungry bones are Fikiri's creations. If Jath'ibaye didn't fight them, they would destroy Vundomu and then advance into the gaun'im's lands. Until now, Jath'ibaye has been the only thing standing between Fikiri and his conquest of all of Basawar."

Joulen's expression turned skeptical. He toyed with his cigarette case.

"I know you find it hard to believe," Hirran went on, "but I swear it's the truth. Say the name 'Fikiri' to anyone in Vundomu and you'll see what a monster he is—how he's tormented these lands!"

"And yet I've never heard of him," Joulen replied.

"But you've seen him," Hirran said suddenly. "In Ourath's tent. He's a gaunt old man with scars all up and down his arms and hands. He has dirty blond hair and skin that looks as if it has been scrubbed raw."

Joulen looked thoughtful but didn't say anything.

"He appears out of nowhere," Hirran went on quickly, "but there's always this terrible rending noise and a flash of fire. And there's a smell afterwards." Hirran shuddered. "I have nightmares about that smell."

"The man you're describing was in Ourath's tent last night," Joulen admitted.

"You see." Hirran's expression was triumphant.

"But that doesn't prove anything," Joulen added quickly. "He could as easily have been your own spy as this Fikiri."

"You have to believe me." Hirran suddenly caught Joulen's hand in her own. "If we don't find a way to stop Ourath within a week, then Fikiri will attack and Jath'ibaye will have to—"

"Have to what?" Joulen demanded.

"He'll have to treat all of the gaun'im as allies of Fikiri's," Hirran said softly. "He'll destroy everything."

"Everything?" Joulen frowned at this. "I don't think we'll just allow him to destroy—"

"What you think won't matter," Hirran insisted. "Ask your captains—the old ones who fought in the Seven Years' War. Ask them what Jath'ibaye can do."

Kahlil could see the worry creeping into Joulen's countenance. Plainly, he already knew the old stories of the wars against Jath'ibaye. Kahlil, too, had heard them when he had lived in the Bousim barracks in Nurjima. Jath'ibaye's sorcery was said to have destroyed armies in minutes, showing no man mercy, allowing no surrender and taking no prisoners. Kahlil now wondered how much of that had been true.

Knowing John, Kahlil imagined that Jath'ibaye would have forced the Fai'daum to adopt some strange Nayeshi code of honor regarding prisoners of war. He would have tried to enforce the Geneva Convention the same way he tried to install democracy and fishing regulations.

But Jath'ibaye was still the Rifter and Kahlil suspected that very few of his enemies had survived his assaults long enough to be taken prisoner.

"If this war comes," Hirran met Joulen's gaze directly, "Jath'ibaye will not restrain himself. He will destroy every last gaunan and all of your lands. The cities will burn and the lands will crumble into the sea. He will not forgive an alliance with Fikiri."

Joulen said nothing for several long moments.

"So what would you have me do?" he asked at last.

"You must remove Ourath Lisam from power," Hirran told him.

Joulen pulled his hand from Hirran's, his frustration plain on his face.

"I don't have that authority," Joulen told her. "And even if I did, I don't have any grounds. All I have is your word."

"I swear that I'm telling you the truth."

"I believe you," Joulen replied. "But I can't act against a gaunsho without any evidence of his treachery. Not even my own family would support me."

Hirran leaned against the iron railing, frowning up at the overhanging blossoms. Joulen watched her.

"Then I'll get you your evidence," Hirran said firmly.

"How?" Joulen asked.

"I don't know, but it has to be done," Hirran replied. "And I will see to it."

Joulen gazed at Hirran intently and then nodded.

"If you can find any proof," he said, "you should turn it over to my uncle, Governor Nivoun. He has the legal power to take action against a gaunsho."

"Can I trust him?" Hirran asked.

Joulen did not answer right away. He seemed uncertain.

"He wouldn't want a war," Joulen stated finally.

"That will have to be enough, I suppose."

"If you can present any proof, I will vouch for your character to Nivoun, I swear," Joulen said.

"If I can't, and the week passes?" Hirran asked.

Joulen frowned deeply and even from a distance Kahlil understood his meaning.

Hirran sighed.

"I was looking forward to meeting you in person, Joulen Bousim," she said. "I wish it could have been under better circumstances."

"Yes," Joulen said. "I'm sorry."

"I had hoped that one day the Bousim house would be an ally to the Iron Heights. I had such hopes…You can't imagine." Hirran looked sad but still quite lovely.

Very carefully, Joulen reached out and brushed a fallen blossom from Hirran's hair.

"I'm glad to have met you." Joulen didn't seem able to take his eyes off her. "Even if this is a terrible time, it's an honor to have met you after only knowing you from your letters."

Hirran smiled at Joulen and Kahlil could see that this was a smile without artifice. He guessed from her expression that she'd harbored her own personal hopes for Joulen Bousim—hopes completely unrelated to trade.

She said, "I will do all I can to ensure that our next meeting will be better."

Joulen couldn't seem to lift his gaze from Hirran, and Kahlil thought the young commander might be on the verge of stealing a kiss. But Hirran straightened and drew back.

"I can't be gone too long," Hirran said.

"Your husband will miss you, no doubt." Joulen scowled at the flower petals at his feet.

"I'm not married," Hirran informed him.

Even from where he crouched in the tree branches, Kahlil could see how this information pleased Joulen. He bowed deeply to Hirran and stared after her as she and her attendant hurried away from the orchard.

Kahlil dropped back into the Gray Space, and several blocks past the Silverlake Gardens, he emerged at Hirran's side. She was startled but managed to retain her dignity. Her young attendant yelped and jumped, almost falling off the walkway.

"You were there?" Hirran asked. The flirtatious tone she had used with Joulen dropped from her voice.

"The entire time," Kahlil said.

"You would make a very dangerous enemy, I think," Hirran said.

"I could say the same for you," Kahlil responded with a shrug.

Hirran seemed deflated. "I'd love to think so, but I don't know that I accomplished much with that meeting."

"The commander seemed impressed," Kahlil said.

"Yes, but it won't do us any good if we don't have any evidence to present to him," Hirran said. "Joulen is fond of women but he's not going to commit treason just because a pretty girl asks him to. We have to find some proof."

"Any ideas how?" Kahlil asked.

"I don't know." Now surly and annoyed, Hirran abandoned all pretense of demure reserve; she eyed Kahlil. "You were a spy. You must have some connections."

Kahlil went silent, thinking that Hirran didn't know much of spymasters or the insulating isolation they imposed upon their agents. In two years of assassinations, he'd never been told another agent's name—he'd never asked. He'd simply done what Alidas had required. Though, considering the political delicacy of certain assignments he'd received, Kahlil had realized that Alidas must control an entire network of informants and agents.

"We only have a week," Hirran muttered.

"If that," Kahlil agreed. They needed to act quickly and directly. If he were going to get anything from Alidas, he would have to return to Nurjima and that meant going into enemy territory.

"I need to see Jath'ibaye," Kahlil said.

"But you aren't supposed to…" Hirran began.

"There are a lot of things neither you nor I are supposed to do," Kahlil said. "And yet here we are. Will you help me get to him or not?"

"How could I say no to such a gallant proposition?"

CHAPTER SIXTY-SIX

Music poured through the long corridors of Jath'ibaye's household. Even from the servant's entry, Kahlil could hear a singer's voice rising above the low murmur of guests. The kitchens were close by and he could smell meats and feast breads. Heat from the huge ovens radiated through the rooms, saturating the air with fragrant warmth.

Servants with trays of baked fish, roast lamb, and precious fruits hustled past Kahlil on their way to the great hall. Ourath and his rashan'im seemed to be receiving quite a warm welcome.

Kahlil's lip curled at the thought. A moment later he schooled his expression into the same neutral interest of the two men ahead of him. They were runners from Hirran's household. Kahlil was taller than either of the two young men and older by a good ten years. He kept his head down. If any of the servants in Jath'ibaye's household recognized him, they gave no indication. Most rushed past after a cursory glance at the Iron Heights insignia on the sleeve of his coat. With his scarlet uniform and his newly cropped hair, he fit their expectations of one of Hirran's runners. No one bothered to examine him much beyond that.

Then again, few of the kitchen servants had seen his face up close. The real trick would be getting to Jath'ibaye without Ourath noticing him. That was assuming he could elude Eriki'yu, Saimura, and Besh'anya.

It would be so much easier if he could just slip into the Gray Space. But he had already pressed his luck too far today. Another disturbance, much less one within Jath'ibaye's own house, would doubtless bring Jath'ibaye roaring down on him. And who knew how many onlookers that would attract?

As he and the two runners stepped through the doors into the great hall, the sound and brilliant light of the vast room flooded over them. Bluish flames burned in the gas lamps high above the gathering. On the tables, expensive beeswax candles offered faint honey scents as well as their warm glow. Silver platters of meats, breads, and fruit filled the wooden tables where high-ranking Lisam rashan'im feasted beside Fai'daum intellectuals and merchants. All were dressed in their finest; for the gaun'im's forces that meant brushed silk and polished amber, while the Fai'daum wore their wool coats and iron rings with obvious pride.

None of the golden splendor of the gaun'im's palaces adorned Jath'ibaye's household. Still, the atmosphere reminded Kahlil of the night he had infiltrated the Bell Dance in Nurjima. Heat and laughter rolled over him. A slim, handsome singer crooned from amidst the circle of musicians gathered near the fireplace. Music poured through the lapses in conversation, creating a sea of contented sound. Servants hurried from the tables to the kitchens and back.

Kahlil glanced immediately to where the guest of honor sat at the high table at the far end of the room. For a moment he couldn't keep from glaring at Ourath's stately profile. His red hair gleamed like copper. His skin seemed to glow with the luster of gold. The close tailoring of his silk clothing offered glimpses of his graceful body as he moved. His full lips parted in a sensual smile.

The woman seated across from him gazed helplessly at him and she wasn't alone. All through the chamber women stared at Ourath. Men stole quick, guilty glances again and again. Servants standing near him lingered too long.

Even seething with anger toward him, Kahlil had to admit that Ourath radiated attraction. A disturbing edge of arousal crept into Kahlil's loathing as he continued to watch. Something cruel and sexual stirred inside him. The sensation infuriated Kahlil, killing what little longing there had been. He wanted to strangle the life out of Ourath for even briefly tainting his desire.

Immediately, Kahlil searched the room for Jath'ibaye. He glanced up and down the rows of tables. People moved, gesturing and laughing. Kahlil took them in dozens at a time and disregarded them just as quickly. Just glimpses of backs, profiles, even gestures, told him that none of these people were Jath'ibaye.

He caught sight of Besh'anya, sitting quite near Ourath. There was an almost glistening flush to her skin. She toyed obsessively with an amulet that hung around her neck.

She and Saimura were supposed to be bearing as much of the effect of the niru'mohim for Jath'ibaye as they could, but Saimura was nowhere to be seen and Besh'anya looked like she was being cooked to death from the inside out. She swayed slightly in her seat and then drained the water glass in front of her.

Out of the corner of his eye, Kahlil noticed Eriki'yu's slender form. Already he made his way toward the runners. There was no doubt that he would recognize Kahlil up close.

"That's the house steward." Kahlil indicated Eriki'yu to the two runners. "You should distract him before he gets much closer."

Kahlil pulled his jacket off and folded it over his arm. Without the Iron Heights insignia he looked less like a servant. Now he waited for a momentary lapse in Eriki'yu's attention. It came quickly enough. Eriki'yu paused as a water boy passed him and then for an instant he gazed sidelong at Ourath.

"Go now," Kahlil told the two runners. As they moved forward, Kahlil stepped back into the crush of kitchen servants. He moved quickly between them, inquiring after the nearest bathroom. In direct contradiction to their brief instructions and the few annoyed gestures that they made, he walked to the back staircase. Then he bounded up the narrow stairs to the balcony overlooking the great hall.

The balcony was dark, and as Kahlil moved past, the bright flames of the gas lamps briefly blinded him. The air around him seemed to stir. Then, suddenly, he felt a strong hand catch his shoulder. He knew the touch even before his eyes adjusted to the darkness.

"You aren't supposed to be here," Jath'ibaye said.

"I know. I had to talk to you," Kahlil said.

"Of course you did."

The noise of footsteps came from above—a servant tromped down the staircase with an armload of beeswax tapers. Jath'ibaye pulled Kahlil away from the stairs. As he allowed Jath'ibaye to guide him into an alcove, Kahlil's eyes adjusted completely to the darkness. At one time sentries had probably been stationed here in order to keep watch over the great hall. Now it was just a recessed area containing nothing but a simple wooden bench.

Jath'ibaye looked strange. Not ill. Rather, he seemed almost too well. A healthy flush colored his tanned skin. The muscles of his long, lean body radiated heat. His motions were fluid and fast, as if every muscle in his body was hungry for action. He looked alert and a little too excited.

"I should have known you wouldn't stay away even one day." Jath'ibaye's voice was low and rough. "Particularly if you were ordered to."

Kahlil couldn't help but remember how agitated Jath'ibaye had been in Nurjima when Ourath had last exposed him to niru'mohim. That had been the night he had choked Kahlil to near unconsciousness.

"Shouldn't Saimura be here with you?" Kahlil found himself surreptitiously edging out of Jath'ibaye's reach and forced himself to stop.

"Saimura is not in any kind of condition to make a public appearance right now."

"Is he sick?"

"No, he just looks like he's walking around with a flagpole in his pants." Jath'ibaye smirked. "I think he's managing it well enough in his room."

"I see," Kahlil said. He supposed Besh'anya was dealing with her own difficulties as well. The thought embarrassed him somewhat.

"Are you…" Kahlil wasn't sure how exactly he should word his question.

"Desperately happy to see you?" Jath'ibaye supplied for him. His smile turned almost shy. "I am. But if you hadn't come I would have managed. You don't have to worry. I'm not going to fuck Ourath, not even if he douses himself in buckets of niru'mohim."

The insecurity that had gnawed at Kahlil's stomach all day melted away. He felt somewhat amazed that this was all that it had taken to dissipate his anxiety. He'd just needed to hear a single reassurance from Jath'ibaye.

"But I am very glad that you did come." Jath'ibaye drew Kahlil close. His breath felt pleasantly hot against Kahlil's skin.

The bench was no use to them. It was too near the edge of the balcony. Instead, they knelt in the deep shadows of the alcove. They said nothing, understanding easily the motions of longing and pleasure. Kahlil exhausted Jath'ibaye's restless body with his hands and mouth. Jath'ibaye responded with assurance and knowing. His quiet skill, both tender and demanding, left Kahlil gasping and certain that Jath'ibaye knew his body better than Kahlil did himself. At last they lay still, curled close atop Jath'ibaye's coat. Their shirts were wildly disheveled; their pants hung open in obvious indecency.

Feeling Jath'ibaye's sticky, hot skin against his own, Kahlil grinned. If Ourath could see the result of his niru'mohim right now, he'd probably tear out fistfuls of his carefully coifed hair. Then Kahlil abandoned any thought of Ourath. He leaned back against Jath'ibaye, enjoying the way Jath'ibaye's fingers stroked the back of his neck and brushed through his hair.

"Your hair was short like this the first time we met," Jath'ibaye whispered. He kissed the back of Kahlil's neck.

Kahlil remembered it distinctly, though he knew that it was Ravishan's past that he recollected. Still with the taste of Jath'ibaye on his lips and the heat of him so close, Kahlil felt the memory as if it were all his own. It had been just a day after he had found a golden key—the ush'hala—one of the three symbols of the Kahlil, lying in the snow. Jahn had looked like a wild man, all lean muscle and knotted hair. Savage. Barely able to speak. Dressed in animal skins and still, somehow, beautiful.

Kahlil almost said that that hadn't been the first time they had met. The first time they had met had been when he had answered John's ad for a roommate. Or perhaps it had been when John had just been a boy, in that briefest instant when the issusha'im had forged the bond between them. But he didn't say anything because it didn't matter right now. At this moment all that mattered was that they had met and now they were here together.

Jath'ibaye sighed and drew back slightly. He dug a handkerchief out of the pocket of his discarded coat and offered it to Kahlil.

"Always prepared," Kahlil commented.

"Well, I was a Boy Scout."

"Yeah, I remember." Kahlil accepted the handkerchief and cleaned himself up. He straightened his clothes and watched as Jath'ibaye finished buttoning up the front of his own pants.

"I don't suppose you'd have a breath mint on you?" Kahlil asked.

Jath'ibaye shook his head, then leaned forward and kissed Kahlil. "Your breath is fine."

"Yeah," Kahlil grinned, "and my hair looks great too."

"Now you're just trolling for compliments," Jath'ibaye replied.

"They help to soothe my seething jealousy."

"Really?" Jath'ibaye cocked his head questioningly. "You're not actually jealous, are you?"

"Yes, but I'm trying to work through it." Kahlil couldn't help but glance past the balcony rail. He didn't want to think about Ourath and Jath'ibaye, but it was hard not to. He just didn't understand what could have brought them together. Maybe it had just been the niru'mohim. Kahlil wanted to believe that. But he doubted that their entire relationship could be blamed on a single potion. Niru'mohim might be strong but Jath'ibaye was good at resisting his own desires if he needed to. Kahlil knew that from the years the two of them had spent together in Rathal'pesha.

It wasn't as if Jath'ibaye was incapable of killing a man who opposed him either. Kahlil could still vividly recall the way Jath'ibaye had broken Esh'illan's neck. He could have been swatting a gnat for all it concerned him. No, if Jath'ibaye had wanted Ourath out of his way, the niru'mohim would not have stopped him. Nothing could stop Jath'ibaye but his own compassion.

That was why Loshai still lived. Jath'ibaye cared for her too much to kill her, even if it would be for his own good. Ourath seemed to have the same kind of hold on Jath'ibaye. That grasp worried Kahlil. It threatened his assurance. He expected to be united with Jath'ibaye against their enemies. But then there were these troubling exemptions. In Loshai's case, years of friendship haunted Jath'ibaye. But with Ourath, Kahlil had no idea. It had to be much more than mere sex. Sex was easy to come by; a man with Jath'ibaye's power and wealth would have to be turning it away. Ourath had to have some other connection to Jath'ibaye—something that ran as deep as hatred and shielded Ourath as if it were love.

"What would you do if I killed him?" Kahlil suddenly asked.

Jath'ibaye didn't have to ask who Kahlil was talking about. He looked troubled.

"I'd hope that you didn't start a war when you did it," Jath'ibaye said at last.

The answer came too late and with far too much sorrow to be honest. Jath'ibaye's concern wasn't just pragmatism. If he had been pragmatic, he would have killed Ourath at the Bell Dance or even before then.

"Why the hell do you care so much for him?" Kahlil demanded.

"I don't. I feel…responsible, I guess." Jath'ibaye caught Kahlil's skeptical expression and went on, "He was young when he met me and I wasn't in the best state of mind." Jath'ibaye leaned back against the shadowed wall. He glanced to Kahlil but then looked quickly away. "You—Ravishan had been gone so long…and Ourath reminded me of him—of you as well—"

"In what possible way is he even slightly like me?"

"It's hard to see, especially now," Jath'ibaye replied, "but when Ourath was younger…he was different." Jath'ibaye went quiet and Kahlil could see him trying to find the words to explain. "He was always beautiful and I'm sure that was the first resemblance I noticed. But he was also so desperate and out of his depth at the same time."

"I'm not out of my depth." Kahlil couldn't stop himself from making the comment. He hated the idea that anyone could look at Ourath and find a likeness between them.

"You aren't out of your depth now, but that night when you—when Ravishan—approached me in Candle Alley, you were. You were hardly a smooth operator in your youth." Jath'ibaye smiled just briefly.

"I wasn't out of my depth. I was—" Kahlil couldn't divide his own youth from Ravishan's. At this moment, he simply felt the truth of his words. "I was in love," Kahlil finished, as if it were an offhanded thing to say.

Again Jath'ibaye gave him that flickering smile.

"Well, I don't know if Ourath was in love." Jath'ibaye looked doubtful. "I like to think that he wasn't. I feel a lot less guilty. But either way it still comes down to the same thing. I wasn't very good to him. I just used him. It made me feel sick with myself and I almost broke it off with him, but then he started wearing the niru'mohim. That made it easy for me to just erase the man Ourath was and see someone else in his body. I started using Ourath like a drug. I called him by the wrong name more than once. He just took it. By then he was involved with Nanvess and Fikiri. He couldn't have gotten out even if he had wanted to." Jath'ibaye looked sad and weary and Kahlil hated to think that it was for Ourath's sake, because the man had plotted to murder him.

"If he'd just met someone else," Jath'ibaye said, "someone who'd appreciated him, maybe he wouldn't have gone to Nanvess for the niru'mohim in the first place. Maybe he wouldn't have ended up like this."

"Or maybe he would have," Kahlil responded. "And ending up like he has isn't as bad as all that. The man is a gaunsho. It's not like he's somebody's slave."

"I know. I've told myself the same thing. But I can't help but still feel guilty." Jath'ibaye's gaze flickered from Kahlil down to the floor. "I shouldn't have been with him at all. I should have waited for you. I just wanted someone."

"Waited for me?" Kahlil frowned at Jath'ibaye. "I was dead." Only belatedly did he realize that he'd spoken up as if he were Ravishan. It was happening more and more and he didn't know if he should fight it or not. Today he didn't, because he needed Ravishan's insight into Jath'ibaye—and he wanted to win this argument.

"And yet here you are," Jath'ibaye responded.

"By sheer luck, yes. But you couldn't have known that. I didn't even know it and I'm me." Kahlil cocked his head slightly as a sudden, new thought came to him. "So what are you thinking? Ourath's murder attempt was some kind of just punishment for your infidelity to your dead lover?"

Jath'ibaye's silence told Kahlil that he'd guessed correctly.

"That's just stupid," Kahlil said. That at least prompted a wry laugh from Jath'ibaye.

"You were always one for tact, weren't you?" Jath'ibaye asked.

"Well, it is stupid." Kahlil shrugged. "You don't deserve to be punished just because you don't die and I do," Kahlil said. "Sooner or later I'm going to die. Then you're going to have to get over my death and move on."

The instant he said the words Kahlil knew he shouldn't have. The mortality of his friends and lovers was the one thing Jath'ibaye had no defense against. His expression was stricken, almost sick.

Kahlil knew that they were going to have to have this conversation some day but not today, not while Vundomu was on the verge of war. Kahlil cursed his own thoughtlessness.

"And as for Ourath," Kahlil said in an attempt to shift the subject, "you're going to have to get over him and not just because I don't share well. We can't afford to play nice with him any longer. He's an enemy to your entire country, not just your personal pain in the ass."

"I know," Jath'ibaye said.

"Good, because I think I may have a way of keeping us from going to war, but Ourath's going to have to die to get it done," Kahlil informed him flatly.

Jath'ibaye didn't object.

"Hirran has an acquaintance among the Bousim gaun'im—"

"Her pen pal, Joulen Bousim," Jath'ibaye said.

"You know about that?" Kahlil wasn't sure why he was surprised.

"I try to keep track of things like that. She's been writing to him for a few years now." Jath'ibaye shrugged. "So something's come of it?"

"If we can bring Joulen evidence of Ourath's alliance with Fikiri and his involvement in the assassination plot, then Joulen's agreed to remove Ourath," Kahlil said.

"On grounds of treason?" Jath'ibaye asked.

"That's right. Even if we can only show his involvement in the assassination attempt against you at the Bell Dance, there are still grounds for treason, because he lied to the rest of the gaun'im and misled them to the brink of war. Joulen will have Ourath executed and the gaun'im will have to withdraw."

"Joulen doesn't have that kind of authority," Jath'ibaye said.

"He believes his uncle, Nivoun, will support him if we can provide some proof of Ourath's treachery." Kahlil moved a little closer to Jath'ibaye. It was difficult to read his expression. Perhaps he was troubled or perhaps he was just thinking deeply. "With Ourath removed from power, the rest of the gaun'im won't fight us. If we can do this, then we'll end a war before it can start."

Jath'ibaye nodded but his expression didn't lighten.

"You came here to tell me you're going to go back to Nurjima, didn't you?" Jath'ibaye asked.

"That's where our evidence will be if there's any to be found," Kahlil said.

"It has to be you," Jath'ibaye said quietly, almost as if he were speaking to himself.

"I can get there the soonest and I have connections with the Bousim house," Kahlil replied. "I think I might be able to convince Alidas to help me."

"Alidas?" Jath'ibaye asked.

"He's the Bousim captain who took me in when I first returned to Basawar. He's a good man."

"Should I be jealous?" Jath'ibaye asked lightly.

"No." Kahlil smiled at the idea that Jath'ibaye would be.

"So, he's a Bousim captain…" Jath'ibaye paused for a moment. "He wouldn't have a limp, would he?"

"Yes, his right leg. You know him?" Kahlil asked.

"Maybe. I might have met him a long time ago. We both did, actually. If he's the same man I'm thinking of, then he took the train with us to Nurjima when you were going to receive your Prayerscars."

Kahlil hardly remembered the journey except for his welcome in Vundomu and that first night he had spent alone with John in Nurjima.

"You'd think he would have recognized me," Kahlil said.

"Maybe, but it couldn't have made sense to him. To be the man he rode with on the train you'd have to be much older," Jath'ibaye said. "It would probably be best not to complicate things with old history if it can be helped."

"Don't worry. Alidas and I have enough fresh history to keep us occupied," Kahlil commented.

Jath'ibaye frowned and Kahlil went on quickly before Jath'ibaye could ask.

"I don't know how long it will take but if it comes to the end of the week I'll return no matter what."

"I'll talk to Saimura. He has friends who may be able to house you. You'll need money and clothes as well," Jath'ibaye said. Kahlil waited for Jath'ibaye to say something more but he was silent. Then suddenly he moved forward and wrapped his arms around Kahlil in a hard, anxious embrace.

"Be careful," Jath'ibaye whispered into Kahlil's ear.

Kahlil returned Jath'ibaye's embrace. He'd been an idiot to bring up his own death. Now it was probably all Jath'ibaye would think about.

Kahlil hugged Jath'ibaye fiercely, as if he could impress his own strength and confidence upon Jath'ibaye physically. He knew he would die someday, but not now. Not for years. He wanted to say as much but knew better than to speak of it. Just as he had to trust Jath'ibaye to have the will to resist and refuse Ourath, so Jath'ibaye simply had to trust that Kahlil would come back alive.

Chapter Sixty-Seven

Nurjima hung beneath Kahlil, silent and colorless as a photograph. For a moment Kahlil simply watched the dark waters roll beneath the Blackbird Bridge. Two years ago he had looked over this same great expanse of river and had gazed out at the winding streets and densely packed buildings knowing that it was all wrong. He had known that he had failed in his duties and destroyed Nurjima's glorious, holy future. And yet the great city had survived his failure.

This time he doubted it would. If Jath'ibaye tore open the earth, Nurjima would crumble.

Utterly unaware of how near their ruin lay, fishermen pushed their boats out into the river to begin their day's work. Deliverymen drove their tahldi across the bridge. Bread sellers were already out on the streets. Soon the roads would be packed with carts and wagons. Clusters of women and children would press through the crowds of men on the walkways. Alidas was already riding the morning patrol of the Bousim districts.

Kahlil had already visited Alidas' private room in the rashan'im barracks, but the captain was gone. Kahlil had left him a note explaining that he would go by Alidas' rooms in Redbrick in the early afternoon before returning to the refuge of the Gray Space. That left Kahlil the remainder of the morning to waste as he would.

Now he stood within the cold, colorless silence of the Gray Space and watched the morning rituals of the men and women of the city. They were each so involved in their own activities—an old man picking at something in his teeth, a girl pausing a moment to catch her reflection in a shop window. Two boys stole buns from a bread seller's cart and ran as the man caught sight of them.

None of them knew of the Great Gate, Loshai, or the Rifter. The vast powers that threatened and protected their lives were as hidden from them as the atoms that underlay their very bodies. In a way, Kahlil supposed their ignorance offered them a luxury that he had personally never known. They were free to indulge in fantasies of their own importance. If they believed in Parfir, it was as a being both too distant and omnipotent to be understood. He was beyond them. They whispered their troubles to prayer stones and imagined Parfir listening in limitless, radiant perfection. They did not want to know that their god had troubles of his own. They did not want to know that he could bleed or vomit or that he might forget their names. It would probably terrify them to see his pain and savage anger or to know that even their god struggled and suffered through life.

Kahlil wondered what it would be like to know none of those things. Would it be bliss? Would it offer deep sleep and easily forgotten dreams? Would it offer security in petty charms and talismans? A few months ago he had been close to knowing. But that ignorance had come at the cost of his own memories. There had been no solace in the restless jumble of his identity. All he had felt then was a pervasive sense of dislocation. For him, it had been a relief to discover the truth. His purpose and place had come with that knowledge.

But he wasn't sure how welcome the same revelation would be to Alidas. No man would want to discover that his god was on the opposing side of a war. It wasn't so surprising that none of the gaun'im recognized Jath'ibaye as Parfir's incarnation. They called him a demon or a profane Eastern sorcerer. But none of them would want to believe he was the Rifter.

In the deep shadows of a huge pylon, Kahlil dropped out of the Gray Space. He strolled from the bridge toward the tightly packed streets of the Redbrick District. All along the walkways he saw clusters of women sitting at simple throwing wheels, turning wet lumps of rust-red clay into delicate cups.

Stacks of glazed and fired dishes filled wooden tables. None of the women even met Kahlil's glances. Brightly dressed sons and husbands proposed a variety of prices as Kahlil passed by. He declined with a polite smile. The deep blue suit he had borrowed from Saimura seemed to convey enough wealth to make the street sellers feel he was worth their time. More than one man followed him a little way, attempting to interest him in a variety of goods and services. Farther down on Water Street, bone vendors called to Kahlil in the same respectfully friendly tones. He glanced at their displays of carved dice and combs without much interest. The delicate knives carved from animal bones gave Kahlil a moment's consideration. All of them were white, obviously untainted by curses. He wondered if anyone but him even knew how to curse bone blades anymore.

A merchant noticed Kahlil's gaze and quickly picked up one of the fine white knives. He smiled and offered it to Kahlil.

"This one was carved from a Lisam bull's thigh bone." The balding man smiled knowingly at Kahlil. "It guarantees success with women."

Kahlil could not restrain a laugh at the notion that he would ever want success with women. He shook his head to decline the merchant's offer.

"But that's no worry for a young man like you." The merchant smoothly replaced the blade with another longer one. "But who doesn't need a little luck with money these days?"

"True," Kahlil agreed. "In fact, I probably couldn't afford that knife."

The merchant seemed about to make an offer but Kahlil cut him off.

"What about something to defeat my enemies?" Kahlil asked. He couldn't help but wonder what the merchant would present him with.

"I'm no witch." The merchant stiffened and narrowed his eyes piously at Kahlil. "We only deal in blessed bones here."

"Of course," Kahlil replied. "I was just curious." He stepped away and crossed the street before the merchant could say anything more.

Many of the merchants displayed carved, blessed bones. All of them were in the form of knives. It amused Kahlil to look at them. Their origin as curse blades was so obvious and yet they were being sold as lucky trinkets. Kahlil couldn't remember how many men he had killed with his own black curse blade. No doubt the mere sight of it would have horrified all these proper shopkeepers.

As he walked on, the merchants and storefronts became more rare. The air began to thicken with the scents of animal carcasses and rendering kitchens. The tightly packed brick buildings lining the street reverberated with the noise of butchering saws. The bone talismans and fine leathers Kahlil had seen in so many store displays were no doubt being produced by the hundreds in the workhouses Kahlil now strode past. Kahlil turned and paced quickly back behind a bone carver's shop. He stopped at the door of Alidas' rooms.

Kahlil couldn't help but wonder why Alidas would rent rooms in this part of the city. It was filthy and loud and so close to the gallows that Kahlil suspected that some of the bone knives could have been carved from the remains of criminals. The noise and slaughterhouse odors could disguise any number of terrible deeds. Torture came quickly to Kahlil's mind. But he couldn't imagine Alidas bothering to fill a torture chamber with all those books and old photographs. Nothing about the small rooms, the worn carpet, or soft bed had seemed conceived with cruelty in mind. And yet the location of the rooms offered no other advantage.

Anyone hearing of Alidas' rooms in the Redbrick District would assume that they were used to interrogate and dispose of enemies of the Bousim family. Perhaps that was what Alidas wanted. Maybe he chose the Redbrick District because it disguised his nature.

Maybe the rent was just cheap.

When it came to Alidas, Kahlil realized that he didn't really know much of anything. Even with everything Jath'ibaye had told him, Kahlil still couldn't guess how Alidas would react to his news. Kahlil wasn't even certain that Alidas would respond to the message he'd left. The last time they had spoken Alidas had warned Kahlil that he had orders to kill him. He didn't want to contemplate what he would do if he had to fight Alidas. He knew where to attack and how the noise and filth of the Redbrick District would serve him. But he didn't want to think like that, not about the man who had rescued him two years before.

He knocked lightly on the door. Almost immediately, Kahlil realized that the surrounding noise of saws, hammers and shouting workmen had probably drowned out such a tentative knock. He lifted his hand to try again just as Alidas opened the door. He stepped back to allow Kahlil to enter, then locked the door behind him.

"I didn't expect you to bother to knock," Alidas remarked.

"I don't have a key anymore," Kahlil replied. They both knew that a key made no difference. Kahlil could have walked right in if he had wanted to. But he owed too much respect to Alidas to trespass in such a presumptuous way.

Several silent moments passed as both of them stood in the small room, surrounded by shelves and stacks of books and Alidas' old photos, staring at one another.

Alidas still wore his riding clothes. Road dust dulled the glossy leather of his boots. He must have come directly from the barracks, Kahlil thought. Alidas studied Kahlil openly, as if he were a new rashan at his first inspection.

"You look good. Life in the north must suit you. That is where you've been, isn't it? In Mahn'illev, at least," Alidas asked coolly.

"Mostly in Vundomu," Kahlil answered. He had no reason to lie to Alidas.

"You seem to have gotten a very nice suit out of it," Alidas commented. There was an almost hurt bitterness in his tone. Kahlil decided to overlook it.

"It's borrowed," he replied.

Alidas smiled slightly at this, as if he had expected as much.

"So, you've come a long way to see me," Alidas said, "and at a bad time as well. What do you need?"

"I don't need anything. I have information," Kahlil said.

"It's too late to buy your way back into the Bousim house, if that's what you're thinking." Alidas shook his head and for the first time Kahlil caught a glimpse of sadness in Alidas' expression. "I can't help you. I'm sorry, Kyle."

"It's not what you think," Kahlil said quickly. "I'm not deserting Vundomu and I'm not trying to buy my way back into your service. I'm bringing information that Jath'ibaye wants you to have, information that you need if we are to avert a war."

Alidas considered Kahlil and then offered Kahlil a seat in one of his two chairs. Alidas himself leaned against the edge of his wooden writing desk.

"Well then," Alidas said solemnly, "tell me what you've come to say."

"The good news is that I've gotten my memory back," Kahlil began.

"And the bad news?"

"I guess the bad news is who I turned out to be."

Kahlil tried to keep things simple. But the truth wasn't simple. Slowly, he unfolded revelation after revelation to Alidas. First there was the matter of his own identity. Alidas listened and even admitted that he had suspected something like the truth but had never known how it could be possible.

"Your face was always familiar," Alidas remarked. "And so were your skills. I remembered them from Amura'taye, when the ushman'im and ushiri'im opened the God's Razor on the Harvest Fair. You were too young, but you looked so much like Ushiri Ravishan."

"I am Ravishan," Kahlil said, "but not exactly the one you knew. I changed Basawar's history when I sent John back from Nayeshi to Rathal'pesha. He arrived years before I even became Kahlil. You knew him as Jahn."

"Yes, until he took the name Jath'ibaye." Alidas' expression darkened. "And destroyed the entire Payshmura faith."

"If it was anyone's right, it was his," Kahlil replied evenly. "He is the Rifter."

Alidas stared at Kahlil in silence. Kahlil could see Alidas' resistance to the idea and then the slow spread of realization as he considered Jath'ibaye's power and history. Jath'ibaye had walked out of the ruins of Rathal'pesha unscathed. He had held Vundomu against all seven of the gaun'im's armies. Rivers rose against his enemies and the earth trembled with his rage. What could he be but the Rifter? Alidas pressed his eyes shut. Troubled creases flickered through his expression like small shocks of pain.

"The Rifter..." Alidas said softly. "All this time he's been here. It's no wonder no one can defeat him. But why didn't he reveal himself?"

It was a good question and one that Kahlil had often contemplated himself. His only answer was a guess, but he gave it to Alidas anyway.

"He doesn't want to be worshiped," Kahlil said. "It makes him uncomfortable to think that people would obey him thoughtlessly. It's odd, but if he weren't the Rifter himself, I don't think he would believe in Parfir. He's not quite what one expects."

"Not quite?" Alidas said.

"When you know him well it makes more sense," Kahlil said. "The man he was on Nayeshi never had faith in religions or churches. I think he only felt reverence for the natural world. So now, even as a god, he doesn't want temples full of worshipers or devotees bowing before him. It's the living world that he feels is sacred and that's what he would have people pay homage to. Not to just one man."

"I knew him but I never even suspected." Alidas picked up a small book that lay on his desk but didn't open it. "How can a devotee be so near his god and never feel his presence?"

"He didn't want to be known," Kahlil replied. "I was his Kahlil and even I wasn't sure until he took Vundomu. After that there could be no doubt."

Alidas looked almost sick. Kahlil had known that learning the truth would be a terrible exertion for Alidas. But there was a resignation in Alidas' expression that told Kahlil that he was prepared to go on. Kahlil felt suddenly proud of Alidas for this. The foundations of his faith had just been crushed beneath him and yet he was willing to accept the truth and even face further revelations.

"He changed the entire world," Alidas said.

"Yes," Kahlil said. He explained the way John's presence had altered their history. How Fikiri had been destined to die but had not because John had saved him.

"Then I should have died with Fikiri as well," Alidas said quietly.

"You were saved by Parfir's own incarnation. If anything, that means you were destined to live," Kahlil replied.

"And all the men of Rathal'pesha were destined to die, then?" Alidas asked.

"They brought the Rifter down upon themselves." Kahlil heard his own voice echoing Wah'roa's flat condemnation.

"Not all of them deserved to die," Alidas countered. "Many were filled with faith."

"Innocent people die," Kahlil said. "You know that. We both do."

"Yes, but you want to believe that it's different in the realm of the divine." Alidas gazed at the book in his hands. "You want to believe that Parfir will sweep down and cradle those who have served him so long and faithfully."

"I think he would if he could," Kahlil replied. "But even he can't protect everyone."

"No." Alidas sighed heavily and set the book aside. "He would have saved his sister and brother if he could have."

"I think he would have saved a lot of people if he could have. But even he can't change death once it comes." Kahlil met Alidas' gaze. "Look, if we don't stop the gaun'im from going to war against the Rifter, then many more innocent people are going to die. And not just soldiers. Nurjima, and everyone in it, will certainly be destroyed in the cataclysm. Jath'ibaye has said as much himself."

Alidas' eyes widened in horror. Without hesitation, he asked, "What needs to be done?"

Kahlil couldn't keep from smiling at that. This courageous pragmatism had been one of the reasons he had always found Alidas so inspiring.

"We need to find a way to remove Ourath Lisam," Kahlil said. He described what he had seen in the gaun'im's camp and what Ourath planned. Their conversation felt familiar and natural. Kahlil had spent two years reporting secrets and assassinations to Alidas. Kahlil relaxed back into his chair. Alidas, too, seemed to sink back into a remembered ease. As he listened to Kahlil his expression grew tranquil; he allowed himself to fall into his private habit of massaging the chronic ache of his right knee.

"Niru'mohim?" Alidas' tone conveyed his disgust. "Only an idiot would use that stuff. I've seen dock whores with burn scars like ropes from using niru'mohim."

"I don't think Ourath cares," Kahlil replied.

Alidas just shook his head and Kahlil went on with his report. He described the council meeting in Vundomu and the arguments of the representatives. Alidas looked a little startled suddenly.

"Wah'roa?" Alidas asked. "The kahlirash?"

"Yes," Kahlil said. "He's in charge of Vundomu's defense."

"I thought he had died," Alidas said.

"You knew him?"

"A long, long time ago." Alidas glanced to an old, yellowed picture. "It doesn't matter. Go on with what happened after the council meeting."

Kahlil described the events of the past two days. Alidas only interrupted him once for the details of Joulen's promise to Hirran. After that he listened thoughtfully. At last, Kahlil came to the end of all he had to say.

"So, you do need something from me," Alidas said. "Evidence."

"Yes, you've got me there." Kahlil offered Alidas a sheepish smile. "Will you help me?"

Alidas studied Kahlil for a moment and then sighed and said, "Yes, of course I will."

"Can you get me the reports on Ourath's treachery?"

"Not directly," Alidas said. "I'm not in possession of any of your reports or those of our other sources. But I do know a man who has access."

"If he knows where the reports are kept, then I can get them." Kahlil flashed his best arrogant grin. "The matter might be settled by the end of the day."

"This isn't something you can just steal," Alidas said. "Joulen will expect the proper seals and signatures. Otherwise you might as well hand him a stack of papers you've written yourself. If Joulen is going to stake his position on this, it has to be convincing. The reports must be genuine."

"You're right." Kahlil frowned in annoyance. Why couldn't this just go easily? "So, you don't think I could find the seals or perhaps reports that have already been signed?"

"I doubt you would find anything you'd recognize." Alidas shook his head. "Hial'luyyn keeps everything encrypted. Any report would need to be decoded before you could even know what you were looking at."

Kahlil scowled even more deeply. He wasn't used to coming up against obstacles that he couldn't affect. But Alidas was right. If the evidence he needed were gibberish, then no amount of walking through walls would change that.

"So what do we do then?" Kahlil asked.

Alidas studied the piles of letters and papers on his desk. He picked up a small white card. It looked like the business card of a dining club. Alidas slipped it into his pocket. Then he glanced back to Kahlil.

"I suppose," Alidas said at last, "that we'll just have to go to Hial'luyyn."

"He's a friend?" Kahlil asked.

"He and I move in a few of the same circles."

"Did he serve with you as a rashan?"

"No." Alidas appeared to be unduly amused by that thought. "He and I simply know a number of the same people. We both belong to the same private club." Alidas seemed oddly reluctant to explain how such a tenuous connection would aid them.

"That will be enough to convince him to help us?" Kahlil asked.

"He will, if we have something to offer him in exchange."

"Such as?" Kahlil asked.

Alidas smiled in a manner that Kahlil had rarely seen. He looked rather handsome but also somewhat sinister.

"Something like what?" Kahlil asked again.

"Something like you."

Chapter Sixty-Eight

The Domu'lam Club inhabited what had once been a Payshmura guesthouse in the wealthy Silver Row District. Like most of the shrines and chapels that had been converted after the ban of the church, this building bore few signs of its past. The golden suns and moons had been chiseled off of the masonry. The blessings that would have been carved into nearly every surface had been sanded down to minute grooves. The few embellishments that remained above the door had been painted over with glossy black enamel.

Kahlil could still feel their presence as he passed through the doorway. Familiar warmth radiated over him with a strength that belied the three decades that had passed since the blessings had last been spoken.

The entry hall of the tall, narrow building was quiet. The walls were papered with a subtle pattern of tiny gray stars. Several subdued prints of tahldi hung in simple frames. There were no signs of the prostitutes and dancing girls who usually adorned men's clubs. Only one pallid young doorman stood there to greet them. He welcomed Alidas formally as 'Rasho Alidas'in'Bousim' and then glanced to Kahlil but did not ask his name.

"My guest," Alidas supplied.

"Welcome to the Domu'lam Club, sir," the doorman spoke softly, as if he were worried about waking someone.

"Thank you." Kahlil kept his own voice low.

The doorman bowed slightly and then escorted them through the hall to a set of double doors that led to the rest of the building. The clink and metallic rasp of the doorman's keys seemed unusually loud in the silence. As Kahlil followed Alidas through the heavy doors, he heard the hard noise of the lock being secured behind them.

"We like to keep the club private," Alidas said when he noticed that Kahlil had turned back to study the locked door.

"I can see that," Kahlil replied.

Much of the ground floor of the building seemed to be taken up with reading rooms and libraries, many of which seemed to be locked, though a few doors hung ajar. Through these openings, Kahlil caught glimpses of stacks of old books heaped beside chairs and across tables. Groups of men, young and old, sat around tables, discussing passages of text in hushed voices. The few men who noticed Kahlil's gaze looked slightly startled but immediately relaxed when they saw Alidas.

The club's dining room was relatively small, seating only forty or fifty men at the dark wooden tables. The chairs were all expensive and new, but none exactly matched the others. They each seemed personalized for particular occupants. Place settings had already been laid out in preparation for dinner service. As they walked past, Kahlil spotted the Bousim crest embroidered along the edge of one folded napkin, while the one next to it was decorated with the Milaun crest. Many more of the settings were emblazoned with the seals of universities. One entire table was inlaid with mother-of-pearl to spell out a scholars' honorific. Kahlil tried to guess which of the seats belonged to Alidas. There was one that was not so deep as the others and a little higher. Kahlil thought that it would accommodate Alidas' injured leg.

"Are we staying for dinner?" Kahlil could smell roasting meat wafting up from a kitchen somewhere in the back of the building.

"Possibly," Alidas said, shrugging. "It depends on how long this takes."

He led Kahlil through the dining room and down another hallway to a locked door. Kahlil wasn't surprised to see that Alidas had a key, though he still found it odd that the club should keep so many doors locked.

Inside the room, shelves of ancient books lined the walls and there were racks for scrolls as well. The space was cramped and only lit by a single gas lamp mounted on the wall. The perfume of incense and age that hung over the books and scrolls was reminiscent of the scent of the archive rooms at Rathal'pesha.

"Have a seat if you like." Alidas briefly laid his hand on the back of one of the chairs.

“Are we going to have to wait long for Hial’luyyn?” Kahlil asked.

“His table was already set, so he’s here,” Alidas said. “Probably he’s upstairs in his room. But I think I should speak to him alone first. This is all going to come as something of a shock to him.”

“You said that he would want me to do something.”

“No,” Alidas said, smiling. “I said that he would want you, the Kahlil. And he will. But I’m not sure he’s ready to just have you and all your revelations sprung on him at once. Let me go up and break it to him.”

“Will he believe you?” Kahlil asked.

“I’ve never lied to him,” Alidas said. “And this would be an odd way to start.”

Not knowing Hial’luyyn or Alidas’ relationship with him, Kahlil couldn’t really say if that was true or not.

“So you just want me to stay here?”

“Yes, I know it’s not in your nature to let someone else act for you, but in this case you must trust me. Hial’luyyn is an old man. We want him on our side, not dead of a heart attack. Just wait here and behave yourself.”

“Behave myself?” Kahlil asked.

“Yes.” Alidas smile faded a little. “Sometimes you seem to have a knack for trouble.”

“Not today.” Kahlil held up his hands in the sign of peace. “I’ll be good and wait.”

“All right then.” Alidas stepped back to the door. “I’m going to lock you in. It should keep most other members of the club from bothering you.”

Kahlil nodded, but he couldn’t help feeling uneasy as he listened to the sound of the deadbolt sliding into place. It shouldn’t have bothered him at all. Normally, doors and locks meant nothing to him. He could leave or enter any room at any time he liked. No prison could hold him except one that had been altered by binding rituals. As he thought of the ritual, he realized what had unnerved him. This club felt so much like a holy place. It reminded him too much of Rathal’pesha and the dark rooms where he had been helplessly confined.

Kahlil placed his hand against one of the walls and silently opened the Gray Space. There was no resistance. If he wanted he could walk out of the room at this moment.

He let the Gray Space snap closed.

He dropped back into a chair, pulled a book from the closest shelf, and flipped through the pages. It was an old book and all of the illustrations were simple engravings. It appeared to chronicle the lives of several obscure Payshmura saints. Kahlil slid it back onto the shelf and grabbed another volume. This one was a history of Jevir, the second Kahlil to unleash the Rifter. Kahlil frowned and chose a third book. This turned out to be a catalog of ancient prayers. Kahlil scanned the titles of the other books. All of them were religious texts and all of them were banned by the Gaunsho'im Council.

The volumes on the upper shelves were tattered and the spines of some were dark with scorch marks. Kahlil stood and took one of them down. He recognized it at once. It was a textbook explaining how to perform an ushman's first blessings and curses. Kahlil held it carefully as he turned the brittle, yellow pages. Many of them were torn or obviously cobbled together with binder's paste and tissue. Kahlil glanced at the dark leather cover and noticed the faint lines of what would once have been gold embossing. At one time the image of the Black Tower had been embossed on the scarred and damaged cover.

Kahlil gazed around the room in amazement. People had been hung for possessing just one book like this one. The gaun'im might bring back the practice of burning people alive for a collection of this size. Suddenly a few locked doors and one young doorman struck Kahlil as far too little security. He couldn't help but wonder about the men in the club. They had to be risking their lives just to read these books.

Kahlil had encountered people who still kept the Payshmura faith. They were often older, like Alidas. Most of them owned a polished stone or kept a tiny carved sun hidden in a drawer somewhere. None of them would have dared to keep even one of these books, much less an entire library. The members of this club couldn't have been men of ordinary faith; they had to be zealots, priests, and ardent believers.

No wonder Alidas had worried about springing Kahlil on Hial'luyyn. It probably could kill a man to learn that his god—whose holy books he had been risking his life to defend—stood in opposition to almost everything in those texts. What would become of a man's faith after such a revelation? Alidas had managed it. But Alidas was not only extraordinarily resilient but also had a streak of pragmatism that allowed him to adapt. How many of the men in this club could be the same? Kahlil didn't think many. He guessed that most of them would rather die as martyrs to the old Payshmura faith than accept Jath'ibaye and his many heresies.

Kahlil gently returned the fragile book to its place on the shelf.

He wondered what Alidas was telling Hial'luyyn. Alidas had said that he had never lied to the man, but that wasn't the same as always telling the truth. Kahlil wondered how much Alidas was leaving out.

Kahlil heard a key turning in the lock and then Alidas leaned in through the doorway, looking happy and relaxed.

"You can come and meet Hial'luyyn now," he said.

Though Kahlil expected to be led upstairs, they instead returned to the dining room. It was nearly full now. With his new insight into the club's purpose, Kahlil had expected most of the members to be Alidas' age or older, but there were a surprising number of men in their late twenties and thirties. Many of them wore scholars' coats and collars. Kahlil took in the interested faces of the men gathered at the tables. It obviously wasn't common to have someone new brought into the club. They watched him with a kind of fascination that Kahlil found a little disturbing.

Alidas led Kahlil to the black table with the mother-of-pearl inlay that Kahlil had noticed earlier. The old man sitting there reminded Kahlil a little of Wah'roa. He was lean with sharp features. But where Wah'roa's skin was tanned to a dark leather hide, Hial'luyyn's was pale and translucent as wax. He studied Kahlil as if admiring a well-made clock.

"Lamansho Hial'luyyn'in'Jitamur." Alidas' voice carried easily in the hush of the room. "I present to you Kahlil Ravishan'in'Vundomu."

Hearing Alidas say his true name and title gave Kahlil a small shock. It seemed to lay him entirely bare. Ravishan, Kahlil allied to Vundomu. Most of his life the title of Kahlil had been his secret, an identity to which he had sacrificed his birth name and all acknowledgment. Now everyone in this room knew. More than that, they now knew that he had come from Vundomu and what that implied. He served Jath'ibaye. Kahlil heard audible gasps and someone made a strange choking sound.

Hial'luyyn remained unruffled. His serene countenance reminded Kahlil of the mystics who sought wisdom through fathi. But his eyes were too focused. He was not a man lost in a dream.

"It is an honor." Hial'luyyn bowed in his seat. The man's words were formal and almost musically elegant. Kahlil knew his own harsh northern speech would never match Hial'luyyn's scholarly refinement. But he couldn't just stand there like a mute, either.

"The honor is mine as well, Lamansho Hial'luyyn."

Hial'luyyn beamed at Kahlil as if his unlovely accent was exactly what he had expected to hear.

"Will you join me for this evening's meal?" Hial'luyyn asked.

"Certainly." Kahlil seated himself in the chair Hial'luyyn indicated. "Thank you."

"Alidas," Hial'luyyn said, "I have been presumptuous in having your seat brought to my table. I hope that you would be so kind as to indulge me."

"It would be a pleasure." Alidas' words were not as elegant as Hial'luyyn's but they were far more formal than what Kahlil was used to hearing from him. Alidas seated himself with a practiced ease.

"So." Hial'luyyn returned his attention to Kahlil. His gaze moved intently over Kahlil's features. "Alidas tells me that you are the Kahlil that never was."

"I suppose you could call me that," Kahlil replied. He wished he knew all of what Alidas had said. He stole a glance to Alidas but simply received a brief smile. He continued, "The ushman'im never wanted the common populace to know that a Kahlil was being trained. They published a denial of my existence the week that I arrived in Nurjima for my final blessings."

"Yes, I remember that there was a great deal of controversy at the time. The Usho and ushman'im were afraid the Gaunsho'im Council would rebel at the thought of unleashing a Rifter. Perhaps rightfully so," Hial'luyyn said. "Very few church documents concerning your existence survived the fall of the Black Tower. Three of them are in my possession. One is a portrait. You hardly look changed at all."

"I'm older," Kahlil said, embarrassed by the old man's warmth. "I was only twenty when I came to the Black Tower."

"Yes, but your eyes, your mouth, even your build are all the same. It's like looking at a document that has come to life."

Kahlil wasn't sure how to respond, but he was saved from having to do so by the entrance of two serving men maneuvering a large silver cart of steaming dishes. The servants, like the doorman, were both pallid and young. They seemed a little unnatural as they swiftly and silently distributed covered dishes to the men at the tables. Once the meal had been served, the two servants withdrew. Absently, Kahlil wondered how the club members ensured the loyalty of those who served them.

The ushman'im of the Black Tower had used holy words and sacred blood to bind stubborn initiates. Though maintaining that control had required the constant chanting of an attendant. Still, the blank expressions of the servants did remind Kahlil of a bound initiate.

"I hope you are not offended, but Alidas took the liberty of choosing a meal for you," Hial'luyyn told Kahlil. "Have you had bull's meat before?"

"Yes," Kahlil replied. "In Nayeshi. It is much more common there than here."

"Really?" Hial'luyyn carefully cut his own steak into small pieces. "Bulls are common there? It must have been a strange world."

"It was," Kahlil agreed. "The sun was blindingly intense and the nights were blacker than you can imagine. It took me years to adjust. Almost everything there was pungent and brilliant and loud. Sometimes it overwhelmed me."

"And the inhabitants, were they like ourselves?" Hial'luyyn inquired.

"Physically, you couldn't tell the difference. But their languages were entirely foreign. They knew nothing of Parfir."

"No, I theorized that they would not." Hial'luyyn looked slightly pleased and ate another bite of his steak. "He is the god of our world, not theirs."

Listening to Hial'luyyn, Kahlil suddenly realized that this man wasn't the ardent priest that he had expected. He was something utterly foreign to Kahlil: a scholar.

"What of the Rifter himself?" Hial'luyyn asked. "What was he like there?"

"He wasn't as powerful but he still affected the world. Even in Nayeshi, the plants, the soil, the water, everything seemed to feel his presence. It responded to him, but in small ways."

"Really? That is peculiar." Hial'luyyn set his knife and fork aside. "I think that goes a step toward proving that the world of Nayeshi is related to our own world. A cousin, if you will."

"Perhaps," Kahlil replied. He had never tried to analyze Nayeshi's relatedness to Basawar. He had simply accepted that both existed as they did by divine will.

"I think Mohimiri may be right that the two worlds were physically connected at one or more points in their ancient histories." Alidas made this comment casually to Hial'luyyn, as if this were the kind of thing he normally spent dinner discussing. Kahlil stared at Alidas for a moment, then speared a tiny herbed dumpling with his fork and ate it.

Alidas continued, "It isn't believable that both worlds should have the same race of people living on them by mere chance."

"Oh, yes," Hial'luyyn replied, "I quite agree. But what is the relation? Did our race cross through a Great Gate to colonize Nayeshi? Could the reverse have occurred?"

This was not at all the conversation Kahlil had imagined having. He had been preparing to talk to a zealot, a religious fanatic. But instead Hial'luyyn was bringing up questions that Kahlil himself had never even thought of pondering. He had simply perceived Nayeshi as a divine world cloaked in mystery. He had never considered why men, or bulls for that matter, existed in both worlds and why tahldi were exclusive to Basawar and cats only existed in Nayeshi. He had just accepted it all as Parfir's will.

He began to have the feeling that he might be the only religious fanatic in this room. As he listened to the quiet conversations of the men at the other tables, he became even more convinced. Many of them were talking about him. But they were not discussing his holy rank or how he had betrayed it. Instead, most of them seemed to be arguing about the extent of a Kahlil's abilities. How much was myth and how much was fact? One young man had raised his voice just enough to carry his words over all the other whispers. He asserted that Nayeshi was not a real place at all but a metaphor which Payshmura mystics dreamed up while indulging in too much fathi. The Kahlil was just a divine drunk.

A deep anger flushed through Kahlil. He had risked his life to reach Nayeshi. He had nearly died returning. It was for access to the wealth and plenty of Nayeshi that Ourath was willing to risk war with the Rifter. Nayeshi was not just some deranged priest's fantasy of women in men's clothes and roads packed with strange machines.

Kahlil turned toward the young scholar unable—and indeed unwilling—to conceal his growing sense of indignation. The young man leaned a little closer to his dinner companions, though he didn't lower his voice. "It's a pity that a sentimental, old man should be taken in so easily. I almost feel embarrassed for him." He glanced meaningfully to Alidas' back.

Insulting Alidas brought Kahlil's tolerance to an end. He snapped open the Gray Space between himself and the young scholar and without warning slammed his fist into the scholar's smug face. The scholar's head rocked back with the force of the blow and he toppled from his seat. He scrambled back to his feet, his face flushed brilliant red.

"Who did—" the young scholar began to demand but then stopped as he at last noticed Kahlil glowering at him. The rest of the men in the room had gone silent. Those who had witnessed Kahlil's fist appear from nowhere gaped at Kahlil in shocked horror. The majority of the men, however, had seen nothing but their fellow club member's sudden fall. They peered around in confusion. Across the table from Kahlil, Alidas shook his head ruefully.

Immediately Kahlil regretted his action. He had come here to ask a favor. Punching one of the club members was hardly going to help him in that. But Hial'luyyn's demeanor had not changed.

"Are you all right, Tevar?" he called out to the young scholar.

"I am, sir," the young man replied, hand still cupped to his face.

"Then I trust you can return to your seat." Hial'luyyn gave the command with a gentle smile. Instantly, the young scholar obeyed. Hial'luyyn then returned his attention to Kahlil. His benign smile took on a hint of genuine amusement.

"I was going to ask for a demonstration of your abilities but I see that they are all that has been written of them."

"I'm sorry I—" Kahlil began, but Hial'luyyn raised a hand to silence him.

"There's no need to apologize." Hial'luyyn's voice rose over the murmurs and whispers that filled the room. "Some of the younger men here are not used to thinking of the immense conviction behind the texts that they study. A holy man of the old faith is a rarity now, and some people do not know how to behave respectfully in such a presence. I hope you'll forgive the rudeness."

"Of course," Kahlil replied.

"Thank you." Hial'luyyn lowered his voice so that just Alidas and Kahlil would hear him now. "When you opened the Gray Space just now, it was so silent. After the reports I have read of Fikiri's comings and goings, I'm quite amazed." Hial'luyyn was again gazing at Kahlil with delighted fascination. And Kahlil realized that for Hial'luyyn he really was an ancient relic brought to life.

"It is rude to ask these things at the table, but would you do me the immense favor of reading something for me?" Hial'luyyn asked. "I know that your time is limited. You must return to Vundomu as soon as the papers you need have arrived from my office, but I would appreciate it."

"Yes, certainly." Kahlil felt a rush of relief. Alidas had already told Hial'luyyn everything and Hial'luyyn had already sent for the papers. Seconds before, the world could have ended in a matter of days. Now, salvation had been presented to him as if it were a common courtesy, as if it were his for the asking. Kahlil didn't think anything in his life had been so easily achieved. It seemed unreal to him. His relief verged on joy.

"Here it is, then." Hial'luyyn lifted a small parcel from his lap. Kahlil could see that it was a book swathed in several layers of silk.

Kahlil pushed his plate aside and took the book. The silk had not just been wrapped around it, he now saw. A finely embroidered case had been sewn for this book. Tiny pearl buttons clasped the case shut. Carefully, Kahlil removed the cloth. He stared at the book for several moments in surprise. It was not an original but an exquisitely detailed duplicate of the Nayeshi text, Dan the Milkman. The drawings had a distinctive Basawar style. The details of Dan's clothing were much too beautiful. His milk truck had taken on a mythical appearance.

"Can you read it?" Hial'luyyn's question came with quiet intensity.

"Certainly," Kahlil said.

"I knew that the Kahlil would be able to read it," Hial'luyyn said, beaming.

"I'd be happy to," Kahlil replied.

After they had finished their meal, Kahlil read and translated the short book as well as two other partial texts from Nayeshi. Hial'luyyn often asked him to repeat lines as he took notes.

"So many of the most profound Payshmura documents were written in the holy language," Hial'luyyn commented. "I almost despaired of ever reading them. But with these translations it should be much easier."

"I'm glad to help," Kahlil replied. Alidas simply leaned back against the edge of the table and looked pleased. He closed his eyes and listened as Kahlil read, first in the holy language and then in common Basawar. The younger men at the surrounding tables sat silently, straining to hear every word.

Three hours later the papers arrived from Hial'luyyn's office. Hial'luyyn signed them and then stamped each one with the Bousim seal. After slipping them into a tough leather pouch, he handed them to Kahlil.

"Thank you," Kahlil said.

"It is my pleasure," Hial'luyyn replied.

"Will everything be all right here?" Kahlil asked Alidas. "The man I hit—"

"Tevar?" Alidas smirked at the name. "That was probably the best thing that has ever happened to him. Don't worry. Even if Tevar did take offense, Hial'luyyn could silence him with a word."

Kahlil nodded. It followed that Hial'luyyn, a spymaster for the Bousim house, would know how to guard his own secrets. Kahlil wondered briefly what word it was that Hial'luyyn could use to silence Tevar. Was it an ancient binding spell from the Payshmura texts or some Eastern ritual, which Hial'luyyn had painstakingly translated?

Kahlil bowed to Alidas. "I must go now, but I wanted you to know that I'm in your debt."

He raised his hands in the Payshmura sign of peace. Alidas nodded and returned his gesture, though slowly, as though his fingers had not formed the sign in years.

"If I ever show up at your door, put me up for the night, all right?" Alidas asked the question lightly but Kahlil knew him well enough to answer seriously.

"You will always be welcome," Kahlil assured him.

Out of habit, he considered waiting until he'd exited the dining room to vanish into the Gray Space but saw in Alidas a certain anticipation building. Of all the men in the room, only Alidas had seen Kahlil's real skills. And everyone already knew who he was anyway. He might as well show off a little, for Alidas' sake. He opened the Gray Space and stepped inside.

He paused for one brief instant, surveying the shocked expressions on the faces of the men of the Domu'lam Club. Then he moved away, through the club walls and out of the city.

It astounded him that everything had gone so well and so easily. For all of the skills he possessed, the Unseen Edge, the Silence Knife, all he had really called upon was his friendship with Alidas. The thought offered Kahlil a reassurance that life was not always hard or cruel. Sometimes it could be miraculously kind.

Chapter Sixty-Nine

Two hours later Kahlil stood at the window of his room in the kahlilrash'im's barracks, watching banks of dark clouds roll in from the distant north. Both Jath'ibaye and Hirran had arrived late and inconspicuously dressed. After Kahlil had presented them with the papers from Nurjima, the two of them had set about reading through them in silent intensity.

In just over an hour they'd both read through every page and sorted the reports into a timeline of Ourath's treachery. Neat piles of crisp pages were spread across Kahlil's wooden table. Hirran's face looked almost luminous with joy. But Kahlil noted that Jath'ibaye's countenance had turned grim.

Outside his window, a fine rain began to fall and lightning crackled.

"No," Jath'ibaye said softly, "it won't work."

Kahlil glanced to him. Jath'ibaye scowled down at a single page with Ourath's name written clearly across it.

"What do you mean? Of course it will!" Hirran eyed Jath'ibaye. "Joulen asked for evidence and this is it. Ourath Lisam is clearly indicated time and time again as a conspirator against the interests of the Gaunsho'im Council. Three of these reports show that he was behind the attempted assassination at the Bell Dance. Just these three could send the gaun'im packing."

"If they got to the rest of the gaun'im," Jath'ibaye replied.

"Joulen swore that they would," Hirran insisted.

"Yes, but Joulen's authority comes from his uncle, Nivoun," Jath'ibaye said.

"Nivoun can't object to these papers. They're from his own house. Even he will have to—"

"Not if he is also in league with Fikiri," Jath'ibaye snapped. Kahlil felt a jolt at the thought of that.

"What do you mean?" Hirran looked startled.

"Here." Jath'ibaye picked up one of the pages and handed it to Hirran. Frowning intently, she scanned the page.

"It says nothing of Nivoun here," Hirran said.

"The agent didn't recognize him well enough to name him," Jath'ibaye replied.

"But you do?" Hirran demanded.

"I know things that the agent didn't. He reports here that Ourath thanked a hidden man for the Tah'iss texts. Ourath got those books from Nivoun Bousim. He told me so himself. The hidden member of the group, the man who introduced the others to Fikiri, is Nivoun." Jath'ibaye scowled. "I should have realized that Fikiri would have sought out an ally here in the north as well as in Nurjima."

"So what if Nivoun is involved?" Hirran asked suddenly. "I say we give the evidence to Joulen and—"

"And then he will present it to his uncle, Nivoun, who will either dismiss it as rubbish or see to it that Joulen has an unpleasant accident." Jath'ibaye collected several pages and straightened them.

"What if we tell Joulen that his uncle is involved?" Hirran asked.

"And what would Joulen do then?" Jath'ibaye asked. "Even if he believed us, Joulen wouldn't have the authority to take action. He can't bring charges against Ourath without Nivoun's authority. How is he supposed to start legal proceedings without Nivoun?"

Hirran sagged visibly. Kahlil watched the northern sky illuminate with sheets of lightning. Jath'ibaye was as frustrated as Hirran. Kahlil frowned out at the storm. They had been so close to success.

"What if we took these reports to another of the gaun houses?" Hirran asked.

"You think they'd just accept evidence presented to them by their Fai'daum enemies?" Jath'ibaye asked.

"They could confirm the authenticity…" Hirran trailed off as she realized whom they would turn to for confirmation of the authenticity of any document from the Bousim house. Nivoun Bousim.

"If we had more time…" Jath'ibaye began but didn't bother to go on. They didn't have more time. They only had a few days. "I'm sorry, Hirran."

Hirran bowed her head into her hands and Kahlil thought that she might be crying. He looked back out at the churning storm clouds while Hirran wiped her face and then straightened.

"What about Ji?" Hirran asked. "Has she had any luck?"

"Some," Jath'ibaye said, but he didn't sound hopeful.

Kahlil scowled at the white pages that littered the table. He had been so pleased with himself when he had brought them back. The ease of obtaining them had overjoyed him. It had filled him with a giddy optimism, an almost childlike sense that the world was on his side. Everything would be all right.

Kahlil silently cursed Nivoun. He hardly knew the man, but at this moment Kahlil hated him with a passion. He wished he could just kill Nivoun and remove this obstacle. But that would ensure a war. If only Nivoun would just drop dead on his own. If only he and Ourath would both fall into a pit and break their necks. Then no one could blame Jath'ibaye for the deaths.

Kahlil paused for a moment to think, not just fantasize. What if he could arrange for Nivoun and Ourath to remove each other? Then these reports might still be put to use. There would have to be more evidence. He would need a weapon that couldn't be traced back to Vundomu. Already, Kahlil's thoughts worked over the details of the execution. The blood would be tricky. His timing would need to be perfect.

"I think we can still bring Ourath down." Kahlil looked to Jath'ibaye. "But I need to know some things about him, about his preferences. I'll need you to get into his rooms."

Jath'ibaye didn't seem pleased by Kahlil's sudden announcement but said, "I'll get whatever you need."

"What are you thinking?" Hirran asked Kahlil.

"I'm thinking that we've been too honest and too kind to our enemies," he replied.

Jath'ibaye nodded just slightly, as if he already knew that it would come to murder.

It would have been relieving, even uplifting, if this one victory had come easily. But Kahlil had not lived a life of easy success gained through great social connections. His strength and skill lay in violence and always would.

Chapter Seventy

Kahlil turned the small pistol over in his hands. It looked absurdly beautiful. Engraved bulls charged over the silver filigree of the barrel. Delicate, curling initials had been etched into the casings of the silver bullets. Kahlil carefully loaded one after another into the chamber. The gun felt heavy but looked sleek. Even in the Gray Space, light gleamed along its edges. The gun seemed almost too attractive to function, but Jath'ibaye had assured him that it shot straight and smoothly.

Kahlil peered down the sight, taking aim at the side of Nivoun's face. It wasn't much of a challenge. Nivoun sat only a foot from where Kahlil stood. Nivoun resembled his son, Nanvess, strongly. He bore the same delicate features, even the same slightly upturned lips, which gave the impression of a smile where there was none. But he was older. Streaks of gray shot through his braided black hair like ribbons. Deep wrinkles cut across his brow and creased the corners of his mouth. Nivoun shifted in his seat. He picked up a supply request from his desk and read it over. Eventually, he signed the document and added his seal to the bottom.

Kahlil moved to the left and took aim again from the new angle. The shot wasn't quite clear. The bronze figurine of a young woman shielded much of Nivoun's bowed head. Kahlil moved again.

As the morning progressed, Nivoun worked through the stacks of papers and letters piled on his desk. More than once he glanced to the empty chair where his secretary should have been seated. Today the secretary was in his own room, feeling sick. One of Besh'anya's potions had ensured that he would remain ill for the entire day.

Kahlil circled the desk, mapping out his best shots. Again and again he took aim at Nivoun and then checked his surroundings. He had to be careful of the windows. They were wide and offered several nearby buildings a view of much of the room. Fortunately, Nivoun had chosen a room on the third floor of Gin'yu's guesthouse. Most of the surrounding buildings were only two stories high.

The cumbersome carved furniture that filled the room was both an advantage and a problem. Huge bookshelves offered Kahlil cover, but the iron studs and thick wood troubled him. The legs of the chairs were so sturdy that they reminded Kahlil of ship timbers. He wondered if the wood was thick enough to stop a bullet. With a small handgun like this one, there was a definite possibility that it could. He couldn't waste his one shot on a piece of furniture. As soon as the guards outside heard the report of a gun they would come rushing in. That meant he had one chance.

The door opened. One of the guards allowed Pesha into the room and then closed the door behind him. Pesha was dressed in the quilted clothes of a common street runner and a bulging courier's satchel was slung across her chest. In one hand she casually held the leather pouch that Hial'luyyn had given Kahlil. Nivoun frowned at the pouch. No doubt, he was recognizing the Bousim crest embossed into its surface.

Kahlil could hear nothing of the words that were exchanged, but he knew what Pesha was saying. He'd tutored Pesha in exactly what to say. He was surprised at how well Pesha acted. As she told Nivoun that the package had come from Ourath Lisam, Pesha's gaze lingered on a pretty figurine on Nivoun's desk. Pesha looked far more interested in the gleaming bronze than her apparent work. There was something inherently believable about her air of unconcerned distraction.

Nivoun took the leather pouch and dismissed her. He closed the door firmly the moment Pesha was out of the room. Kahlil watched Nivoun's features as he pulled out the pages of evidence and slowly read through them. Even from the Gray Space, Kahlil could see Nivoun go pale. An expression of growing horror spread across his face. Halfway through one of the reports, Nivoun suddenly strode to the windows and pulled the curtains closed. He collapsed back into his chair and continued reading. After he finished, Nivoun simply sat in his chair staring at the far wall.

Then, in a sudden burst of energy, he gathered the pages and stuffed them back into the pouch. He stood and paced around his desk, glancing again and again at the leather pouch. He had to be wondering what Ourath had meant by sending this to him. How had Ourath gotten his hands on these reports? Why hadn't he destroyed them?

Kahlil moved close to Nivoun, keeping pace beside him. Now everything depended on what Nivoun would do. If he were the kind of man who waited, then Kahlil would have to force the situation. But Kahlil was betting that Nivoun would not allow events to simply unfold. He would act. He was, after all, a man who plotted assassinations and planned to seize power over two worlds.

Nivoun went to the door and shouted out to the two rashan'im standing guard. Kahlil watched his lips form Ourath's name and demand that he be brought at once. Nivoun slammed the door shut. Kahlil smiled to himself.

Nearly two hours passed. Nivoun paced. He sent his lunch away untouched.

Ourath arrived looking impeccably groomed and annoyed. A boyishly pretty secretary trailed behind him, as did two guards. Kahlil didn't like having so many people in the room and neither did Nivoun. He snapped something at the secretary and the young man flushed. Almost immediately Ourath sent his attendants away.

As soon as the door was shut, Nivoun hurled the leather pouch to Ourath. Kahlil watched as Nivoun demanded to know what the meaning of it was. Nivoun's face was dark and Kahlil knew his voice was raised enough to carry through the door. The guards outside would know something was wrong. They would hear an argument brewing.

Ourath opened the parcel. He read a few lines and then looked up at Nivoun in outrage.

Kahlil's pulse raced. He cocked the pistol and stepped out of the Gray Space. The heat of the room surged over him. Ourath's voice roared in his ears.

"How dare you—" Ourath demanded of Nivoun. Then he went suddenly silent as Kahlil appeared almost on top of him.

Nivoun opened his mouth, began to call for his guards, and Kahlil fired the pistol. Nivoun's head rocked back. A gush of scarlet blood sprayed up from his forehead. He stumbled on his feet and then hit the floor. A breathless gasp escaped Ourath.

Kahlil dropped the pistol and threw himself back into the cold silence of the Gray Space.

The guards came through the door instantly. Nivoun lay on the floor, dead but still bleeding. Ourath stood staring in horror, spattered in Nivoun's blood. His pistol lay at his feet. The guards seized Ourath. He offered them little resistance. His face was white with shock. He still gripped the leather pouch in one hand. One of the many pages declaring him a traitor had fallen to the floor where Nivoun's blood began to soak through its white surface.

Joulen arrived minutes later. His expression was both sickened and lost as he knelt beside his uncle's body.

Kahlil watched Joulen's face as Joulen noticed the blood-stained page on the floor. In accordance with their plan, Hirran had already informed Joulen that she had sent the evidence against Ourath to Nivoun. Joulen caught sight of the pouch Ourath held. His sorrow contorted into raw fury as he tore the leather pouch from the other man's hand. Joulen dropped one hand to the holster at his hip, pulled out his gun, and aimed it at Ourath's face. For a moment, Kahlil thought that Joulen might shoot. Instead, Joulen holstered his weapon and turned away. He ordered the guards to shackle Ourath and remove him.

After the guards had gone, Joulen knelt back down beside his uncle's body. He bowed over the old man and wept.

Kahlil left him his privacy.

☾☾☾

Kahlil hunched under the water spigot, scrubbing at the dark brown spatters of dried blood. The water was almost steaming hot, but he still felt cold. A slight tremor passed through his hands as he brushed the soap into a lather and washed his hair. He thought he might vomit. The feeling passed.

This happened sometimes, after he had killed a man. When he was a boy it had been far worse. Now, this sick self-revulsion rarely came over him. It never lasted long.

Kahlil closed his eyes and rinsed the soap from his hair. The image of Joulen bowed in grief came vividly into his mind's eye.

He hadn't wanted to witness that. Kahlil had known, watching Joulen sink to the floor, seeing the way Joulen's hands touched Nivoun's body with such tenderness, that he would be sick with himself.

He did not regret killing Nivoun. Nivoun had needed killing.

Kahlil regretted the pain that Joulen had to suffer. The thought of mourners always disturbed Kahlil. He knew what they felt. The shock. The desolation. Their grief resonated through him. Kahlil usually went to pains not to witness the aftermath of his murders. But this time he had needed to be sure that Ourath was accused of the killing.

Another unwanted image flickered through his mind: his little sister screaming as the black smoke of their mother's witch's pyre rolled up before her. Rousma had screamed as though she had been in that fire herself. She had shrieked like she was dying, but the murder of their mother had saved her life. It had saved his life.

At times like this that knowledge did not console him. If he were honest with himself, it had never consoled him.

At times like this, he wondered if it would have been better if they had all died that day, so that his father, his mother, Rousma, and him could all be cradled in the arms of Parfir together.

There was a little song that the street girls used to sing in Amura'taye.

No one likes the butcher
No one likes the hunter
No one likes the man
With blood on his hands

He did not remember the rest of the song. But he recalled, even as a youth, thinking that people might not like a butcher but they still wanted to eat their meat. It was work someone had to do. It was work that took courage to do, because it was hateful and it left a man feeling ugly. But it had to be done; and it had to be done right.

Kahlil had done his work right. Neither Nivoun nor Ourath could now threaten Vundomu. All of the people of Nurjima would be saved because he'd had the strength to get blood on his hands. He could be proud of that. He had to be proud of that.

He stood and stepped out of the bath. The tremors that had shaken him so badly were nearly gone. Kahlil toweled his hair to a damp mass. His face looked pale in the shaving mirror.

He dressed. The clothes were new. They smelled of nothing and felt stiff in his hands. His old clothes were now ashes in the fireplace of the adjoining bedroom.

The bedroom was cold, the fire having died out completely. He must have lost track of time. He sat down on the bed. The room Wah'roa had given him was more spacious than most in the kahlirash'im's barracks, but it was still simple and unassuming with its bare, gray stone walls. A writing table and shelf had been crammed close together in the far corner like decorations that no one was ever expected to use. The old botanical tome that Kahlil had been translating sat alone on the shelf.

That was work that didn't leave a wake of orphans and widows. Of course, it was also work that in no way suited Kahlil. It bored him. He could only translate a page before his thoughts wandered and he began to long for something else to do. As a rule he approached it like a kind of penance. When he knew he had done something wrong he worked on it. The last time he had gotten more than a few pages done had been after he had infuriated Jath'ibaye by disappearing off to the northern chasm.

Kahlil stared at the book. No, he didn't feel that guilty. In fact, he didn't feel guilty at all. He just felt sad that a lying traitor like Nivoun still had people who cared for him. He wondered suddenly who would mourn Ourath. He had wives and children. Would they feel the same deep loss that Kahlil had felt when his own parents had been killed?

Would Jath'ibaye mourn? Kahlil hated to think that he would. Kahlil stood and walked to the window, trying to read Jath'ibaye's reaction to Ourath's death in the sky. A few faint white clouds clung to the horizon, telling him nothing.

Ourath didn't deserve Jath'ibaye's sympathy. He had betrayed Jath'ibaye unforgivably. He had planned the ruin of Vundomu and risked the destruction of all of Basawar. There should be parades and celebrations to mark Ourath's death. Kahlil couldn't help but imagine himself riding through the streets of Nurjima, hearing the joyous roar of the surrounding crowds cheering him for saving the whole world.

He had ridden into Vundomu like that once.

Kahlil smirked slightly at his own fantasy. In reality, he had been incredibly uncomfortable when the crowds of priests and kahlirash'im thronged around him in open worship. He had been overwhelmed by the walls of strangers who shouted his name. He had hated how their admiration had taken Jahn from his side.

Outside, the sinking sun began to streak the sky with gold and orange. Ranks of kahlirash'im filed into the big, brick dining hall. Kahlil supposed that he should join them. His nausea had long since passed and he was beginning to feel hungry. He wondered what would be served and hoped it wasn't dog.

There was a knock at his door. Kahlil guessed that it was Pesha coming to get him for dinner. Kahlil strode across the room and opened the door. Jath'ibaye stood with a heavy tray of covered dishes in one hand.

"I thought you'd be hungry," he said.

"I am." Kahlil stepped aside to allow him in. "If I had known you'd be delivering it, I'd have called for room service earlier."

"Well, you know, I can always use the tips." Jath'ibaye set the tray down on the writing desk. He turned back to Kahlil. "Joulen presented the evidence to the leaders of the other gaun'im's armies."

"Already?" Kahlil asked.

"He has the authority to do so now that he's inherited Nivoun's position," Jath'ibaye said. "They found Ourath guilty of murder and treason. Joulen executed him about an hour ago."

"How did that go?" Kahlil asked.

"Fast," Jath'ibaye replied. "Joulen's a good shot."

Kahlil nodded. He had expected more distress in Jath'ibaye's voice, more sorrow in his expression.

"I thought it would be worse than it was," Jath'ibaye said after a few moments. "It's funny. I almost feel guilty for being so relieved that he's dead."

"You shouldn't feel guilty for anything."

"I don't, really. I'm relieved that you did what I couldn't do. You saved countless lives today." Jath'ibaye frowned down at his own hands. "I don't always express myself all that well…particularly not when it's something that I feel strongly about."

"Yeah, I've noticed that." Kahlil smirked at Jath'ibaye's understatement.

Jath'ibaye offered him a wry smile in response.

"Well, today I want to make sure that you know that I'm proud of you and I'm incredibly thankful that you are here with me. I wouldn't—I don't want…anyone else." Jath'ibaye lapsed into a sheepish quiet.

"You said it well enough." Kahlil felt his cheeks warming. This was all the parade he could have wanted, Jath'ibaye standing before him with such open admiration and affection in his expression.

Kahlil stepped closer to Jath'ibaye and began unbuttoning his shirt. The tension melted from Jath'ibaye. He kissed Kahlil deeply.

The food could wait.

Chapter Seventy-One

The gaun'im's withdrawal reminded Kahlil of an awkward apology. Everyone involved wanted it over with quickly. The forces, which had so dramatically converged on Vundomu, now hurried away in disorderly regiments. No banners flew. Some rashan'im didn't even bother with formal formations. They simply packed and rode for the ships that would carry them downriver.

Kahlil watched the steady stream of departures from his vantage point in Jath'ibaye's watchtower at the height of Vundomu. He focused his telescope on the road south of Mahn'illev. A convoy of Milaun supply wagons came to a sudden halt. Two of the tahldi had become tangled. The driver jumped down and went to straighten the harnesses. He shouted angrily. Anyyd riders filed past the man. None of them offered any assistance. They were all far too demoralized to care about a Milaun supply wagon.

The gaun'im's armies had come as a unified force, bent on avenging their own, and then they had discovered that it was their own who had betrayed them. Ourath, Nanvess, and Esh'illan had plotted an assassination and died for it. There was no honor or justice in avenging them and certainly no grounds to demand compensation. That knowledge had destroyed more than the gaun'im's cause. It now fueled the petty rivalries and grudges that they had attempted to put aside. No doubt, many of them would have preferred to remain ignorant and justified. Now they looked like fools. And they could only blame themselves.

Small squabbles regularly broke out between the retreating ranks of the rashan'im. The clashes were particularly violent between the Lisam riders and those from the Bousim house. Their usual rivalry was blossoming into outright hatred. More than once the kahlirash'im had to intervene to avert bloodshed.

Oddly, there were very few transgressions against the people of Vundomu or any of the surrounding river towns. The gaun'im's armies seemed almost too embarrassed to involve themselves with even cursory looting.

"It's nice to see so much dissent among our enemies." Kahlil glanced from the telescope to Jath'ibaye.

"It's just good to see their backs," Jath'ibaye replied.

"Particularly with each other's knives in them," Kahlil added.

Jath'ibaye smiled in response.

"Do you think things will have settled down by the Bell Dance next year?" Kahlil asked.

"Why? Are you hoping I'll take you?"

"Well, the last one I attended went so well…"

"Yes. It went so well that I doubt either of us will be attending another for a few decades, at least," Jath'ibaye said.

"Decades? You really think it will take that long for the gaun'im to accept you again?"

"No, they're too greedy for iron," Jath'ibaye said. "But it might take that long before I'm willing to attend another of their social functions."

"At least you have an excuse for declining now. Before, it probably just seemed like you were some kind of a stick-in-the-mud."

"Stick-in-the-mud," Jath'ibaye repeated. "You remember the oddest phrases."

Jath'ibaye gazed thoughtfully out the wide window. Kahlil returned to his study of the stranded Milaun supply wagon. The driver appeared to be hurling filthy rags at the Anyyd riders as they passed by. Kahlil guessed there would be another fight soon.

"I couldn't have imagined that we would find a peaceful way out of this," Jath'ibaye said.

"Peaceful for us," Kahlil commented. "I think this Milaun boy is going to get his head knocked in."

Jath'ibaye gazed out over the scene, then asked, "Is that underwear he's throwing?"

"Don't know. I can't make it out," Kahlil replied. "If it is, where did he get it all?"

"No idea." Then after a moment, he offered, "Maybe he's the launderer for the Milaun camp."

"All of them? No wonder he's so blithe about throwing his life away." Kahlil set the telescope aside.

Jath'ibaye leaned out the window, closed his eyes, and drew in a deep breath of the warm spring air. Kahlil couldn't remember the last time he had seen Jath'ibaye simply enjoy a breeze. For the last week Jath'ibaye had closely controlled the weather, balancing the need for future crops with the threat of hungry bones in the north. He had manipulated the wind, humidity and cloud cover so intensely that Kahlil had almost forgotten that Jath'ibaye could let the weather do as it would. Watching Jath'ibaye now, Kahlil remembered how much John had loved the feel of wind on his skin.

Kahlil wanted to relax as well, but he didn't trust the sense of relief that pervaded him. Though the gaun'im might be leaving, Fikiri and Loshai remained, and as long as they lived, Kahlil's work was unfinished.

He turned to the northern windows of the watchtower. The hungry bones would be hunting soon.

Jath'ibaye glanced up at him. He frowned as he noticed the direction of Kahlil's attention.

"I need to practice moving through the Gray Space north of the Greenhills District," Kahlil said. "The last time I tried to follow Fikiri he lost me out there."

"You don't have to..." Jath'ibaye began but then stopped himself, studying the northern horizon.

"I must do this," Kahlil said. He expected an argument.

"I'll go with you." Jath'ibaye suddenly looked tired again.

Kahlil felt like an ass for ruining Jath'ibaye's carefree mood. But they couldn't allow victory on one front to lull them into a sense of safety while the other front still plotted their doom. Once Fikiri and Loshai were dead, they could enjoy spring breezes.

Kahlil said, "I'll get my coat."

Chapter Seventy-Two

At the northern tip of the Greenhills District, the Gray Space was thick and damaged. Scarred. The farther north Kahlil went, the worse it grew. The Gray Space here had a dense, ropey texture that resisted his passage. Other areas folded over the landscape, distorting Kahlil's view as if he was looking at it through warped glass.

A mile from the white edge of the northern chasm, Kahlil discovered another phenomenon. Each time he attempted to move forward through a particular patch of the Gray Space, it tossed him back twenty yards to the left. The motion sickened and disoriented him. Kahlil remembered it from the time he had attempted to follow Fikiri from Nurjima.

Kahlil studied the patch of the Gray Space. It hung in front of him, severed from the rest. As he moved around this thin, dark irregularity, he watched how the colorless world outside distorted. The irregularity was two fingers wide. It was as if someone had taken a narrow slice of the hills just to Kahlil's left and pasted it over the snow-flecked plain in front of him.

He could see a section of the abandoned stone path that he and Jath'ibaye had passed by earlier. Tough spring weeds edged the broken flagstones. Jath'ibaye stepped into Kahlil's view. He followed the path down the hill, passing out of the glimpse afforded by the fragment in the Gray Space.

Kahlil looked back to where Jath'ibaye approached. Jath'ibaye searched the Gray Space. Every day for last six days Jath'ibaye had tracked him down and brought him lunch. Perhaps it was an excuse just to make sure that Kahlil was still alive, but Kahlil appreciated both the company and the food. Today, Jath'ibaye only carried a rifle.

Kahlil stepped into the distortion. For a sickening instant he felt his body whip back. He dropped out of the Gray Space a few yards behind Jath'ibaye. Jath'ibaye instantly spun on him. A hard look flickered over his features, then disappeared.

"I could have sworn that you were up ahead of me," Jath'ibaye said.

"I was." Outside the Gray Space, the sun shone bright. The air felt hot. The few thin crusts of snow that remained on the ground glistened with beads of water as if they were sweating. "The Gray Space here has displaced patches. Almost like windows. They jump from one spot to another. I'm working out how to use them."

Kahlil strolled down the path toward Jath'ibaye. A warm breeze rolled over him and he could feel the sun on his face. After so long in the Gray Space, the fresh moving air felt cleansing.

"How's the planting going?" Kahlil asked.

"Good. The ground is warm enough to till." Jath'ibaye closed the remaining distance between them. His eyes lingered on Kahlil's neck. "You're cut."

"I hit a rough spot earlier. I had to force my way through." Kahlil was beginning to see why Fikiri moved through the Gray Space the way he did. "I got a couple scratches. Nothing bad."

Kahlil moved close to Jath'ibaye so that their shoulders brushed against each other. Jath'ibaye touched his hand lightly.

"No lunch?" Kahlil asked.

"I thought we should eat back at the Greenhills watchtower." Jath'ibaye studied the distant white strand of the northern chasm. "Hungry bones will be waking soon, and the district guards are testing the new landmines today. I don't imagine it'll be particularly peaceful out here."

Kahlil disliked the fields of mines that surrounded the northern front of the Greenhills District. In his youth, those same fields had been filled with golden taye. Minefields seemed like a terrible misuse of the land. When the people of the Greenhills District no longer had to protect themselves from hungry bones he'd be happy to see them again fertile, though he had no idea how they were going to remove all the landmines.

As soon as he had the thought, he knew the solution. Jath'ibaye would do it, of course. Probably using nothing but a shovel.

"Anyway," Jath'ibaye said, "Ji thinks she may have worked something out with the yasi'halaun, but she will need more of my blood to test it."

He lifted his arm, displaying his bandaged wrist. The fact that Jath'ibaye's wounds always healed quickly and mostly perfectly didn't make the sight of them less disturbing for Kahlil.

They followed the broken path back to the narrow dirt roads that the men and women of the Greenhills District used. Low stone walls lined the roads, creating a patchwork of crumbling old bricks, new black iron, and stone.

They walked close and at an easy pace. Jath'ibaye wasn't in a hurry to return to the Greenhills watchtower. Kahlil paused to study the collapsed remains of a cottage. It had to have been abandoned decades ago. The cracked weasel hutches now sheltered dozens of birds' nests.

"Blackwing flycatchers," Jath'ibaye said.

"It's amazing that anything lives out here," Kahlil said.

Just ahead of them the weedy plains gave way to open fields. Row after row of small white flags and earthen mounds filled the fields for miles. The flags designated newly laid mines. The only irregularities in the fields were random, blackened craters. Powdered ash and pieces of pale bone stood out starkly against the scorched soil. There used to be small farms all across these lands.

Now the inhabitants of Greenhills lived behind huge walls and kept vigil from their watchtowers. Kahlil looked up to the south. Even at this distance, the watchtower wall looked huge. Heavy guns and godhammers stood out from the red walls like black spines. Kahlil noticed a flash of reflected light from a telescope lens. Guards always stood ready at the watchtower waiting for movements from the north.

Kahlil waved.

"Making a new friend?" Jath'ibaye asked.

"Maybe." Kahlil wondered what kind of people chose to remain in the Greenhills District. He knew that many did not. Most of the people he'd met at the Greenhills watchtower were older. Perhaps they had faced worse odds in the first years of Vundomu. Or maybe they were just too stubborn to move.

Jath'ibaye began walking again and Kahlil strode next to him.

"Hirran arrived today," Jath'ibaye said.

Kahlil accepted the new subject without concern. Jath'ibaye was not a fluid or subtle conversationalist.

"She wants me to attend Nivoun's funeral in the Bousim lands," Jath'ibaye added.

"She probably wants you to show your support for Joulen. I think she has far-reaching plans for that unsuspecting fellow."

Jath'ibaye nodded but didn't say anything.

"But you're worried about the hungry bones and about leaving when you know Fikiri could still attack," Kahlil told him.

Jath'ibaye gave a slight nod.

"We should see what Ji has managed to come up with. We may be able to deal with the hungry bones and still allow you to go," Kahlil said.

Again Jath'ibaye nodded, though more reluctantly than previously.

"Your presence at Joulen's request would help to cement his authority. If you can go, you should." Kahlil watched Jath'ibaye's profile for any kind of telltale nod or headshake however minute. None came. "You don't want to go, do you?"

Jath'ibaye smiled a little as if appreciating a private joke.

"What?" Kahlil asked.

"You're so easy to talk to," Jath'ibaye said.

"I'm easy to not talk to," Kahlil offered, since Jath'ibaye hadn't really said much at all.

"That too," Jath'ibaye agreed. He seemed to be studying the tall, red wall ahead of them. They were close enough now that Kahlil could see two figures moving between the gun turrets that lined the top of the wall. A woman in scarlet strolled beside an angular, older man. It had to be Hirran and Tai'yu.

Hirran ducked under the barrel of a heavy gun. Catching sight of Kahlil, she waved. He returned the gesture.

Jath'ibaye turned off the main road and onto a side path that ran parallel to the Greenhills wall. Kahlil followed. The new path was sunken and so narrow that Kahlil had to walk behind Jath'ibaye. A low wall ran alongside, giving it the feeling of a trench.

"So is there anything I left out?" Kahlil asked.

"I hate these kinds of things."

"Funerals or state functions?" Kahlil asked. Then he added, "Or days that people test land mines?"

"I'd be hard pressed to say which I hate most," Jath'ibaye said. "Funerals, I suppose."

"I can't imagine that you'd be expected to do more than stand there looking somber," Kahlil said. "You do that all the time. There will be nothing to it."

Jath'ibaye stopped and looked back at him.

"I do not just stand around looking somber," Jath'ibaye said. "I also wander around looking somber."

Kahlil laughed and said, "Maybe Hirran can tether you to a spot."

"Maybe," Jath'ibaye said. "Could you come with me?"

"Possibly." Kahlil's attention strayed as they passed a crumbling section of stone wall. Pieces of bone jutted from it like shrapnel. Kahlil thought he heard hissing voices rising from the bone fragments.

"You don't want to?" Jath'ibaye asked.

"What? No, I'd like to be with you," Kahlil said. "I'm somewhat nervous about Joulen Bousim seeing me right away."

Jath'ibaye shot him a questioning glance.

"He noticed me when I was spying in Ourath's tent. Only for a moment, but I'd like there to be more time before he sees me again," Kahlil said.

"You shouldn't come then." Jath'ibaye stepped closer to Kahlil. "Let's not go back to the watchtower. We could spend the day away from everyone else." Leaning forward, Jath'ibaye kissed the side of Kahlil's neck and then his lips.

Kahlil's initial flush of embarrassment ignited into a rush of desire. He slipped his hands inside Jath'ibaye's coat and traced the lines of his body. He unbuttoned the top of Jath'ibaye's shirt. Jath'ibaye's skin was hot. His heartbeat quickened under Kahlil's touch.

"If you lean back against the wall—"

The rest of Jath'ibaye's whispered proposal was interrupted by shouts of, "Clear the field! Clear the field!"

Kahlil and Jath'ibaye both turned to look.

A group of heavily bundled men and women came running over the slight hill and threw themselves over the low wall onto the path. An instant later, a low muffled explosion sounded and a geyser of dirt kicked up into the air. Heavy clods plunged directly back to the ground. A spray of fine grit and dust rose on the wind and blew over both Kahlil and Jath'ibaye.

"Did I mention that they would be testing the new mines today?" Jath'ibaye asked.

"Yes, I recall now that you did," Kahlil said.

Kahlil glanced to the group of men and women crouching behind the wall. Several of them returned his gaze with expressions of confusion and surprise. His and Jath'ibaye's embrace was clearly not the sort of sight they expected to encounter on the narrow roads between their cratered minefields.

"Maybe we should keep moving," Kahlil suggested.

Jath'ibaye nodded. He looked to the group of men and women.

"Anything up ahead we should know about?" Jath'ibaye asked.

One younger woman shook her head.

They turned and continued walking. Behind them, Kahlil thought he heard someone mumble Jath'ibaye's name and his own with a tone of slight uncertainty. He wondered how long it would be before everyone at the watchtower knew. Then he wondered if it would matter if they did.

"I'm going to give you a bad reputation," Kahlil said.

Jath'ibaye shrugged. "It couldn't be worse than some of the things people just make up about my sex life."

"Like what?"

"Bones, demons. A few years ago, someone started a story about how I went out impregnating mountains and rocks." Jath'ibaye slipped his hand into Kahlil's.

"Rocks." Kahlil smirked. "That's a little macho, even for you."

"Just a bit," Jath'ibaye replied with amusement.

They walked farther along the winding path. A few stands of black saplings occasionally broke the barren minefields. The black trees were familiar to Kahlil. He studied the gentle hills, imagining them once again cloaked in forest. He knew this area, he realized. They weren't that far from where Amura'taye had once stood.

Kahlil was sure of it when they reached an old stone bridge. The bridge and narrow stream below were exactly as he remembered. He stopped.

Jath'ibaye looked back at him.

"I think I've been here before," Kahlil said. "We've been here before. Together. In the winter."

Jath'ibaye glanced at the bridge and then nodded. Kahlil studied the aged stones. He wasn't surprised to find his own initial awkwardly scratched into one of them. He crouched down and carefully pulled a single cracked stone aside. For a moment he actually expected to see the key still lying there, where he had hidden it so long ago. But only cobwebs filled the nook now. Kahlil stood back up, feeling oddly disconcerted.

"I'm confusing his memory and mine again," Kahlil murmured. He hadn't spoken to Jath'ibaye about his memories since the first night they'd slept together. He wasn't certain that he should now, but he wanted to be honest, if only with Jath'ibaye. "I keep thinking that I've got my life and his separated and then I come across something like this bridge and his memories all come back to me like they were my own." Kahlil closed his eyes only for an instant, but the memory poured over him. "I can smell the veru oil and blood. I remember how cold you felt in my arms…" Kahlil looked up at Jath'ibaye and recognized that careful stillness in him.

"It's not just his bad memories," Kahlil assured him. "There are glorious, wonderful moments of his that I recollect as well, like the week he spent in Nurjima with you—"

"But you don't want those memories?" Jath'ibaye asked.

"Of course I want them. Who wouldn't want the happiest memories of two lives? I just—I don't know that I deserve Ravishan's memories," Kahlil admitted.

"Because you aren't the same man?" Jath'ibaye asked.

Kahlil nodded.

"But you are the same man." Jath'ibaye held up his hand, cutting Kahlil off before he could object. "I've been thinking about this for a while now and just for a moment hear me out, will you?"

Kahlil felt an odd nervousness at the prospect of what Jath'ibaye might say, but he nodded.

"You've lived through two different histories and you've taken different paths in different circumstances," Jath'ibaye said. "But you have always been the same courageous, reckless, beautiful man."

Jath'ibaye moved close, placing his long hands on Kahlil's shoulders gazing intently into his face.

"I don't know if you remember this, but when we were in Rathal'pesha, I told you that I knew you'd become a fearless Kahlil. I knew that because I'd met you—Kyle. And you are fearless and resilient and loyal and strong and…" Jath'ibaye sighed as if he couldn't find a word to sum up all that he wanted to say. Then he pressed on, "No matter what circumstances have been thrown at you—whether I was with you or not—you've never stopped being any of those things. You are Ravishan and you are Kyle. It isn't one or the other."

Kahlil could feel his face flushing. He hadn't expected such an outpouring of adoration and emotion from Jath'ibaye.

"You have been giving this some thought, haven't you? Who knew you had so much free time?" Kahlil commented, if only to save himself from being drawn into further analysis of his own character. He'd known such failings and been so weak, but he didn't want Jath'ibaye to know those things about him.

"I have a vested interest in you, you know." Jath'ibaye seemed to sense Kahlil's desire to let the subject go because he added, "Where else am I going to find someone who can understand my pained memories of the Chicago Cubs?"

Kahlil laughed then and the two of them continued walking together. They conversed easily about unimportant things and absurd notions. Many of the intersecting paths they crossed offered more direct routes back the Greenhills watchtower, but Jath'ibaye didn't take them. Kahlil didn't mind. The two of them hadn't had much time alone lately. And he enjoyed the way Jath'ibaye's thoughts moved over such a range of subjects.

One instant he was noting the origami-like folds required for a beetle to hide its wings within the confines of its glossy wing case and the next he was pondering the Gray Space.

"It makes you wonder if the weave of time and space does unravel in places," Jath'ibaye commented.

"You think about the strangest things," Kahlil replied. "The weave of time and space?"

"I know it sounds odd, but don't you think that the connection is exceptionally tenuous within the Gray Space?"

"The connection between time and space, you mean?" Kahlil asked. He suspected that if Jath'ibaye and Hial'luyyn ever met they'd have a great deal to discuss.

"Yes," Jath'ibaye replied. "When you move through the Gray Space, it seems like you slip out of sync with normal time. Not as much as when you travel between worlds—"

"Through the White Space," Kahlil supplied.

"The White Space," Jath'ibaye said, "may be pure space stripped of all relation to time."

"But the Gray Space?" Kahlil asked and he found himself truly interested.

"It seems to only be loosely linked to time. Obviously time passes when you're in the Gray Space. And it always moves forward, doesn't it?"

"Yes, always," Kahlil replied. He had never really thought of the Gray Space like this.

"So, time exists in the Gray Space, but just barely. In a few seconds, you can move across distances, which in normal space would encapsulate days or longer." Jath'ibaye sounded thoughtful. "I wonder how exactly it functions."

Kahlil thought as well, trying to find an adequate answer as they continued along.

It made Kahlil smile. Here Jath'ibaye was, a god, attempting to understand the holy world as science.

And yet, Jath'ibaye's words made Kahlil think as well. If he traveled through space without time, then the issusha'im traveled through just time. They never left their physical location but they saw hours, years, decades, even centuries beyond the realms of their bodies.

"Damn it." Jath'ibaye's quiet curse snapped Kahlil out of his contemplation.

A large party of familiar people walked up the path toward them. Ji was in the lead. Behind her Kahlil could see Saimura and

Besh'anya. Tai'yu and Hirran, as well as their various attendants and secretaries, followed. Kahlil even thought he glimpsed Pesha at the back of the long procession.

Besh'anya waved. Kahlil reluctantly waved back.

"Someday you and I are going to go somewhere where no one else will find us," Jath'ibaye muttered.

"Who'd cook?"

"We'll pack sandwiches."

"Jath'ibaye!" Tai'yu called out as they came closer. "Ji said we would find you here."

Kahlil noticed the brief annoyed glance Jath'ibaye shot at Ji and her responding smile.

"What is it that you need?" Jath'ibaye asked. His tone had lost the relaxed warmth of his private conversation with Kahlil. Even his posture altered. His back was suddenly rod straight, his shoulders squared. His grip on his rifle tightened as he lifted it so that the barrel rested against his shoulder. He strode forward with mechanical precision. Kahlil followed Jath'ibaye but gave him a little more room.

"Hopefully we won't need anything but blood," Ji replied. "If the rituals I've used on the yasi'halaun don't hold, then we may need you to deal with hungry bones, but otherwise, just blood."

Jath'ibaye began to unbutton his cuff.

"I've already used the yasi'halaun to destroy the souls trapped in shards and fragments of bones," Ji went on. "Now we need to see how it will affect those that are still intact."

Kahlil took in the gray hilt that jutted up from the sheath strapped across Saimura's back. It looked longer than Kahlil remembered. Kahlil wondered how big it would get after devouring hungry bones the size of fishing boats. They might need a cart to move it after a while.

Jath'ibaye turned back to Kahlil. "We'll have to go back to the chasm. It could take all day. You don't have to come along if you don't want to."

"I'll come," Kahlil said firmly. The thought of Jath'ibaye and the yasi'halaun both so close to Fikiri and Loshai worried him. "But maybe you shouldn't. The yasi'halaun was created to—"

"I know. But I have to go. Ji is right about needing me to deal with the hungry bones."

"Then we'll both go," Kahlil stated. "Together."

☾☾☾

Afternoon sun radiated off the white sands running along the edge of the northern chasm. Waves of heat distorted the gray line of the horizon. Kahlil pulled off his coat and folded it over his arm. Pesha had already discarded her jacket in a heap along with Besh'anya's medical bag and Saimura's coat.

Kahlil glanced to Jath'ibaye. His face was flushed with heat.

"Give me your coat. I'll put it with the others," Kahlil said.

Initially, he thought that Jath'ibaye hadn't heard him. Jath'ibaye simply stood, staring out past the edge of the chasm where the mist rose up from the ocean far below like a bank of clouds. Kahlil could just make out the faint silhouette of a tower. Jath'ibaye was never at ease near the northern chasm. Here, almost at its edge, his agitation intensified into a fixation on a single point. He watched the mists writhe over the remains of Rathal'pesha. He seemed almost unwilling to even look at Kahlil.

"You're going to smell like an old sweat sock if you don't take your coat off," Kahlil said.

Jath'ibaye automatically removed his coat. The cuffs of Jath'ibaye's shirt barely hid the mass of bandages that wrapped his wrists. It embarrassed Kahlil to feel so sickened by the sight of them.

Jath'ibaye's gaze remained fixed on the tower in the north. He shifted the weight of his rifle against his shoulder. His expression was set in a hard frown. When his gaze did flicker to Kahlil, he flinched as if seeing him here, and remembering Ravishan's death in Rathal'pesha, caused physical pain. Kahlil took Jath'ibaye's coat and said, "It's not going to happen again."

"I know." Though Jath'ibaye's expression softened, he didn't relax his vigilance.

Far south of the white bone sands Kahlil saw the flash of glass lenses in the brilliant sun. Both Hirran and Tai'yu had chosen to wait with their attendants and secretaries far back on the plains. There they would be safer and probably more comfortable as they observed the demonstration through telescopes.

It was hard to believe there had been snow on the ground that morning. Saimura moved slowly around Ji, enclosing her in a circle of carved stones. The ring would protect Ji when the yasi'halaun drew the souls from the hungry bones. Besh'anya followed Saimura, whispering Eastern incantations and daubing each of the stones with blood from a large brown glass bottle. Kahlil couldn't help but stare at the bottle full of Jath'ibaye's blood. Besh'anya carried it almost like a child, slung between her hip and the crook of her elbow. Ji lay on the sand, stretched out and panting.

Kahlil strode to where Pesha sat guarding the yasi'halaun. Kahlil tossed his and Jath'ibaye's coats into the pile with the others.

Pesha squinted up at Kahlil.

"Do you think the devil will come?" Pesha asked in a whisper. Like Jath'ibaye, Pesha scanned the horizon, but Pesha didn't know what she was looking for. Her dark eyes darted from one rolling mass of mist to another.

"He might," Kahlil admitted.

Pesha shuddered.

Kahlil crouched down next to her. The sand was searing hot and for a moment Kahlil wondered how Pesha managed to sit cross-legged on it. Then he realized that Pesha was sitting on Besh'anya's coat.

"If Fikiri does appear, you aren't to stay here, you know that?" Kahlil said.

Pesha glanced at the long sheathed blade of the yasi'halaun.

"I take the yasi'halaun and get back to Vundomu," Pesha said quietly, as if Fikiri might somehow overhear the plan.

Kahlil nodded. Pesha had managed several crossings through the Gray Space now. She couldn't go far, but she would be able to get the yasi'halaun out of Jath'ibaye's physical proximity. That would leave Kahlil free to deal with Fikiri.

"What about Besh'anya and everyone else?" Pesha asked.

"They know what they're doing," Kahlil replied. He glanced to Jath'ibaye's back. "You have to trust them to defend themselves, you know."

Pesha frowned down at her scratched hands.

"What if Fikiri comes after Besh'anya? He tries to make women like her into hungry bones."

"So, you'd rather stay and defend her?" Kahlil asked.

Pesha flushed a little.

"I know how you feel," Kahlil said. "But you have another duty."

Pesha looked up at him with a startled expression.

"You like Besh'anya?" Pesha asked.

"No, that's not what I meant." Kahlil almost laughed at the flustered jealousy in Pesha's tone. "I'm not attracted to Besh'anya. I just meant that I know how it feels to want to protect someone."

Pesha nodded, seriously.

Kahlil watched Saimura and Besh'anya. He could hear Ji whispering low invocations beneath Besh'anya's chanting. Saimura stayed silent, but he swayed with the distinct rhythm.

Kahlil thought he could hear other sounds. Tiny whispers rose from the thousands of bone pebbles all around him. Kahlil listened intently, trying to pick out a coherent sentence or a single voice. There were just noises, animal growls, groans, and gasps. They drifted into each other, becoming an ambient hiss that sounded like the breaking waves of the ocean far below the chasm.

Kahlil's attention drifted to Jath'ibaye's back. He studied Jath'ibaye's broad, straight shoulders and gazed at the way his body tapered down to lean hips. His heavy black pants hid the muscle of his buttocks and thighs, but Kahlil knew how taut they would feel under his hands. Jath'ibaye's skin would be hot.

"What's he like?" Pesha's question suddenly intruded into Kahlil's thoughts.

"Who?" Kahlil asked. Then he saw that Pesha, too, was studying Jath'ibaye. Her expression was troubled. "Jath'ibaye?"

"I've never seen him smile," Pesha said.

"Surely you have."

"Only at you," Pesha responded. The truth of Pesha's words embarrassed Kahlil.

"He's very private."

"He's so powerful. Why does he need a Kahlil?"

"To protect him," Kahlil responded.

"What could hurt him?"

"Anything that hurts a man can hurt him," Kahlil informed her. "Almost nothing can kill him, but hurting him is a different thing. He feels everything you and I feel. Sometimes I think he feels more. If you become his next Kahlil, it will fall to you to keep him from harm."

Pesha stared at Jath'ibaye solemnly. "Wah'roa says that the Kahlil must be bound to him."

"Yes, that's true."

"What does that mean exactly?" Pesha asked.

"It's a ritual."

"But what does it do?" Pesha moved slightly closer to Kahlil.

"It links the two of you. You feel his presence and it draws you to him." Kahlil shrugged as if it were nothing. He knew that it would only worry Pesha to tell her how Jath'ibaye's presence electrified his body and aroused his spirit. When he was near Jath'ibaye, the wind felt alive and the air tasted lush and exotic.

"Does it hurt?" Pesha inquired.

"No," Kahlil assured her.

"Will it change me?" Pesha asked. She glanced briefly to Kahlil, then looked quickly down at her hands.

"Of course," Kahlil said. "But it won't make you into someone you aren't."

"But could it make me feel different about Jath'ibaye?" Pesha's voice was so quiet that Kahlil had to strain to hear her. Kahlil studied Pesha's bowed head, unsure of what Pesha was attempting to ask. Then he remembered Jath'ibaye's comment about Wah'roa lecturing the kahlilrash'im on the sacred bond between the Rifter and his Kahlil.

"It won't make you his lover, if that's what you're worried about," Kahlil said.

"It won't?" Pesha's relief was visible.

"No." Kahlil shook his head. "But being Kahlil means that your life is dedicated to him. You don't have to be his lover but you must love him. That doesn't come from the bond. It has to exist within you. Either the feeling is there or not."

"If it isn't?" Pesha asked.

“You shouldn’t be his Kahlil. There are lots of other things to do with your life,” Kahlil said.

“Would you still train me, if I didn’t…” Pesha’s question drifted into embarrassed silence.

“So long as you are willing to be trained, I will train you,” Kahlil replied. “I’m not going to throw you out just because you’re attracted to Besh’anya and not to Jath’ibaye.”

“I tried to feel that way about him,” Pesha admitted. “But I just couldn’t.”

“There’s no point in forcing yourself.” Kahlil smiled at Pesha. “I wouldn’t really appreciate the competition, anyway.”

Pesha looked up at him, startled. Then she shyly returned Kahlil’s smile. “I guess you wouldn’t.”

Besh’anya painted the last stones with Jath’ibaye’s blood. The blood glowed as it soaked into the carved surface of the stones. Black symbols seeped out from the stones, letters of Eastern script. Kahlil couldn’t read them. They twitched like tiny spiders.

Besh’anya and Saimura both went silent. The low murmurs of Ji’s voice rolled through the air. Her words throbbed like the echoes of thunder.

Ji spat on the ground and the black symbols rushed in over her like a swarm of insects. The symbols crawled through Ji’s yellow fur and dug down to her skin. Tiny black forms crawled over her face. They swam over her yellow eyes. Her tongue and the pink flesh of her mouth darkened as she continued speaking strange Eastern words.

“Is that supposed to happen?” Pesha whispered to Kahlil.

Kahlil glanced to Saimura.

Saimura watched the black symbols with calm interest for a few moments, then returned to his own work. He braided copper wires around a pure white stone. Besh’anya watched Ji in fascination. Jath’ibaye glanced back once and then returned to studying the northern horizon.

“I think so,” Kahlil replied.

Ji went suddenly silent. With a loud crack, all of the stones split and a wave of searing wind rushed in over Ji. The black symbols encased her, glowed red, yellow, and at last, a blinding white.

"Bring the yasi'halaun. Now." White light glowed from Ji's mouth and throat as she spoke. Kahlil grasped the yasi'halaun and brought it to her.

"That's good," Ji said once Kahlil had come within reach of her. "Unsheathe it."

Kahlil did as Ji instructed. The yasi'halaun was longer than it had been and also thinner. The hilt in particular had changed. It had shaped itself into a sharp tip, like an ice pick.

"Drive it into the ground, blade up," Ji said.

Carefully, Kahlil pushed the hilt of the yasi'halaun into the pebbled ground. He expected it to fall but it remained upright. The tip of the blade nearly reached Kahlil's chin. It was flatter than before and there were marks that had never been there. Hundreds of long parallel lines etched the surface of the blade.

"Besh'anya," Ji called, "anoint the blade."

Immediately Besh'anya moved to Kahlil's side. She lifted the jar of Jath'ibaye's blood and poured just a few drops over the blade. The blood trickled down the tiny grooves in the blade. The bloody trails began to steam and glow.

"Get back!" Ji commanded.

Besh'anya rushed behind Ji. Kahlil strode toward the chasm, keeping his body between Jath'ibaye and the yasi'halaun. Jath'ibaye stepped closer to him and their hands brushed against each other.

"Don't go too far," Jath'ibaye said.

Ji began chanting again. This time she spat words quickly, with the angry intensity of commands. The yasi'halaun shuddered. The needle-thin grooves in the blade began to separate into long spines. They spread like fingers fanning out. Arcs of light leaped from the tips and danced over the ground. Kahlil could hear the pebbles of bones gasp and then go silent. The bones looked powdery, like the ashy remains of coals. They crumbled and scattered on the breeze.

Arcs of light bolted from the yasi'halaun toward Ji. The blazing symbols that covered her flashed like lightning. The yasi'halaun's hungry arcs split and speared the surrounding ground. Steam rose off of Ji's hide. She clenched her eyes closed and continued her furious chanting.

Saimura stood and held up the stone he had bound in copper wire. It resembled a skull but was far smoother. Saimura whispered something over the stone and then he laid it down on the ground. Kahlil felt a soft throb pass through the ground.

"It will summon hungry bones," Jath'ibaye said. "Hopefully no one else."

The arcs of light from the yasi'halaun danced and bolted over the ground, devouring hundreds of trapped souls at once. The arcs snapped and crackled and split into more and more tongues of light as they continued feeding. Again and again the yasi'halaun attempted to feed on Ji but her protections held.

Jath'ibaye tensed slightly and turned to the east and said, "The bones are coming."

At first the waves of heat rolling over the white sands disguised the hungry bones. But steadily Kahlil differentiated the white serpentine form from the white hills around it. It moved like a centipede and with alarming speed. Most of its massive body had come from some huge undersea creature. A skull that was nearly all teeth gnashed through the pebbled sands. Long quills of bone arched from its spine. Kahlil imagined that they might have once been the supports for huge dorsal fins.

The bones that supported the creature were obviously the remnants of dozens of tahldi. Their legs bounded over the sands. Their skulls snapped furiously from where they hung amidst the huge sea creature's ribs. The bodies of animals it had already devoured hung inside the hungry bones like organs. Some were newly impaled and still bleeding. Kahlil thought he could make out the form of a human torso. The roar of the hungry bones drowned out the distant ocean and split through Ji's chanting.

Jath'ibaye lifted his rifle.

A sound almost like a sigh came from the yasi'halaun. Suddenly the arcs of light shot out and burst through the hungry bones. The roar of the hungry bones became a wrenching scream. It writhed and jerked as the bones of its body crumbled to ash. Kahlil could feel its body slamming into the ground as it tried to shake free. But the light of the yasi'halaun was like a voracious disease. It leaped from bone to bone in thousands of blazing arcs. It flashed across the surface of the bones and the bones blew away in streams of ash.

It was growing stronger, Kahlil realized. He glanced back to Ji. Her head was bowed. Steam rose from her body and escaped her open, gasping mouth.

The moment that the hungry bones collapsed completely, the yasi'halaun's lights arched back and slammed down against Ji. The symbols protecting her burned a dull yellow. She swayed slightly but continued her chanting, her voice low and commanding.

Steadily the yasi'halaun folded closed. Its greedy tongues of light flickered, crackled, dimmed, and then disappeared.

Ji sighed heavily. Saimura went to her side and offered her water from his canteen. She flopped down on his lap.

"I'd call that a success, wouldn't you?" Ji asked breathlessly.

"It was amazing!" Pesha's voice and face showed her unabashed awe.

Kahlil looked to Jath'ibaye, whose attention remained fixed on the distant ruins in the north. The gray mists churned and rolled. Flickers of red light exploded through the darkening clouds. Kahlil wondered what sort of sorcery those lights portended.

"We should get back to the watchtower," Jath'ibaye pronounced.

Kahlil went immediately to retrieve the yasi'halaun. It had grown still longer and the fine lines that had marked the blade were now pronounced grooves. Kahlil felt an electrical hum pass through his hands as he pulled it from the ashen ground. The buried hilt had grown as well. It stretched out like a thirsty taproot. It was too long for its scabbard now, stretching up almost as tall as him. Kahlil wrapped it in his coat.

Jath'ibaye walked to his side.

"You want me to carry it?" Jath'ibaye gestured to the yasi'halaun.

"It's not as heavy as it looks," Kahlil replied. He studied Jath'ibaye. "You look worried."

Jath'ibaye nodded. Kahlil knew he was thinking about Loshai and Fikiri. Kahlil didn't want to bring it up, particularly in front of other people.

"Can't figure out what you're going to wear to Nivoun's funeral?" Kahlil asked.

Jath'ibaye smiled at the question. "Yeah, that's what I'm wondering about."

As they marched back over the ash and sand, they heard cheers rising from the rocky plains. Tai'yu whooped. Hirran bounced up and down, waving her arms and grinning like an overjoyed child. The line of a dozen attendants and secretaries had easily tripled. Common men and women as well as guards clapped and hooted. Kahlil thought he recognized several of the people from the group who had been testing mines. There were no traces of confusion or horror in their faces now. They laughed and grinned as joyously as the rest.

Chapter Seventy-Three

Kahlil sprinted forward. Behind him, hungry bones tore through the dunes of white sand and dark ash. The hisses and growls of the hungry bones rolled over Kahlil like waves breaking above his head. Sand slid under his feet. He stumbled and forced himself to keep running. His lungs burned. His thighs felt like they were turning to liquid as he broke over the rise of the last dune.

Below, he could see white arcs burst up from the yasi'halaun's dark form. Ji looked tiny beside it. Besh'anya, Saimura, and Pesha were farther back. Kahlil threw himself forward, half-running, half-sliding through the sand and ash.

Behind him, the hungry bones surged over the rise. They leaped down after him. Their immense bulk loomed over him, blotting out the sun. Kahlil dropped into the Gray Space. The frigid cold struck him like a shock of ice water. The hungry bones slammed into the sand and tumbled down the dune.

Even from within the Gray Space, the arcing white lights of the yasi'halaun were blindingly brilliant. They shot out instantly, ripping through the hungry bones and devouring the souls trapped within. In seconds only heaps of ash remained.

Kahlil stepped out of the Gray Space and collapsed down next to Pesha.

"That one was huge," Pesha said.

Kahlil just nodded. His heart was still hammering in his chest.

"Have some water." Besh'anya handed her canteen to Kahlil. He drank deeply.

"Thanks." Kahlil returned the canteen to Besh'anya.

"Are nine enough or are you up for another run?" Saimura only glanced up briefly from the stones and wires in front of him. "None of these summoning stones are ready yet."

Kahlil looked to Ji.

Arcs of the yasi'halaun's light lashed continually at Ji's defenses now. Eastern wards flared from Ji's body, forming luminous halos around her. Ji ignored them and continued to chant the ritual that controlled the yasi'halaun. Steam rose off her as if she were cooking from the inside out. Three days of controlling and resisting the yasi'halaun's hunger had burned away what little flesh there had been on her body. Her hide hung over her bones like a discarded washcloth. The few remaining hungry bones were those hunting along the edge of the chasm. They had to be lured closer to the yasi'halaun by a living body.

The sooner they finished with the hungry bones the better.

"I can try for another if Ji's up to it," Kahlil said.

Ji didn't even bother to open her eyes. She gave the briefest nod of her head. Kahlil got to his feet and dusted the ash off his legs. The muscles of his thighs trembled. Just one more run. There couldn't be many more hungry bones remaining.

Already the white sands of the northern chasm were transforming into miles of gray ash. Twilight breezes easily lifted the fine ash and sent vast plumes rolling across the yellow sunset, turning it orange. The air smelled of fires.

Pesha coughed. Besh'anya handed her a kerchief to tie over her nose and mouth.

"I told you that you'd want one," Besh'anya said.

"And you are as wise as you are lovely," Pesha replied. "Thank you."

"You're welcome." Besh'anya laughed at the flirtation and offered Pesha a motherly smile. "Though you should save a little of that flattery for the Greenhills girl you were charming last night." Then Besh'anya's attention shifted to Kahlil.

"If it gets much darker, you won't be able to see." She stepped closer to Kahlil and lowered her voice to a whisper. "Ji needs to rest. She just won't say so."

Kahlil nodded.

"Yeah, now that I'm standing I can really feel the strain in my legs," he said. "I don't know if I could make another run like that last one. Sorry, Ji, but I think we'll have to call it a day."

Kahlil noticed the look of relief that flickered over Saimura's expression. He wondered if Saimura had purposefully refrained from finishing any more summoning stones.

Again Ji offered only the slightest nod of her head. The low words of her chant changed. Slowly the needlelike spines of the yasi'halaun began to fold back down into a massive blade. Kahlil sat back down next to Pesha.

The knowledge that he wouldn't have to run again was like a release for the exhaustion he had been holding back. Now fatigue flooded his body. He closed his eyes, forehead resting on his arms. Maybe tonight he would sleep well. It had been hard with Jath'ibaye gone. His dreams had been more troubled. That voice kept calling him, whispering to him all night.

"Kyle'insira?" Pesha's whisper unnerved him, but he didn't open his eyes.

"Yes?"

"I wanted to ask you about something."

"Is it important?" Kahlil asked. He prayed it wasn't more about Besh'anya. He didn't know how much more he could manage to speculate about her attributes with Pesha.

"I don't know," Pesha said. "It's just a strange patch of space I've been watching."

Kahlil instantly opened his eyes and sat up.

"Where?" Kahlil demanded. "Don't point. Just tell me."

"Just in front of Ji," Pesha said. "All afternoon the yasi'halaun kept striking that spot, but there's nothing there, is there?"

As Kahlil watched, a last tongue of the yasi'halaun's light crackled at the empty air again and again. Something there attracted the yasi'halaun's hunger. None of them could see it, but the yasi'halaun sensed it. Something was there, waiting in the Gray Space.

"Shit." Kahlil bounded to his feet.

The yasi'halaun had already snapped closed. Ji knelt down on the ground in utter exhaustion.

"Ji," Kahlil shouted. "Move!"

The Gray Space screamed as it ripped open wide. Ji shoved herself back up to her feet. She swayed unsteadily. Geysers of flame licked the torn edges of the Gray Space and the massive centipede-like bulk of hungry bones surged out. Behind it, Kahlil caught a glimpse of Fikiri.

"Pesha," Kahlil yelled, "move your ass now!"

Behind him, Kahlil heard Besh'anya's startled cry. Saimura screamed Ji's name.

The hungry bones smashed down on top of Ji. Her body crumpled under them. Kahlil heard her yelp. Then he plunged into the silence of the Gray Space. The hungry bones pounded over Ji's broken body as they bounded toward Pesha, Saimura, and Besh'anya.

Fikiri was still somewhere in the Gray Space. Kahlil concentrated on the texture of the Gray Space. Then he caught Fikiri's movements. A faint ripple passed through the colorless landscape as Fikiri moved just beneath its surface.

Fikiri strode toward the yasi'halaun. Kahlil raced through the Gray Space after him. Fikiri was closer but Kahlil was faster.

Fikiri dropped out of the Gray Space. His form became perfectly clear. He smiled in triumph as he extended his hand toward the yasi'halaun. Kahlil only had an instant to stop him. He lunged into the space occupied by Fikiri's body and slashed through the thick Gray Space, aiming to rip the other man in half from the inside out.

Fikiri felt Kahlil's presence a moment too soon. As Kahlil tore his way out of the Gray Space, Fikiri dropped back into it. For a sickening instant, their two bodies passed through one another.

Kahlil burst out of the Gray Space. Nausea and dizziness rushed over him. He staggered and almost fell. His vision briefly blurred into a haze. He clenched his eyes shut to help them clear.

"Pesha!" Kahlil shouted blindly. "Get the yasi'halaun out of here!"

He could hear the roar of the hungry bones and Besh'anya shrieking out a string of Eastern invocations. Finally, his vision cleared.

The hungry bones arched up over Besh'anya. Besh'anya stood with her hands raised, gripping a heavily engraved stone. With each word Besh'anya shouted, a dull gold light pulsed from the stone. Saimura knelt beside Besh'anya, desperately drawing symbols in the ash at her feet. His low voice droned beneath Besh'anya's. The hungry bones swayed back and forward in time with the pulses of the stone in Besh'anya's hands. Steam rose from between her fingers.

Neither Fikiri nor Pesha were anywhere to be seen.

Kahlil turned back to the yasi'halaun. The long dark blade still jutted from the ashen ground. Beside it, Ji's crushed body lay in a pool of dark blood. A sharp pang of anguish shot through Kahlil. This time he would find Fikiri and kill him.

Kahlil plunged back into the Gray Space.

He found his enemy at once. Fikiri had broken into the Gray Space that Pesha occupied. Their desperate movements sent waves of distortion through the colorless landscape. They heaved and rolled as one mass. Kahlil made out the shadows of thrashing limbs.

Kahlil moved next to them and punched through the membranous wall of the Gray Space. He tore deep into the Gray Space but not through to the outside world. His entire body ached from the exertion. The texture of the Gray Space bit into his hands as he ripped it farther open.

His fingers brushed over moving bodies. He groped for a hold on Fikiri. At last he caught hold of a mass of Fikiri's dirty blond hair. He gripped tightly and jerked Fikiri back from Pesha. The membrane of the Gray Space tore further as Kahlil wrenched Fikiri through it. The ragged edges slashed them both.

Kahlil caught only a glimpse of Pesha. Dark blood poured from her nose and mouth. Her eyes were wide in fear.

The opening between them snapped closed, leaving a ropey scar in its wake. Kahlil prayed that Pesha would have the presence of mind to do her duty.

Fikiri twisted in Kahlil's grip and pulled free. He spun to face Kahlil. Both of them drew their black curse blades. Guns were worthless in the Gray Space. The bullets simply didn't move quickly enough. They circled each other. Kahlil needed this to be a fast fight. He didn't have the strength left for a drawn out battle. He guessed that Fikiri knew as much.

A strangely smug smile flickered over Fikiri's features. Fikiri bolted backwards. Kahlil lunged after him. Fikiri threw himself through a faint distortion in the Gray Space. Kahlil charged past it. He wheeled around, searching for Fikiri.

Yards ahead, Fikiri dropped out of the Gray Space almost on top of the yasi'halaun. He grabbed the hilt and jerked it up from the ground. Kahlil raced for Fikiri, but he knew he was already too late. Fikiri staggered slightly as the full weight of the yasi'halaun slumped against his body. He would be gone in an instant.

At Fikiri's feet, Ji suddenly jerked upright. Her hide was black with blood and pieces of her bones jutted up from her flesh. She pushed herself up onto her broken hind legs.

Fikiri started back at the sight of her. The weight of the yasi'halaun kept him from moving quickly. Ji fell as much as lunged forward. She sank her teeth deep into Fikiri's forearm and jerked him back violently. Fikiri's mouth opened wide in a howl of pain. The yasi'halaun fell to the ground. Fikiri plunged his curse blade into Ji's throat.

Kahlil burst out of the Gray Space. He heard Ji's soft whimper like a roar. Ji fell limply to the ground. Kahlil wanted to kneel beside her, to pull her into his arms and protect her. But he knew she was already dead. Not even she could survive such a wound.

Fikiri thrust forward with his curse blade. Kahlil barely managed to block the blow with his own blade. Fikiri fell back, breathing hard. His blade arm drooped slightly. Kahlil started after Fikiri. Then he caught the flash of Fikiri's smug smile. Fikiri wanted him to advance. Kahlil stepped back. His heel bumped against the hilt of the yasi'halaun.

It was like Fikiri to try and draw him away. In battle practice he had always relied on feigning. Kahlil refused to be drawn. For a moment Kahlil and Fikiri stood simply watching one another and waiting.

Behind Fikiri, Kahlil caught the huge mass of the hungry bones striking at Saimura. He felt the force of the hungry bones' impact against the ground. He heard bones breaking. Saimura rolled to his feet and hurled a summoning stone away into the hills. The hungry bones surged after it. Again there was an earth-shaking crash as the hungry bones smashed themselves into the ground.

The noise almost drowned out the sound of the Gray Space wrenching open. Kahlil's attention flashed back to Fikiri. He hadn't moved. Instead Pesha burst out a foot from Kahlil. She looked terrible. Dried blood colored her nose and mouth. Deep scratches crisscrossed her face and arms. She stumbled toward Kahlil.

Fikiri seized the moment. He charged Pesha, curse blade forward. Kahlil instantly dropped into the Gray Space and threw himself between Pesha and Fikiri. He sliced the Gray Space open. Fikiri came hurtling in. Kahlil pounced on him and drove his own curse blade into Fikiri's body. His blade skidded across a hard surface. It was that damn armor he wore beneath his tattered black robes.

Kahlil stabbed again, this time aiming for the soft joint of Fikiri's groin. But Fikiri jerked back. Kahlil's blade ripped through the fabric of Fikiri's robe and tore a deep furrow into the white bone armor beneath it. Fikiri kicked at Kahlil. An inscription on the armor flashed. The kick landed incredibly hard, pounding through Kahlil's body like a hammer blow. Kahlil staggered back and Fikiri stumbled free of his grip.

At the edge of his vision, Kahlil saw Pesha lift the yasi'halaun and then drop into the Gray Space. Fikiri noticed the motion as well. He spun from Kahlil and immediately charged the faint shadow of Pesha's movements.

Kahlil lunged after Fikiri, slamming into him. Pain exploded through his beaten chest as the collision sent the two of them sprawling forward. Rough patches of the Gray Space slashed Kahlil's arm. His curse blade slipped from his grip.

Then suddenly he and Fikiri were jerked wildly through space. A sick sensation flooded Kahlil. The landscape surrounding him changed completely as they fell through another distortion.

Carved pillars jutted through crumbling stone walls. Archways of marble steps rose from cliffs and stretched out into empty air.

A huge doorway stood alone on a stone stoop. Payshmura suns and moons decorated nearly every surface. They were in the ruins of Rathal'pesha.

Corded scars twisted and tangled through the Gray Space like spider webs. Kahlil jumped to his feet. Countless rough patches of the Gray Space scratched his skin and ripped through his clothes. It would be insane to move more than a few feet through the Gray Space here.

He saw Fikiri drop out of the Gray Space a few feet ahead of him. With an intense effort Kahlil tore his way free of the Gray Space as well.

The heat of the outside world rushed over Kahlil. His injured right arm burned. A shallow gash ran from the back of his hand to his elbow. He took a deep breath and pain shot through his chest. He couldn't allow Fikiri to land another kick like that last one.

Fikiri spun on Kahlil. His weathered face was scratched and bloodied. He glared at Kahlil in open fury.

"You will die, Ravishan!" Fikiri growled. He drew his curse blade and sprang forward.

Kahlil's own weapon was lost. He flicked his fingers apart, ripping the intensely resistant Gray Space into a Silence Knife. He thrust the Silence Knife into Fikiri's curse blade. The curse blade shattered. Kahlil plunged his Silence Knife up into Fikiri's chest. Fikiri's armor sent Kahlil's hand skittering. Kahlil struck again and felt the armor crack. His Silence Knife slash through flesh.

Fikiri cried out then bolted back from Kahlil and sprinted for the cover of the ruins.

The foolishness of pursuing Fikiri into unknown territory gave Kahlil momentary pause. He didn't know what could be lurking in the ruins. And his body was already at the edge of collapse. But he couldn't bear to turn back. Not after what Fikiri had done to Ji. How could he tell Jath'ibaye that he'd let Fikiri escape?

The muscles of Kahlil's legs shuddered, but he forced himself to rush after Fikiri. He pushed himself harder, closing out the sharp cramping pain. He'd endured worse hurt for less.

Cracked flagstones littered the ground. The footing was uneven but also innately familiar. Kahlil recognized the ring of broken stones that had marked the common baths at Rathal'pesha. Water still bubbled up from the natural hot spring, but now it reeked of sulfur.

Kahlil raced after Fikiri through familiar and strange corridors. A crumbling hall filled with eroded statues and apple trees led into an old library. Rotting shelves slumped against each other. Tatters of ancient scrolls lay on the floor. All the books were gone.

Kahlil chased Fikiri down a long hall. Shafts of light shot through holes in the roof. Kahlil noticed the remains of priests' bodies. Hand bones, ribs, cracked skulls, and even a few complete skeletons littered the floor. The remnants of clothes still clung to some of them. Kahlil saw Fikiri briefly crouch down beside one body. He clutched something and raced through a doorway.

Kahlil rushed after him. His chest burned with each breath he drew but he forced himself to sprint ahead despite the pain. Fikiri was slowing down already. His hand still bled badly. Kahlil easily picked out the fresh splashes of Fikiri's blood from the ancient dried stains that discolored the stone floors. Fikiri couldn't run much longer.

Kahlil burst through the door only seconds behind Fikiri. He sensed something different in the air of this room. It felt dank and subterranean. Dull green light glowed from corroded lamps hung high in the vaulted ceiling. Kahlil's eyes adjusted to the dim interior quickly. The stone walls were dark and covered in minute inscriptions. The only door in the room was the one behind Kahlil.

Fikiri had run himself into a dead end.

He stood against the far wall, gasping for air. As Kahlil advanced, Fikiri lifted an old Payshmura pistol. Rust caked the side of the barrel. Fikiri must have taken it from one of the priests' bodies. Fikiri took aim with his left hand.

Kahlil continued his advance. Even if Fikiri managed to get the corroded pistol to fire, Kahlil could destroy the bullets with an Unseen Edge. Kahlil lifted his hands. He expected the Gray

Space to resist. Instead he felt nothing, as if the Gray Space were not there at all.

Suddenly, Kahlil realized why the air in the room felt so disconcerting. This was one of the chambers where the ushiri'im had been trapped and punished.

Fikiri grinned as he saw the look of shock on Kahlil's face. Then he fired the pistol. Kahlil dodged to the side but outside of the Gray Space he could not outmaneuver a gunshot. The bullet punched deep into the muscle of his right bicep. Kahlil clutched his arm as hot blood welled up from the wound.

Fikiri cocked his pistol and took aim again.

Fury surged through Kahlil like strength. He refused to die like this. He would not allow Fikiri to have this cheap, easy victory over him.

Kahlil charged Fikiri. He heard the loud burst of a second shot and felt a sharp pain tear across his abdomen. Kahlil ignored it. Fikiri attempted a third shot, but the pistol misfired. Then Kahlil seized him.

He punched Fikiri in the face and the man's head smacked back against the wall. Kahlil punched again. Fikiri brought up his armored arm, blocking Kahlil. But all Kahlil felt was rage. He threw his weight against Fikiri and slammed him back into the wall again. Fikiri attempted to kick freel. Again Kahlil hurled Fikiri against the wall with brutal force. Blood smeared across the stone. Fikiri buckled. Kahlil gripped his throat and hammered his head back into the stone wall over and over.

He continued beating Fikiri's skull against the stone, until Fikiri's weight went dead in his hands. Kahlil's arms failed him. He let Fikiri's body slump to the floor.

Kahlil swayed on his feet. His hands were caked in blood, hair, and a pulp of flesh and bone. Exhaustion welled through him. His legs trembled under him. His arms and side throbbed with pain. He wanted to collapse.

He couldn't afford that. Not in this room. He had to get back to Vundomu.

He turned. In front of the door stood two large spiderlike hungry bones and a small blond woman. Even swathed in heavy black robes, her body looked unnaturally thin. Her face was surprisingly young and pretty. Her eyes were nearly as bright blue as Jath'ibaye's. She lifted a delicate skeletal hand and pointed at Kahlil.

"Hurt him," Loshai said to the hungry bones.

And for a long while, they did.

To be continued...

Characters from John's Story

Ashan'ahma~An ushiri studying at Rathal'pesha.
Alidas~A rider for the Bousim family; partly crippled.
Amha'in'Bousim~Lady Bousim, 3rd wife, exiled to the north.
Bati'kohl~A servant of Lady Bousim; brother of Ohbi.
Bill~Called Behr in Basawar.
Dayyid~Second ushman at Rathal'pesha.
Fikiri Bousim~An ushiri candidate; son of Lady Bousim.
Hann'yu~An ushman exiled to the north— specializes in healing.
Inholima~Spy in Lady Bousim's household.
Issusha'im~The Payshmura oracles.
Ji Shir'korud~Dog demon; one of the Fai'daum.
John~Jahn
Laurie~Called Loshai in Basawar.
Mosh'sira'in'Bousim~Gaunsho Bousim.
Mou'pin~A rider under Pivan.
Nuritam~The ushman at Rathal'pesha.
Ohbi~A loyal servant to Lady Bousim.
Parfir~The earth god.
Pivan~The second in command of the Bousim rashan'im.
Rifter~The destroyer incarnation of Parfir.
Ravishan~The most promising of the ushiri at Rathal'pesha.
Rousma~Ravishan's sister.
Sabir~The leader of Fai'daum.
Saimura~Ji's son.
Samsango~An elderly priest at Rathal'pesha.
Serahn~Powerful ushman in the Black Tower of Nurjima.
Tashtu~Pivan's commander.
Wah'roa~Leader of the kahlirash'im at Vundomu

Character from Kahlil's Story

Alidas~Captain for the Bousim in Nurjima. Member of the Domu'lam.
Besh'anya~Fai'daum witch. Student of Ji's. Daughter of Tanash.
Chyemon~Fai'daum sailor. Brother of Besh'anya. Son of Tanash.
Desh'oun~The house steward in the Lisam Palace.
Du'rai~Musician and scholar. Evacuated Nurjima with the Fai'daum.
Eriki'yu~Jath'ibaye's house steward at Vundomu.
Esh'illan Anyyd~A young gaunan killed while attempting to murder Jath'ibaye.
Fikiri Busim~An ushiri from the fallen Payshmura Faith. Called 'The Devil' by the Fai'daum.
Gethlam Anyyd~High Commander of the Anyyd Rashan'im. Brother of Esh'illan.
Gin'yu~Fai'daum representitive of Silverlake Islands.
Hial'luyyn~ Spy Master for the Bousim. Mamber of the Domu'lam.
Hirran~Fai'daum representitive for the Iron Heights. Daughter of Tai'yu and the witch, Kansa.
Jath'ibaye~Fai'daum war hero and protector.
Ji Shir'korud~Fai'daum war hero, escaped issusha and witch.
Joulen Bousim~Bousim heir after Nanvess. High Commander of the Bousim Mountain Forces in the north.
Kahlil~ Kyle'insira also called Kyle.
Litivi~Fai'daum representitive for Westcliff. Son of Gin'yu.
Loshai~The Lady whom Fikiri serves.
Mosh'sira'in'Bousim~Gaunsho Bousim; aged and weak ruler.
Nanvess Bousim~Son of Nivoun, and heir to the Bousim house. Killed while attempting to assassinate Jath'ibaye.
Nivoun Bousim~Governor of Bousim Northern Territories. Nanvess' father.
Ourath Lisam~Gaunsho Lisam.
Parfir~God of the banned Payshmura Church, his worship is now forbidden.
Pesha~Student of Kahlil's. First female ushiri. Attacked as a young child and nearly killed by Fikiri.
Piam~Fai'daum sailor.
Rousma~Kahlil's sister. Lost with the rest of the issusha.
Saimura~Fai'daum war hero. Son of Ji. Jath'ibaye's house steward in Nurjima.
Shira~A captain serving under Joulen Bousim.
Tai'yu~Fai'daum war hero and representitive for the Greenhills District.
Wah'roa~Leader of the kahlirash'im and representitive of the Fortress District.

Dictionary of a Few Useful Words

and ⁓ iff
animal/it ⁓ shir
asshole ⁓ wahbai
bark (tree) ⁓ -istana
bee (honey) ⁓ behr
best ⁓ sho
black ⁓ yasi
blond hide ⁓ jahn
blood ⁓ usha
blue ⁓ holima
bone ⁓ sumah
bones (holy) ⁓ issusha
book ⁓ lam
brothers ⁓ ashan
but/however ⁓ hel
chasm ⁓ kubo
city ⁓ tamur
cold ⁓ polima
dead ⁓ maht
death-lock key ⁓ maht'tu hala
deer (mount) ⁓ tahldi
delicious ⁓ mosh
dog (domestic) ⁓ kohl
dog (wild)/wolf ⁓ sabir
exhausted ⁓ renma
fast ⁓ sam
fire ⁓ daru
food ⁓ nabi (grain)
friend ⁓ pashim
from/of ⁓ in
fuck ⁓ faud
goat ⁓ fik
good/ pretty ⁓ domu
grain plant ⁓ taye
green ⁓ ibaye
harm ⁓ ratim
hawk ⁓ alidas
hill ⁓ rousma
holy ⁓ ushmana
hot ⁓ niru
how/because ⁓ ahab
idiot ⁓ bai
joy ⁓ amha
key ⁓ hala
knife ⁓ halaun
lazy ⁓ pom
little/diminutive ⁓ iri
lock ⁓ tu
lost ⁓ gasm'ah
love ⁓ mohim
man/male ⁓ vun
meadow ⁓ pivan
meat ⁓ nabi'usha
medicinal tree ⁓ yasistana
monastery ⁓ ushmura
money ⁓ jiusha
mountain ⁓ rathal
no ⁓ iss
noble ⁓ gaun
none ⁓ illin
orchard ⁓ umbhra
peace ⁓ tumah
place ⁓ amura
quiet ⁓ itam
rain ⁓ parh
red ⁓ daum
river ⁓ fai
road ⁓ nur
run ⁓ sango
sacred books ⁓ ushmana'lam
sacred drink ⁓ fathi
same ⁓ -kin
shit ⁓ jid
similar ⁓ ro
sky ⁓ loshai
snow ⁓ pelima
solitary ⁓ jath
speak ⁓ vass
spill ⁓ ra
spoil ⁓ lafi
still ⁓ tash
stop ⁓ nahara
strike ⁓ bish
terrible ⁓ **tehji**
time/year ⁓ ayal
to be lost ⁓ gasmya
to drink ⁓ siraya
to eat ⁓ nabiya
to harm ⁓ ratimya
to kill ⁓ rashiya
tree (fruit) ⁓ isma
tree bark ⁓ istana

Dictionary of a Few Useful Words

ugly/bad~mulhi
unholy/unclean~korud
water/drink~sira
weasel~ganal
what~bati
when~bayal
where~bamura
white~pesha
who~ban
why~bahab
wine~ vishan
witch~tahjid
woman/ female~vur
gold/yellow~jima/ ji
yes~du

Pronouns

he/him~vun
his~vun'um
they(all male)~vun'im
she/her~vur
hers~vur'um
they (all female)~vur'im
they(mixed)~pun'im
theirs~pun'um
I/me~li
mine~li'um
we/us~li'im
ours~lim'un
you~yura
yours~yura'um
you (plural)~yura'im
yours (plural)~yura'un
it~shir
it (plural)~shir'um

Declensions and Conjugations

positive~dou
negative~iss
question~ sa
object of action~hir
source of action~ati
one who does~hlil
plural~im
possessive (singular)~um
possessive (plural)~un
future tense~ad
past tense~ah
present tense~ ya
(Ya literally means 'to do' or 'to be'.)
possible~at
hoped for (future)~atdou
hoped against~atiss
command form~hi
gerund~yas
adjective~an
adverb~al

Titles

Usho~Leader of the Pashmura Church.
Kahlil~Holy Traveler and Companion to Parfir.
Ushman~High Ranking Clergy; often in a position of great responsibility.
Ushiri~Talented Priest studying to become Kahlil'im.
Ushvun~Priest.
Ushvran~Nun.
Kahlirash~Military sect devoted to Parfir's destroyer incarnation.
Gaunsho~Lord of one of the seven noble houses.
Gaun~Nobleman.
Gauniri~Noblechild.
Gaunvur~Noblewoman.
Gaun'im~Nobles (as a group).
Laman~Scholar, Doctor or anyone learned.
Lamiri~Student.
Rasho~Military leader, particularly calvary.
Rashan~Soldier.
Vunan~Common man.
Vuran~Common woman.
Shir~Animal; derogatory when used to address a human being.

His Sacred Bones

Book Three of the Rifter

October 2013

Works by Ginn Hale
Available from Blind Eye Books

Wicked Gentlemen
ISBN 978-0-9789861-1-7

Tangle (Featuring the novella** Feral Machines**)
ISBN 978-0-9789861-0-0

Lord of the White Hell (Book One)
ISBN 978-0-9789861-6-2

Lord of the White Hell (Book Two)
ISBN 978-0-9789861-7-9

Irregulars (Featuring the novella** Things Unseen and Deadly**)
ISBN 978-1-935560-16-6

The Shattered Gates (Book One of the Rifter)
ISBN 978-1-935560-23-4

The Holy Road (Book Two of the Rifter)
ISBN 978-1-935560-25-8

His Sacred Bones (Book Three of the Rifter)
ISBN 978-1-935560-26-5

Print and digital editions of these books and many others can be found at blindeyebooks.com.

Blind Eye Books
Look for them, because they can't see you!